Fiona Collins studied Film and Literature at Warwick University and after stints in Hong Kong and London returned to the Essex countryside where she grew up, with her husband and three children. She is the author of four romantic comedies including *A Year of Being Single*.

You can follow her on Twitter @FionaJaneBooks and find her on Instagram @fionacollinsauthor

www.penguin.co.uk

YOU, ME AND THE MOVIES

Fiona Collins

CORGI BOOKS

TRANSWORLD PUBLISHERS
61–63 Uxbridge Road, London W5 5SA
www.penguin.co.uk

Transworld is part of the Penguin Random House group of companies
whose addresses can be found at global.penguinrandomhouse.com

Penguin
Random House
UK

First published in Great Britain in 2019 by Corgi Books
an imprint of Transworld Publishers

A CIP catalogue record for this book
is available from the British Library.

ISBN
9780552176385

Typeset in 11.5/13pt Garamond MT by Jouve (UK), Milton Keynes.
Printed and bound in Great Britain by Clays Ltd, Elcograf S.p.A.

Penguin Random House is committed to a sustainable future
for our business, our readers and our planet. This book is made from
Forest Stewardship Council® certified paper.

MIX
Paper from
responsible sources
FSC® C018179

1 3 5 7 9 10 8 6 4 2

To anyone who ever loved the movies . . .

NOW

Chapter 1

I never thought I'd see him again. The man I loved all those years ago. The man who inspired me, dazzled me, adored and betrayed me. But on a damp and darkening afternoon at the end of December – when I think nothing surprising or dramatic will ever happen to me again, thank God – there he is.

It isn't really a day for miracles. An hour before mine I am walking through a drizzle-drenched London park, blisters on my heels from wearing in new shoes I've bought myself for Christmas and sweltering under a fuggy-bear of a belted, checked wool coat in the unseasonably mild weather. I am also attempting to rock a beret, although I spilt coffee on it at work and have swivelled the stain to the back, hoping no one will notice. I like to look put together, each day, however I feel when I wake up in the morning.

People *won't* notice, I think; I am just walking home early from work, through the park. There is no audience, no one watching or judging. After all this time, it still feels like a huge relief.

As I walk, a stray piece of bedraggled red tinsel, probably in residence since the beginning of December, flicks off a tree branch in the half-hearted breeze and drifts to the ground in front of me like the feather in *Forrest Gump*. Without the symbolism: it's just tinsel.

'Smile, love, it might never 'appen!' a jolly botherer in

1

hi-vis calls from somewhere under the spiky umbrella of the tree. He walks towards me, grabs at the stray tinsel with a litter picker and twitches it into a gaping black bin bag.

'Let's hope not,' I reply, granting him a smile that is wry and half-formed, and I know he is thinking, *Miserable cow*, though he wouldn't dare say it these days. I probably do seem that way, to the outside world, but I'm not miserable, although I was for a long time. 'Happy' might be a bit of a stretch; 'relieved' – yes, that's certainly applicable on a daily basis. Miserable? No. If I remotely wanted to answer this man honestly, I'd say everything that could happen to me has happened already, pretty much. All the bad stuff, anyway, and I'm not expecting anything particularly fantastic to come my way now. If I didn't want to bat my stock response back to his stock barb (has a *woman* ever said 'Smile, love!' to a *man*, by the way?), I would say I'm on an even keel these days: I am level, steady and certain to be unruffled.

There aren't the usual hordes of people about. London is in the sleepy grip of a post-festive no-man's-land – that dreary period between Christmas and New Year when you've done the paper hats and the enforced jollity and you're yet to do the party poppers and the reluctant midnight kissing of swaying, drunken strangers. (I'm so glad those days are over, there were far too many of them. *Thanks, Christian.*) Commuters are straggling home after heart-not-in-it days at the office. Sales shoppers bag listless bargains in half-empty shops. London's soundtrack, a week ago loud and raucous – ram-packed with Slade and Wizzard and Shakin' Stevens on a loop – is muted, waiting for the feverish New Year's Eve pitch of 'Hi Ho Silver Lining' and 'Auld Lang Syne', where nobody knows the words beyond the first verse and chorus so they just repeat that over and over until their party hats fall off, and they step on someone else's toe, and the chain of arms break with a laugh and a stagger, and a husband snarls and says 'You're *drunk*' although the reason you are drunk is him.

I flash a bright smile to the dimming sky, long after I've passed my heckler, as a silly act of freedom and rebellion. No one need demand a certain look, a smile, or a line on cue any more. If I look dreary and bored to the man on the street, then that's OK; I like my face's new capacity for lack of expression.

The soft drizzle frizzes up my already electric hair as it spirals from under my beret, my once natural blonde curls now from a bottle but doing a passable impression of their former selves. I don't think I'll ever succumb to grey, not appearance-wise, anyway; in most other aspects of my life it's the only shade that surrounds me.

I walk, the comfortingly unexcitable weather perfectly matching my perma-grey, comfortingly unexcitable mood. It's certainly *not* the kind of weather to offer an emotion-saturated, high-colour background for miracles to occur. For the giant surprise of a man you once loved until you *ached* to come back into your life.

'Arden!'

I look round. It's Becky, and I am no longer unruffled. I immediately reel under the dual stab of emotion I experience, now, when I see my old friend. Deep unassailable fondness and crushing guilt. The feeling that I want to say 'sorry', but I don't know how. Becky and I met at university, thirty years ago, and she is standing further up the path and wielding a bulging M&S carrier bag. She's always in that place, perusing Meal Deals and single men; it's where I finally bumped into her after years of not being allowed to see her.

'Hi,' I say, as she trots up to me, the plastic handle of the bag twisted round her gloved fingers. My voice sounds hesitant, but it does around her, these days.

'You OK? I'm on my way to St Katherine's,' she puffs. 'Dominic's in there with a broken leg.'

'Oh no! Is he? I didn't know!' Well, why would I, when I spend much of my life avoiding my friends? 'How did he do that?'

'Fell off a lighting rig or something. You know what he's like! I'm sure he'd love to see you. It's been ages. Do you want to come and visit him with me?'

She is smiling but her eyes are slightly narrowed, as though she is expecting me to say no. I look back at her, already ashamed. My voice is even more hesitant. 'I don't know. I've been to work. I'm just on my way home.' St Katherine's hospital is only about fifteen minutes' walk from here and it's true, I haven't seen Dominic, our old friend from university, for ages: I turn down a *lot* of invitations.

'You've finished early.'

'The office closed.' I shrug. 'Nothing much was going on.' It was true; we'd pretty much all been kicked out, though I wouldn't have minded staying.

'Come on!' Becky shoves an optimistic arm through mine, the wet slipperiness of her navy raincoat colliding with the damp woolly check of mine. 'We'll only go for an hour. You'll be home by half five. Come with me!'

'OK,' I mutter. I like the familiar feeling of her arm through mine, but I really don't want to go to the hospital. I have a date with a Sky-Plussed *Coronation Street*, a Netflix movie and the remains of a heavenly Christmas tin of shortbread my son Julian bought me. I do like Dominic, though. He's been cheering up life since the late eighties. I really like Becky, too, of course – I just don't deserve her any more.

We walk, Becky's arm still through mine as she leans into me and enthusiastically confides all her latest news, mostly dating disasters. By day she's Front of House Administration at The Royal Opera House in Covent Garden; by night, she dates – trying to find Mr Right before her 'face slides into a middle-aged puddle at her feet', as she puts it. She has a whole string of catastrophic dates she loops around herself as funny anecdotes, until she is a ball of them.

'So, last night, this guy turned up wearing a green jumper with suede patches on the elbows like he was a seventies

4

geography teacher and on the bottom half he was wearing pleather trousers and combat boots like something out of the bloody *Matrix*!'

'Oh God!' I can't help but laugh. Becky is still very funny.

'Then he had the cheek to say I looked nothing like my photo! OK, I've had a haircut since I posted it' – she pats her spiky pink pixie cut – 'but *he* had completely defiled the Trade Descriptions Act!'

I laugh again.

'And then during dessert – God knows why I was still there; well, actually, the food was really nice – he asked me if I wanted a foot massage. At the bloody table! Reader, I married him.'

I laugh really loudly this time. It reverberates into the colourless air. It's not a sound I hear very often, my laugh, but I appreciate the lightness of it.

'Actually, I went to the loo and didn't come back. You know what else he did? Kept saying "lol" and referring to me as "m'dear". Big mistake,' she adds.

'*Colossal*,' I agree.

Becky grins at me and I grin back, but then I look away, guilty. It doesn't feel right to be lapsing into our old banter. *I* don't have the right to enjoy what once came so easily to us.

We are vaped as we walk up the final road to the hospital in the wake of a tracksuited man dawdling in front of us; he emits a dramatic cloud of steam from his e-cigarette panpipe like something from the boiler room of the *Titanic*. In the past I might have worried about signalling my offence by crossing the road. Now, I just cross.

Becky, linked to me in our arm chain, crosses too, then resumes her bubbly chatter. I used to be bubbly; it's a quality I really admire. I don't think I'll be bubbly again, or have an outside chance of *feeling* that way again, since bubble after bubble was burst by the man who swore he loved me but reduced me a little more each day. It's OK. Becky can be bubbly enough for the both of us.

'Ah, *It's a Wonderful Life*!' she says. We are walking past The Parade and James Stewart is dashing through the snow on one of the tellies in the hi-fi shop. They're showing it about a week too late; no one is in the mood any more. I'd be home by now, I think, in my house. With it blissfully quiet, as always, the soft whirring of the fridge the only sound. Peace and quiet, but mainly peace. The warring part of my life is over. I am now beholden to no one, accountable to no one. Except my fantastic nineteen-year-old son, of course – but he is on the other side of London now in new and blissful co-habitation with his girlfriend, Sam, *so* happy he's even helping load the dishwasher. I tried to bring Julian up so he wouldn't be domestically useless. I didn't want to *inflict* him on some future partner – a man-child who doesn't know where the washing machine lives. He's done really well so far, considering all he's been through – my son already has a job in the City with great prospects, a relationship that seems happy and equal and the ability to wash his own pants.

'Come on, we need to get a Scooby on, Ardie!'

I'm not worthy of Becky's familiarity; the awkwardness I feel around my friends is like a disease. I was forced to gradually distance myself from them while married to Christian, to eventually shut them out of my life. I became an expert at evasion, ignoring, hiding. Christian doesn't like confident, bubbly women (he certainly muffled all that nonsense out of *me*). He doesn't like cheery, tactile men. He doesn't really like anyone, actually. He once accused the *postman* of flirting with me, when the poor bugger was passing the time of day with me, one Saturday morning, asking how I kept my grass verges so straight (answer: Christian standing over me and directing how I used the nail scissors). The postman was *frightened*, after that. He never knocked again; just signed for any parcels himself and left them on the doorstep.

I still don't know why they've taken me back – Becky, my former best friend, and Dominic, our old friend from university. If I hadn't bumped into Becky in Marks & Spencer in Oxford Street, in the summer of last year, I don't think it would have happened: after I left Christian I was too ashamed to go crawling back to them.

'Crawling' was Christian's word. He said it while I packed my final bag – zipped up my make-up, my hair mousse, my fears. He said if I went crawling back to them they wouldn't want me and at that point I was prone to believing every word he said. Part of me still is. I'm aware I'm quite unlikeable. There's not much left of me to like. I'm really not sure why Becky perseveres with this odd reincarnation of our friendship and wonder if she is weary of trying. Perhaps she hopes the old me – the fun one – will come back. Perhaps she's just a far better person than me.

We arrive at the hospital, a five-storey modern block with every window lit. After we walk down what seems like an endless series of over-heated yellow corridors, some trailed with overhead silver garlands that resemble stretched-out Slinky toys, some with walls zig-zagged with flagging green tinsel to look like the lines of a heart monitor, Becky stops outside Ward 10, announces herself as a friend of Dominic Klein at the intercom and we are buzzed straight in.

'Becky! Ardie!' shouts Dominic, way too loudly, from a bed halfway down the ward, and there are several frowns and a few disapproving coughs. Ward 10 is packed, crammed with patients and visitors and gaudy post-Christmas decorations. The nurses' station is a fuzzy tinselled sleigh of gold and red; there's a plastic tree in the corner struggling under dragging baubles; more tired silver Slinkies ribbon over the beds. Most of the men here are under their covers – those crisps white sheets and pale blue blankets. Some have their hands silently held by their visitors; some are talking softly, giving those who've come to see them small smiles and

7

hopeful laughs. A couple of more hearty-looking men, in jaunty striped pyjamas, perch sideways on their beds, sharing a joke with wives and children and grandchildren. With friends. My eyes fill with tears, inexplicably, as we walk through the ward, and I blink them away.

It's bright, busy and hot, the sort of warmth that will have visitors nodding off in ten minutes, but Becky has brought M&S prosecco to keep us awake. As we slide on to plastic chairs at the side of Dominic's bed, she pulls a mini bottle and a small stack of disposable cups from her carrier bag and pours the contents of the bottle into two of them, her back turned to a passing nurse.

'None for you, Dominic,' she says, mock sternly.

'Spoilsport,' he replies. Dominic is ebullient and has a cheeky look on his face, in spite of the fact that his left leg is encased in thick plaster from the thigh down. I knew he would be cheery. He's always the same.

He turns towards me and flashes me a kind smile. 'OK, Ardie?' he asks. I nod and return his smile, feeling guilty again. 'This *is* a nice surprise! Did Becky have to drag you?'

'Of course not,' I say. I glance at Becky and she's giving me a look that says, Yes, I *did*. 'I couldn't pass up the opportunity to see you bound and captive.'

'Ha. Quite right. It's a rare state for me, that's for sure.'

His face is all rosy and his brown hair, grey at the temples, is curly. He looks like a grown-up, middle-aged cherub. Despite being a bit of a Casanova, Dominic is living proof that not all men are abusive bastards. He became a fun and brilliant friend to us at university, when he wasn't busy in the students' union, roadie-ing for visiting bands; he's a real roadie now, touring with rock stars like Bruce Springsteen.

'How long will you be in here for?' I ask.

'They're letting me out tomorrow. For good behaviour. Then I have to sit at home on my arse for six weeks. Will you two come and visit? There's someone suspiciously like Nurse

Ratchet here – it's the white rubber shoes – and I'm a bit scared.'

'It's Nurse Ratched,' I say quickly. 'Not Ratchet.' Then I immediately regret it; I can't afford to go around correcting old friends. I am an idiot.

'Pardon me, movie buff.' Dominic grins and I smile back at him, relieved he's not cross. 'It does feel a bit *Cuckoo's Nest* in here, though,' he says, looking around. 'I can't wait to get out.'

I look around with him, and see several beds have switched-on television sets suspended above them, with visitors gawping up at game shows and property programmes. Others are blank screens, patients stowed underneath. Two men on the ward do not have visitors, I notice: an old boy, two beds away, who stirs in his sleep, muttering something, and a man opposite us who lies as still as an Egyptian mummy.

I know Becky will visit Dominic at home with his broken leg, but I'm not sure about me. Small talk deserts me unless there's a third or more party to spur it on. I furtively look at my watch, not wanting to appear rude. It's five past five; I would really like to be at home. *Coronation Street* followed by *The Shawshank Redemption* is waiting and, more importantly, nobody that stamps on my soul. My quiet house – quieter still without Julian – is a home to me again.

We sit for a while. Talk and joke. I try to contribute. I know I am a survivor, that I have survived so *much*, but I don't know how to move on from it. How to get the old me back. I want to be funny and optimistic. I want to be someone people are happy to spend time with. It seems I have forgotten how to be that person.

'What time are they feeding you, Dom?' asks Becky, draining the last of her prosecco. I have been sipping at mine steadily and it has gone, too.

'Oh, I've had it. Mush and chips. Actually, it was OK. Not bad for institutional slop.' Dominic does a giant yawn, loud and characteristically over the top.

'Are we keeping you up?' laughs Becky.

'Yeah,' says Dominic. 'It's pretty tiring, this broken bones business.'

'We'll go,' says Becky, standing up. Her chair makes a hideous scrape and a nurse – petite, short dark hair with blonde at the tips – looks round and gives a conciliatory smile. 'I'll call you, Dominic.'

'OK. Thanks for coming.'

We both kiss him on the cheek and start to head out, Becky stuffing the empty prosecco bottle back in her bag and zipping it up.

'Oh, look at that poor bugger!' she exclaims.

She tilts her head over to the other side of the ward, about halfway along. I follow her head. It's the man lying prone like an Egyptian mummy. There's a sheet up to his chin and his eyes are closed. His hair looks like it's been freshly combed off his face and his cheeks are pink and a little raw, as though one of the nurses has recently given him a wet shave. He looks comatose: his body so straight, his arms so rigid and flat at his sides.

'Do you think he's all right?' Becky asks in a stage whisper.

'I suppose so,' I say, thinking if he wasn't surely someone would have noticed.

Becky looks again. 'Bloody hell, Arden,' she says, narrowing her eyes, 'you know, in a certain light that could be Mac Bartley-Thomas!'

'What?' I glance at the man's face again and my insides lurch and then petrify. 'Of course it isn't!' My voice doesn't sound real; it sounds like it's coming out of one of those suspended televisions; a sort of fizzing is going through me like I'm a cathode. 'No *way* is that Mac Bartley-Thomas!' Saying that name out loud sounds even odder, when it's a name that's been locked in a back chamber of my brain for so many years.

Becky and I have both come to a stop. I stare at the man with the sheet up to his chin. 'No, it's not him,' I conclude, attempting to sound breezy. 'I don't think he'd be in London. And that man's way too old.'

'Not really,' says Becky, as we set ourselves into motion again and bustle out of the door – Becky with certainty, me with reluctance. It clanks softly shut behind us. 'He was – what? – early thirties then, so early sixties now?'

'Yes, you're right,' I say. 'It's definitely not him, though. Oh God, hold on a minute, I've forgotten my phone!' I'd taken it out to check the weather for tomorrow, at a point when my conversation was at the height of lacklustre. I'd put it near the foot of Dominic's bed. It had half gone under a corner of the cellular blanket when he'd shifted his good leg and I'd thought to myself, Don't forget that – and I hadn't, as it's in my bag.

My heart thumping, I quickly buzz again, say Dominic's name and dash back into the ward, making sure Becky is not in my tailwind.

'Sorry, Dom. I'd forget my head if it wasn't screwed on,' I say, in lame idiom mode, as I pretend to retrieve my phone and slip absolutely nothing into my coat pocket. 'See you.'

'Don't be a stranger,' Dominic says, reaching for a magazine, but I'm ashamed to know I absolutely might be.

Despite my sins, some kind of god is smiling at me as a nurse approaches to pull a curtain round Dominic's bed and I cross the ward hurriedly, to stand at the end of the bed of the man who's lying there like a mummy. The lights are dimmed over his head. I look at his face and feverishly consult my memory. Is it him? Is it Mac? Of course I'd seen him many times without his glasses, but without them now he looks like a scrubbed pickle. His hair is silver, but there are still traces of the dirty blond; his eyes are closed so I can't see if they are watery, iridescent blue, with flashes of pistachio; his lips – once so soft and giving – now look set and half vanished. I think it's him, though. I think it's Mac.

There's a clipboard at the end of the bed, the sort that

says 'nil by mouth' and other depressing things. I haven't been in a hospital since my mother had her hip operation, but they *are* eternally depressing, aren't they? I find it trite when people say they don't like hospitals because is there anyone who *does*? But I have to linger on this ward a little longer. I have to look. Shaking, I pull my reading glasses from my bag, put them on and bend down.

'Can I help you with anything?' A male nurse is smiling at me, but there's a certain steel behind that smile. He's seen me, hasn't he, visiting Dominic, and is wondering what the hell I'm doing nosing at another patient's clipboard.

'No, no, I'm fine, thanks,' I mutter, mortified. I straighten up, shove my glasses back in my bag and hurry out of there on hot coals.

'Come on!' chides Becky, as I emerge. She attempts to link her arm through mine again and I resist the horribly ungrateful urge – so familiar to me, now – to wrench it free, escape from her and run all the way home, the damp wind in my hair and the many, many questions jolting round my mind. 'Do you want to go for a drink?'

'No, thank you,' I manage to say and somehow I spring a bright, bright smile on to my guilty face. 'I've got some stuff to do at home. Do you mind?'

'No, not at all,' says Becky, although she looks disappointed again. 'Another time.'

I nod. Becky's feet don't walk fast enough. Her lovely bubbly chatter is not speeding us along the streets at the right pace. Finally, we reach the point where she has to say goodbye and with a kiss and an attempt at a quick tight hug she is gone, leaving me to run back to my empty house, the damp wind in my hair, and let out the mighty exhalation of breath I am holding on to very, very tight.

NOW

Chapter 2

I'm at work. I don't have to go in these limbo-ish days between Christmas and New Year, but I want to. I quite like the listless post-holiday feel to these quiet days in the office. Drooping decorations. An artificial tree missing a branch that no one can be bothered to stick back on. Half-empty tubs of Heroes lying around, in case anyone fancies a quick shot of palm oil.

I work at the production office of a long-running police series, *Coppers*. I'm assistant to the Locations Manager. It can be fun, I suppose; it can be tedious. It's a job. I'm chatting to Charlie, who *is* fun. He's the sort of bloke to wear a spinning bow tie at the work Christmas party (he did) and have a sign on his desk saying 'You Don't Have to be Mad to Work Here But it Helps' (he does). He's tall, fair and rangy, a young blond John Cleese – I can just see him striking a Mini with half a tree.

'You've got something between your teeth, Hall,' he tells me, perching on the front of my desk.

'And *your* flies are undone, Hipworth,' I retort, without even checking my teeth as I know that today I'm not remotely guilty as charged. I haven't eaten since breakfast and that was half a yogurt. I'm not very hungry today. I'm also really tired, as I didn't sleep a wink last night. To counteract this I'm wearing my smartest white silk blouse and black pencil skirt combo, which hopefully yells 'wide-awake professionalism' to anyone who might be interested.

Charlie's flies aren't undone either, but he checks them anyway. 'Oh, good one, Hall,' he says. 'Have you got the file on Three Hill Court? Michelle wants to cross-check who was in that burglary scene. I wish I'd taken these couple of days off, after all.' He sighs, looking round the ghost-town office with its skeleton staff. 'It's *dead* in here.' He huffs like a sulky teenager. It's funny, really, how we get on so well. He's like the younger brother I never had. 'My wifey's off; we could have gone to Winter Wonderland.'

'I can't think of anything worse,' I reply – Christian once dragged me there, plied me with false kisses and candyfloss, then terrorized me on the Ferris wheel – 'but then again, I am really old.'

'You're not old; you've just lived longer than a load of other people.'

'Thanks,' I say, mock tersely. He's twenty-seven; I'm forty-eight and have wrinkles and a *whole* lot of baggage to prove it. 'That file's in my in-tray. Help yourself. And tell Michelle she can give me a call if she wants a hand with anything.'

I always wanted to work in film and television and this is where I ended up: a back-room office with ridged charcoal carpet and a view of the local gas depot. All the *Coppers* action takes place elsewhere – in the studio sets in the aircraft hangar-esque building down the road, or out on the streets, or at the locations I help to book but rarely get to visit. Nigel the Loca-tion Manager does that and he goes out on the days they film, too, to make sure everything goes smoothly. I sit in the office. I keep everything logged and on file. I do spreadsheets. I make phone calls and bookings. I make sure the people who own the locations – the lock-ups, the terraced houses, the news-agents, the garages – get looked after and paid on time. I go begging to the relevant London borough for permits to film on local streets, for all those chases, both on foot and in cars. My job is just another boring admin job, really, here in the office – despite the snazzy-looking LinkedIn profile Nigel made me set up – except we occasionally get people dressed as police constables popping in.

Charlie works in casting. He's good at spotting perfect faces for roles in *Coppers*, especially villains; he has a knack for finding just the right bald head and the right curled-up snarl. He's also good for keeping me cheerful, even when I was at my lowest ebb.

'Thanks, Hall.' He refuses to call me Arden. It is a silly name, I agree. I was named after Ellen Wagstaff Arden, the character played by Marilyn Monroe in her last ever movie, *Something's Got to Give*, with a short nod to Elizabeth Arden cosmetics. Arden Hall sounds like a stately home to me. My mother has a lot to answer for.

Charlie picks up my hole punch and shakes its confetti contents. 'So, still joining everybody for the works' pre-New Year's Eve drink tonight? You know it's tradition.'

'No, really sorry, Charlie; I can't make it now.' New Year's Eve is on Monday, not that it matters.

'You're such a bloody killjoy.' He raps me gently on the knuckles with the file then looks immediately sheepish. 'I thought you would come. I know you're a complete lightweight and half a shandy finishes you off, but you said you would!' Now he sounds like a child. If I could reach it I'd be tempted to give the top of his head a little pat.

'I know, I know. But I can't now, sorry. Have my half a shandy for me?' The phone on my desk is ringing. I let it ring three times and Charlie pulls an 'I hate you' face at me which makes me smile and then he backs away like a comical, shambling ape, swinging his arms like Liam Gallagher. I *can't* go out tonight. I was forcing myself to anyway, to try to join in, to try to be normal, like everybody else, but now I have other plans. I *have* to have other plans.

I answer the phone.

'Ms Hall?' says a clear voice. Scottish accent, although I know from the caller ID she's calling from Walsall. 'It's Connie from The Cedars. Your mother is asking when you might be coming up next to visit. I'm sorry to bother you with it, but she's talking about it all the time and it's getting a little . . .'

'Shrill? Irritating?' I prompt. I can't help myself.

'*Trying*,' says Connie. 'Sorry. So, when do you think you'll be able to come?'

'In the next couple of weeks, hopefully?' I sigh. I really don't want to. Visits to my mother these days are the absolute embodiment of Duty Visits and kill me a little more every time. Who wants to sit in a pink room and hold hands with someone they never really liked and who never really liked *them*?

'Fabulous,' says Connie. 'So Marilyn can look forward to seeing you very soon?'

'Absolutely,' I say. 'Thanks, Connie.' *Thanks for looking after Marilyn. Thanks for looking after her far, far away.* It means everything to me that I don't have to.

I put the phone down with a sigh. I don't have time to think about my mother. It's two o'clock and there are about twenty phone calls to make, six contracts to organize and a whole lot of data to put into a spreadsheet before I can get on with my plans.

The hospital is quiet tonight, as I make my way to Ward 10. It's just as bright, though, the yellow light flooding everything in over-jolly, artificial sunshine. I pray Dom was right and has already been let out for good behaviour. I don't want him to see what – or rather who – I've come here for. I do feel the lack of Becky's breezy presence, though, tonight; in another life I'd feel able to lean on her for support. Instead, I am alone. I can hear crying from somewhere and the soothing sing-song voice of a nurse.

I've been in a bit of a state since this time last night. I haven't known what to do with myself. I've barely eaten, I couldn't face *Shawshank*; my head's been all over the place and full of Mac Bartley-Thomas. If it's him, then he's in *London* – this alone is incredible. If it's him, why is he at St Katherine's? What's wrong with him? *If* it's him, why, in a ward full of visitors, did he have no one at his bedside? And why is thinking I've seen him again having such an effect on me? My equilibrium – which took so very long to restore – has been shunted sideways. I am sidelined, derailed and other ridiculous train metaphors. I have come to Ward 10 to get answers to all these questions and the biggest one burns into my brain like a hot poker: is the man I saw last night the man I once loved?

Realizing I am trembling, I press the buzzer.

'Ward Ten?'

'I'm here to visit Mac Bartley-Thomas,' I say, and I hold my breath.

There is a pause – quite a long one – then the door jamb clicks, just like that, and I push the door open and step into the ward.

My heart is pounding, my thoughts racing, as I cross the ward as interloper, imposter, terrified visitor. I immediately glance to the other side to make sure Dominic has gone and he has. There's now a friendly-looking man sporting a beard that looks painted on in his bed, pouring himself a glass of water.

It is definitely quieter on the ward tonight, too; have all the visitors been and gone? It's only six o'clock. I can just hear the murmur of televisions and the clank of equipment and the tinkle of teaspoons in mugs in the nurses' station at the end of the ward. And some soft coughing.

I head towards Mac's bed, half-expecting a heavy hand to land on my shoulder and a voice to ask what the hell I am doing here: wasn't I here last night, visiting someone else?

Am I some sort of weird Munchausen-type person who likes breaking into hospital wards? But there is no hand and no voice. I make it to Mac's bedside unscathed, despite the shockingly, un-Ratched loud noise of my heels on the polished floor, and I sit down, terrified.

Mac – here in London, here at St Katherine's – has his eyes open, which is an initial surprise and makes me feel like running away, and he is staring up at the television screen hanging above him in a giant, royal blue plastic box. Alexander Armstrong is chuckling at something *Pointless*. Will Mac recognize me? What will we say to each other? I haven't a clue, except why is he here? Does he *live* in London? Does he live *near* me? If he does, how have we missed each other until now, and what would we have said to each other if we hadn't?

I wait. I keep my coat on, over my blouse and pencil skirt, my feet in black suede court shoes tucked under the chair. I wait for him to notice I am here, and after what feels like a very long forever, Mac looks down from the television. He looks at my face and stares at me for a moment, then his eyes crinkle into a soft smile of recognition – it *is* recognition, isn't it? God, I hope it is – and finally, slowly, his mouth joins in. He knows who I am.

Still petrified, I smile back at him. He's older but the ghost of his beautiful, younger face is still there. His eyes are still periwinkle pale blue, with fair eyelashes. His mouth is still a delight, a promise. His hair is not back from his face today, some of it has flopped forward and it makes my heart contract a little, as though squeezed by an eager hand. I loved Mac's floppy hair. I would run my fingers through it and let it fall, in soft layers, into his eyes, before he would blow it up into the air again, his mouth a soft 'O'. I hope I don't disappoint him; I'm in my late forties, I have my own crinkles, an uncertain jawline, possibly an air of not long-departed despair . . . But *he* doesn't disappoint *me*.

He creeps his hand forward, at the side of the bed, so

18

gradually I could be imagining it, but I place my own over it. His hand is warm and I am taken by a faint echo of the electricity I used to feel, a distant current, like the ripples from a skimmed stone on a faraway lake.

'Hello, Mac,' I say, my voice quavering. 'It's really good to see you.' He smiles at me again, and I squeeze his hand gently until it stops mine from shaking. 'It's been a long time.'

He nods very slowly.

'How are you feeling?' I know how *I* am. Nervous, shy, scared stiff, nothing like how I was when I first spoke to him, in the Arts common room, at university, thirty years ago. He, the charming, maverick Film Studies lecturer; me, the overconfident English Literature student. God knows what happened to *her*...

Mac doesn't answer. He just smiles at me, those blue eyes creasing until the irises nearly disappear.

'I was visiting a friend last night,' I gabble on. 'He's gone now, broken leg. I saw you were here. I came back to visit you. It's so weird seeing you again. After all this time.'

Mac nods again. He smiles. I can see his teeth, still a little crooked, something he always said he would fix, one day. He liked the idea of a Hollywood smile. He always joked that in the right light he'd look like a young Nick Nolte.

Why is he not saying anything?

'He can't speak,' says a nurse, pausing at the foot of the bed. It's the nurse I saw last night, the one with the spiky hair dip-dyed blonde at the ends, although the blonde bits look more orange tonight. Her badge says 'Fran'. 'He damaged his left hemisphere in the car accident.' I nod, needing to give the impression I already know some of what she's saying. Like the fact he's been in a car accident. Poor Mac. How awful. 'We don't know if his speech will come back or not,' says Fran. 'The doctors say we can't be certain of anything at this stage.'

I nod again. I look at Mac; he smiles as though he is sorry.

19

I am flooded with feeling and memory. I'm almost in tears at the thought that he can't speak to me. I have so much I want to say and so much I want to hear.

'Would you like some water?' I say to him.

I look to his bedside table but Fran is already standing at it and pouring water from a clear plastic jug with a blue lid, into a beaker with a straw in it.

'I'm Fran,' she says, as she passes me the beaker, 'and you're his first visitor. Friend or relative?' She makes it sound like Friend or Foe and I almost laugh.

'Friend,' I say. 'Though it's been years.' I go to pass Mac the beaker, but I don't think he can lift up his arm so I place it under his chin and, with what a hopeful person might construe as a slight wink, he sips from the straw.

'Good you're here,' says Fran and she moves silently off to the next bed. I wonder why I am Mac's first visitor. Where is his family? His friends? I put the beaker back on the cabinet. We look at each other. I long to hear his voice. Still, if he can't talk to me, I can talk to him. He looks at me – those crinkly eyes – and I almost blush, remembering all that we did and all that we had. 'I have no idea what you're doing in London,' I say. It's hot – I take off my coat and slip it over the shoulders of the plastic chair. 'Do you live here?'

He nods, almost imperceptibly.

'Do you work here?'

He nods, then tips his head to the side as if to say 'kind of'. I regret asking him – he looks so tired – but I thought he'd still be working. I can't see Mac ever giving up work altogether; he lived for it.

I have no further questions. Well I do, Your Honour, I have a million of them, but I don't want to exhaust Mac further and this has felt like dreadful small talk. Mac and I never did that. Everything we did was *big*. I decide to be as silent as him. Companionable silence, that's what they call it. It was something Christian and I never went for. We could be silent but even that felt like a war, with him watching my every move, my every expression, challenging me to do something he wouldn't approve of. But Mac and I sit for a while, in silence, and I search his face for all the parts of it I loved.

Fran bustles back past. I stand up and go over to her, feeling guilty for stopping her in her important tracks. 'Excuse me, *Fran*? Sorry. What's Mac's prognosis? How long has he been here?'

'Just over a week. He came in five days before Christmas. Two days in intensive care before coming to the ward.' Poor Mac – Christmas in this place. Mine hadn't been the most exciting, but at least I had spent it in my own house, with Julian. 'And the doctors don't know at the moment. On their last round they said fifty per cent chance of a full recovery.'

'And the other fifty per cent?' I ask.

Fran smiles a smile I know she has given a million times before. 'Uncertain' – she shrugs – 'as I said before. But we hope for the best.'

'Thank you,' I say. 'Thanks, Fran.'

'You're very welcome. He's a nice man,' she says. 'We can tell. And I get the feeling he may have had quite a *twinkle*, once upon a time.'

There's a sudden strange noise from behind us, like the clearing of a throat. Fran and I both turn round and look at Mac. There's the glimmer of a twinkle going on right now; his eyes are glinting and his lips slowly part.

'Bunny,' says Mac, or at least it sounds like it. His voice is low and rumbly, like cracked pepper.

I look at Fran and we step towards him. 'Mac? Did you say something? What are you trying to say?' I ask.

Mac's lips move again. His eyes flash and he looks directly at me. 'B-bunny soup,' he says.

'What did he say?' asks Fran. 'Something *soup*?' but I am staring at Mac and laughing out loud, delighted at hearing his voice again and knowing *exactly* what he said, although it is unbelievable, after all these years.

Bunny soup.

I sit down and retake Mac's hand. A full grin is lighting up his face. He grins till his eyes crinkle to almost nothing. We beam like idiots at each other, the background murmur and clunk of the ward an applause.

'It really sounded like "bunny soup",' says Fran, at the end of the bed, 'how odd,' but she is obviously as delighted as me, as she adds, 'But he *said* something! Well, I never! Well done, Mac,' she says to him, as though speaking to a child. She comes to the side of the bed and pats his other hand. 'Why is he talking about soup?' she asks me.

I laugh again. I laugh far too loudly for a hospital ward and receive several looks. Anyone would think I was once bubbly. 'He's talking about a film,' I say. 'Mac and I watched a lot of films together, back in the day, when I was a student. He's referencing one of our favourites.' Actually, it was the first film we watched, Mac and I. And I would never forget a second of it.

'Oh, right,' says Fran, stroking Mac's knuckles gently and looking thoughtful. 'How odd. You know, it might be possible Mac has a form of aphasia. I used to work on the Stroke Ward and some of the patients there have something called non-fluent aphasia – they can't manage normal speech, but they can call up expressions or memorized phrases from the long-term memory. It's all in the right hemisphere, you see,' she says, tapping the side of her head. 'Quite amazing, really. Some of them can't utter a word but can sing whole verses of "Love Me Tender". Which film is it?' she asks.

'*Fatal Attraction*,' I say. I'm gazing at Mac.

'Ah, yes.' She nods. 'I get it . . . *bunny soup*, the whole "bunny boiler" thing . . . Glenn Close in a white nightdress, *Madame Butterfly* . . . Great movie.'

'Yes, great movie,' I say. I smile at Mac and he smiles back. *I remember*, his eyes say; and I remember too.

22

THEN

Chapter 3: Fatal Attraction

I didn't get good enough grades to study Film Studies at university so I did the next best thing: I had an affair with a Film Studies lecturer.

In 1988, the year in which Margaret Thatcher became the longest serving prime minister of the twentieth century, Kylie Minogue became a pop star and Phil Collins became a movie star, I made my own news by scraping into Warwick University. I'd known I'd been optimistic, filling in my UCCA form with 'Film Studies' at Warwick as first choice; I was optimistic putting *any* course down for that university, as it was one of the best in the country. But I was a chancer, and a grafter when I wanted to be, and although I'd had torpid results in my mocks, I managed to pull something out of the bag for the real things and achieved the required grades for my second choice at Warwick: English Literature. I liked literature, it was all perfectly OK. But I loved film.

I met Mac at the end of the autumn term – after I had already studied Tennyson and Milton and Joyce, and danced at the discos and drank at the bars, and made friends with Becky, a very funny girl on my course with a severe, bright pink bob and a propensity to *not stop talking*. But the Film Studies lecturer's reputation preceded him, like an invisible trophy held aloft by a trail of adoring students with blinding all-white T-shirts bearing his name. Everyone knew who

Mac Bartley-Thomas was; he was one of those lecturers who was just a *phenomenon*.

'Mac Bartley-Thomas? Oh, he's brilliant,' they would whisper, in lectures. 'Mac the Film Studies lecturer? He's a legend!' they would say, in the students' union. 'That Film guy?' they would utter, queuing for the bus into Coventry. 'Yeah, he's fit!'

As I learnt from word of excited mouth, he was highly charismatic, a genius, a beacon, a luminary and a superstar – and 'only thirty-one', the youngest lecturer at the university, although to be honest that sounded ancient to me. Hearing how great he was only made me feel more piqued that I hadn't got on to his course. I had not yet clapped eyes on him – this academic giant of a man, this hot shot, this campus *celebrity* – but I was jealous of students who got to devour his words of cinematic wisdom in lectures and pick his infinite brains in intimate seminars. He had all the knowledge I ever wanted; he knew everything I needed to know. It should have been me, I protested to myself and, sometimes, to anyone willing to listen to me harping on like a glowering ex-girlfriend of the groom at a wedding. If I was in the students' union and had a cider and black in my hand, I could be quite effusive on the subject, though I tried to make it comical.

'Never mind,' I'd say faux-dramatically, 'I'll just weep in a corner for three years over my bloody Byron and my sodding Shelley.' (I was definitely being over-dramatic; I had a tiny soft spot for both.) 'I'll just sob over what *could have been*.'

'But you're *here*!' said one random, earnest lad, a Philosophy student in a Smiths T-shirt, in the third week of term, who I had just batted away when he attempted to drunkenly snog me while I'd been queuing at the bar. 'You made it to university! Thousands didn't. Be happy about it!'

I tried to be happy. I got on with my studies, attended my

lectures, enjoyed my new friends – the best and brightest and most hilarious being Becky, who halfway through the term had her hair cut into a choppy Mohican with shaved sides dyed purple. I was walking with her to the loos in the Humanities Building one afternoon when I first saw Mac Bartley-Thomas. He was walking down the corridor holding a stack of books against his chest. And he was whistling. I was pretty sure it was the theme to *Love Story* but that could have been projection on my part.

Becky raised her pierced eyebrows and whispered, 'That's the famous Mac Bartley-T.'

'Right,' I whispered back, taking him all in. 'So the rumours are true. He *is* fit.'

I never knew he was exactly my type until I laid eyes on him. He was ridiculously tall, broad, loping, cute, a little shabby, but that was OK as so was I. He wore clear-rimmed glasses and slightly too baggy cords. Plum-coloured desert boots and a grandad cardigan with those buttons that look like tortoises. A white twill cotton shirt undone one button too far. His hair was floppy and he was very, very sexy.

As he passed me he raised his eyebrows ever so slightly, so slightly it was almost imperceptible. I don't think Becky noticed, but I did. As I was having a day when I was feeling pretty confident and was in one of my favourite outfits – black dungarees, stripy top, scuffed DMs, denim jacket and my hair bouncy as Shirley Temple's – I raised my eyebrows ever so slightly back at him, bold and fearless.

'He drives an MG *and* he lives on campus,' Becky said, after we had passed him. I resisted the temptation to look back. 'Sometimes he has parties.'

'I bet he does,' I replied.

A week later the Film Studies common room was closed for emergency repairs – a leak in the café or something – and for a few days its students shared ours. One morning, in late November, I found myself standing behind Mac

Bartley-Thomas in the queue, anticipating a cup of tea and a piece, or maybe two, of shortbread. He was laughing with a man almost half his height who had a bald head and was holding a book in his stubby hand called *What is Cinema?*. I realized the queue in front of them had moved forward but they had not.

'Sorry, we're yakking for England,' Mac Bartley-Thomas said suddenly, turning round. His eyebrows lifted a tiny fraction again when he saw me. 'Do you want to go ahead of us?'

'Oh right, yes, thanks.' We looked at each other for just a second too long. His eyes were crinkling at me, behind his clear-rimmed glasses, but they also looked curious. I was looking at him because he was beautiful. A surprising kind of dazzling. I was really susceptible, though, to this kind of *moment*; after all, it was one of the ones I had lined up for myself to have at university. Being dazzled by someone. Except I thought it might be a boy in an Aran sweater with an interesting postcode I could visit in the holidays, not one of the staff. Not a *lecturer*. I blushed a little and hated myself for it. Marilyn always said to never give yourself away by blushing, unless you wanted the other person to see you had come undone.

Eventually, Mac turned back and carried on chatting to the man. They were talking about Sigourney Weaver. The man with the bald head was making a point about the actress's hair in *Alien*, how it not only emphasized her vulnerability but masculinized her, as they wanted to make her as tough as a man. Mac Bartley-Thomas said he disagreed, that their intention was to make her as tough as a *woman*, and the other man looked thoughtful. Mac had a strong Northern accent, which, combined with how he looked, thrilled me. I was from Essex and the North was a country I had not yet visited – it was so exciting to me: dark, visceral, gloomy skies and factory gates and spires, whippets and flat caps and pale ale . . . I'd only made it as far as the Midlands, here at university, but even the Midlands was exotic as far as I was concerned. Coventry, the campus's nearest city: grey and municipal and concrete and sullen, was also 'other' and rather exciting – it had been sung about in a Specials song. I was a million miles from Essex and its flat boringness and its try-hard green spaces. The promise of further north, as spoken in accents like Mac's, was even more thrilling.

'A survivor and a heroine as opposed to a victim,' I said, out of nowhere, and I was suddenly terrified I had said it. What was I *doing*?

'Quite right,' said Mac, turning round and looking at me again, more than curious now. 'Some theorists would argue that Ripley was Hollywood cinema's *first* action heroine.' He looked at me a little longer, and I looked at him, then he turned back and he and his companion moved forward in the queue.

The next time I saw Mac was at a Christmas party he held in his flat on campus. Becky and I were drunk at the end of an unfathomable Robert Plant gig we had pretended to enjoy, and someone in a Ramones T-shirt said they were going on to a party, so we just sort of followed along behind and before we knew it we were on the walk to Westwood, the other side of campus, and heading to Mac's staff accommodation. A bloke in a denim jacket we were walking with said Mac had a real house in Sheffield but he always lived at Westwood during term time, that there was a whole block for staff and lecturers and wardens; some even had their families living with them. I'd been to Westwood only the week before, with Becky. There was a weekly disco there called The Westwood Bop. The queue to get our hands stamped had been so long we'd climbed in through the window and waited behind the long curtain until we could make a run for the dance floor.

Mac's little flat was very warm. Lots of people were smoking – the smoke was circling round a terrible shiny bell-shaped garland of red and green that had been Sello-taped to the middle of the ceiling. There was a straggly Christmas tree – an artificial one – which stood on a table in the corner of the room, already decorated with empty wine and beer bottles. The windows had venetian blinds, which were closed. In another corner of the room a telly, no sound, was showing – randomly – *Bugsy Malone*: there was some joyous custard pie slinging going on.

Mac was holding court in the centre, the garland wilting above his head, and Becky and I drifted towards him – the party's nucleus; I had the feeling he would be, wherever he went. I experienced a frisson – a chill – as I got near him, like something portentous was going to happen, which was undoubtedly stupid. Why should it just because I wanted it to? But I felt powerful tonight – a feeling that had been simmering since the beginning of term, fuelled by freedom and escape, and it bubbled up inside me as soon as I walked into this party. I *knew* from just looking at him – white shirt, blue jeans, floppy hair, clear-rimmed glasses, crinkly eyes and a bottle of tequila, held insouciantly in his right hand – that my simmering feeling of power was going to rise to the top of me, spill over into the world and claim something amazing.

'Hello again,' he said. Oh, he remembered me. That made me feel ridiculously good. Despite being drunk, all my nerve endings were scrabbling upright to attention, like tin soldiers. 'Have you got a drink?'

'No,' I said, and he turned to somewhere behind him and shoved a bottle of Budweiser in my hand. I swayed to the music – Grace Jones? Something sophisticated – but Becky annoyed me by grabbing my hand and pulling me into the kitchen. A boy she liked was in there; she started a stilted conversation with him about what grades they got at A level and which subjects, although this topic really should have been exhausted by the end of Freshers' Week. The *man* I liked was in the living room. I left the kitchen, happy to be

28

drunk and with only a few inhibitions still standing. It was a heady feeling. I marched back up to Mac, daring. I put myself right in front of him, confident. His hair was flopping into his eyes and he was laughing.

'Hello, again,' I said, 'hello,' wondering if he would get my little reference to Neil Diamond's emotive song from *The Jazz Singer*. 'Dance with me.'

It was a command not a question. I was full of this new heady power, despite my ridiculous outfit. Becky and I had decided to wear Santa hats, with tinsel round our necks like a tie. I was wearing this over an unseasonal lilac T-shirt with a rainbow on it and a pair of teeny-tiny jeans shorts over woolly tights. Plus my obligatory DMs. Actually, maybe I felt that heightened rush of delicious power *because* of my crazy outfit – I looked pretty cute and like no one else in the room, seeing as Becky was in the kitchen. All the other students were in dreary student garb – greys and blacks and long cardigans and, yes, Aran sweaters.

I was primed and I was ready. I knew he would be here; my Big Love. I had yet to experience one in my life and I was ripe for it, receptive, ready to yield and to feel and experience it *all*. Again, I had been imagining an earnest, curly-haired Heathcliff type in a fisherman's jumper as the receptacle for this, a boy who would enjoy poetry and cider and black with me; not Mac Bartley-Thomas. But here he was.

Mac laughed. He wanted to dance but was reluctant, I could tell. I knew he wouldn't want to choose a 'favourite' amongst all his adoring minions. I gyrated a little, anyway. The music was now the Rolling Stones' 'Brown Sugar' – it was one my dad liked and played on hot summer days in the car, with the windows down, to show the neighbourhood he was not really a too-gentle middle-aged cuckold, but rather cool.

Mac offended me by moving away a little – there was a shifting circle around us, mostly girls, others to catch his eye – a small step back, a turned head. I wasn't having that, so I put on a show. He was the real deal to me – older, fiercely intelligent, the king of Film Studies, with everything to teach me. And sexy as fuck. Mac laughed again, handing his bottle of tequila to a girl next to him, who took a glug from it, but he was watching me dance. I could tell he wanted to put his hands on my waist, to get closer, now. And I was ripe. I was ready.

'Dance!' I commanded again and I wondered if I could get him into bed by the end of the night.

The party went on until very late. It was a Friday night. No lectures or seminars the next day – only single beds to be lain in until half three or hungover trips to McDonald's to slouch off to. We could stay up all night if we wanted.

Becky had long since disappeared with Two As and a B Boy.

'You coming?' she had asked, her fingers entwined in the belt loops of the boy's jeans while he nuzzled like an eager spaniel into her neck.

'No,' I'd said. 'I'll be all right here for a bit.'

'Sure? It's quite a way back.'

'Sure,' I said. 'I'll come back with BJ.' BJ was Boring Jason, a Physics student on my floor – we had all sorts of nicknames for people we hoped they would never find out. 'Don't forget I'm helping you with that *Othello* essay tomorrow afternoon? After three, maybe?'

There was no way I was leaving yet. I still hadn't had a proper conversation with Mac. My attempt to dance with him had largely failed – I had been swallowed up by a load of drunks pogoing to the Buzzcocks and he had become out of my reach.

Mac was over by the CD player, fiddling with something. A girl in a short black dress was talking to him. For the past few hours I had not been able to get close. Too many people dancing, the music too loud, too many others jostling for his attention. Why was he having this party in the first place? I wondered. But I knew the answer. To get close to students. To bask in their admiration. He was a very willing magnet, I thought, a man like Mac.

And then I thought, *Sod it. I'm making my move.*

I strode over and stood right next to him, blocking the girl in the black dress. 'I tried to get on the Film Studies course but they wouldn't have me,' I shouted over the music.

'Oh.' Mac smiled, glancing up from the CD player and looking amused. 'And why was that?'

'I'm too much of a handful,' I shouted, pleased with myself. It sounded great, didn't it? Being too much of a handful? It implied so many, many things, most of them quite naughty. I reckoned it was the *perfect* thing to say in the pursuit of a seduction.

'Or did you not get the grades?' suggested the girl in the black dress. Damn, she was still here. She'd sidled back to Mac's side. I smiled brightly at her.

'Yes, you're right,' I said, brittle, and I turned exclusively to Mac. 'But I would have loved to have done it. I'm especially interested in the History of Cinema. You're doing that this term, aren't you? *Birth of a Nation*? *Battleship Potemkin*, all that?'

'Yes,' said Mac, still looking amused.

'I would have had a lot to offer.'

'Really?' He was laughing at me but in a really pleasing way. The smile he was bestowing on me lit me up inside, like the fairy on top of that pathetic Christmas tree. God, he was sexy. He was sort of leaning against the wall now, his feet crossed at the ankles. He was just so casual, so effortless, so *everything*.

'Yeah.' I swayed a little. I had to steady myself on his arm. It was warm. He had the sleeves of his white shirt rolled up. His arm was excitingly hairy. 'I'm really interested in *mise en scène*.'

31

Mac laughed out loud. It was like a cannon going off and I was thrilled to have lit the fuse. 'Are you now?' God, that accent . . .

'Yeah. I could probably do it on this room. Your venetian blinds – they're very noir, aren't they? I bet you peer from them at night, looking all furtive, with shadows on your face. You've got that framed quote by Truffaut – *I have always preferred the reflection of the life to life itself* – to show how arty you are, but on the opposite wall you have a *Ghostbusters* poster, to show you're accessible and down with the kids.' Mac is laughing, looking entranced, I hope; I am on fire. 'But, pray tell, sir, what is the significance of that lame wind chime thingy hanging by the door? Does anyone actually *care* you've been to Goa? Why do you have a yucca plant next to your stereo? Are you showing off that you can keep things alive? Everything means something, Mac.' And I actually winked. I was brazen; I was absolutely full of it. Mac laughed again. The girl in the black dress had given up and melted over to a ball of dancing drunks. Good.

'Well, you know your stuff,' he said, and I knew he was teasing me and I loved it. 'You're right; everything means something. Although the blinds are nothing to do with me – they were already here when I moved in. The *lame* wind chime was a present from a mature student last year – I hung it there because I didn't know what else to do with it. The plant, well, it's just a plant. But, yeah, you got me on the Truffaut and the *Ghostbusters*. I'm a pretentious Peter Pan just trying to be *down with the kids*.'

It was my turn to laugh. This was delicious. 'A plant is *never* just a plant,' I said solemnly, looking Mac right in the eye and revelling in just how *enraptured* he looked.

'So, what course *are* you doing?' he asked.

'English Literature.' I scowled.

'That's a good course.'

'Not as good as yours,' I said.

32

'What's your name?' he asked suddenly, like he really wanted to know.

'Arden,' I said. 'I'm named after a Marilyn Monroe character. My mother is . . . a little challenging.'

'It's a lovely name,' he said, concentrating. 'Don't tell me? Ellen Wagstaff Arden from *Something's Got to Give*?'

'The very same,' I said, impressed, although I knew he'd know it. 'It would have been "Ellen", but a neighbour when my mother was growing up had a yappy Jack Russell called that, and she said she couldn't shake the association.' The cannonball went off again. 'Marilyn Monroe died during the making of that movie. You could say my mother inflicted me with sadness from the moment I was born,' I said melodramatically.

'You don't *look* sad,' Mac replied. 'You look' – he stared at me, his eyes full of curiosity, probing – 'full of beans.'

'Full of beer,' I corrected. I knew, then, that he liked me. I knew I was safe to proceed.

'Shall we dance?' I suggested again, with a mock-shyness that was fooling no one, least of all Mac. He raised an eyebrow at me, like the lifting of a portcullis.

'OK,' he said. And surprising me, he grabbed my hand and pulled me to the middle of the drunken throng.

At 4 a.m. there was just me, BJ and a couple of female Politics students in Mac's flat. Mac and I had been talking – or more like sparring – for the past two hours, drinking and flirting, and I'd been pulling out all my wit and charm, so he could examine it in the half-light of the pathetic Christmas tree. *He* had just been bloody captivating. I couldn't take my eyes off him, although I pretended to. I knew every single one of his eyelashes by around two fifteen.

We were squished on a kind of beanbag thing, my legs under me, Mac's long legs splayed out to the side. The warmth of his body was like balm to me; I just wanted to get closer.

33

'Do you like thrillers?' Mac asked suddenly. We were ignoring the looks of the other students, the whispers. Actually, I wasn't, I was enjoying every single barbed glance.

'Yes,' I said. I liked pretty much everything. I'd not met many movies I didn't like. Even if they were bad I enjoyed their badness. There was always *something* to appreciate.

'I'm planning a new course, for the year after next. "Women in Hollywood". Ten films. *Fatal Attraction* is the first one. Have you seen it?'

'Everyone's seen it,' I replied.

'Would you like to see it again?'

'Yeah, sure. When?' I looked around me, as though it were about to appear from somewhere. The TV was now showing *Scarface*: Michelle Pfeiffer was throwing a drink at Al Pacino in a restaurant.

'Now. I received the print of it today. I was going to go to one of the screening rooms – earlier than this, I didn't realize the party would go on for so long. I want to start making some notes. Do you want to come with me?' He stood up and from a cupboard behind him, with three open shelves at its base, he slid out a stack of three large, shallow blue cardboard boxes.

'What's that?' I asked, like a fool.

'*Fatal Attraction*,' said Mac. 'Three reels.'

Movies came to me through the television or on video tapes, or appeared at the cinema from mysterious projection rooms I sometimes turned round to look at, intrigued, from the stalls: a letterbox of golden light, way up high; a glimpse of a shadowy figure moving around; the dust-particled cone of a magic beam, beaconing into the darkness. I had never seen an actual film reel before and I was strangely excited.

Mac placed the stack of boxes on the floor and removed the lid of the top one. Inside was a dull grey metal canister, circular, and inside that – as Mac showed me – was the wheel of a film reel, the tightly packed brown tape wedged and grooved

34

between the radial arms. On the central axis was a white circular sticker on which was handwritten, *Fatal Attraction*.

Mac looked as excited as I did. Did it still thrill him, to open a film canister and see the reel inside?

'Wow,' I said. Yes, I wanted to watch *Fatal Attraction* again. To be honest I would do anything this man suggested. I would even watch *Neighbours* while drinking Bovril with the guy.

'Come on, then,' said Mac, pulling me up from the beanbag by the hand. 'Let's go.'

Leaving BJ and the others to it (they looked like they were never going to go home, quite frankly), Mac grabbed his keys and we walked out of his door and down his wooden steps, then along the pathway back to main campus. I was in a state of excitement, I was desperate to hold his hand, but I knew he was already playing with fire, walking around campus with me at four in the morning like this. I had to make do with walking close to his side. Basking in his light, in the dark. It was December – freezing – but neither of us had coats; I couldn't imagine Mac in one, to be honest. He looked just perfect in the tweedy blazer he'd grabbed.

'What texts are you studying?' he asked me.

'The usual. *Beowulf*, *Paradise Lost*, Chaucer, Shakespeare . . .'

'*Northanger Abbey* and *Middlemarch* next year?'

'Yep.'

He nodded. 'All the good stuff.'

'Yeah.' There were approximately three working streetlights between Westwood and the main campus. We were walking under one now. I studied Mac's face in profile. It was a good profile. Strong. 'How did you become a Film Studies lecturer?' I asked.

'BA in English at Cambridge. PhD in Film at Birmingham. And a spell in New York at the Film Academy.'

'Cambridge in the seventies . . .' I mused.

'Yes, the seventies.'

'Did you wear flares and ride a bike?'

'Yes, at the same time. Thank God for cycle clips.' His long, slow smile melted me inside. Every word he said tantalized me. I was totally bewitched. 'I also had a beard,' he said, 'if you're interested.'

'I'm very interested,' I said and he looked at me and I raised my eyebrows at him, high. Then I laughed.

'Why do you like films so much?' he asked me.

I shrugged. 'I've seen a lot of them. I've had a home life I needed lots of diversion from.'

'The challenging mother?'

'Yes. And a very lovely but pretty useless father. So I'm always at the cinema; I watch everything that comes on TV. I rent a lot of videos. I have a player in my room, at home.'

'What's your favourite movie?'

'Don't ask me that!' And I swiped him quickly on his tweedy arm. 'Don't *ever* ask anyone that! I simply couldn't tell you, it changes day to day, hour to hour.'

'Me too.' Mac nodded. 'Me too.'

We were at the Humanities Building. Mac opened the door with one of the keys from a giant, jangling bunch he pulled from his jacket pocket. We walked down a darkened corridor to the screening room, which he opened with another key.

'Soundproofed,' he said. He flicked one light on, at the front of the room, illuminating several low, dark material chairs – some sort of velour; squishy, with high backs and no armrests – and a large Formica table at the back.

Mac took three steps up to the rear, which was behind glass, and switched the lights on in there. I followed him. It was a projection room. There were two massive and complicated-looking metal film projectors side by side. A pile of blue film boxes. Messy shelves with gadgets and empty film reels and topples of small cardboard boxes.

'I've caught many a student asleep on a denim jacket on that table at the end of a screening,' said Mac, gesturing to the table through the glass before carefully taking the first reel from its box. He attached it to a wheel on the projector on the right and fed the end of the brown film, with those familiar perforated edges, through a succession of rollers and cogs and into the workings of the grey metal beast, where it was held by a kind of metal gate. 'Hangovers. A student's occupational hazard.'

'Really?' I was amazed, not at the hangovers but at the sleeping – how could anyone *sleep* during one of Mac's films?

'Perhaps you haven't seen *Tokyo Story*,' Mac said, 'although I love it.'

I smiled as if I agreed with him, although I had never heard of it.

Mac went to the projector on the left and threaded in the second reel. The remainder of the reels were put to wait on the floor.

'Reel to reel,' he said, walking back to the first projector. 'You normally have two people. We train the Film Studies students to project the films on their course, on a rota. Some are better at it than others.' He laughed. 'Last week a couple of lads thought they'd done brilliantly but when they looked down an entire reel was spooled on the floor, like spaghetti. We start one projector, then when the reel is finished, we change over to the second. You know, when you see the dots in the right-hand corner of the screen? You have eight seconds from that point. It's *fraught* with jeopardy.' And he winked at me.

'How do you do it?' I asked, enjoying his enthusiasm and trying not to stare at his magnificent forearms. 'Change over?'

'This pedal,' said Mac. 'Here. And a few switches. Then you load up the third reel on the original projector, so it's ready, and so on.'

I wasn't paying attention any more. All I could see was Mac, and I was looking at his hands, the tips of his fingers, imagining them on me. Mac started the motor of the first projector. It shuddered into life with a surprisingly loud and rather frantic tick-tick-tick. I watched, through the glass, as scratchy images appeared on the screen before us in quick succession: random words and symbols that made no sense. Then that familiar countdown from eight, with an accompanying beep per number and a line sweeping round a circle, filling it in with grey. A zero, a final beep, and then slightly wobbly, slightly juddering, the movie started. The snow-capped mountain, the circle of stars. *Paramount Pictures*.

Mac adjusted the focus and, his arm at my back, just above the waistband of my shorts, directed me down the three steps and to the screening room, where he hauled two of the armless chairs together so they formed a makeshift sofa.

'Enjoy, mademoiselle!' he said, with a sweep of his arm, and I sat down. He took a notepad and pen from his bag and sat down next to me, not close enough. There was a hand's span between our two thighs and I didn't like it. He *liked* me, didn't he? He must do, to want to do this with me. I needed to get closer. I could smell him, all warm and beery and with some delicious aftershave I was now picking up, but I wanted to get closer.

'Ready?'

'I'm ready.'

Things moved fast. As Dan and Alex flirted in the restaurant I was aware of Mac's leg, closer to mine. I could feel the heat of it. By the time Dan and Alex were in the lift, it was touching the side of my thigh – deliciously – so I placed my hand on Mac's and looked across at him, in the dark. He was smiling, facing forward, so I left my hand there, feeling sparks of fizzing electricity I prayed he could feel too. By the time Alex cooked pasta for Dan, Mac turned to me in the dark, placed a hand on the side of my face and kissed me softly. By the time Alex was flicking the light switch on and off, I was practically on Mac's lap and we were snogging each other's faces off. We were still snogging when Mac missed the dots and the first reel came to a spluttering end, as the film tape whipped angrily from the spool.

'Oops,' said Mac to a blank screen, in his beautiful northern accent, and all I could hear was the tick-tick of a disgruntled motor and the beating of my heart.

I returned to Mac's lap after he had fired up the second projector and snuggled into his neck for the rest of the film while he tried to take notes.

'So, what did you think this time around?' asked Mac, finally, the third reel having been successfully launched and the film having reached its dramatic conclusion. We stopped kissing for the rabbit in the saucepan and the bathroom and the blood.

'Good,' I said. 'I fully appreciated the bunny soup on this second viewing.'

Mac laughed. '"Bunny soup", I like it.'

'Would you like my thoughts on the film's portrayal of women?'

'Desperate for them.' Mac's pen was poised delightfully sarcastically above his notebook.

'I felt sorry for *both* women,' I said. 'I think Alex was perfectly justified in her persistence with Dan, her unwillingness to accept it was over. Her resistance to just being a cheap one-night stand. Of course, she went a bit crazy at the end, but they probably had to satisfy audience expectations of Woman as Psychopath.' Oh, I loved this. I hoped I sounded super intelligent. 'They had to make her a monster or there would be no story to tell,' I continued, totally warming to my theme. 'She couldn't have just gone away quietly. She *had* to make bunny soup!' I postured, and Mac laughed again.

'Very good,' he said, scribbling on his pad. 'Very good indeed.' He sucked on the end of his pen. 'Let's see, crazy . . . psychopath . . . cheap one-night stand . . .'

'I hope you're not referring to me,' I said, mock-challenging. I knew I was none of these things, and also that one night with Mac would probably not be enough. He looked directly at me, making my insides crumble.

'No,' he said evenly. 'I don't believe you'd ever be a cheap one-night stand.' He was gazing at me so intently, I had to briefly look away. 'What did you think of Dan's wife?'

'Lovely. A victim. Justified in protecting her family, I suppose. But, actually, I also think she let Dan get off lightly.' This was just occurring to me and it was genius. 'She treated him like some kind of naughty boy, like a prize, while the wicked woman who he cheated with had to be totally *destroyed*. He did it *too*, you know? Beth should have shot *him*!'

'Really?'

'Yes, really.' I was so brave, so on fire Mac had to be loving all this! 'And I think there was some ambiguity at the end, wasn't there? About whether they stayed together or not. The family photo – it almost seemed ironic, to me, too staged.'

'Hmm,' said Mac thoughtfully and he wrote something else on his pad. I glowed; he was noting, storing away things *I* had said. 'You're quite the interesting character, Arden,' he added, eventually, 'with your *bunny soup*, and now I'll walk you back to your halls. Where are you?'

'Twenty-one Whitefields.' Oh, I was disappointed. I thought tonight was to be the first of several non-one-night stands. My heart sank to my DMs and I felt crushed. Denied.

'OK.'

Mac didn't kiss me on the corner of the building. He didn't say much to me at all. But from how he looked at me and the way he said, 'Goodnight, Arden,' my faith in what was going to happen between us was restored. There would be more kissing between Mac and me. More of everything. I could just tell.

'Will we do this again?' I asked him, confident enough to know his answer.

'Yes.' He smiled, taking one of my curls and twisting it round his finger. We stood, for a few seconds, just looking at each other. Then I opened the outer door and skipped up the stairs to my room on the first floor.

NOW

Chapter 4

Thirty years ago, I think, as I close my front door and set off down the street to work on Monday morning. That's a long time ago. Eighteen was a whole other land. I was young and optimistic, with grand ideas about love; I knew nothing but thought I knew everything; I had a driving licence but no car and a Sony Discman loaded with songs for the uninitiated . . . and both of my parents were still very much alive and in a marriage almost as soul-destroying as the one I've escaped. Yet, for me, at eighteen, the possibilities for life and love seemed limitless.

At eighteen I didn't hide away, like I have this weekend. Mac didn't say anything else in Ward 10 on Friday night despite me talking at him on and off for another hour or so. He let me hold his hand, he looked into my eyes, he drank water; he managed to eat a couple of custard creams. We watched an episode of *Eggheads*. But he didn't say another word. Nothing. I had to make do with 'bunny soup'. But that funny little reference couldn't have been more full of meaning for us. How we met. How we started The List of the films for his course, for his lucky, lucky students. And how he eventually betrayed me.

I left in a bit of a daze. Mac fell asleep towards the end of the visit and I can't even remember what I said as I left, something inane like, 'nice to see you', that he probably didn't hear. Since then, I've spent the whole weekend thinking about him. Absolutely, totally thinking of nothing and no one else. 'Bunny soup' nearly had me running straight back to the hospital on Saturday morning, but I needed time to process that it is him and he is here. What it means for me to see him after all these years. Thrilled, overwhelmed, scared and sleep-deprived; the weekend hasn't seen so much of a derailment as me pulling, breathless, into a siding, to consider what to do next. Do I go back? Do I go and see Mac again?

I slept better last night and this morning, finally, I rumbled off the siding. An onlooker might almost say I have a spring in my step, as I walk to work, despite the stretched layers of graphite cloud squatting on the horizon and giving it an ashen gloom. I have thought and I have remembered and, as a result, I have plans once more, for tonight, and it feels good to have plans. I'm going back to St Katherine's to see Mac. How can I not? My mind has been almost blissfully blank for such a long time. Five years, in fact. Five years since I have escaped Christian. Now it is etched with Mac and movies and *Fatal Attraction* and, although it scares me, it delights me, too, and I know I have to see him again.

I blush a little as I walk along Trinity Road. I won't be told to 'Cheer up, love, it may never 'appen!' today as I know I am smiling. Fancy *Fatal Attraction* being the first film Mac and I saw together! *So* much sex, when we hadn't even 'done it' yet (student vernacular), so much lust and intensity and drama, when we had that all to come, too, but were unaware of it on our horizon. Although, I think we were, actually. Mac knew it and I hoped for it. I recognized, even then, there was both art and design in Mac holding that Christmas party; casting himself as the older, wiser, highly charismatic object of desire for all those wide-eyed ripe and ready female students. I felt I had been *recruited*, that there must have been others before me, but I didn't care, because it was me he'd chosen that night. And I was on entirely the same page. I knew *exactly* what he was doing because I was doing it too.

Mac would also have been conscious of how sexy and thrilling it was to watch a sexy and thrilling movie in the middle of the night. The nightie, the hair, the lift, the sink, Alex's leather coat . . . The eighties gloss. But I was on board anyway. I would have gone anywhere with him. That's who I was back then. Up for excitement, up for escape. Up for it all.

I use my key fob to buzz myself into the production offices of *Coppers* and walk to my desk, politely saying hello to the colleagues that I pass. I have a reputation for being 'head down', quiet. Funny how much of a brazen seductress I was thirty years ago. How unapologetic. How fearless. I don't recognize that girl now. She slipped out of view a long time ago.

Charlie is hovering by my desk.

'Hall! You missed a good night the other night!'

'I can tell, by the bags under your eyes and the Red Bull in your hand.' I smile. I place my bag under my desk and sit down, turn on my grubby computer. I really must get some of those special wipes and give it a good clean. 'I'm glad it was a good one, though.'

'It was! It got totally messy – Joe from Scripts got tanked and Lou and Teresa from Accounts got engaged! Wedding bells are on the cards . . . I can hear them chiming.' He cupped his hand to his ear. 'I wonder if we'll get an invite . . . So what *did* you do that night? A little light telly? Some reading? Knitting?'

'Knitting! How dare you,' I say, mock-affronted. 'No, I went to visit an old friend.'

'Interesting . . .' teases Charlie. 'Say no more!'

'Then I won't.'

'You're such a *moody* cow,' he says, and I laugh. I have no moods to speak of at the moment, I'm all evened out. At least I was until Mac came back into my life. Now I feel like I'm pulling down the metal bar and buckling myself into an unpredictable rollercoaster. 'Only joking; you know I love you, Hall. Now, New Year's Eve tonight,' he says needlessly. How could anyone *not* know? 'What are you up to? There's a few of us going down The Long Good Friday if you fancy it.'

I haven't been to The Friday for years. And I won't be going tonight. I've already declined invitations to a meal and a tribute Michael Jackson at the Taj (with Becky) and a night on a boat on the Thames (with Dominic). I'm not a big fan of New Year's Eve, never have been. Growing up it was a raided drinks cabinet and the under-eighteens' disco, which was always a disappointment, then it was pubs, clubs and extortionate tickets, no taxis, no coats, freezing walks home and more disappointments. Years and years of them. In the early days of Christian there was one mad party, somewhere, which was fun, as he was still in 'love-bombing', reel-me-in mode, but once we were married, New Year's Eves anywhere with Christian were hell. When I couldn't even glance at another man or say remotely the wrong thing. When love-bombing turned nuclear.

'I can't,' I say, 'I'm going to visit the same friend. He's in hospital.'

'Ah,' says Charlie. 'Sorry to hear that. Nothing serious, I hope.'

'Well, it is,' I say, 'but I'm hoping he'll be OK.'

'You've got egg in your hair, by the way,' says Charlie. He knows I occasionally start the day with an egg burrito from the canteen.

'Have I?' I pretend to reach up to check. I enjoy Charlie's cheeky chastisements – at least I no longer live in fear of having my faults dragged out for examination and scoured into my face.

'Right, I'd better go.' He grins. 'I have a drug addict and a teenage runaway to cast. See you later.'

'See you, Charlie.'

*

The streets are quiet tonight. Everyone is at home glamming themselves up. Squeezing themselves into bodycon dresses and skinny-legged *TOWIE* suits in electric blue. Dousing themselves in perfume and aftershave. Getting into that party spirit – the horrifying one where you have to be all overexcited and hyped-up to toxicity . . . before it all turns to too-much-vodka and disillusionment. I'm a little nervous, but happy to be swished in through the quiet automatic doors of the hospital and into its lemon light. Cocooned inside the embrace of its low voices and purposeful activity and the muted soundtrack of both hope and resignation. No party hats and shouted song lyrics here. No 'Hi Ho Silver Lining's. I feel guilty, though, about Becky and her Michael Jackson night – once upon a time we would have had a right giggle at something like that; especially as she doesn't even like Michael Jackson. I wonder who has gone with her.

As I wait to be buzzed into the ward, I spy through the small square of glass in the centre of the door a man standing by Mac's bed. He's wearing a dark suit and has dark hair. He's tall. Is he a consultant or another visitor? He doesn't *look* like a consultant. He has no files in his hands or lanyards around his neck. I'm a little disappointed it won't be just me, really, if he's not. If I was Mac's first visitor, is this his second? Is it his son, maybe?

Fran opens the door before I get the 'click' to let me in. She's wearing a turquoise party hat, one from a cracker, and has eye make-up on. She looks pretty.

'He's got someone else visiting,' she says, looking incomprehensibly furtive and darting her eyes around like a member of the French resistance. 'A man.'

'Yes, I can see,' I say. I'm trembling a little at the thought of the man being Mac's son, considering our history, and it may be a little bratty, but I don't want Mac to have another visitor. I want to have his full attention. I don't want someone else sitting there on a plastic chair, making inane chit-chat and nodding at Mac and expecting Mac to nod back. I want Mac to look at me and I'm hoping he will say something else to me tonight. I can remember the second movie on The List and I hope Mac does, too.

'I'm off on my fag break; see you in a bit.'

'Yeah, see you, Fran,' I say absent-mindedly. I make my way over to Mac's bed, aware of my heels on the floor again. Under my checked coat I'm wearing a green, sleeveless shift dress, one of my favourites, in a vintage-y boiled wool. It's a bit tight as I ate so much of Julian's shortbread over Christmas and I'll need to hold my stomach in, if I remember.

The ward has had its decorations refreshed. Intertwined with the Slinkies are now paper chains, the old-fashioned ones you lick and stick together, which also drape between the metal headboards of the beds. Shiny new concertinaed garlands hang optimistically from the ceiling; one or two are in the eighties style of the terrible bell at Mac's party, which makes me smile. The nurses all have party hats on; some are wearing sparkly deely-boppers. There are pops of colour all over the ward and it looks cheery; hopeful.

The man by Mac's bed has his tailored charcoal back to me. He is still standing.

I approach, wave a weak 'Hello' at Mac, although he appears to be asleep, and take off my beret. The man is still standing there, slightly awkwardly. He's very good-looking. He has the face of a movie idol – chiselled, strong jaw, salt-and-peppered temples. I am suspicious of very good-looking men; they are usually hiding something. Does he look like Mac, though? He is dark to Mac's fair and holds himself very differently – he is straight-backed, composed-looking.

'Hello, I'm Arden,' I say, holding out a hand I am trying to steady. 'Are you Mac's son?'

'No, I'm his neighbour,' says the man. Of course, he's too old to be Mac's son – this man is forty-something. Forty-four? Forty-five? He actually looks like an estate agent. A bit of a wide boy. Wide boys are the ones to avoid. I know this, having called on my knees to one through a locked bathroom door, begging for next week's housekeeping. 'I'm James.'

'Pleased to meet you,' I say.

'I've been away since before Christmas,' James says. 'Eleven nights at my mum's down in Kent. Just got back. The roads were terrible. The nurse says he's only had one visitor on the ward so far; was that you?'

'Yes.' *And thank you for the information about the roads.* I take a few steps closer to James so a sleeping Mac can't hear. I notice he has soot-grey eyes; dark eyelashes. 'I wonder why his family haven't come,' I say.

James frowns. 'I don't know,' he says. 'I've never seen any family. Mac lives alone.'

'He's not married?'

'Not that I know of.'

Oh. 'How long have you lived next door to him?' I ask. I'm still a little nervous but I'm being really nosy; this is not like me, these days.

'Four years. I haven't known family come to visit. No kids, no grandkids . . .' James appears to be almost talking to himself and has a northern accent, a little like Mac's, though not as strong.

'How strange,' I say. No children, no wife; I'm surprised. 'Whereabouts in London do you and Mac live?'

'Larkspur Hill.'

'Oh, right.' Then Mac does live near me. He lives very near. How miraculous but terribly sad it is that Mac and I have been living mere streets away from each other, but never met. We could have bumped into each other. We could have looked surprised, then delighted, refused to make small talk and only talked about the big stuff in our lives, then, after a while, Mac could have smiled one of his long, slow smiles and pulled me into him for a hug . . . 'That's not far.'

'No, not far.' James smiles, a little unsteadily.

'Where are you from?' I add. Now I'm being *really* nosy. What's *wrong* with me?

'Macclesfield, originally. Why?'

'Oh, I like accents,' I mutter, feeling foolish.

'He's a nice man,' says James, obviously deciding to ignore what an absolute nosy twit I am. I can't believe myself. Years of barely saying boo to a goose and now I'm interrogating some poor stranger. 'How do you know him?'

'I'm a former student of his,' I lie.

'Ah,' says James. 'I believe he was quite the legendary academic, back in the day.'

'Yes, a Film Studies' lecturer.' I am still reeling from the fact that all this time Mac has been living so close to me. I could have reached out and touched him, almost.

'I met one of his former students at a barbecue he held once. I don't think it was you.'

'No, it wasn't me.' And I wonder who it was, and what she was doing there, and if the tequila came out.

'Do you want to sit down?' James has a formal way of speaking, I think. And he doesn't look me in the eye.

'Thanks.'

He pulls the sole plastic chair by Mac's bed forward for me and I sit. He drags over another, marooned by the next curtain, apologizing for the awful noise, and sits down next to me. He stretches out his legs, a little self-consciously, I think, and with a small smile I see that under all that charcoal he is wearing a pair of red and white stripy socks. Where's Wally, I think. Or *The Cat in the Hat*, one of Julian's favourite films when he was growing up. He watched it over and over; knew every line. It became a kind of comfort blanket and escape for him, when life became very hard. I will text Julian 'Happy New Year' at midnight, and I do wish him a very happy one. I know he's fine, but I worry about him, still. He's a confident grown-up man now but I sometimes worry that that terrified little boy, under Christian's regime, might still be there, in the shadows.

Mac's eyes are still closed. He has one foot sticking out of the bed which makes me grin and wonder if he asked one of the nurses to move his leg for him. His foot always had to be out; he got too hot in bed otherwise. The telly is on, above us, *The Review of the Year* or something similar. It's mostly bad things, some silly stuff. Famous people who have done things. Other famous people who have sadly died.

'I don't really like New Year's Eve,' says James, watching as an athlete breaks the ten-minute mile again or something (I don't do sport). He really *is* handsome, I think, in just that matinee-idol way I know is dangerous. Good-looking men hold too much power; they think they have it all and want to crush anyone who dares think otherwise. I wonder if he's kind to his wife or girlfriend. Or whether he puts all her money in a joint account and only lets her have £75 of it a month. 'It's always such a massive disappointment.'

'Me too,' I say. 'I'm happy to be spending some of mine here. I've got a son I could impose myself on – he's nineteen – but I don't want to cramp his style.'

James nods. He's not forthcoming about why he is here on New Year's Eve. 'I guess you know all about the car accident and Mac's injuries,' says James. 'I've been talking to – Fran, is it? She says he can't talk?'

'No, apparently he might have some form of aphasia. The non-fluent one, or something. He can only say the occasional phrase. He spoke last night – just a few words – but nothing since.'

'Oh, what did he say? Was it something important?'

'Only to me,' I say. I don't want to tell him about 'bunny soup'. It will sound utterly ridiculous. 'It was just something silly.'

'OK.' James nods. I imagine he might say something next like, 'I'm not one to pry.' 'Ah, you're awake.'

Mac has opened his eyes. He looks surprised to see me, at first – perhaps he thought I wouldn't come again – then he smiles at both his visitors, reserving the tiniest of tiny, imperceptible winks for me, as a little extra. Well, I like to think so, anyway; it banishes the remainder of my nerves. I'm glad he's with us. Talking to James is a little . . . awkward. He talks slowly as though measuring up each word before it comes out. I realize he has the formal language of a very polite, elderly man. At least he's not rattling off his day to me, though, I think – whatever it is he does – or banging on about the weather.

'Sorry I couldn't make it in before now, I've been away. So, how're you doing?' James asks Mac. 'I know you can't answer, probably, but you look well,' he says. 'Oh God, I'm dreadful at this sort of thing,' he adds, turning to me. 'Mac knows what I'm like, though. Or doesn't, rather. I keep myself to myself, really. I'm not a good neighbour.' He must be, I think, as he's here, but someone so good-looking being introverted as he describes is unusual. Someone who looks like him would normally be braying against shiny bars every night, breaking people's hearts. I notice his mouth turns up slightly at the corners even when he's not smiling and wonder if his hair would be inclined to curl if left to grow.

'I'm sure Mac is just glad you're here,' I say, not that I can speak for him. Perhaps he can't stand the sight of this James. It doesn't look that way, though; Mac looks pleased to see both of us. He lets James squeeze his hand briefly. To me, he again gives what could almost be a wink, which having remembered what I do of us, makes my heart give a little hitch. I enjoy the sensation, my heart having been unbothered for so long.

Fran, faintly smelling of cigarettes and, if I'm not mistaken, Anaïs Anaïs (ah, old school), bustles over with a lidless tin of Quality Street.

'Want one?'

There are only the duff ones left so I decline. James takes a toffee penny.

'I can't bear New Year's Eve,' she says, taking the wrapper from James and stuffing it in the pocket of her tunic. It's pretty universal, then, I note. 'But you have to make the effort. It's not so bad being here at work, though. It's warm, it's dry, I don't have to stagger anywhere and the punters are not *too* much trouble.' She grins at Mac.

'No bouncers required,' I offer.

'No, though I suspect if he got the chance young Mac here could get a little rowdy.' She winks at Mac and he smiles slowly back, his eyes crinkling at the corners like a closing fan. She bustles away again.

'I have to leave at eight,' says James, to no one in particular. He is very unrelaxed, I think. Other male visitors have legs plonked confidently across knees, hands laced behind heads – elbows out – assuredly taking up Man Space. James is sitting up straight, looking slightly anxious and apologetic for being here, a bit 'out of sorts', as Marilyn used to say about people, when she was being generous. When she wasn't, she just used to say they were arseholes. 'I've got to show a couple round a house. No rest for the wicked, not even on New Year's Eve.'

'Oh, you *are* an estate agent,' I say, then realize I sound like an utter fool yet again.

'Why do you say that?' James looks defensive; he's gone really northern and deadpan.

'It's the suit,' I say. 'Sorry.' *Keep digging that hole, Arden.* 'Sorry,' I repeat – old habits die hard. 'Why are you doing that now? Showing people round a house, I mean?' Now I sound not only nosy but bossy; I really don't know *how* to be, it seems.

He shrugs and says, 'It's when the clients are free. I have to be available at any time. Would you like a coffee?'

'OK. Yes. Thanks very much.'

There's a vending machine in the corridor outside the

ward. James levers himself off the chair with an apologetic smile and walks towards the door.

'All right, Mac?' I ask, squeezing his hand. He applies a very slight pressure back. 'It's nice what they've done with the place, isn't it? The decorations. Remember your party? That Christmas tree you had?'

He nods. Does he remember?

'Remember your *Ghostbusters* poster? You'd put tinsel round it, I think.'

He nods again, a tired smile. I feel like I'm in a tragic comedy sketch, suddenly. A drunk person in an art gallery trying to make conversation with a statue, or something. It makes me feel foolish. It's also warm, so I shrug my cardigan off. I believe Mac notices my dress as his left eyebrow twitches up ever so slightly. Not much of a repertoire, is it, I think. A smile, a wink, the faintest squeeze of the hand. I will him to get better. I will him to *come back*. I want to ask him how the past twenty-eight years have been for him, how it all worked out. If he has forgiven me like I have forgiven him.

But most of all, if he had *forgotten* me.

James returns with the coffee. He has a hot chocolate; the steam rises into his face as he sips from it. The three of us just sit for a while, an odd triangle. Someone on *The Review of the Year* has just won an Oscar and the replay of their speech is comically awful. A man opposite breaks – randomly – into song, from his bed. 'We'll Meet Again', and no one tries to shush him. His voice is noble, determined. A couple more low, timorous, wavering voices join in. A nurse – not Fran – lends her off-key chime, as she adjusts someone's drip feed. It brings tears to my eyes. I now feel like I'm in some kind of wartime epic by David Lean.

At eight fifteen James gets up to go. He looks tired now, I think; he actually looks worse than Mac. He has purplish shadows under his eyes, like the beginnings of a bruise. 'Right, well, I'm going. I might see you again, Arden. Nice to meet you.'

'You too, James.' I'm not sure if it has been, really, but then again, I doubt I've made much of an impression on him, either. With a stride of charcoal and a flash of Where's Wally, he leaves the ward.

'Is visiting still finishing at half eight tonight?' I ask Fran, as she passes by with a big tub of Haribos.

'Half nine tonight,' she replies, 'we're extending it for New Year's Eve. Call it a lock-in.' She grins.

'Ooh, exciting,' I say, returning the grin.

'Get it where you can find it,' says Fran.

At nine o'clock Fran slips a DVD into the bottom of one of the suspended tellies and turns the volume right up so we can hear last year's Big Ben and watch some pre-recorded fireworks.

'We're doing it early!' she calls out. 'So you lot don't have to burn the midnight oil.'

The patients try to look vaguely interested or, some of them, excited. One sweet old boy is attempting to blow on a given-out party horn but it doesn't make much of a dent. The nurses are huddled in a weird group hug; I spy a bottle of contraband prosecco and think, *Good for them.* I am holding Mac's hand and I feel strangely . . . happy, like I belong here, on this warm, bright ward where life, although interrupted, seems to be ticking along quite merrily in its own suspended vacuum of safety and care. Where faces are – albeit briefly – animated and alive. I feel safe and almost cosseted.

The premature countdown starts – ten, nine, eight . . . and I am reminded of the screening room and the ticking, rattling countdown to our movies on The List. I wonder if Mac remembers too. I join in the chorus of numbers – some voices hoarse (the patients), some high and raucous (the nurses). As an early Big Ben chimes I take the liberty of kissing Mac briefly on the cheek and then, feeling brave, I place my hand on the other side of his face. We remain like that for a few seconds; my mouth close to his cheek, breathing him in, then I move my hand on to his, at the side of the bed – warm, a tender pressure. Where has he been all this time? Where have I? And why has he come back to me now?

Like the changeover of reels between the two old movie projectors in the screening room, the old year sputters out, spinning until its end tick-ticks to nothing, and the 'New Year' is kick-started into life, it's motor already running at pace, loud and juddering. And I am with Mac. Again.

He smiles at me and then his lips part a little. I lean in further towards him, although we can't get much closer. 'What is it, Mac?'

Only just audible and with lots of false starts and hesitation, Mac says, 'That's . . . lot of . . . birds.' And a huge smile dawns slowly on my face.

He remembers. He remembers the next movie. The one where everything truly began.

I brave a wink back at him as though I am the old Arden.

'A *lot* of birds,' I agree, as last year's fireworks continue to explode over London and the nurses break into 'Auld Lang Syne'.

THEN

Chapter 5: The Birds

Mac and I watched *The Birds* at the beginning of the spring term. Despite him saying we'd 'do this again' – words I clung to like a child to unwrapped Christmas presents – I didn't see Mac Bartley-Thomas again after his party; there were only a few more days of term and they limped on infuriatingly, without me so much as catching a tantalizing glimpse of him. But thoughts of him, and my determination to make things happen again in January, kept me going during the Christmas holidays. University holidays, I soon realized, were to be *endured*.

When I arrived home, after that first term at Warwick, with my enormous bag – more like a backpacker's rucksack – Marilyn was at the kitchen table fuming over a round robin.

'Bloody show-offs!' she raged, like she always did when she received the Christmas card from the Bankses with the photocopied, two-page letter inside. She seemed neither to have noticed nor to have cared that I had come in through the back door. The tap was dripping. The kettle had just boiled and there was steam hanging in the air, with no particular place to go, by the window. 'Who cares about Timmy's PhD and his humanitarian mission to sodding Uganda,' she spat with the disdain of the seasoned, trodden-on proletariat. 'And Meredith's fucking handcrafted sodding mittens? And Tarquin's badminton scholarship?'

None of these were their real names, but Marilyn was prone to embellishment. She was not dressed. She was in one of her ubiquitous grubby slips, her hair up in a tangled topknot, secured with a claw clip; her veiny legs bare and crossed. I felt cross with myself that – clearly delusional – somehow on the train journey home I'd almost started to look forward to seeing her, and, after my ten-week absence, I'd entertained the stupid notion that she might be looking forward to seeing *me*. Her scowling face, projected down to the offending missive on the table, told me I was a fool. Her refusal to even be dressed laughed at my misguided hope, and she banged and stubbed a red Bic biro on to the table until the end snapped off. She'd been 'marking' the round robin, I noticed, had crossed bits off, added angry exclamation marks here and there, scribbled out bits furiously. She did it every year.

She still hadn't noticed me, in the doorway, despite the door being wide open. She never really noticed me – not now – and I'd given up trying to make her.

'Hello, Marilyn,' I said. She wouldn't let me call her Mum, but I didn't mind as I didn't really think of her as one any more. She was certainly nothing like my friends' mothers. They actually cooked the tea and didn't behave like constant narcissists.

'Oh, it's you.' She tore up the letter and threw it dramatically into the tiny bin which was suckered to the inside door of the cupboard under the sink. A kitten-heeled patent slingback on the end of one pale, veiny leg kicked the door shut with a bang. I could hear an empty tin of beans, or something, fall with a clatter inside. Marilyn always wore heels, even when she wasn't wearing much else. *Standards*, she called it. 'I hope you haven't brought a ton of washing home,' she said and I waited for the classic line about treating 'the place like a hotel'.

'No, none,' I said. 'I used the launderette at Warwick

57

before I came home.' I wouldn't have asked her anyway, but I knew she wouldn't want to do it. Marilyn was not big on domestic tasks. She was not big on much apart from doing her hair and flirting with anyone with a male set of chromosomes.

'Oh, *Warwick*,' she parroted. She thought I had got 'above' myself even applying. 'You sound a bit la-de-da,' she added, narrowing her false-lashed eyes, 'a bit posh. Bet you didn't want to come home to us commoners.' She laughed, as though she was sharing an excellent joke with me, then winked at me so I managed a smile back. 'It's been terrible here.' She sighed, fluffing up her hair with a taloned hand. 'Dull.'

Somehow, my mother was furious she wasn't a film star. She was christened Marion but she didn't want to be the mum from *Happy Days*; she wanted to be Marilyn Monroe – despite having neither the talent nor the drive to become anything resembling a Hollywood star. When she was twenty-two she won a beauty contest at Butlin's; when she was twenty-four she was in an advert in the free paper for a local car showroom. Apart from that she worked as a cashier in a hardware shop, and at twenty-five, she had me. But she made everyone call her Marilyn, for as long as I could remember, and she looked the part, with a fierce relentlessness.

It was the late eighties, but there was no mullet-y bubble perm or flicky helmet for her. No chenille jumpers, jeans and soft flat loafers, in burgundy. No blue eyeshadow. She had the blondest of toxic short blonde hair, which she rolled into waves and giant curls, like Marilyn's – except hers were slightly frizzy and calmed with Vitapointe, before mousse was invented. A spit-in-it black eyeliner, in a block, that she winged her eyes with. Capri pants and off-the-shoulder, python-tight black tops and itchy, high-necked mohair sweaters. With heels, and a pointy bra and to-the-waist silk, frilly knickers hidden underneath.

She liked to pretend she was special and either furious with those who couldn't see it or wheedling and conniving with those who showed a hint of being remotely willing to go along with it. *I* would have thought she was special enough, just being my mum, but unfortunately being someone's mum wasn't enough for her.

I put my giant bag in the hall and went up the stairs. I didn't want to say anything else to Marilyn. She would only accuse me of putting on university airs and graces. She didn't want to *see* me, either. I was the literal embodiment of 'nothing to see here', like they always said in crime films. It hadn't always been like this. I believed she once looked kindly upon me. The photos in our dusty old album with the seventies-print cover seemed to suggest so; there were several of her actually *smiling* at me, as a baby on her lap. She looked quite happy to have me there. I also believed that from about the age of five I became an irritant to her.

'I used your room as a dressing room!' she called upstairs after me. 'I'll move my gear later.'

My bedroom had been surprisingly immaculate, for me, when I'd left it. I'd spent hours taking down all my teenage posters, making my bed, dusting and picking up crap from the floor and hoovering. For the first time I had seen the carpet and had clean, clutter-free surfaces; I wanted it nice for when I came back so that *something* would be. Now her 'gear' was strewn all over the place. There were make-up bags and rollers and brushes and combs scattered all over my bed. Dresses and tops hung from window latches and door knobs, and draped over radiators. Shoes toppled against each other like fallen dominoes on my cream carpet. There was a spilt lozenge of bright red nail varnish on the carpet like a faceless beetle.

She hadn't always been this way – a slut and a slattern. Dad agreed it was sometime after turning thirty that she changed. The distraction of my baby and infant years had passed; the unformed dream of her being the next big thing in Hollywood was now a painful joke. She started to panic about not being young, about not *being* somebody; she had nothing to cling to except perpetuating a bad Marilyn Monroe pastiche, and cultivating a growing resentment towards everyone in her life. Dad said she needed self-created drama and validation from other men or she was afraid her very own sense of self would slip away. That she became cruel because it gave her a warped kind of control, and credence to the illusion of being someone special. I wasn't sure what any of that meant; I just knew Marilyn used to love me but now she didn't.

I gingerly lifted a silky chemise thing – pilled and frayed at the hem – from my dressing-table stool and there was a three-pack of Durex condoms under it. I shook my head, with a grimace, and as I tidied all her stuff into a pile which I dumped out on the landing, I wondered just how many indiscretions Marilyn had chalked up since I'd been away. She was a master seductress – we all knew it – a champion. If seduction was an Olympic sport my mother would win Gold and then try to get off with the bloke putting the medal round her neck.

'He fancies me,' she'd say, about everyone, and then she'd try to do something about it. It didn't matter that she had a husband who adored her and would take her back each and every time she cheated, and a child who used to adore her, until the child realized how fruitless that was – Marilyn always wanted more. Sometimes there was a calm period of three or four months, maybe six (I came to think of it as her 'resting'), when she came back to us and she and Dad were all lovey-dovey, and things were fine. But then she would scour for men and succumb again.

'I've put it all out on the landing!' I called down. I knew, as usual, she would later try to appease me for her rudeness, her disinterest. She'd appear in my bedroom doorway with a box of Milk Tray and a disarming smile – she had a stash of both hidden away, ready to be pulled out, like a rabbit from a hat, when she needed to get round me. She would make me open the chocolates and watch me choose my favourite one, something that used to make me feel nice but didn't now; she'd ask me to save her a hazelnut whirl for when she got back from her shift at the leisure centre.

She'd worked there for three years – another in a series of jobs. In the little reception area next to the turnstiles. Stage front, she called it, as though she worked at the theatre. It *was* her stage, though. She got up from her office chair a lot – pencil skirts, sheer blouses over that pointy bra, stockings with those seams up the back; always slightly on the wonk. A steady stream (a pool, if you like) of men to flirt with went clanking through those turnstiles: dads, sporty young men, lifeguards. Dad and I knew when she'd been up to no good. She'd slink home with her jaunty MM curls a little messed up and stinking of chlorine, despite a good layer of *Charlie* over the top, sniffily declaring a pool party or a late session she'd had to stay on duty for. This was code for shagging a poor lifeguard senseless in one of the filthy private cubicles in the changing room. We weren't stupid. We knew she was as dirty as one of the changing-room drains matted with dark, wet hair and a rubbery week-old verruca plaster.

'Arden!' she shouted up at me, her voice shrill. 'Don't touch my cerise baby doll, it's very delicate!'

It was somewhere at the bottom of the pile on the landing, its pompom hem crushed under a red suede court shoe. I hated her saying my name. Why would she call me a name which suggested she wanted me to be exactly like her? A Marilyn clone? I didn't want to be her or be like her. By now I was repulsed at the thought of even being in her womb.

Right up to my departure for Warwick there was Marilyn drama. We just couldn't escape it. Dad was a mild-mannered, loving and genial man who always turned an eye so blind to Marilyn's misdemeanours he needed a guide dog, and took her back every single time. He loved her; that was always his excuse. He couldn't imagine life without her. You had to admire the man for his staying power. *I* did. I loved him for sticking with her as it meant he stuck with *me*. I'm sure it was one of the reasons he did. But, until I left home, I had no choice but to be privy to all the drama and the constant ups and downs. His everlasting hope she would stop being such a cow; her everlasting refusal to be worthy of such a steadfastly loyal man.

Three days before I made my blissful escape to Warwick, for that first autumn term, I came in through the back door after the pub to the sound of high-pitched weeping. Marilyn was in a terrible state at the kitchen table (*Happy Days* are here again?) and wailing like an air-raid siren. It seemed a boy had nearly drowned at the pool during one of her shifts.

'Where was the lifeguard?' Dad asked, with as much world-weary inquisition as my poor father could muster. He was at the table eating an early portion of fish and chips out of the paper, his hair flat to his head, his faded New York Yankees sweatshirt looking too hot and tight for him. He had massive biceps just ripe for hitting someone with, but he never did. He had been a hippy in the sixties, had travelled to San Francisco during the summer of love. He was a lover not a fighter, but this of course made him a loser, too, my lovely Dad. He had lost in the game of love with Marilyn, big time, and over and over again.

'He was there, of course he was,' she said, sniffing, but she wouldn't look at us. She never did when she'd been caught out.

Dad and I looked at each other instead and Dad took another slug from an ever-to-hand glass of beer. It didn't take an over-active imagination to fathom what had really gone on, did it? She'd been shagging the lifeguard out the back somewhere and someone's poor kid had nearly died.

'Oh, Marilyn,' I said, and she lit up a fag, blowing smoke all over Dad's chips.

But an hour later, once she'd made a furtive call to her colleague, Debbie, from our dual-decorated hall (striped wallpaper and floral sponge-effect, separated by dado rail) and had ascertained she wasn't going to get into trouble, she was dishing up Findus crispy pancakes and frozen peas to me without a care in the world.

It was a miserable Christmas. Awful. Christmas Day being an absolute low point. Marilyn was drunk and, with no flirting outlet for it, was trapped with Dad, me, a dried-out turkey and *Morecambe and Wise*. She became snappy and morose. She refused to wear the cracker hat as she said it made her look unattractive; she stropped over the Brussels; she laddered her stockings and swore like a sailor. Dad got on the cider just to make it bearable; drink to me was all about fun so I abstained. They were both snoring by the time a safari-suited Roger Moore whizzed through the swamps on an air boat, chasing baddies, in the Christmas-afternoon movie; Marilyn's fluffy mule slippers hanging off the end of her stockinged feet and Dad stuffed endearingly into his worn velour armchair.

I couldn't wait to get away. I couldn't wait to go back to Warwick and my freedom. When the film ended, I sneaked out of the room and called Becky – we had exchanged numbers on the last day of term. She sounded happy; I could hear *Top of the Pops* on in the background, her cousins were over and it all sounded terribly festive. I was jealous as hell.

I slept with Mac the first Tuesday of the spring term. I know it was a Tuesday because we always had a morning lecture on a Tuesday, followed by a lunchtime seminar. I caught him in the corridor outside the Humanities Lecture Theatre with a book in his hand, whistling the theme from *The Guns of Navarone*. He looked boyish, cheeky, delicious, and I was utterly in lust. I wanted to rake my hand through his floppy hair and kiss him until he begged me to stop.

'Here's that book on film theory you wanted to borrow,' he said, as I went and stood chirpily in front of him, giving him my best smile.

'Did I?'

'Yes.' He thrust it into my hands. It was called *Sculpting in Time*. 'I hope you get a lot from it.'

'I'm sure I will.'

'There's a very good chapter on "yearning for the ideal".'

'Splendid.'

This exchange of words between us was entirely and immediately sexual and it completely thrilled me. I was grinning; there was delight in Mac's dancing eyes; my heart was thumping in my knickers, which childishly declared 'Tuesday' on the front, accompanied by a cartoon bear.

'What are you doing now?' he asked, while the thumping and the grinning continued.

'Going back to my room. Staring at my Einstein poster. Rifling through my Letts notes on *The Canterbury Tales*. Lying on my bed and dreaming of Fellini.'

Mac laughed. 'Do you want to come for a coffee with me? Maybe a muffin?' The word 'muffin' had never sounded so sexually charged before. I liked it. 'Harvey's should be quiet at this time.'

'OK,' I said, and I knew exactly where it would lead and, God, I hoped it would.

We walked to the café, me daring anyone and everyone to notice us together. I felt like I was walking on air. Air that had a massive power surge crackling through it, like those clouds in *Flash Gordon*. Mac ordered coffee and toasted English muffins, with butter, although I was too excited to eat mine. I toyed with a tea, two sugars. I looked around the sparsely populated café – students eating all-day bacon and egg baguettes, nursing strong coffees for their enduring hangovers – hoping people were wondering what we were doing together, considering I wasn't one of Mac's students. I was challenging someone to give us 'a look'. There was zero chance we appeared entirely innocent. I felt as far from innocent as I ever had.

Forty-five minutes later we were in his double bed in the bedroom of his flat and we had already had sex twice. A half-finished bottle of wine was on Mac's bedside table, along with two torn condom wrappers, his glasses – still slightly steamed – and my watch.

'So,' said Mac. He was lying prone, his head on the pillow, looking up at the ceiling and catching his breath. His chest was pale above the white sheet. There was just the right amount of hair there for me to circle into cute whorls of tumbleweed with my finger.

'So,' I said. I was on my side, my legs flanked against his; my chin nestled in his sweet and sour armpit.

'You're sure you're OK?' he said, sticking one foot out from under the covers. 'With the whole lecturer/student thing? It's not against university rules but it *is* frowned upon.'

'I'm used to being frowned upon,' I said into his armpit. 'It's fine by me.' My bra was on the floor, my Tuesday knickers were screwed up at the end of Mac's bed and I had come three times. It was academic to be talking about rules and regulations at this stage, quite frankly.

'You're absolutely sure? I'm certain we won't get caught.'

'I'm absolutely sure. Are you saying you want to carry on with this?' I held my breath, praying he would say 'yes'.

'Yes, I do. Do you?'

'Oh, definitely. I've got one question for you, though.'

'Go for it.'

'How many students have you slept with before me?' This was what I really wanted to know: did I have predecessors or – worse – a rival, here on campus.

'None,' said Mac.

65

'*None?*'

'None. Have there been rumours?'

'Loads,' I said, 'but if you say I'm the first, then I'm the first.'

'You're the first.'

'OK.' So I *had* been recruited, but as the first, not as the *next*. I was really happy.

'And you? There's no one else at Warwick you're seeing?'

'No.'

Actually, I had a boyfriend at home I hadn't quite got around to dumping yet. He wasn't up to much, Steven from Home. But I had been determined to lose my virginity and he was sometimes a good laugh and he had a decent car. We'd sit and snog in it after he dropped me home from the pub, him putting on a Whitney Houston CD, for mood. When it got too boring and unsensual, I'd go in. I'd hate it if Marilyn was still up as she'd be all giggly and ask if I'd been 'necking', which was excruciating. She'd be sitting at the kitchen table in her flimsy silk dressing gown, a 'fag on' and an open Arthur Miller in front of her so she could pretend she was a semi-intellectual, like the real Marilyn.

We only had sex a couple of times, Steven from Home and I. It was pretty awful; I felt sorry for all the missionaries who had ever lived. I did it with him again, just the once, in the Christmas holidays, when the boredom of being at home with Dad and Marilyn got too much. I needed to get around to writing him a letter to end it.

'Would you like to watch another film with me?' asked Mac, playing with my hair.

'Which one?'

'*The Birds*?'

'Hitchcock? Yeah, sure. Haven't you got a lecture or something to go to, though?' It was gone three in the afternoon.

'No, all done for the day. You?'

'Nada,' I said, raising my chin – any essay I should be getting on with could wait. 'I'm free as one of dem *birds*.'

'You're funny,' he said. I knew this. I had cultivated my wit to see me through life: a drawbridge against Marilyn's bitter complaints; a swinging saloon bar against school's hard edges: pretty robust, but not always effective. 'Have you ever watched it?' Mac took the fag end of a packet of Polos from the side, peeled back the foil with his neat fingernail and offered me one before popping the last mint in his mouth. I was glad Mac wasn't one for a post-coital cigarette. I hated smoking, because of Marilyn. I hated yellow ceilings and shell ashtrays and the kind of breath, combined with coffee, which could make a girl heave before school in the morning.

'Yeah, a couple of times. It's scary.'

'What other Hitchcock films have you seen?' He played with the Polo mint, speared on the tip of his tongue. I was mesmerized.

'*Rear Window*, *North by Northwest* – the one with the cornfield, that's the one, isn't it? *Dial M for Murder*. I love that one. I think that's possibly my favourite.'

'That's interesting,' said Mac, looking surprised. 'It's not his most popular. Critics call it "Lower Case Hitchcock".'

'Really? Well, I'm an interesting person.'

'Indeed you are.' Mac looked rather pleased about that. 'What do you make of Hitchcock's portrayal of women?'

'A bit dodgy,' I said. 'He treats them as sex objects while pretending he reveres them as strong women. All those icy blondes . . . He was a bit of a sex pest, wasn't he?'

'No one's really said so, in so many words . . .' said Mac. 'I know he put Tippi Hedren through a fairly sadistic ordeal for that attic scene of *The Birds*, though. She had her eye clawed at, got pecked at by real birds. She described it as the worst week of her life. Hey, I hope you don't think of *me* as a sex pest.' He was grinning; he knew there was no way I did.

'You're not a sex pest if it's mutual,' I said and I pressed my body closer to his and trailed my finger down the central groove of his chest.

'Very true.' He smiled lazily. He shifted his body so he was facing me. 'Can I ravish you one more time and then we'll go? We'll really have to sneak in this time, like fugitives. We don't have the cover of darkness to skulk around in at this time in the afternoon.'

I liked his use of the word 'skulk'. I was most certainly up for a spot of it. After the ravishing we got dressed and left Mac's flat, separately. We crossed the courtyards and the open spaces of campus, the wind tunnels between square-bricked buildings, at a steady distance from one another. I entered the Humanities Building a minute after Mac, looking left and right like a spy. I had the urge to turn up the collar of my denim jacket. This was fun.

I decided it would be even more fun to kiss Mac on the threshold of the screening room before he had even unlocked the door (he had got somewhat delayed; a student had stopped him to briefly pick his illustrious brain), which was deliciously dangerous, as three other students had only just slipped from view round the corner. We kissed for ten more minutes on a squishy chair, the door locked, before he opened the faded cornflower-blue box he'd brought with him, where the reels of *The Birds* lay. These reels were older, a duller metal, the name on the middle of them faint and in scrawled handwriting. He took the top reel out and I held it in my hands. I ran my fingers over the metal, grooved my nail over the stack of brown film.

Mac looked at me as though I were a curiosity. 'You're really hard to resist; you know that, don't you?' he said.

'You don't have to resist me,' I replied. 'You can have me any time you like.' And he took the reel from me and placed it carefully back in the box. Then he hoisted me up on the Formica table and pushed my satin fifties skirt up to my knees. We did it silently; the last thing we wanted was a red-faced research assistant knocking on the door.

'Let's watch the master at work,' Mac finally said, as he did up the buckle of his belt and I yanked up my red woolly tights.

'I thought I just had.'

He laughed, bounded up the steps to the projection booth in one stride and began loading up the reels. I waited on one of the squishy chairs, pulling up another to make a sofa again, next to the wall.

The movie flip-flapped into life. Mac trotted back to me and plonked himself nearest to the wall as the countdown rattled down and the movie began; dark flitting birds skittering and battering across the screen as the credits rolled; the words splintered and disintegrating, as though pecked at; the only soundtrack the foreboding flap of wings and desolate, scrappy cawing and cheeping. I felt the opposite of foreboding and desolate. I was full of excitement, my body charged; my mind was swimming with great moments to come. As Tippi walked elegantly through Union Square in San Francisco and into the pet shop and Hitchcock did one of his famous cameos, coming out with two dogs on a lead, Mac took my hand and smoothed each of my fingers in turn with his forefinger and thumb.

Tippi Hedren was so beautiful as socialite Melanie Daniels. Her face, the elegant chignon her hair was rolled into, her green sleeveless dress with matching jacket. I was fascinated by everything, seeing this film anew with Mac – I was determined to *notice* everything. Stoic Mitch whose face didn't move much, the shrill women of the weird town on the coast. All those ominous faces. Never-ending, treacherous skies. Even the children were freaky-looking, before anything had even happened. Last time I'd seen it, I'd been wedged between Marilyn and Dad on our grubby mustard chesterfield, the central overhead light on, Marilyn noisily sucking on Fisherman's

Friends in my left ear. Mac and I were in the dark. The sound-track was as loud as we dared have it, despite the soundproofed room. It made it all wonderfully scary.

I tried to pre-empt what Mac might ask me afterwards. What was the significance of the lovebirds that Mitch fails to buy in the pet shop but which Melanie takes to his door, in order to woo him? What was with all the cage imagery? The significance of Tippi's green suit? I wanted to impress and excite him; I wanted to both challenge and contribute to his magnificent knowledge.

'She definitely brought them with her, didn't she?' I whispered, as Tippi crossed Bodega Bay in the tiny motor boat, with the lovebirds in the cage, to Mitch's house by the lake. 'Melanie Daniels. She brought the evil of the birds to Bodega Bay. She's being punished for being a woman who goes for what she wants.'

'Some would argue that,' Mac whispered back and I felt pleased as Punch. I was impressing him already. I had *The Birds* sussed.

When the first reel ended it made me jump – the little jolt and the bright dots pocking the screen, in the top right corner – even though I knew it was going to happen, as Mac had already left me and bounded up to the projection booth. It was jarring, how one reel ended and another one started. Precarious. *Jeopardy*, that's how Mac had put it. It seemed I was partial to it. Someone tried the door handle just as Mac sat back down, giving it a good old waggle, and I pretended to look horrified and then started giggling, my hand over my mouth.

'You *like* danger!' Mac said to me, his eyes flaming behind his glasses.

'A little.'

In the second reel, in a quiet bit, when Melanie was talking to Annie, the jealous schoolteacher ex of Mitch's, in her living room, there was a tapping noise. *Tap tap tap. Tap tap tap.* Over to our right.

'What the bloody hell's that?' I asked.

'I don't know,' said Mac.

Melanie and Annie continued their tense interplay. The tapping continued.

'Seriously, I'm freaking out. What *is* that?'

Mac burst out laughing and showed me his biro, tapping against the wall.

'You sod,' I said, appreciating the man's childish streak, and he put his arm round me and pulled me in close as Annie and Melanie discovered a hideous dead gull on Annie's doorstep. I liked snuggling in and feeling unsettled in Mac's arms as the movie got more and more eerie. Deliciously on edge.

'You enjoying it?' he asked me, as Melanie smoked on a bench in front of the schoolhouse, a jungle gym in the playground behind her – crow after crow alighting on it until there's a terrifying *murder* of them (clever, that Hitchcock).

'Yes,' I said. 'Bloody hell, that's a *lot* of birds!'

Mac laughed. 'I'm going to write that down,' he said, pretending to reach for his pen. 'I like your insights.'

'Yeah,' I said. 'Get used to them.'

And so the affair began. We didn't go for coffee again; Mac didn't hang around outside my seminar room, whistling and on spurious pretexts. I just used to go back to his little flat at the end of every night. I'd say goodbye to my friends, leave the students' union – the Monday-night disco, the Friday-night disco, the frequent gig nights – then head alone to Westwood. Afterwards, I would run home, back to my halls, the thrilling Midlands wind in my hair, my scuffed DMs flying over the concrete slabs of sixties municipal glory. Hoping no one would see me.

Luckily I didn't live in the same halls as my fellow disco buddies, people on my course or – worse – students on Mac's course (I knew who all of them were, lucky bastards,

71

although now *I* was the lucky one). I didn't research properly when it came to living on campus – typical me, impetuous, impatient, easily swayed – I went by the prettiest accommodation name and the prettiest boy who showed me round. The best place to be was Rootes, a long block facing the main university building. I was in Whitefields, a series of weird, angular buildings, like bashed-out hexagons, which were two storey and had two shared bathrooms and the obligatory hideous kitchen with 'don't touch me' labels on all the boxes of cereal. Gone-off milk. Fray Bentos pies in tins. There were halls with en suites, for God's sake, on other parts of the campus – why hadn't I known about them?

Still, number 21 was close to one corner of the students' union, where there was an exit, so it was noisy all the time, but close to stagger in and out of. And, better yet, my route from Westwood back to my room meant I could run there, like a mad, wind-swept homing pigeon (who really didn't want to go home; I would rather stay with Mac) without having to pass through other halls and the threat of someone I knew looking out of a window.

The sex was . . . illuminating. Mac did things that were totally new. He would go down on me, which was always a wonderful surprise; he'd hoist my legs high into the air, or over his shoulders, making me laugh and yelp; he would shunt up behind me, like a lazy locomotive, to assume the spoons position and do me that way, and as he did I would clutch the iron railing of his bed base, my thumb grazing the edge of his mattress, or bite at the nail of my left forefinger. I felt *other* to myself, I felt beautiful; I felt I had been cast in a sexy love story as the tantalizing lead. I experienced the world revolving all the way around me.

The experience was different every time with Mac. Sometimes I was thrashing around in the eye of a storm, everything torrid and frantic; sometimes it was like lying in a meadow on a dreamy summer's day while the sun drifted over me in soft waves; other times I was drowning like Ophelia, drunken and sated and dragged down by heavy pond weeds into a heavy elixir of bliss. Oh, I felt all sorts when I was with Mac. But most of all, I felt that life held infinite possibility, as long as I was with him.

'Would you bring lovebirds to *my* door?' he asked me once, after a particularly lively session.

'Of course,' I said, all cocky. 'I kind of did, didn't I? I pursued you. And I got what I wanted.'

'The Melanie Daniels spirit?' he suggested.

'If you say so,' I replied. 'Though I'd call it my *own* spirit. Yes, I would bring you lovebirds – would you bring them to *me*?'

Mac smothered me in kisses. 'Always.'

When I wasn't with him, I was bored, grumpy, biding time, treading water. I would laugh with people at McDonald's in Leamington Spa, but think about being in bed with Mac. I would stomp to the Fine Young Cannibals at the Monday-night disco, but I would be plotting how soon I could leave to go to Mac's room. I would scribble notes in lectures about Shakespearean verse, while resisting the childish urge to doodle our names on the back of my notebook, inside a biro love heart.

I had to tell Becky quite early on. She was my friend; I cared what she thought of me. And the way I was acting *was* really weird: declining to go back to anyone's room for bacon sandwiches after the union. Turning up for 10 a.m. lectures (10 a.m.? Good lord, it was the crack of dawn!), wild of hair and eye, struggling to repress an enormous grin as I opened my A4 notebook and pretended to concentrate. She was even wilder-eyed when I told her.

'Bloody hell, Arden!' she said. I was cross-legged on her bed, in Rootes. She had a duvet cover with hippos on it and was wearing something spectacular in tie-dye. 'Can you get kicked out for that?'

'I don't think so,' I said, separating my toes through the foot of my tights. 'I don't think he can, either. Frowned upon but not a sackable offence, apparently. Mac says keep it discreet and everything will be OK.'

'I can see the attraction,' she said, and I knew she was shaking her dyed purple head in impressed disbelief. 'He *is* fit. And cute. And *so* bloody clever. Lucky you, I suppose. Is he married?'

'Yes.'

'Oh, Arden!'

I had never felt more like my mother's daughter. But I wasn't ashamed. I was determined, resolute, unrepentant. There was no way I was going to stop. 'So? What does it matter? She's a hundred miles away. I don't know her. She's never going to find out.'

That he was married had never even entered my head, but someone I knew had mentioned in passing, while going on about the great Mac Bartley-Thomas, like everyone always did, that he had a wife and she was a fellow at Sheffield University. I had been taken aback – momentarily – at the news, had felt a slight chink in my brazen bravado – momentarily. I was in the students' union at the time, propping up the bar with a pint of dry white wine. The same Mac-adorer had then added, in passing, that Mac's wife did Classics, which had always sounded deathly boring to me – all that nonsense about Greek gods. It was enough for me to swallow down my momentary misgivings, along with my revolting wine, and imagine Mac's wife as a hippy, an over-earnest academic with a steely bob (possibly prematurely grey) tied on top with a jaunty ribbon, sensible shoes and long skirts. It wasn't giving Mac much credit, but that wasn't the point. The point was I just didn't care about her. I didn't care that he was married. I was in too deep: I wanted Mac and he wanted me; nothing and no one else had to be on my radar.

'How long do you think it will go on?' Becky wanted an

end to it already, I could tell. She wanted me back being like everyone else. Snogging blokes our own age, partaking in those bacon sandwiches until 3 a.m. But I couldn't be the same as everyone else.

'Who knows?' I replied, but I thought it would go on for as long as I wanted it to.

NOW

Chapter 6

I try not to think of my ex-husband too often any more. It's best if I don't. I prefer to erase our eleven-year relationship and our ten-year marriage from my mind, if I can. Sometimes, though, I get a little reminder of it – a snippet, a soupçon, like this morning, when a letter plops through the letterbox like a hand grenade – a missive from Christian's solicitor asking me to send on Christian's collection of football annuals. I finish my tea and, my hands trembling despite themselves, go to my laptop and quickly compose a letter back – I have work in an hour – saying Christian really should have taken all his possessions with him when he moved out of the marital home five years ago, not leave most of them behind so he would give himself a reason to continually harass me. With fake bravado, I remind Mr Tobias of the restraining order. I tell him I have got rid of all traces of Christian now, *including* the football annuals. The very last thing of his was a pair of shoes I found wedged at the very back of the wardrobe. They had 'Help Me' written on them in Tippex and he wore them on our wedding day, when he didn't need help as he was getting everything he ever wanted. *I* should have worn the bloody things.

See, fake bravado.

I don't want to receive any more letters bearing that man's name. *Christian*. Not for the first time I think how highly ironic the name is for the man who couldn't be further from one. It's almost amusing; I can almost hear the laughter now, all the way to the women's refuge . . .

I need to get ready for work. It's the second of January; I spent yesterday, New Year's Day, with Julian and Sam. They invited me over, cooked me a roast and we played Monopoly, one of Julian's childhood favourites. I enjoyed seeing how in love they are; how close. They have a lovely kind of teasing relationship which suits Julian, I think. I'm proud of him. When he wanted to go into the City like his errant father, Felix, and his ex-stepdad, Christian, I was worried about several things, including him not going down the university route, like I had, and the possibility of him turning out like either of those terrible father figures, but he wanted to get out there, start earning, save for the property ladder; build his own walls around him. Julian's in something called Futures – I'm probably being naïve but that sounds kind of *hopeful* to me – and I'm convinced he has a great one. He certainly has things a lot more sussed than *I* had at nineteen. He's working in a great job, being half of a rewarding relationship; not playing up, guzzling cider and black and seducing married Film Studies lecturers . . . I am fiercely proud of my boy.

I send him a quick text.

Hi J, I know you're at work already but wanted to say thanks again for a great day yesterday. Mum xx

A text pings back.

My pleasure, mum, was great to see u. Sorry I thrashed you at Monopoly (again)! X

I smile; he loves that game. My heart also contracts a little: Christian used to play it with him, when he was in our lives, as a kind of sadistic humouring. He'd let Julian assemble a

77

decent property empire around the board, from Whitechapel to Mayfair, including a handful of Utilities and a couple of train stations, then accidentally on purpose put a bomb under it all, aggressively swiping the board clear with his arm ('Oops! Clumsy me!') or standing up and announcing he was bored and he had to go ('Sorry, *son*!' The way he called my boy 'son' used to kill me). What hurt the most was Julian's simple and eternal optimism that Christian wouldn't do it again the next time (hope over experience as misplaced as mine). In the end, I gave the game to the charity shop, but I rebought it last year, and when we play now, I'm thrilled to see my boy's face light up with childish delight when he's able to buy a hotel for Pall Mall or something, unhindered.

I didn't get home until late last night. At about seven o'clock, as my iron landed on Free Parking for the seventh time, I thought of Mac and Ward 10 and wondered if he was wondering where I was. But I would go tonight.

I shower, get dressed in my strict-looking grey skirt suit and pussy-bow blouse, eat my microwave porridge. On the way down the street I post the letter to Christian's solicitor, wishing I could post all my remaining thoughts about that man along with it. The divorce was a dragger – all those letters going back and forth between his solicitor and mine; all those unreasonable demands of his, right to the bitter end. I won't countenance one more of them. I have to be brave. Still.

Work is dull and is also a dragger today. No one is really in the mood. The Cedars call again, saying Marilyn is complaining about the food. I do what I can to try to fix things, which is to gently tell the staff she'll just have to put up with it. At almost nine hundred pounds a week – funded by the selling of her bungalow – The Cedars is as good as it gets, I'm afraid. Mum was never bothered about food anyway, as her cooking from about 1975 testified. Before that, if my memory serves me right (something *she* never did, *after 1975* . . .) she had some good moments: coconut rock buns, a killer moussaka, a vanilla-y cake in the shape of a lopsided Paddington Bear on my fourth birthday that was delicious. Things made with love and care from a warm kitchen where a hug from a floury apron over a fifties sundress was not unknown. Those moments did not last.

I allow myself to get hauled to the pub at lunchtime – not The Long Good Friday, but The Crown, the tiny pub across the road from us – an early two fingers stuck up to Dry January, apparently, or 'Cry January' as Charlie has decided to call it. I haven't been here for a long time, either. Years, in fact. It's been done up and now has wooden floors and high stools with smooth walnut-veneer seats that cup your bottom. Charlie and I decide we don't want our bottoms cupped and move to stand at the bar.

'So, Hall,' he says, leaning against the bar with his lager and lime, like Del Boy, 'I've finally got you out. Now when are we going to get you back in the saddle?'

'The saddle?' I ask, sipping at my lemonade. 'What kind of saddle?'

'The man saddle.'

I almost splutter my lemonade over the bar. 'I hope you're not offering!'

'Of course not!' he says, frowning impishly and tapping over-dramatically at his giant gold wedding ring. 'But it's been quite a long time now, hasn't it? Since that bastard? It's a whole new year now and you need to get out there, girl. Get some action.'

'Some *action*? Sounds horrendous.' I laugh.

Charlie grins. 'Romance, then. *Romance*. Come on, my friend. You must have one more Big Love in you.'

'I don't think so.' Two was enough, I think. Mac, which didn't end, as I'd hoped, with us riding off into some multi-hued sunset together – quite the opposite. And Christian – *that bastard*. I don't think three's a charm or even a possibility.

I can't see me falling in love ever again, or imagine any kind of man on this earth who would fall in love with *me*. Don't I have 'Damaged' written on my forehead, like in that party game where you have to guess who you are? ('Am I sub-human, half alive . . . ?' '*Yes*.' 'Do I want another relationship, ever . . . ?' '*No*.') Aren't there warning lights flashing all over me saying 'Keep Clear'?

'You never know, though,' says Charlie. 'You never know what's around the corner.'

'Round the corner from me is the post office and the news-agent's that never has any milk,' I say, 'and that's about it.'

Charlie chuckles. 'OK, I take your point. But you could keep an open mind, couldn't you? You're still young, ish. Would you like another lemonade?'

When I get back to work there's a note on my desk that Becky has called. I'm scared to call her back – I'll end up telling her about Mac and she'll be curious and want to know why I'm visiting him, and why he still means so much to me, and I don't have an answer for her because I don't really have one for myself. I flit around all afternoon, trying to settle to something – guilty that I'm not calling her. I'm always guilty when it comes to Becky. I continue to treat her badly, it seems, even though I now have a choice. I just seem to be *stuck*, unable to recover the Arden of old that Becky remembers.

I finally settle to googling Mac Bartley-Thomas on my PC to see if I can find out about any family and where they might be. Wikipedia is my first point of call. It talks about Mac, where he studied, the years he lectured at Warwick University. The word 'maverick' is mentioned, as is Sheffield University and UEA – the University of East Anglia – although there's a question mark next to it and no years are detailed. There's a bibliography listing a book he wrote, *The Language of Celluloid*. I scroll down. *Here*. Here it is. He has one son. His name is Lloyd Thomas. *Lloyd*. I roll the name around my mind and while it settles there I wonder where the 'Bartley' went to; that's a bit odd. The name was edited three years ago. Was it by him? You can't click on Lloyd Thomas and when I google him there are about a million of them. Googling his name and Mac's together just brings up the Wikipedia page again. I am at a dead end already. The internet knows nothing about Mac's son. Where is Lloyd, why has neighbour James never seen him and does he know his father is in hospital?

After work, and a jacket potato at home – done in the microwave – I walk to the hospital. It's raining and my umbrella is little defence as the rain has decided to spitefully come down in a horizontal slant. I now have jeans on, and knee-high boots and an afghan coat with a huge shaggy fur collar. I should have worn my enormous cagoule thing but I want to look nice.

Fran is at the nurses' station as I come into the ward. It's no longer a tinsel-y sleigh.

'Hello, luvvie,' she says, snapping shut the lid of a Tupperware box. 'He's really sleepy today.'

'Is he? Is that a bad sign?'

'Well, he's unsettled. His bloods are up, too.' I have no idea what this means. 'Until they sort themselves we can't do a lot. I wanted to give him a bath today but that will have to wait.' I don't like the thought of Mac being given a bath, like a baby. I flick through the images in my mind and select one of him laughing in the shower at the Wiltshire Hotel in Soho, his chest hair all soapy and water falling from flattened hair into his face.

'When did the doctors last come round?'

'This morning. They're happy with him, I think, generally. We just need to keep an eye out, you know.'

'OK. Well, thanks, Fran.'

Mac is asleep when I go over. I smooth his hair away from his face and brave a quick, light kiss on his cheek. I hope he doesn't mind; he has been in my head all night and all day.

His cheek is papery and soft and warm. The man in the next bed calls over something but I can't quite hear it.

'Sorry?' I enquire.

'I said, he's Rip Van Winkle today, that boy,' responds the man.

'Ah, is he? Thank you.' I sit anyway, as Mac sleeps. I watch a bit of telly; the London news, *The Chase*. I'm near to closing my eyes myself – my eyelids feel heavy. But I'd rather be here than at home. What would I be doing there? Whiling away the hours watching TV until I can go back to work again? Privately nursing wounds that have stayed with me too long? I'd much rather be here.

After an hour I wonder if James is coming tonight. Perhaps he's busy showing people around houses. Perhaps he doesn't want to come again. Why would he? He's only Mac's neighbour. He's not a lonely ex-lover like I am, with a bruise for a heart.

I study Mac's face. His eyelids are still closed; he's softly breathing. He looks peaceful. I select another image from my mind and hold it in front of me for a good look: Mac, sleeping in that white bed in his flat at Westwood, the night after a funny Valentine's dinner we had in a pub – the sheet and blankets helter-skeltered round him; his foot hanging out the bottom of the bed. I hadn't been able to take my eyes off him. He was a blond prince. An angel without wings. A slumbering god . . . or I expect I had used such over-the-top imagery to describe him at the time. Precocious, I was. Pretentious. I miss that girl a lot.

I think about sending Becky a quick email – saying what, I don't know – but before I reach down to the phone in my bag, Mac's eyes open. He smiles gently at me. I take his hand and hold it in mine. His lips are moving; is he trying to say something? I bend down so my face is next to his and he croaks to me so softly I can barely hear him.

'Give . . . me . . . the . . . skinny, Ilsa.'

I grin, my lips close to his cheek. Rick and Ilsa. *Casablanca*. The next film on The List. There's a scene where Humphrey Bogart asks Ingrid Bergman who she really is, what she was before she met him, but she enigmatically refuses, saying she doesn't think they should ask questions of each other. In my usual cheeky fashion I'd paraphrased Bogart's famous line to 'Give me the skinny!', which had amused Mac no end. He said they should have let me write the script and he started using that line on me himself, until it became a bit of an in joke – him asking me for the 'skinny' – but he got it, more or less. I told him about Marilyn, my dad, my home life before I went to Warwick. I kept it light, though; I didn't go into the full extent of the misery, the boredom and the despair. Conversely, I knew very little of Mac, but that was fine by me, at the time. There was a lot I didn't *want* to know, until I found out everything.

I wonder if Mac's asking me it because once again he wants to know the answer. Who am I now? What have I been doing for the past thirty-odd years? He closes his eyes again; he is asleep.

'Mac's just spoken,' I say to a passing Fran, raising my head away from Mac's. I want to give her some good news today. I want to tell her he has said something – it might reflect an improvement in those 'bloods'.

'Oh, fantastic! What did he say?'

I stand up and move towards her. 'A reference to another movie. Well, an in joke, really.'

'Oh?' She stops, a file in her hand. 'Which one?'

'*Casablanca*,' I say, proud on Mac's behalf.

'Another of the films you watched together?' she says. 'Wow. He's really pulling things from that right hemisphere.'

'He saw the same films time and time again.' *And every time he must have remembered the things I said*, I think. 'He was a Film Studies lecturer at Warwick University. I was one of his students,' I lie.

'Ah, really? I could tell he was something fancy. The chap just looks bloody clever, you know?'

'He does, doesn't he?' I agree. Mac has always been so very, very clever. 'I wonder why he's not at least *trying* to say something else,' I say to her. 'Why only these little snippets from films? Can't he at least say "hello" to me, or something? That must be in his long-term memory, too.'

'No two cases are the same in this kind of thing, but non-fluent aphasia patients sometimes only speak in idioms, swear words, occasionally numbers,' ponders Fran. She clasps the file to her neck and drums her fingers on it. 'I had one stroke patient who would only mutter stock phrases about the weather. Sometimes there's no rhyme or reason to it, but, you never know, Mac might be saying what is most important to him.'

'Perhaps,' I say. Is that what he's doing? I wonder, or is he saying what is most important to *me*?

'Talk to him,' she suggests. 'He's got good comprehension and will understand everything you say. He can't fill in *his* gaps but you can fill in *yours*. Tell him about your life, tell him your story, I'm sure he'd like to hear it.'

'It's not a very *happy* story,' I say.

She shrugs. 'I'm sure he won't mind. Who has one of those, anyway?'

Fran heads to the next bed and I sit down and take Mac's hand. I suppose I could talk to him, tell him a bit about my life. Not all of it, just some edited highlights. I don't want to make him feel worse than he already does, poor bloke. I can tell him the decent stuff. The stuff that doesn't make me fear my soul will never dance in the streets again, or, sometimes, even get out of bed. I can give him the *skinny*.

'I have a son,' I say, and Mac opens his eyes and looks at me. 'Julian. He's nineteen. He's the best thing in my life.' Mac continues to gaze at me, giving nothing away. I wish he could tell me about *his* son, about Lloyd. 'I have a house,' I continue,

84

'not far from here, on a lovely tree-lined road. It's all mine and I live alone, which is really great.' This is lame and not strictly true, I think. I don't really like living alone and I am lonely. I have alienated my best friend and now she has come back to me I feel so guilty I am continually pushing her away. I know I'll never fall in love again and despite what I said to Charlie, it actually makes me feel incredibly sad.

Oh sod it, I think, I will tell Mac the *unhappy* story. He can't give me pity, as he can't speak. He can't express his disappointment things didn't turn out that well for me, as he can't express much of anything. But I can tell him who I am, really, and what I was before.

'My life . . . since you, has been, well, a little bit rocky.' Mac continues to look at me, his blue eyes steady and with those flashes of pistachio light. 'I went utterly textbook,' I say, 'after you. As in, I did that thing after the end of an affair where you go for the complete opposite to someone.'

I had. After Mac, I pitched myself at non-clever wide boys, in the sense they had no academic sheen but they glittered bright in other brittle and exciting ways and in other places; in the City, the Stock Exchange, on dance floors and in bars and hot new restaurants. I hoped there would be safety in them, after the end of our affair, and I dated a lot of them: party boys who loved a pint and a good boogie, who promised a few laughs and a carefree, easy-going kind of love, with no accompanying toad of angst or drama on its back. Plus, I had little career myself to distract me during these seemingly carefree times.

'The country was recovering from a bad recession the year I left Warwick,' I say. 'Well, you know that. Jobs were still thin on the ground, despite the Milk Rounds and the jolly jobs conventions and all the promises.' Mac smiles slowly in recognition. Those 'bloody Milk Rounds', he used to call them. 'I could have got a role as a dogsbody in a publishing house or something – if I could beat off the competition of the other three thousand girls applying for it – but the money was terrible anyway, so I got a job in tele-sales, selling advertising space in women's magazines, and I started dating these good-time boys. Boys who were fun and uncomplicated, not like you. Although you *were* fun, you know, sometimes . . .' I'm teasing. He tries to give me a wink but can't quite do it. Hey, I'm *teasing*, I think. I haven't done that for a while.

'I met someone called Felix. I never loved him but we got on well. He was uncomplicated, made me laugh. We moved in together and I got pregnant. I had Julian. My boy.' Behind me a nurse drops a metal dish and it clatters to the floor. Someone from a bed shouts jauntily, 'Sack the juggler!' I turn back to Mac. 'But we split up when Julian was three. Felix cheated on me, twice – I guess he was more compli-cated than I thought. He moved away, kept bare contact with Julian. Not a great father. And then I met Christian.' Only this morning I had been trying to banish thoughts of him from my brain, now I was unburdening myself to Mac about him, as though he were that therapist I had refused to see. 'He was positively a Good Samaritan when we first met. I was still working in telesales, I'd been running across the street one lunchtime, late back to work, and my heel snapped. You would say it was like something out of the movies, Mac, as he picked me up off the ground and took me into a bar and got me a drink while he dashed to Tesco's down the road and bought me a pair of plimsolls, guessing – rightly – my size. Well, the Tesco wouldn't have been in the movie but the rest of it was classic, don't you think? He came back and put them on my feet and we fell in love. It was all kind of breezy and light. Not intense, like us.' Mac manages to raise one eyebrow, ever so slightly, and I laugh and tuck his hospital blanket further around him.

'He asked me to marry him after a year, and I said, "Yes." He was so, so nice to me.' I know my face is falling now from that laugh, my heart sinking way, way down. I have to remind myself that's not where it is now. That things are now OK. 'He made me feel so special. He said he wanted to be a dad to Julian and . . . and, well, then it all went wrong.'

'Sorry, love.' It's Fran, bustling in. 'Just need to take the fella's temperature.' She slips a glass thermometer under Mac's tongue – old school. He looks sleepy again as she checks it. 'There we go. That's better. Oh, not too bad. Carry on.' *Carry On Nurse*? I think, although Fran doesn't have the titter or the dreadful puns.

'Once we got married, it was . . . insidious,' I continue, once she has bustled away again. 'He was a recruitment consultant in the City, a big man to take both of us on. Very, very charming. He started small, like I expect they all do.' I take Mac's hand again; I need to anchor myself to him. 'And his shrinking of me – because that's what it was – took *years*. He started with making little comments, about things he didn't like, things I had to *adjust*, to make him feel better. He suggested I close my bank account, move all my money and savings into his. He let me have housekeeping; I had to ask him for everything, on bended knee – school stuff for Julian, pencil cases, football socks, everything. I had to distance myself from my friends. I had to report to him, let him know what I was doing every hour of every day. I got accused of all sorts – affairs, mostly. But it was all OK, because he was *looking after me*. Because he was *providing for me and my son*.'

Mac says nothing, of course. His pale blue eyes just look, and absorb. I suddenly wonder if I should have made up some brilliant life to tell him all about, but it's too late now. I have no choice but to carry on with my disappointing, pity-inducing monologue. 'I was with him for eleven years. *Eleven years* . . . When things got really terrible he'd say, "I don't hit you, Ardie," as though that made all the other shit all right. That it wasn't that bad. And because it wasn't *that bad* – that, in between the bad stuff, he could be so, so *nice* again, turn it on, just like a tap, or he'd say he was stressed, I was over-exaggerating, he wouldn't be like that again, "promise" – I was stupidly, catastrophically, with him for all those years, until I couldn't be any more. I missed my friends, I missed being a person. He was either horrendous to Julian or ignored him – totally ignored him – and it broke my heart. How could I let that happen, Mac? How could I let it happen for so long . . . ? My dad died – remember me talking about him, Mac, my dad? He died and it tore me apart but Christian was cold, so cold. He told me that I was pathetic to cry, that I was weak and irritating to be utterly devastated. And on it went . . . on it went, until one night he went mental because I was twenty minutes late home from work. He started throwing stuff; he ripped up my favourite dress. There was a moment – just a single moment – when there was a knife on the kitchen table between us – I had been making a tomato salad, I think – and I thought he might kill me.' I am no longer looking at Mac now; I am looking down at my lap. 'I tried to throw him out but he wouldn't go. Refused to. Julian and I had to go to a women's refuge while all the house and stuff got sorted out with the police and everything, because he got quite nasty, and it was two weeks before we could move back in. It was *my* house. I'd paid for it from my telesales job.' I pause, take a breath. 'I've got a new job now, Mac.' I look back up at him. 'I got it not long after my son and I came back home. It's not quite Hollywood but I work in locations, on *Coppers*, the police drama. You might be quite proud.' I shrug. 'I don't know. It's nothing much. But that's it. That's my story.'

I sigh and feel a relief that it is all out. 'There,' I say, like I am a nurse too. 'I should have stuck with you, kid, if you'd let me. Because even though we were in some kind of *Educating Rita* fuck-up, as well as the obvious deceit and betrayal, it was an equal relationship, wasn't it? I had a *say*, didn't I? In fact, most of it was my doing!' I know Mac is struggling to keep his eyes open; he is tired. I need to stop talking. 'So that's who I am and what I was before. I won't be the person you remember, nothing near. But I'm trying to be stronger now, though I'm not sure *how* a lot of the time.'

Mac's eyes hold mine. It feels like an eternity but I won't look away. I drink him in. I want to see inside his soul, to know him, again. He doesn't blink; I want him to see into *my* soul, to know me, once again. We look and we look, then, finally, with the flicker of the beginning of a smile, his eyes close. I feel drained. I am as exhausted as he is. He has heard me, though. He has *heard* me. I don't want to go; I still feel the need to draw strength from him, though he has no strength to give. 'Aren't you going to say something, kid?' I ask, to his silence.

'Hello.'

I whip round, caught out. 'Oh, hi, James.'

James is wearing a different suit. It's a very dark navy. His hair looks like it's been parted on the other side. I feel the need to compose myself, but all I can come up with is patting one side of my springy hair and saying brightly, 'You've just got here?'

'Yes.' Oh God, how long has he been standing there? Did he hear my confession? I can't imagine him as a creeper, though. I imagine he's the kind of bloke to stand well back when someone is pouring out their heart in an over-the-top, melodramatic manner. 'There's not long left,' I say, fiercely trying not to blush, 'for visiting.'

'No, I know. Just thought I'd pop in. I wanted to let Mac know someone came to the door about his car.'

'Oh, right.'

'I've got some documents to show him,' he says, patting the inside jacket of his pocket. 'I'll read them to him when he wakes up. So, you're here again?' he says, sitting down.

'Yeah, I've got nothing better to do,' I say and I like it

when James gives a dry little smile, even though what I've said is the truth.

'Would you like a biscuit?' He pulls a packet of chocolate digestives from a kind of man bag he has over his shoulder. I wonder what else he has in there.

'Thanks.' We munch on the biscuits. I, unexpectedly unburdened, am suddenly ravenous; I ask him for another. I notice he has pink socks on tonight – bubblegum pink. I like to think they are a small rebellion amongst all his estate agent-ness, making me feel less awkward in his company, somehow. Like there's a spark there he mostly likes to keep under wraps but allows others a glimpse of, to put them at ease. We sit and stare up at the television in almost companionable silence for the remaining fifteen minutes of visiting, then I put on my coat, James fastens his man bag and we leave the hospital, him to turn left, me to turn right.

'I'll be here again tomorrow. I'll see you then?' James asks.

A bit presumptive, I think, but, 'Yes, I expect so,' I reply.

THEN

Chapter 7: Casablanca

'The thing with *Casablanca*,' said Mac, 'is that Ilsa was always going to go back to her husband, because of film censorship. It was 1942 when that film came out, the midst of the Second World War. The censors never would have allowed her to go off with another man, even if he *was* Humphrey Bogart.'

We were walking back to Westwood, in the dark. None of the lights in the alleyway were working that night. It was chilly; my flimsy denim jacket felt laughingly insubstantial in the mid-February air. I longed for Mac to put his arm round me but knew it was risky enough him walking beside me at this time of the evening, talking about old black-and-white movies.

'Ultimately, Bergman had to be wholesome and admired by the audience. She had to do the right thing for the greater good of the country. Nobody gets what they want in *Casablanca*. She was only allowed to have an affair with Rick in the first place because she believed her husband was dead.' I was taking this all in; it was fascinating. I had the fleeting thought that Mac was always going to go back to *his wife*, but it *was* fleeting, and largely redundant; I had no concern for the greater good, there was no censorship for Mac and me. I was getting what I wanted. 'The Hays Code,' concluded Mac. 'It had a hell of a lot to answer for.'

'What's the Hays Code?' We were passing the entrance to the tiny path, edged by prickly bushes, that led off to Sainsbury's, the trees overhead looming and pleasurably menacing. I felt we were in our own film noir, although Mac had told me *Casablanca* wasn't a film noir but had noir-ish *elements*. I was learning a lot.

'Hollywood was forced to clean up its act in 1934, before that it was a little racier, immoral, even a little feminist. Marlene Dietrich and her tailored suits, confounding expectations of femininity – all that. You know who she is, right?'

'Of course I do.' I loved the way Mac said her name in that sexy northern accent.

'It imposed a code on itself. No sex, violence, no crimes that could be imitable. It's why Mae West became a star – all that innuendo, to circumvent the restrictions. Everything was highly sanctioned, sterile. I'm putting *Bonnie and Clyde* on my Women in Hollywood course – I'll show it to you at some point, Arden. By then – in the later sixties – the Hays Code was on its way out, and that particular firecracker exploded away the final remains of it, right off the screen.'

'Boo to the Hays Code,' I said.

'Exactly,' replied Mac, taking my hand and putting it in his trouser pocket. That was as good as it was going to get, and the moon had gone behind a cloud again, so we could get away with it. 'Interesting times, though.'

It was a Tuesday, about half seven. We had watched *Casablanca* early. The coast had been pretty clear; all the students had gone back to halls or were getting ready to rave it up at the Edwin Starr gig in the students' union. I wouldn't be going. I had snuggled up to Mac in the screening room and felt all romantic and cosy as we settled down to watch one of the most famous movies ever.

'What do you think of black-and-white films?' Mac had asked me as the opening credits started to roll, showing us the globe, the war in Europe, Casablanca, its market streets.

'Love them.'

'Me too. You can say so much with an absence of colour. Did you know the human eye can detect between one and ten million different colours? Black-and-white distracts from all that . . . busyness. It enhances things. Loneliness becomes that more lonely, romance becomes that more romantic.'

'Black-and-white reveals people's souls,' I said, almost casually – I had read it somewhere – but I was searching Mac's face for a reaction and was thrilled when he served me a gratifying grin and an impressed eyebrow hitch. I was spurred on. 'Although there are some *brilliant* films that go from black-and-white to colour and vice versa. *The Wizard of Oz*, *A Matter of Life and Death*, *Raging Bull* . . .' I thought for a moment. '*Singin' in the Rain*.'

'Bloody hell, you're good, Ms Hall,' said Mac, looking thoughtfully at me as the camera swept through the streets of Casablanca. 'You're really good.'

'Tell me about it, *Mac*,' I replied, in my best Olivia Newton-John.

The movie had been as epic as I remembered. I'd seen it once before, with Dad, on a rainy Sunday afternoon. He'd fallen asleep halfway through and I'd enjoyed the rest on my own, with a bumper bag of mini Mars Bars. It was sweeping. Sad. I loved Rick's Bar – I wanted to go there, especially with Mac. We could order spider crab and drink Moroccan martinis . . . Tonight I had to settle for dinner at The Moody Cow, over in Kenilworth, if we ever made it. I'd booked a table for half eight, but if we didn't get back to Mac's flat soon we'd be horribly late. He'd been a bugger to persuade off campus in the first place.

'What did you think of Ilsa?' Mac asked, as he changed his desert boots for a pair of shoes, in his bedroom. I was already in my 501s and my best top. 'As a character. Did you like her?'

'I'd like to go *out*,' I said. 'Hurry up!'

'Come on, Film Studies interloper,' he persisted, sitting down on the bed with only one shoe on, stalling, 'imagine you're writing an essay on *Casablanca*. What did you make of Ilsa, apart from the whole goes-back-to-her-husband thing?'

'OK. Well, she was always slightly out of focus,' I said.

'Intentional. So she can be ethereal, nostalgic, other-wordly. What else?'

'Stop it and put your bloody shoe on!' I said. Normally, I would adore all this film talk; now I just wanted to get Mac away from his flat. I wanted to go *out* somewhere with him, like we were real. 'I feel like Rita in bloody *Educating Rita*!' Not for the first time.

'I'm just being Frank,' quipped Mac.

'Michael Caine did it much better . . . All right, Ilsa's an idiot! And I *will* talk about the whole goes-back-to-her-husband thing.' Writing an essay on *Casablanca* would be so much more fun than the essays *I* had to write, I thought. 'I don't believe she *should* have done the right thing for the war effort! I think she should have followed her heart and gone off with sexy Rick. Go for what you want! Like Tippi in *The Birds*.'

'Is that what you do? Go for what you want?'

'Do you even have to *ask*?' I had my hands on my hips, all sassy, and I knew Mac loved it.

'You could also argue it's for her safety.'

'I don't *like* safety.'

'Clearly.'

I flung my arms in the air. 'She's a damsel in distress; I don't like those. She reacts to things, she doesn't *do* any-thing!'

'She points a gun at Rick.' His second shoe was finally on.

'Yeah, I suppose.' I was full of bluster and swagger and overconfidence. Mac looked highly amused. 'She's too young for Rick, anyway.'

'Er, *hello*!' said Mac, in an American accent, holding out his arms in mock-stupefaction. 'Tell me about your mum and dad,' he asked suddenly.

'What the hell are you asking that for? Are you Philip Larkin? A therapist?'

'I want to know things about you. Who you are. Who you were. Like Rick asks Ilsa in that flashback.'

'When he wants the skinny?'

Mac laughed. 'The skinny? One of Humphrey Bogart's most famous lines in *Casablanca*, in one of the best scenes, when he asks the enigmatic Ilsa for her history, and you're reducing it to him asking her for the *skinny*?'

'It's more concise,' I laughed back. '*Give me the skinny, Ilsa!*'

'Another one for my notes,' he teased. 'Right. Let's have *your* skinny. Mum and Dad. Come on.'

'There's not much to say,' I said. 'They're just my mother and my dad. Now can we please get going to the pub? *Please.*'

'OK,' said Mac, grabbing his blazer, 'I can see I'm not going to get anything out of you right now. We'll go to the pub.'

The Moody Cow's dining room was far too pricey for students so we were safe there, as far as detection went, but it was surprisingly packed.

'Oh shit, it's Valentine's night!' I said. How had we forgotten? The tables were all wedged in together, like rows of desks at school. Every table but one had a doe-eyed or already-bored couple stuffed either side of it and there was a hopeful red rose in a wine bottle in the middle of each table.

'Where's cupid, stupid?' said Mac.

'I'm with stupid,' I retorted, like one of those T-shirts. Steven from Home had taken me for a meal the February before, on Valentine's Night, to a little Italian in the next village. It had felt ridiculous, like we were going through a set of pointless motions. I didn't feel enough of anything for him to be one of those couples gazing into their heart-shaped soup and struggling for conversation.

Despite his quip, Mac hesitated, on the threshold – a dark wooden wonky beam underfoot and a low door frame he had to stoop to get under – like he didn't want to walk in any further. I bet if I'd suggested we go straight back to campus he would have leapt at it. *Campus Man.*

'Let's get a drink at the bar first,' I said, taking his hand and dragging him there.

He ordered a beer and I ordered a Kir Royale, which Marilyn was always going on about as some kind of fantasy drink. I was glad I had worn my best silky top over my jeans and had boots with little heels on them, not that I needed any extra elevation; I was on an absolute high, being out with Mac.

'Interesting, what you didn't say about your mum and dad,' said Mac, as we waited for our drinks. 'Nobody is *just* anything. You need to give me something.'

Did I? I sighed. 'OK, potted *skinny*. My mother is awful and has fidelity issues. My dad is lovely but puts up with them too easily,' I said.

'"Fidelity issues"?'

'That's me putting a gloss on it. The truth is she appears to be addicted to a series of grubby encounters with disposable men. Next?' Our sandwiched-in table was ready. We were shown to it by a waiter and our drinks were brought to us by another. My Kir Royale had a plump drunken strawberry floating in it.

'Why does your dad put up with it?'

'Because my dad is my dad. He drinks too much and loves her too much. It's fine. Now come on, let's get into the Valentine's Day spirit. Let's link our arms through each other's like they do at weddings and make a toast.'

'What would you like to toast to?' asked Mac, linking his arm through mine and raising his glass.

'Entirely up to you,' I replied nonchalantly, but my heart was beating fast when he looked me in the eye, making the room dissolve away to nothing, and said, 'To us; always to us.' Then we tried to drink from our glasses and it all turned instantly comical. Like a couple of inept contortionists, I spilt some of my Kir Royale and Mac almost elbowed the man at the next table in the face.

'Sorry, mate,' he said, deadpan northern, and I thought it was the cutest thing I'd ever heard. 'What are you grinning at?' he asked.

'You,' I replied. We sipped at our drinks and scanned the Valentine's-themed menu. I quite fancied the Love Boat mushrooms and the Romeo and Juliet steak, whatever that was.

'Helen doesn't believe in Valentine's Day,' said Mac, looking around the room.

'Who's Helen?' I asked absent-mindedly. I was reading all about the desserts while simultaneously trying to work out if the couple by the door were having a row or not.

'My wife,' said Mac, sounding surprised, and I wondered whether he was surprised because he thought he'd already mentioned her somewhere along the line, or surprised with how casually he'd just come out with her name.

'Oh,' I said. His *wife*. It sounded strange: alien, wrong. Why was he bringing her up when we were having a nice evening out together? I had forgotten all about her. Well, I had barely spent any time thinking about her at all – only fleetingly, of course. Now I knew her name I was in danger of having all sorts of thoughts I didn't want, like how many times did he phone her, what did they do in the holidays? How many times a year did they have sex? Mac looked a little flustered. 'It's OK,' I said, cool as anything. 'I know you're married.'

'Sorry,' said Mac. 'I shouldn't have brought her up.'

'It's OK,' I said again, and, not wanting him to think I was

97

in any way pissed off about him mentioning her, I added, 'What *does* she say about Valentine's Day?'

Oh, I was cooler than cool. I was *good*.

'Not much.' He grinned. 'That it's consumerist fallacy at its worst. That it's the beginning of the end of modern civilization, or something.' He looked a little proud, which I hated.

'Well, good for *Helen*,' I said, going to polish off my drink. I spilt some more on the table. *Clumsy clots.* I mopped it with my sleeve and laughed a high, bright laugh.

'Sorry,' said Mac again.

'Don't mention it,' I replied. 'I mean, really, don't mention it!'

He looked contrite, guilty even; I liked this even less so I laughed again and called the waiter over to order more drinks.

Despite this shaky beginning, where a lesser girl would have thrown the remains of her Kir Royale right over Mac's head (but I was determined *not* to be a lesser girl, ever), this was probably the most romantic night of my life. I decided to throw myself head first into the evening instead and banish *Helen*, the invisible hippy rival. We saw off the other couples in the dining room, too. There must have been at least three that came and went from the tiny table next to us. None of them looked as happy as us. No one laughed as much. No one drank as much, or had as much fun. I bet none of *them* had a shoeless foot in their crotch for half of the evening.

Mac had never looked so handsome; I had a 100-watt bulb lit up right inside me. I was aglow, I was on fire; I was indestructible . . . Compared to us, everyone else just looked dimmed, somehow, and downright miserable. This night, this moment, was *everything*.

We ordered loads of food – potato skins and scallops and steak and fat chips dripping in sauce. We let sauce slide down our chins and we didn't care. We ate off each other's forks; we dipped fingers in each other's cream. I trailed my finger round the rim of my glass, then brought it slowly to my lips like I'd practised with mugs of milk, as a teenager, for when I came to restaurants as a grown-up, with sexy men.

Our waiter flirted with me, which I loved. 'He fancies me,' I said, then wished I hadn't as this was Marilyn's line.

'Not half as much as I do,' Mac replied. He studied my face, drunk it in. He looked at me as though I was the most captivating person he'd ever met. He fed me petits fours from a dessert spoon. He even bought me a rose from one of those ridiculous sellers that came wandering in.

'What's your favourite movie genre?' I suddenly asked him, the rose behind my ear. 'You haven't told me. Or are you not allowed to have one? Do you have to be impartial and love all genres equally?'

'Westerns,' said Mac. He put the rose between his teeth and did a growl.

'*Westerns?* Ugh. They're my worst.'

'Love 'em,' said Mac. '*The Searchers, High Noon, The Magnificent Seven.* I'm going to get myself out to those prairies one of these years, see it all for myself.'

'*Really?* Do you own a pair of cowboy boots?'

'Yes, ma'am.'

'Jon Voight in *Midnight Cowboy*,' I said, showing off again. 'I bet you really fancy yourself as some sort of stud in those boots.'

'One of my favourite films,' said Mac, 'and if you play your cards right, I'll put them on when we get home,' he added, with a wink.

I giggled and everything inside me turned somersaults. 'I'll hold you to that.'

We were *so* ramped up for some huge explosive sexual encounter when we got back to Mac's flat, but it didn't happen. Which was a shame, because I'd just gone on the pill. I'd sat in the campus medical centre just over a week ago at the ungodly hour of nine o'clock, yawning my head off and praying I wouldn't see a student I knew, which of course I did. Two, in fact, who *both* made the cardinal faux pas of asking what I was there for. I had coughed tragically and said I had the flu and they had moved away from me.

Mac and I had eaten way too much to make use of my new contraceptive powers. My stomach, under my silky top, was all popped out like a cute egg. We were burpy and full and giggly and we wrapped ourselves in each other's arms, like koalas, and went to sleep on Mac's bed. I never *did* see the cowboy boots that night.

Mac woke at 2 a.m. and so did I. He put Kate Bush on his stereo. Before I arrived I was not at all studenty in my music tastes. I was a pop girl, an occasional soul girl. I wore neon, I liked mild hip hop and songs that were in the charts; the intro to Wham's 'Club Tropicana' was the best thing I'd *ever* heard. Mac changed all that; he introduced me to The Smiths, The Cure, Kate Bush, The The – my ears were opened.

'"The Man With The Child In His Eyes", that's you,' I said, as Kate sang.

'What are you trying to say? I'm the boy who will never grow up?'

'Something like that.'

Mac looked strangely sad. And I must have suddenly felt *completely* masochistic because I said, 'Tell me about your wife.' God knows what I needed to know. I had already formed my opinion of her personality: fiercely intelligent, confident, deeply unsexy, a bit dull, blah, blah, and, most importantly, nothing like me. Perhaps it was my inflated self-confidence that made me brazen enough to ask about her. I mean, you couldn't get more brazen *or* more confident than being in her husband's bed. Or maybe I just wanted some of Mac's *skinny*, too, however self-destructive that was.

'She's very clever.' *Check.* 'Very sure of herself.' *Check.* I drew my leg from under the sheet and rubbed it up and down Mac's. He smiled lazily at me. 'Interesting.'

Oh, she was supposed to be dull. She'd *sounded* dull – all that Valentine's Day stuff. This threw me a bit. Still, she couldn't be a lecturer if she couldn't get people interested in what she had to say, so I let that one go. I was safe. I could listen to him talking about his wife with a feeling of glowy smugness. I was younger than her, better all round. She was *old* and I was *new*.

'She is amazing, sometimes. Kind, affectionate.' *Uh oh.* He'd be looking all wistful in a minute. 'She also sometimes makes me feel smaller than I have ever felt.'

Ah, now, this *was* interesting. She was sometimes a cow, *good.* 'You don't have any children?' I asked. The less to tether him to her the better, I thought, and I was pretty sure he didn't.

'We've tried for many years, but Helen has had several miscarriages.'

I was sketchy on these. I didn't know anyone who had had one. Although Marilyn said there was a boy, before me, who hadn't made it; she never elaborated on why but perhaps it was another reason she found it so hard to tolerate me.

'I'm sorry,' I said, but it came out as though it had a question mark on the end, which sounded a bit dodgy. I wasn't that hot on empathy; in fact, I was hopeless at it. I had a certain skill in not being able to come up with a single, appropriate thing to say when people brought up their sadness or troubles.

'They all happened quite early, around thirteen weeks, actually one was at sixteen,' he said. I nodded, but this didn't mean much to me. I remained clueless on the subject. 'It has been quite tough, and men are not supposed to open up on these sorts of things, are they? We have to be *strong*.' He looked so downcast, so vulnerable, it made me want to leap on him, which I knew wasn't the right call at this particular juncture. 'But I know, however I've felt about it, it has been a lot worse for Helen.'

Helen, Helen. I rolled the word around my brain with distaste. I wish I'd never conjured her up again, like a witch.

'I'm very sorry, Mac,' I said and I tried to say it properly this time. He lay on his back and stared up at the ceiling.

'I feel I have lost children out there,' he said unhappily, 'somewhere – just out of reach. I wanted to have loads of them. A whole brood.' He turned and raised himself up on one elbow, looked at me. 'Have you ever read *The Water Babies*?'

'No, thank God. Well, I tried to, as a kid – I couldn't get on with it.'

'The ultimate Victorian didactic fable,' said Mac, looking at me with those pale eyes. 'I read it as a boy. Cover to cover, it sucked me in, although I sort of hated it, and it has never left me. I feel like my lost children – and I imagine them all as boys, somehow, although of course we'll never know – are swimming somewhere like the Water Babies. Held prisoner by that bloody shark and eel.' He took a deep breath and I rubbed his arm sympathetically although I was totally out of my depth and had no idea what he was going on about. 'It makes me feel I can't breathe when I think about it. I hate that book. It bloody well haunts me.'

'Oh, Mac.' My words were empty. I couldn't understand less. I didn't want children; couldn't see I ever would. They just seemed like a pain. My mother's legacy again – *thanks, Marilyn.* I hugged him anyway. I sensed it was the right thing to do. 'I'm so sorry,' I said again. I couldn't bring myself to say something like 'you can always try again', as of course I didn't want them to. Him and *Helen.* I didn't want him anywhere near her.

We lay there for a while. Kate Bush had moved on to 'Cloudbusting'. 'Do you think that was really it for Rick and Ilsa?' I said eventually, as a stab at changing the subject.

'How do you mean?' Mac was staring at the ceiling again. There was a branch outside his bedroom window tap-tap-tapping at it. I hoped Mac wasn't still lost in the land of the Water Babies. I didn't want him there.

'Do you think they really walked away from each other on that tarmac and never saw each other again? Do you think she would have been happy staying with Laszlo?'

'I don't know,' he said. 'I don't think you're supposed to think beyond the movie. I never do.'

'Really? I like to,' I said. 'I like to imagine what Melanie and Mitch did after *The Birds* had buggered off. And did Dan and Beth survive or did they break up anyway years later, after she kept throwing the whole bunny thing back in his face? I want to know *what happened next*.'

'Interesting,' said Mac. Yes! I hoped I was as interesting as *Helen*. 'I live within the movie and when the movie is over I let it go.'

'I'm quite envious of that,' I said. 'I always have massive questions. Mostly, will love survive? I mean, all those big loves – they can't just disappear!' And I know now I am talking about me and him. Love was not something we had talked about – why would we? Love was not something that had even flickered on any sort of horizon. Until now. But now I knew it was a possibility. I felt it; I felt I could love him.

Mac pulled me down into his arms and spoke with a tenderness I had not yet heard from him. It was early days, wasn't it, after all?

'I think you'll have a bigger love than me.'

'I doubt that,' I said, and there, I had admitted it. He was my Big Love, or at least he was damn close to it; the one I had been looking for, and I was telling him so. Was what *he* said just arrogance – 'a bigger love than me'? Or was he open to the wonderful, terrifying possibility of it, too? 'I already have a feeling this is pretty much it.'

And just like that, my coolness disappeared in a puff of smoke. I was now officially vulnerable.

'No,' he said. 'You will. Your life is just beginning. There'll be so much more for you. You'll be so much more than *this*.' What was it? Was it *love*? What was he saying to me?

'You're not going to tell me there's a big wide world out there, are you?'

'Well, yes I am.'

I preferred my world being in this room: the Victorian ironwork bed with its cowboy blankets and its in-need-of-a-wash white sheets; the ticking clock on the bedside table; the poster of *Betty Blue* opposite us an aphrodisiacal equivalent of a mirror on the ceiling; the knee-high stacks of *NME*s . . . And the possibility of love. 'I'd rather stay here with you.'

'Well, me too.' He leant down to kiss me and I turned my face to his. 'But you know things don't last for ever, don't you?'

'They bloody well should,' I said.

NOW

Chapter 8

James is outside Ward 10 waiting to be let in when I arrive at half six on Thursday evening, fresh from work, although fresh is hardly the word I'd use to describe myself. Today has been . . . challenging. Nigel has been in a strop most of the day; a much-needed file went missing; there was a fire drill when we all had to troop out to the car park and waste one whole, precious hour standing around saying how fed up we were to be standing around in the car park; and the kettle broke. From about half two this afternoon I've been dreaming of working in other departments; I quite fancy Scripts, in my more delusional moments.

I'm in a long black wool coat and grey beanie; James is in a similar suit to before, dark navy again. White shirt. His hair is slightly smarmed down; so different to Mac's 'flop', I think. I can't tell whether he is pleased to see me or not. He has a face that reads as largely unreadable. Handsome, though. I've never met a man so handsome yet so unaware of it.

'Hello, James.'

'Hi, Arden. Here again?'

'Here again,' I echo. 'How was your day?' I ask, as we are buzzed in. 'Sold any houses?'

'A couple,' he says. We walk down the ward towards Mac. 'Not all estate agents are wankers, you know,' he says, looking sideways at me.

I laugh at the word 'wankers' and say, 'I didn't say they were.'

'It's an unwritten law. I get it. I'm actually a nice estate agent,' he adds, giving me a short smile. 'There are a select few of us.'

'Sorry,' I say, feeling tremendously guilty as I *have* always thought estate agents are wankers, when I have thought about them at all.

'Don't worry about it.' He sounds clipped but he is still smiling at me.

Mac is very sleepy again tonight . . . he lies motionless, his eyes flicker open now and then, but only briefly. I take off my coat and hat and James and I sit on either side of the bed and volley looks of uncertain resignation to each other, accompanied by giant shrugs. Mac's TV, like the kettle at work, is temporarily broken and is a silent black rectangle suspended above us. I wish I *did* knit; I feel awkward and not sure what to do with myself. I also fear there will be no celluloid pearls of wisdom coming from my former lover during this visit. To my shame I can't quite remember which movie is the fourth from The List is anyway. I keep looking at Mac's mouth, waiting for him to say something, but I know nothing will happen. Eventually I get up from my plastic chair to go and get hot drinks for James and me. On the way, I corner Fran at the nurses' station, where she is briskly ticking things off on a long list.

'Mac's very sleepy tonight,' I say. 'What are the doctors saying?'

'He's doing OK,' she says, not looking up. 'He's just on a bit of a shutdown. We're observing him, doing all the checks. Everything is stable.'

'So he hasn't gone downhill, or anything?' I ask.

'No, not downhill,' she says, 'just a slight dip from a plateau, really. He's doing OK,' she repeats.

'How long has he been here now?'

She looks up. 'Two weeks.'

'Is that bad?'

Fran gives a medicinal smile. 'Mac is currently stable,' she says and she returns to her list.

'Thank you, Fran,' I say to the top of her head, and I leave the ward for the coffee machine. James has requested a hot chocolate, and I get myself a tea.

'It's been two weeks,' I say, as I hand James his hot chocolate before returning to the other side of Mac's bed. 'Since Mac has been in here. I don't know whether to be worried or not.'

'We're worried anyway, aren't we?'

'Yes.'

'Then why worry more?'

'I suppose so. But the longer time goes on . . .'

'I know.'

'It's just . . .'

'Let's just be with him. Show him we care. What more can we do?'

We stay for an hour, sit and continue to throw the occasional downturned shrugging smile at each other, across Mac's sleeping form. I can feel my eyes going, too; it's so warm in here, so yellow. I get the crazy urge to pull back the scratchy covers, get into bed with Mac and have a little sleep next to him, and I wonder if he'd like that or be absolutely horrified. Would he even really notice? I wonder what he thinks of me, visiting him all the time? Of the confession I made, telling him how my life has turned out? I could be just this annoying middle-aged woman who keeps turning up. A crazy person from the past he'd actually like to get rid of. But then, why the movie references? Why remind me of all those amazing times and some of the times that weren't so amazing . . . ? The Valentine's dinner, when I sparkled like crystal. The moment when he told me about Helen's miscarriages and my attitude was cavalier, if not heartless.

Everything is being brought back, everything about how I was then, for me to hold up and examine against how I am now. Can he still see something in me? Does he see more than I do? I feel he remembers everything, things about myself I may have forgotten.

'I want to go to Mac's house tomorrow,' says James. 'Pick up some pyjamas and some more toiletries for him. He's still in that hospital gown and he might like to get out of it. I don't suppose you want to come with me? We could go straight after work tomorrow, then come to the hospital afterwards? Well, I don't even know what it is you do, but would you be able to? Would you like to?'

He's so damn awkward, I think, adding once again, in my mind, because I can't help it: *for such a good-looking man.* We're a right pair of bumbling, unconfident misfits; perhaps Mac attracts them, not that I was anything like this when he *first* did. Lordy, no. You couldn't get less bumbling or more confident. Funny how twenty-eight years and a bastard of a husband can knock the stuffing right out of you.

'I work on *Coppers*,' I say to James. 'Production office, and yes, I'd like to,' I add, and then I nearly laugh because I sound like I'm accepting the offer of a date, or something, which is hilarious because he wouldn't fancy me in a million years and a first date would hardly be going round some old bloke's house to pick up his pyjamas, would it? My first date with Christian was in a loud, brash bar – all chrome and coloured lights, people out on the pull and the lash, shouting into each other's ears and Christian a witty and attentive, benign manufacture of his later self. I am clearly a horrendous judge of character.

'*Coppers*? The police drama? What do you do there?' asks James.

'Locations assistant,' I reply. Mac's eyes are flicking so I stare at him, but they go still again and he sleeps. 'Whereabouts in Larkspur Hill do you and Mac live?' I ask.

'Ford Road, do you know it?'

'No, not really.'

'Ten minutes' walk from here,' says James. 'It was barely worth waiting for an ambulance.'

He gives a dry smile, but I am confused. 'Hang on, what do you mean? Did Mac have the car crash near his house?'

'Yes, just outside.' It's something I haven't asked, how it happened. It's not something you want to revel in the details of, is it? How the man you once loved came to be prone in a hospital bed, unable to speak. 'He was reversing out of his drive when a car came hurtling up the street and crashed into him, side on, driver's side. It was a young lad. Drugs, by all accounts. He's being prosecuted for it.'

Immediately, I wish I didn't know the details. I will have an image of Mac now in my mind, merrily pulling out of his drive, the radio on – Radio 2, perhaps – maybe whistling, and a souped-up sports car driven by a grinning, drugged-to-the-eyeballs youth with rap music at full blast smashing into him. 'Were you there?' I ask James.

'No, I was already away, at my mum's. A neighbour down the road called the ambulance. It was pretty awful, I've been told. I didn't find out until I got back today. I feel terrible, actually. That I didn't know.'

'I'm sorry,' I say. 'I'm sorry for Mac and the neighbour, and for you.'

'Thank you,' says James, offering another shrug. 'I appreciate that.'

We sit in silence for a while. James pulls a book from his bag – an autobiography, Freddie Flintoff's – and I send random texts to Julian asking him how his day was and what he's cooking Sam for dinner. We leave Ward 10 when visiting time is over and Mac is still fast asleep.

'So, I'll give you the address and meet you outside at, say, six?' says James. We're at the main hospital exit; me about to turn right, James about to turn left.

'OK,' I hear myself saying, although I am suddenly nervous about meeting James outside Mac's house, and going inside. 'I'll see you then.'

Mac's house is an almost pretty Victorian terrace: No. 6, Ford Road. His front drive is gravel, there's a paved garden in a square next to it. A rockery? This fits with Mac; I can't imagine him as any kind of gardener. Behind it is Larkspur Hill, the little sister to Primrose. It's less of a hill and more of a low-rise hump, really, with a winding path ambling up to a little bench on the top, but it gives pretty good views of the city. I've been up there a few times before, in the summer, not for years, though. I smile to myself as I remember something Mac said once, about British films set in the north of England – like *Kes* (love it!) and *Rita, Sue and Bob Too* (brilliant!) – how they often included a scene on a hill, where an introspective character would look down on a city and its smoky factory chimneys or grey and grim housing estates and reflect on their circumstances. He loved all that realist, Northern angst, mirrored in the setting, and so did I, by proxy. I'm glad to see Mac now has his very own view from a hill . . . perhaps that's why he moved to this house.

'He loves it up there,' says James. 'Says it's perfect for when a moody sod wants some time alone.'

I grin as I look up at the hump and the bench – I enjoyed how James said 'moody sod' in his own northern inflection – although I can't imagine Mac being moody; he certainly never used to be. But it's perfect, this Larkspur Hill. Mac probably comes up here with a book on film theory and lords it up over London, surveying his kingdom, moody sod or not.

'That's mine,' says James, pointing to an identikit house to the left of Mac's. 'We have each other's keys for emergencies.' He pulls a key from his inside jacket pocket and we walk up Mac's front path and James unlocks the door.

We step into the hall. James croupiers up the post on the

mat and puts it on a small console table. I never went to Mac's real house, of course, back in the day. I'd only seen his little flat, the academic surroundings of Mac, where he held parties, made his notes, kept his books, slept with me. I never saw his real life.

The hall is clutter free, but there are framed movie posters. *To Catch a Thief, High Noon, The Philadelphia Story* . . . I smile when I see a famous poster of *The Birds* – Tippi, in her green suit, being attacked by crows – and wonder if Mac thought of me every time he passed it. I hope so. I can see into a dining room, to the right; dark green walls, stacks of books on the table, piles of papers. A tiny galley kitchen at the end of the hall, tiled in blue and white, dark granite surfaces; no feminine influence. James turns left into a square, teal sitting room and I follow behind him. There's a small brown leather sofa, a matching chair. Venetian blinds like the ones Mac had at Warwick. A coffee table, bare but grained with giant knots. And, facing us, a huge bookcase lined and jumbled and stacked with books. *Loads* of books. Books perched horizontally on side-stacks of vertical spines; books leaning on one another and wedged into every conceivable space; books scattered along the top, layered and overhanging each other like coins in that arcade game.

I step towards the bookcase. There are some works of fiction – Jack Kerouac, Ernest Hemingway, Sylvia Plath – but most of them are film theory books and biographies of Hollywood stars. Here, Greta Garbo collides with Gregory Peck. There, Rita Hayworth nestles up against Robert Mitchum. And Dean Martin chinks against Richard Burton with a wink and a cigarette.

'I like biographies,' says James. 'And autobiographies. I've read that one,' he said, pointing to Richard Burton. 'Quite a colourful read.' He gives a rueful smile. 'I read all sorts about all sorts of people,' he says, 'cricketers, soap stars, celebrity chefs. I like seeing how people started out and where they ended up. Their reasons behind things, I suppose,' he adds. 'It's interesting.'

'Absolutely,' I reply. I flick through the Richard Burton then put it back. Something about the smell of the books makes me sneeze, although they don't look particularly dusty.

'Bless you.'

'Thank you.'

I wonder how James started out and where he ended up. For the first time I wonder what *his* story is. From what he's said and *hasn't* said, he lives alone. Why is such a good-looking, seemingly nice guy on his own? 'I'm not a big fan of biographies,' I say. 'I prefer made-up stuff to real life, I think. Oh look, this is Mac's book!' I pull out a red book with a navy spine, Mac's name both there and on the front cover. *The Language of Celluloid*. He wrote it when he was quite young, in the early eighties. It became a kind of bible for Film Studies students, for a while.'

'I didn't know,' says James. 'I mean, I know he's a lecturer. I don't know much else. I've never been in here. I've only been in the garden, for a barbecue once, and in the hall, bringing a parcel in for Mac when he's been away.'

'If you were a woman you'd have gone for a good nose round,' I say, then I wonder why I'm being so horribly sexist. It was the sort of thing Christian used to say, with an awful, mitigating chuckle: that women were nosy, unreliable gossips and bad drivers. Soon after we married, he was suggesting ways in which I could 'improve' myself – my untidiness being an obvious bone of contention, but others were dug up – how I watched television, my loud laugh; the 'annoying' way I breathed . . . and the list of faults he quickly found in Julian and my friends never had an end. I would never nose round someone's house, uninvited; I don't even know who my neighbours *are*. 'Sorry,' I add weakly, and I'm aware that sounds strange, but I'm sure by now James thinks I'm a complete weirdo anyway.

112

There are photos, on the bookcase – only a few, in frames, squeezed at odd angles between books. One of Mac up on stage doing a talk at the BFI, which makes me both smile and feel incredibly sad, another of him on a sunny pebble beach – Nice, maybe? – with his top off, looking tanned and happy. He looks about forty; he still has all his 'Macness' going on. There are no family photos. No wife. No Lloyd.

'Is this you?' asks James. He has slid out a Polaroid photo from where it was sneaking between two books.

'Oh God, yes!' I cry. In the yellow-green-tinged eighties Polaroid I am grinning, all teeth and crazy hair, from under a neck-high white sheet. Mac is looking amused, studious even, next to me, from behind his round, rimless glasses. This is the only photo ever taken of Mac and me – there were no selfies in those days, of course, and no one around to witness our secret relationship, let alone record it. But one lecture-free afternoon, he had set up his camera on a tripod and taken a photo of us under the white sheet of his bed, as though we were John and Yoko on one of their Bed-Ins, minus the chocolate cake. Mac looks handsome and clever, as always. I look ridiculously young, silly and in love, and as Keira Knightley famously and annoyingly – to some – says in *Love, Actually*, 'quite pretty'. We look guileless, when we were not. We look simplicity itself – a deception, in hindsight.

I am amazed to be here, in Mac's sitting room. After all this time, and all that passion and all that hurt, he has found a place for me in his house in London and I feel sheepishly delighted by it but, more than that – much more – a great, great urge to go back to that moment in time right now. Back in that bed. Back under that white sheet. When things had seemed so uncomplicated and love had not yet become a wounding double-edged sword.

Of course, news of our relationship is a novelty for James.

'Oh,' he says, looking at the photo like a forensic scientist . . . I wonder if he is appreciating the *mise en scène* . . . 'Not just a former student, then?'

'No,' I say and I can't help but smile, though I wonder if James thinks I should look more ashamed. I *should* feel more ashamed, but they were such ridiculously happy times, in Mac's bed, in his arms. 'And I wasn't even *that*. Are you shocked?'

'Not really.' He shrugs. 'I'm not shocked by much.' For the second time in ten minutes, I wonder what his story is. He's an enigma, really, but aren't we all? We are all a sum of our untold stories. He looks at the photo again. 'You look really pretty here,' he says, 'but I prefer you now.' Now *I* am shocked. I wouldn't think anyone in a million years would prefer the current version of me.

'Thanks,' I say, at a loss. I daren't look him in the eye. What a funny thing to say! He continues looking at the photo, the scene of all our crimes. 'What did you say we needed to pick up?'

'Pyjamas and some toiletries,' says James, and I watch as he slides the photo back between biographies of Lana Turner and Gene Kelly. 'Are you coming up?'

Briefly pondering if he's a psycho, with a Swiss Army knife in his inside jacket pocket and the heart of an evil serial killer under his crisp white shirt, I follow him upstairs. I'll be surprised if Mac *has* any pyjamas, to be honest. His bedroom is neat and masculine – a white bed – nothing changes, then? – and a dark wood wardrobe and chest of drawers, more film posters – *They Live by Night*, *A Fistful of Dollars*, *On Golden Pond*. The same blinds. A navy carpet. Neat and ordered.

'I don't feel right going through his drawers,' I say, and then I laugh as it's a silly innuendo, especially in the light of what James now knows.

'Well, quite,' he says, with just the flicker of a smile, and

I silently thank him for not cashing in on my comment. '*I'll* do it.'

James has a good look through Mac's drawers and wardrobe, almost a rummage, I think. He'd give Becky a run for her money. She's a rummager. If something's not worth rummaging in her bag for, for twenty minutes, then it's not worth having. I must email her. James puts everything back exactly as he found it, though. He stacks and he folds.

I sit on the edge of the bed, feeling awkward. I look around the room. It looks fairly freshly decorated; the window panes are clean. Mac always was more house-proud than me; most people are, to be honest. My eyes alight on something that makes me grin but I try to hide it. James has already seen me in Mac's bed wanton and half naked; he doesn't need to witness me grinning shyly over a pair of cowboy boots in the corner of Mac's bedroom and possibly shamefully blurting out I once wore them to have sex with him.

'He hasn't got any,' James finally says. I knew it! Same old Mac. It's weird, being here, though. I'm being given a sense of who the Mac of today really is – not the man in the hospital bed, who, apart from the past he shares with me, has no context, no imprint, no footprint. It makes me wonder about Helen and about Lloyd, both why there are no traces of them here and what sort of an imprint *I* may have left on them.

We go back downstairs and get ready to leave. James picks up the pile of Mac's post.

'Just want to make sure there's nothing important,' he says, flicking through. I notice the top envelope has a red stamp across the top.

'London Film School,' I say, peering at it. 'A newsletter?'

'I believe he might do some lecturing there,' says James. 'I think I met a man at Mac's barbecue, that time, who was from the London Film School.'

Mac had signalled to me he was sort of still working.

Maybe he lectured only occasionally; the London Film School hadn't come up when I googled him. 'What was that barbecue like?' I ask.

'It was OK,' replies James. 'Odd bunch of people. I've never seen any of them again.'

'What was Mac like?' I imagine him roaming around, waving his hands in the air, keeping everyone entertained.

'Quiet.' He shrugs. 'Mac is always fairly quiet.'

This surprises me as it's far from how Mac used to be. No visitors at the hospital (apart from us), no visitors at home, *quiet* . . . ? Has Mac's light dimmed in recent years; have we both changed irrevocably? But I've seen that twinkle at the hospital; I know the old Mac is still there. I pick up the envelope and wonder. I also wonder if someone at the London Film School would know about Mac's son. Where Lloyd Thomas is.

We stack the post back on the hall table, lock up and James suggests a quick trip to Marks & Spencer, before they close, to pick up new pyjamas – I expect Mac will probably hate them but never mind. It's an amusing experience, shopping with James. He doesn't do the usual, male smash-and-grab shop, but takes his time, picking things up and putting them down again, making sure the piles he has disturbed are re-neatened, even sniffing at fabrics like a curious terrier. I wonder if people think we are a couple, then wonder if that tickles me, as a notion, or totally horrifies me. He's handsome, yes, but so *awkward*.

'What about these?' says James, holding up a paisley pair in burgundy silk that come with a matching silky robe, all on the same hanger.

'Perfect, if you think Mac wants to channel Robert de Niro in *Casino* . . .'

James laughs, and it takes me by surprise because I haven't seen him laugh yet. His teeth are very even and his laugh temporarily crinkles his entire face. He looks nice when he laughs, and I laugh too because he got the reference. He hangs the 'mob boss' combo back on the rail and we carry on looking.

Finally, we walk to the hospital and troop in, laden with bags. Mac is awake and his left eyebrow twitches at seeing us come in together, but I may be imagining this.

'We've brought you some stuff,' I say, pleased to see he is with us today. 'Toiletries and some new pyjamas.' I take the pyjamas from my bag – plain pale blue cotton, with top and bottoms joined together and suspended from a plastic hanger – and hold them up against me with a coquettish tilt of my head. 'What do you think?'

'Cute,' says James, and Mac's eyebrow could be twitching again.

I wonder about the logistics of actually getting them on Mac – I suppose the nurses will do it. It will be nice for him to get out of that undignified backless hospital gown. James goes to find Fran so he can give the bags of booty to her and I pour Mac some water. I watch as he sips from his straw, I tuck one corner of his pillow back in the envelope flap of his pillowcase; I gently smooth back his silvery, floppy hair. I remember that photo as I look into his eyes and smile – me and him, so carefree and so happy – and wish I had slipped it into my coat pocket to study at home. I sit down. Mac's lips are moving. He makes a small noise, a muffled croak. Does he want something? Does he want to say something to me? I lean forward and bend my face down to his, so my left ear is close to his lips. He smells of toothpaste and something lemony.

He whispers in my ear. Oh, he is flirting with me, even now.

'Damn, you're the ... best girl in the Midlands,' he whispers.

THEN

Chapter 9: Bonnie and Clyde

It was boiling hot, the day we watched *Bonnie and Clyde*. It was the summer term, June. We had planned to smuggle ice lollies into the screening room, from the tiny freezer compartment of Mac's fridge, but they had melted to stumps in our fingers long before we'd got there. We'd had to wash our hands in the loos opposite; for fun, and a spot of jeopardy, I'd dashed into the men's with Mac. We'd been tempted to *do it* in one of the cubicles – well, I had; Mac had looked mildly horrified – until I'd conceded we could do it after the film, in more comfortable surroundings. And without the accompaniment of the hand dryer, which appeared to have got stuck at warp factor 10 and reminded me of the one Madonna cools her armpits under in *Desperately Seeking Susan*.

I hadn't seen *Bonnie and Clyde* before; I'd only ever seen some of the iconic stills from it, but it didn't disappoint. Right from the opening shot of Bonnie naked in her bedroom, it had me. I was absolutely hooked; I barely moved a muscle for the entire film. God, I was obsessed with Faye Dunaway. Who could not be? Her ethereal sensuality and almost brittle beauty were mesmerizing – I wondered if I could dry my hair straight into a style like hers with a huge hairbrush. And then there was Warren Beatty's swagger, the berets, the coats, the brutal final scene of the movie. It helped that the screening room was hot, as hot as Texas; it added to the mood. Despite my cute cotton sundress with the straps that tied into dinky bows on the shoulders and the white plimsolls that I'd slipped off my feet on to the floor, I was as sticky as Bonnie and Clyde were in the southern American heat. And I took every breath with them.

'Wow,' I said, at the end, turning to Mac, who was fanning himself with one of the pale blue reel boxes. 'That was *intense*.' The tragedy of it appealed to me. Bonnie and Clyde's Big Love. I felt it right in my heart.

'Yup,' said Mac, speaking American. He had not mentioned Big Loves or Bigger Loves or any kind of love at all since our middle-of-the-night chat on Valentine's Day. I was in love with him, though. Every time I looked at him, I thought, *I love him*, but I didn't dare say it out loud. What if he didn't feel the same, and why would he? This was an *affair*, something that wasn't supposed to last for ever, however much I wished that it might. I didn't want to make a colossal fool of myself; I had already gone too far saying 'this is pretty much it' and hoped he didn't remember that. I'd gone all light and bolshie since that night – well, more than usual – to cover my tracks.

'Not the usual cultural signifier of women,' I added, layering on the 'bolsh' with a flick of my hair over one shoulder.

'Nope.' Mac was grinning at me. I could tell he was gratified that I loved the movie as much as he did.

'Bonnie is sexually vivacious,' I said, 'and *totally* on an equal footing with Clyde.'

'Yup.'

'Although I hated it when he made her change her hair, in the diner,' I added, and Mac nodded. 'I mean, he said he didn't like it and she just *changed* it.'

'I can't imagine *you* doing that!' he chuckled. He lazily slid an arm round me and pulled me in close to him, although the back of my neck was already too hot from the itchy velour of the sofa-seat.

119

'Well, no.' I leant forward, away from him, and pulled my sweat-dipped curls into a hand-held temporary ponytail. 'But, in general,' I said, 'both Bonnie and Clyde were just so brazen, so unashamed.'

'The director Arthur Penn liked to portray outsiders,' said Mac, and I released my ponytail and sat back against his arm. 'He said something like, "Society would be wise to pay attention to people who don't belong, if it wants to find out where it's failing."'

'Yes.' I lapped up the words, let them digest within me. God, I loved this! Sod being on the Film Studies course – this was better! I was closer, closer to all the knowledge and I adored it. Who cared that I was barely scraping by on my *own* course? That there was an overdue and unfinished essay waiting for me, back in my room, I was in no rush to return to? 'What was America like at the time?' I begged, eager to learn.

'Well, the Hays Code was on its last legs and in came the sexual revolution and women's rights, set against the backdrop of the Vietnam War and frequent riots across America. The movie is such a good reflection of all that was going on, as Hollywood so often is. Was Bonnie satisfying herself or satisfying the male gaze? Was she expressing sexual power or was she a victim of it?'

'The male gaze . . . ?'

'Oh, it's all about the male gaze,' said Mac. 'Coined by theorist Laura Mulvey. I'll lend you her book.'

'Yes, please. Do you like gazing at me?'

Mac laughed. 'Of course I do.'

The male gaze . . . I totally got it, and probably didn't even need to read the book. I loved seeing myself through the prism of how Mac saw me – sexy, fun, irresistible. Perhaps that's why I had started things with him in the first place – from the very moment he raised his eyebrows at me in that corridor I liked how he *viewed* me. He immediately put me in a sexual, seductive frame and I adored being there; in the lens of Mac's viewfinder I was more than I had ever been.

These discussions with Mac made me feel alive. I felt I had something to add, too, which thrilled me. I never had the chance to debate with anyone before, not all this stuff that I loved. Marilyn imagined herself as a semi-intellectual but it wasn't semi, it was a big fat zero. Dad never said much at all – he didn't have the confidence for tackling *issues* – and Steven from Home had never exactly been a debate buddy. He talked about football or whether he was going to have a battered or plain sausage from the fish and chip shop. I'd asked him once if he liked Brando and he thought I was talking about the shop in the precinct that sold knock-off Fred Perry T-shirts.

'So you liked *Bonnie and Clyde*, then?' Mac stretched out his legs. He was wearing a white T-shirt with the sleeves rolled up – a little Brando-esque himself, I thought. He'd spilt a little green ice lolly on it – he had a cute exclamation mark near his left nipple.

'Absolutely.'

There was chatter outside the screening room, a gaggle of students passing. We waited until they had gone then Mac leapt up the steps to the projection booth to extricate his reels and box them up. I waited, twiddling one of the straps on my dress and planning that night's seduction. I was hoping it would involve a quick trip to Sainsbury's to pick up some Lambrusco (Mac) and a lying naked-in-wait in his bed (me). There was only a week to go until the end of term. I felt hollow at the thought. A return to Dad and Marilyn, boredom, nothing to do, nowhere to go, an atmosphere of varying unpleasantness . . . I'd hoped to meet up with Becky this holiday – but she had arranged to spend the summer on a kibbutz in Israel and was deserting me. I'd been too wrapped up in Mac to organize anything. Besides, I had no funds: I couldn't go Interrailing, I couldn't afford a cheap quickie to the Med, I had not researched fruit picking as I really didn't fancy it, and I had failed to look into Camp America because the thought of spending time with a load of American kids in baggy shorts and back-to-front baseball caps appalled me.

I wanted to stay in Mac's viewfinder. I didn't want it slipping from me, in case it never came back.

'Can we meet up in the holiday?' I asked him, later that night, after the seduction. I was lolling in his bed, the sheet completely off. 'Just once. To keep me going? I can't bear to not see you for the whole zillion-whatever weeks.'

So much for covering my tracks and not revealing my true feelings, but my confidence was borderline off the chart since twenty minutes before, as he'd entered me, Mac had whispered something similar to a line Clyde had made to Bonnie, in the movie, except that I was apparently the hottest girl in the Midlands. Not quite Texas, but I'd taken it. I'd giggled and so had he. I felt invincible, like I was riding the crest of a wave on a jaunty surfboard and could shout anything while I was up there, without risk.

'I could try,' Mac replied, sitting up and munching on cheese and crackers, a glass and a bottle of red wine at his side. An after-shag snack.

'When, where?' I demanded. 'How?'

He trailed a tickling finger up my arm. I stole one of his crackers and devoured it, whole. The only way we could do it, we decided, ultimately – after more cheese and crackers and another roll in the cool hot sheets – was to return to Warwick. Mac could pretend to come and do some pressing preparation for next term; I could tell Dad and Marilyn I was meeting a couple of friends for a night out in Coventry and we were hiring rooms in halls. People did that, apparently, in the university holidays.

So that's what we did. One day, in late July, after a month

of flopping aimlessly around at home, wandering shopping precincts and cornfields, avoiding old school friends and getting under Marilyn's feet (shudder), I stole £100 from her tea caddy (only used for sundries, i.e. her face cream and condoms, probably), caught the train to London, survived a startlingly hot tube journey across the capital and then boarded a fast train from Euston to Coventry.

Mac was waiting for me in his car – a red MG – at the station. I felt like Audrey Hepburn; I should have been wearing a headscarf and slingbacks. No matter that I was in rolled-up jeans and a Lloyd Cole and the Commotions T-shirt; Mac looked pleased to see me, anyway. He had sunglasses on and a thin chambray shirt I could almost see his chest hairs through. We sped away like, well, Bonnie and Clyde.

The campus was dead, eerily quiet, but quite exciting, in a way. It had become its own micro ghost town; tumbleweed city. We parked in the car park by the medical centre, in case anyone saw Mac's car at Westwood, and walked to his flat.

I dumped my quirky floral carpet bag, he his leather bowling one and we went to Sainsbury's and bought a picnic to have back in Mac's room: a bottle of red for him, some hock for me, pre-packed sandwiches, crisps, dips, cheese and crackers and cherry tomatoes. We were coming out laughing, with our distended carrier bags, when Mac said simply, 'Jesus.'

'Where? What?'

'The Dean.'

'Where?'

'There.'

The Dean – Alistair something, a rotund figure in round tortoiseshell glasses I'd only ever seen smiling myopically from the Student Newsletter – was about ten feet ahead of us, scuttling between the trolleys and the cashpoint like an engorged beetle and stuffing something in his back pocket. We hid behind a scuffed grey pillar, like in a comedy scene.

I crouched behind Mac, my head down, clutching on to him and giggling. We were definitely Bonnie and Clyde, without the stupidly good looks. And I doubt Bonnie would have been seen dead with a bottle of hock in a Sainsbury's carrier bag.

The Dean took ages at the cashpoint. He must have been checking his balance, asking for a receipt, everything. Finally, he left it and exited, stage right, towards the footpath that led back to the main campus.

'What would he have done?' I asked Mac, when I dared to speak and had returned to a standing position. 'If he'd seen us? What would you have said?'

'He would have said "hello",' replied Mac, exhaling with relief. 'Asked me what I was doing here in the holidays. Asked me to introduce you. Tried to make it obvious he didn't know you were a student I was having an affair with. Pulled me in for a chat. Told me it was frowned upon, that my reputation would suffer unless we were discreet, that he couldn't promise it wouldn't get out . . . None of it would have been good.'

'He might have thought we'd just met up for extra tuition,' I said, with a clear and present glint in my eye.

'You're not on my course.'

'Oh yeah, sometimes I forget.' I grinned.

'But he didn't see us,' he said. 'I want to keep you under wraps for as long as I possibly can. My wraps, under my covers.' His eyes looked all far away, disturbed. 'My cards would have been marked. It would have made things very uncomfortable. Difficult.'

'Me too,' I said, although I wasn't sure I liked what Mac was saying. That he was thoroughly relieved not to have been caught with me. Although I was relieved too, it would have been nice if he'd said he'd be all defiant, all stand-by-me and fight-for-me until death. I supposed that stuff only happened in the movies, but still. I detected a note of fear and almost *cowardice* in Mac that chimed awkwardly with my view of him. 'So what do we do now?'

'Skulk around here for a while. Wait until the coast is clear.'

Skulking again. I wished I had a trench coat and dark glasses. 'I feel like a fugitive,' I said, shaking off my disappointment at his relief. 'This is exciting.'

'Trust you to find it *exciting*!' Mac rolled his eyes and I played up to my part by giggling and clutching at him again. We loitered for ten minutes then made our way back to Westwood, me looking left and right and pretending to jump at things and generally winding Mac up.

'Did I put my card back in my wallet?' asked Mac, slapping at his back pockets as we rounded the last corner. 'No, I thought I hadn't.' He pulled his credit card from his right back pocket and his wallet from his left. As he opened his wallet, something fluttered down to the tarmac and I picked it up.

It was a photo. It was a photo of a blonde woman sitting on the end of a seesaw and the seesaw was high in the air as there was the top of a tree behind the woman's head, and she was laughing.

I hadn't asked Mac what he had done the day before, or what he was going to do the day after. I wasn't going to say anything about *Helen*. But here she was, and she wasn't a dry and academic husk with glasses, hippy hair with a centre parting and a scarf tied on top of her head. She was Timotei blonde, with long straight hair and a pretty fringe that fell in her wide-set, earnest-looking (probably blue or possibly green) eyes. A small mouth. A delicate chin. And something surprising. A darker strip of skin across the top of her nose – a birthmark, a blemish – like Adam Ant's make-up or the marking of a strange and beautiful tiger. Oh God, she was not only spectacularly pretty but she was striking, unrepeatable; unique.

I felt the first stirrings of despair. It was quite a shock, and seas and oceans and continents apart from what I was expecting *Helen* to be.

'Is that Helen?' I asked, trying and failing to sound breezy. I had *competition*.

'Yes,' said Mac, and he slipped the photo into the card section of his wallet and tucked it back in his pocket.

'She's pretty,' I said.

'Yes.'

'So what are you doing with me?'

'Helen is Helen and you are you,' he said, as though that explained everything in the whole universe and beyond.

I had to be satisfied with that. I tried to remember that despite him saying Helen was kind and affectionate, he had also said she sometimes made him feel small. I clung on to that like a drowning woman to a plank of wood; if she was evil in some way, then I could win. I *had* to win. So in an attempt to make myself feel secure, I went big; I leapt at Mac as soon as we got back into his apartment, clawed at his chambray shirt and thrust my hand down the front of his trousers.

'Hey! Steady on!' he cried, but I was determined in my quest to override Helen, to put myself so far in the foreground she would be a mere speck on the horizon; to make love to Mac over and over again, with only small intervals to drink hock and munch ravenously on brie and crackers with slices of tomato, until a watery sun came up the next morning and a giant bird started chirping outside our window, making us laugh. Mac put a pillow over his head and yelled for it to 'Shut up!'

'Don't, he'll come and peck you,' I said, lying in my post-coital haze, my knickers stuffed to the foot of the bed. 'Remember Tippi?'

'Tippi was – *probably* – being punished,' said Mac. 'I don't think we are, do you?'

'No,' I said, remembering the Dean, his beetle-like form. 'Not yet.' And I whacked Mac with that pillow, full of gaiety but already dreading our goodbye later that morning. It was a hundred years until October and the beginning of the autumn term. How the hell was I going to survive that long?

'When you see me next I might be wearing a beret, like Faye Dunaway,' I said, as I pouted by his car in the medical centre car park, having flung my bag in the boot. He was giving me a lift to the station, then he was driving home. To *Helen*. It seemed she could only ever be temporarily dispelled and I hated that.

'I look forward to it,' said Mac. 'You'll look cute.'

We kissed there and then in the car park, by his car, with me instigating, and then Mac motioned for me to get in, so we could kiss some more. I couldn't bear the thought of him driving this car home to Helen. To spend the rest of the summer with her, to make prospective babies, to flick that blonde hair out of her eyes and run his finger softly over her tiger stripe. To do whatever it was two academic geniuses did together – *The Times* crossword? Chilli prawns with an avocado dip at sophisticated dinner parties? High-brow barbecues with other learned scholars, chuckling about paradigms and intricate world views? The more I thought about her, as we were kissing, the more bitter I felt inside until I was kissing him quite violently, in a pre-emptive strike. I wanted to leave a mark on him, a brand so deep he would feel it all the way to October.

'Steady on!' he cried again, as I devoured him alive.

'No!' I said.

Finally, I released him, to let him drive, and when we got to the station I had a cloud of anger so black and massive around my head I'm surprised a passer-by didn't alert the Met Office. I *wanted* to be all surly and feel all martyr-ish. I *wanted* to show him I was upset that we had to be apart for so bloody long, while he kept house and a baby-making sex schedule with another woman. It was childish but I didn't care.

I was glad of my short shorts and my little shirt which tied at the waist. I was glad my hair was big and wild and cute and my shirt a little too far unbuttoned as I got out of his car. I wanted to look sexy and angry and tragic and beautiful. I wanted him to see me that way – through his prism, his viewfinder – and I wanted him to *know*!

'Bye,' I said, slamming first the passenger door then the boot and walking away. I may have been the best damn girl in the Midlands but I sure as hell didn't feel it.

NOW

Chapter 10

Maybe it's good Mac can't speak to me properly, I think, as I leave work on Monday. Perhaps he would tell me just how bloody awful I used to be. Precocious. Demanding. Quite the little brat. I wonder exactly what he *saw* in me back in the day. Oh, I was a sexy little thing and all that, and maybe that transcended everything else, but, boy, was I hard work! I'm embarrassed by lots about my old self. I hope he can see I'm different today. I have a conscience, I'm not so selfish; I have baggage dragging at my heels that has qualified and altered me. I wonder how surprised he was by the story I told him, of what has happened to me since him. I wish he could tell me *his*.

The former best damn girl in the Midlands didn't make it to the hospital this weekend. My sneeze turned into a two-day stinker of a cold that I didn't dare bring to St Katherine's as I was terrified of giving it to Mac and the other patients. Instead, I hunkered down with my cold, a huge box of tissues and Sky Movies, where I watched loads of black-and-white films I hadn't ever seen with my ex-lover in Ward 10. I missed him; I missed taking my seat at the hospital, and I hoped he didn't mind too much that I wasn't there. I even phoned and asked one of the nurses to pass on a message to him, that I hoped to be back on Monday.

I feel much better today – apart from a slightly croaky

throat – more like my old self if not my *old* old self. I dive in my bag as I walk, checking I've got my phone. Funny, I think, that there were others who seemed to like the old, wild, selfish Arden, or at least tolerated her. Becky did. (The thought of her gives me a pang to the heart. How we used to be together. The fun we used to have. I have a sudden vision of us dancing to Terence Trent D'Arby in the students' union. Laughing. Throwing our arms round each other.) The other people on my course. I can't have been all bad. Yet, I had an affair with a married man, without guilt. I betrayed another woman, however far away she seemed. I don't think I'm heightening my past image in any way, making it more dramatic or playing up to the retrospective camera of my own mind. I can see clearly who I was. At the same time, knowing I am nothing like the girl I was – good and definitely *not* so good – makes me sad. That girl was confident: she was sassy and she was feisty. My sass and feistiness have long since fled the coop; my spirit, once so free and eager and full of its own potential, crushed underfoot like a wandering beetle. Telling my story to Mac may have been a mistake. I have admitted how much of an empty shell I now am and he may not be surprised, but disappointed with me.

I'm popping home to get changed before I go to St Katherine's. I've got my phone. It's snug in a side pocket. The last text on it is from Julian telling me that *Rain Man* is on telly tonight and that I've seen it a hundred times but he knows I'll want to see it again. The last call I had on it was some woman from Newcastle telling me I'd had a car accident and I should be claiming for whiplash injuries (oh, the irony). The last work call I had today was Becky, just before I went home, and I answered it by accident because I was distracted by Nigel wittering on about the key to a lock-up for a DBS (Discovered Body Scene) and didn't look at the caller ID.

'There you are, stranger!' she said as I felt my face redden. 'You don't write, you don't call . . .'

It's been fairly easy to avoid Becky as she's one of the small handful of people on this earth who don't have a mobile phone. She called me about a year ago – on my work phone, so I didn't have a chance to not answer – saying she'd got rid of her mobile as she wanted to simplify life, so all our one-sided communication is now between her desk phone at the Opera House and mine at *Coppers*. It suits me, of course: there have been no texts to not reply to. Even when Becky had a mobile, though, during the hell of my marriage, it wasn't difficult to bend to Christian's will and shut her out. All I had to do was ignore all her messages and calls and not answer the door to her when she came round to the house. It killed me, but that's what I did. I have one particularly awful memory of hiding in my own kitchen, squatting down by the worktops, heart pounding, as she rang and rang on the doorbell. It was a Saturday. My car was there; she knew I was in. I hid until she went away. Seeing her just wasn't worth the anger and the recriminations and the sulky, endless silent treatment I would get from Christian. The scales of my life inexorably tipped fully in his direction; it was just easier that way, and I was rewarded, by him, for getting rid of Becky. I was told how happy Christian was when he had me all to himself, that he hated sharing me, that I was special. The usual.

'What are you doing tonight?' she asked, and I had to admire her eternal optimism. She keeps asking; I keep shoving her away.

'Working,' I lie, and I find myself back on the well-trodden, somewhat slippery path of the consummate liar. I became such a good one it began to be instinctive.

'Ah, that's a shame.'

'Yes.' And then I decide I don't like it on that treacherous, worn path. Would it really harm to step off it? To dare to tell some sort of truth to Becky? I *can* now – it's so stupid really; after all this time, sometimes I forget that I am free. 'Well, not working, actually, but I have plans.' Now she will hate me for the initial lie, but she probably does anyway.

'What are they, chickee? Because there's a cool new bar called Gatsby's opening in the West End and I think we should go,' she says, skating over the fact I've just fibbed to her and proving once again she's a far better person than me. 'Don't say you're washing your hair or doing your nails, or I shan't believe you for a bloody second. Will you come?'

'It's a Monday.'

Becky sighs. It's like the sound of a seashell to my ear, at the beach, not a gentle sound, though, but rather blistering. I'm sorry I've made her sigh. 'Monday is the new Friday,' she says.

'I've got plans,' I limply say again, although I suppose I could go to the hospital a bit earlier and go out afterwards, if I wanted to. Do I *want* to? Maybe I do. 'But I suppose I could be free about nine.'

'Great!' And while I'm thinking her voice has a slight edge to it, that it has the whole phone call, I feel relieved she hasn't made me say what these plans are, as I would have chickened out of telling her. I've been an idiot really; I should have just told her I was still ill. 'Dominic's going to come as well,' she continues, 'and I've got a *kind of* date I need moral support with – well, checking out, really. Well, he's not actually a date at all but someone I really like. I need you there, Ardie!' she says, and the edge seems to disappear. 'It should be a laugh.'

An actual *laugh* – for a whole evening – may be beyond me, but it is just the sort of thing I used to love, a thousand years ago. And Becky says she needs me, which makes me think. It would be nice to be needed, not as a cowering, flattened mat to have huge, bruising boots stamped on, or a human dartboard braced for sharp words, but for support and for friendship. If only I had it in me to provide them.

132

'OK, yes, I'll come,' I say, and *damn, damn, damn*, I think, as I put down the phone. I'm going out, to a bar, at night, for the first time in years.

There's a card waiting for me on the mat when I get home. It's a card with a little cartoon on it of a pathetic-looking bird and inside, in spidery, looping writing, are the words, *When are you next coming to visit me?*

My mother. Again, she's just so *wheedling*. The address is written by someone else – she obviously got one of the staff to do it. And fetch a stamp for it. And post it. Haven't they got better things to do? The card makes me never want to go and visit her again, but I check my calendar hanging on the back of the kitchen door and resignedly write 'visit Marilyn' on Saturday 12 January in red biro.

I shove the card in a kitchen drawer and then I call the London Film School, wondering if it's too late and if anybody will be there. Somebody answers – a woman with a lilting Welsh accent – and I realize I have no idea what I'm going to say.

'I'm a friend of Mac Bartley-Thomas's,' I say; the wavering croak in my voice not only due to the vestiges of my cold. 'He's in hospital and I'm trying to trace his son. I believe Mac might lecture with you – is there anyone there who might be able to help me?'

'I'm sorry to hear that,' she says. 'We didn't know he was in hospital. Yes, he does lecture with us occasionally, although he's not due with us again until February. I'm not sure we can help. All we have is Mac's contact details, address and so forth. I don't know anything about a son. Well, perhaps you could ask Stewart Whittaker – he's the closest to Mac here, but he's in New York at the moment, I'm afraid. Hang on . . .' There's a slight rustling sound, as though she has to go off-camera and blow her nose. 'I have his email address if you'd like it?'

'Yes, please,' I say breathlessly. 'Yes, I'd love his email. Thank you.'

She recites it to me and I note it down and as I end the conversation my brain is scrolling through its roll-call of people I have ever met. *Stewart Whittaker* . . . I've met him, haven't I? He's the man who Mac and I ran into that time, in Soho. I'm pretty sure of it. A little scared of doing so, I go to the laptop and compose an email to him, saying I'm a friend of Mac's and does he know the whereabouts of Mac's son. As I sign off I wonder if Mac ever told this Stewart about me – properly. Will he recognize the name Arden Hall and think, Oh, *her*?

I go upstairs to have a shower and then put on what I call my Notting Hill outfit, as it's very similar to what Julia Roberts wore when she went to Hugh Grant's friends' house for the birthday dinner in *Notting Hill*: dark blue jeans, kimono-type satin blouse and low ankle boots. It's a bit fancy for the hospital but perfect for the bar later; and when has that ever stopped me, anyway? Clothes are my armour and my disguise and my freedom.

James is at Ward 10 again tonight, looking all stiff in his suit, but he smiles as though he is pleased to see me.

'You weren't here this weekend.'

'No, I had a bad cold. Check out the red nose and the lingering air of Lemsip.' He gives that brief, wry smile again, but his grey eyes look amused. 'I'm all right now, though. Which day did you come?' I ask him.

'Both days. Saturday and Sunday.'

'Oh, right.' I wonder if he'd wondered where I was. He can't have much of a social life, I think, if he's propping up Ward 10 on a Saturday night, not that I can talk. I spend all my Saturday nights gawping at the telly then drifting upstairs at 10 p.m. with a book I've usually read before and might manage two pages of.

'It's nice to see you back.'

'Thanks.'

He makes no mention of my dressy outfit, although Mac looks like he may appreciate it. There's an unhurried smile from him as I approach the bed. He is almost sitting up tonight, the upper half of his body shored on about four pillows. His eyes are shining and his cheeks have good colour in them. Has his condition improved since I was last here?

'Oh, you're looking bright and breezy,' I say, as I sit down in my usual chair, half-expecting him to just say, 'Hello, Arden,' and start chatting, but of course he doesn't. 'Sorry I couldn't make it at the weekend.'

'A good day today,' says Fran, passing the bottom of his bed. 'Chipper, our Mac has been, haven't you, Mac?'

Mac smiles and nods a little, as though he's taking the piss, which I hope he is.

'Any talking?' I ask her.

'No, sorry,' says Fran.

'You're far too quiet these days,' I say to Mac cheekily, remembering what James said about him. 'I miss you going on and on and on about films.' I do. I miss our discussions; I really want to talk movies with him. I'd talk anything with him, to be honest. I would just really love him to speak to me.

'So, how was work today?' James asks me, flipping up the back of his suit jacket and taking his own seat at the other side of the bed. Fran has decided to stop and take Mac's temperature, top him up with water. She clucks around him like a starchy hen. 'That's if you were there, after your cold?'

'Yes, I was there. It was quiet, fairly dull, a bit croaky, in places. How about you?'

'Not too bad, I sold a house on Brompton Road.'

'Oh, great. That's good.'

'Yeah, nice people, too. The buyers, I mean. The sellers are arses.'

'I see.' I'm finding James's polite manner with the occasional swear word chucked in quite amusing.

'No thrills at *Coppers* since I last saw you, then?'

'Thrills are always thin on the ground at *Coppers*, to be honest. At least in my office . . .'

'What is it you do there again?'

'Locations,' I say, 'you know, arranging to go and trash people's houses with equipment and muddy trainers – that sort of thing.'

'Oh, we're quite similar, then' – he nods – 'dealing in property. *You're* a wanker too.'

I laugh. 'Why, thank you very much!'

His grey eyes are dancing. 'Oh, while I think of it,' he says, and he pulls his phone from his inside pocket and clicks something on it. 'I won't be able to come to the hospital this Saturday. I've got to go to an expo and I'm not sure I'll be back in time.' I notice he does a contemplative little frown sometimes, just a subtle knit of his brows. He's doing it now. *I* contemplate this is a lot of superfluous information and wonder why on earth he is telling me. Perhaps he fears I won't turn up at the weekend again, either, and wants to make sure someone is on shift, for Mac.

'Is it on how to fleece people?'

He knows I am joking. 'Yes, absolutely.' He grins, giving a short laugh.

I decide to be superfluous too, why not? 'I probably won't be here on Saturday either. It will depend what time I get back.'

'Oh, where are you going?'

'To visit my mother in a nursing home in Walsall.'

'Ah. My expo's in Birmingham. Twenty minutes from Walsall on the M6,' muses James. 'Do you want a lift up there?'

I am taken aback. 'Why? Oh no, I don't expect so!' I say primly but far too loudly, with a touch of the wartime harridan; next I'll be wielding a broom and a head full of curlers and seeing rapscallions off my doorstep.

'Oh, OK!' Now *he* looks surprised, like it wouldn't be at all odd for us to drive up to the Midlands together, just like that. I've been planning to take the train, as I always do. Do I really want to sit in a car for two and a half hours with someone I barely know?

'Plastics,' says a raspy voice from the bed.

'What?' I say. Fran has moved off down the ward now and I turn to Mac who is sitting up on his pillows and staring at me. 'What?' I start to laugh. I pull my chair closer to him and I laugh and laugh. 'Is that all you've got to say for yourself,' I tease. 'Is that *it*?' My cheeks are probably now rosy too. The silk of my jacket rustles as my shoulders vibrate. I haven't laughed like this for a long time.

'*Plastics?*' parrots James, bemused.

'Plastics is a famous bit in *The Graduate*. Have you seen it?' I ask James.

'No. Never seen that one.'

'That's a shame. And well, you haven't lived, quite frankly. You should watch it tonight; it might be on Netflix or something. Ben – that is, Dustin Hoffman – is saying he wants his life to be different and his future to be something brilliant and the advice he's given by a well-meaning neighbour of his parents is "plastics".' James looks like he doesn't get it. 'It's all in the context,' I say, grinning at Mac. I am excited; I am talking too fast. 'Ben has just graduated, he's listless, terrified of the future and of ending up like his parents – "plastics" is the last thing he'd ever want to get into. The line is also indicative of the age, how plastic everything was. All that disgusting sixties consumerism. Isn't that right, Mac?'

Mac nods, just a little, and smiles. I'm almost feeling like my old self – the good part. I have to resist the urge to tell him that I am filled with everything about our time together, that my body and brain are swirling with images from the movie and the Simon & Garfunkel soundtrack and Ben and Elaine on the bus and the knocking on the church window and the *everything* of us. But I can't, can I? With James here? And maybe it's for the best. Who wants a gushing nostalgic fool at their bedside anyway?

We sit for a while. Me full of Mac and *The Graduate*, James full of a packet of salt and vinegar crisps and a can of Coke he got from the vending machine in the corridor. He's a noisy slurper but it doesn't offend me.

'Ooh, you look dressed up!' says Fran, later, after we have said our goodbyes to Mac and are making our way to the door. 'You two going anywhere nice after this?'

I am horrified. Does she mean *together*? And James *always* looks dressed up; he wears a suit every time he comes to the ward!

'Well, I don't know what *James* is doing tonight,' I say carefully, 'possibly watching *The Graduate* . . .' I look at him and smile. 'But I'm meeting a friend and going to a new bar in the West End.'

'Oh, which one?' asks James. He really is a very strange man sometimes.

'Gatsby's.'

'Oh, yes. Used to be The Chapel,' he muses. 'It's supposed to be pretty good.'

'Sounds like he wants to come,' says Fran, looking all excited and happy, like she's in a bloody romcom. And she actually winks at me. Oh, bloody hell. She's the matchmaker in *Fiddler on the Roof*, finding me a find, catching me a catch, when I don't bloody want one.

James shrugs again, like he is not denying it. Really? He wants to come out with me and Becky and Dominic and the mystery man who needs checking out – although I'm not sure why Becky is trusting *my* judgement. She must know it to be supremely off.

'Do you want to come?' I ask, in the manner of a huffy child having to invite the class bully to her birthday party.

'OK,' he says.

'Right, OK. Bye then, Fran,' I say through clenched teeth. *Thanks a lot.*

Talk about awkward. Despite what Becky said about needing me, I'm not sure if she wants me here after all. She's in a foliaged corner with the 'prospect'. They are talking and laughing; she is flinging her head back and showing all her teeth, knocking back the vodkas. I haven't seen her like this for a long time, but at least she looks happy, I think. I check out her date from a distance. All I can gather is that he's wearing a pair of red velvet slippers with no socks and likes to put his hand on her shoulder, while laughing, but she can probably clock that for herself. Dominic's off doing his own thing, too – he's at the bar chatting up a waitress and using his broken leg as a flirting aid, which seems to be playing its part well; the waitress is currently scribbling something on it with a black marker pen.

And I appear to be stuck with James.

'All right?' he says, a bottle of Beck's in his hand.

'All right,' I reply, stirring a passionfruit and chilli mojito dispassionately with a straw.

Gatsby's is packed. Monday really *is* the new Friday. I'm already wincing at the high-decibel laughter, shrieks and over-loud music. I wish I wasn't here; I wish I was home in bed, or still in the hospital with Mac, under dimmed amber light. It is an amazing venue, though, any fool can see that. It has been accurately and exuberantly done up like an original 1920s speakeasy: there's a jungle of tropical plants performing botanical theatrics in every corner; printed tropical-plant wallpaper, so you're not sure where plant ends and wall starts; studded leather bucket chairs and a marble floor; lazily flicking ceiling fans; cloisonné lamps suspended over tables in cosy corner booths; American jazz; cocktails in tin cups; and a New York style bar. New York . . . I wonder if Stewart Whittaker has seen my email.

It's all colour and light and up-for-it boys and girls – lots and lots of girls, all done up to the nines, tens and elevens. Becky looks almost subdued in comparison, in her pale aqua stretchy dress – these girls are in a riot of colour, each trying to outshine the next. And James seems to be getting a lot of attention from them. They are glancing at his salt-and-pepper handsomeness, then looking away. Flicking their hair in the direction of his smart-suited oblivion. Grinning at their friends, then risking another look. Even Becky's eyes expanded to dinner plates when we met her outside and as she scuttled me to the bar, while James kindly took coats to the cloakroom, she hissed, 'Where the bloody hell did you get *him* from? He's gorgeous!'

'It's nothing like that!' I said.

'Who is he, then?'

'A friend, an estate agent.'

'Are you *moving*? Where do you meet friends like *that*?' She quickly ordered two vodka and tonics at the bar – doubles, despite my protestations – and I knew I would have to tell her.

'I met him in the hospital.'

'The hospital? Which hospital?' She was already sipping noisily through her straw, mining it through the rim-high crushed ice in her vodka and tonic.

'St Katherine's. I've been visiting someone. Someone we saw the night we went to see Dominic.'

Becky stared at me. I could see her brain whirring under her choppy blue quiff. 'St *Katherine's*? Who?' The brain kept whirring. She bit at the top of her straw and frowned. 'The night we saw Dominic . . . Hang on . . . ? Don't tell me that man who looked like Mac Bartley-Thomas *was* him!' she exclaimed. 'Oh my God! You went back in to get your phone.

What? Were you checking it was him . . . ? Arden! Bloody hell! What on earth's been going on?'

'He was in a car accident,' I said, sipping at my own drink, and hating how meek I sounded. How ashamed, although the only part I was ashamed about was not telling her. 'I've been visiting him. James has, too – he's Mac's neighbour.'

'Oh, *right*,' said Becky. She waggled her straw and inhaled from her glass. 'Blimey. So Mac lives in London? Bloody hell. Wow, Arden. This is pretty huge.' And pretty huge that I hadn't told her . . . 'You really loved him.'

'Yes, I did.'

'Is he OK? How long has he been there? And what does he say about you turning up in his life again?'

'Not a lot! He can't speak, you know, because of his injuries. He's in quite a bad way, really.' I won't tell her about the whole List thing. The movie references. How I've been reliving mine and Mac's affair. 'He's been in hospital for a couple of weeks. Brain injury.'

'Wow,' she said again. She shook her glass, hoovered once more through a stack of crunchy ice with her straw. 'You're such a dark horse.' She looked cross, then thoughtful. 'Poor man,' she said. 'What a thing. I wonder where this is going to go.'

'How do you mean?'

'Well, it's like something out of the movies you used to watch with him. Him turning up like that. Some kind of serendipity.'

'John Cusack, Kate Beckinsale,' I said, almost flippantly, referring to the movie of the same name. But I am so sad Mac and I met each other again so late, and under such circumstances, and sorry Becky was the last to know.

'Er, yeah. What do you think will happen?' She excavated the last of her vodka, leaving the pole of her straw standing in its siphoned arctic nest.

'I have absolutely no idea. I don't even know if he's going to be all right.'

'And the gorgeous James?'

Two hands suddenly appeared on Becky's shoulders and she jumped two feet in the air, a splatter of crushed ice jerking over the rim of the glass and landing on her dress. She whipped her head round and then grinned.

'Simon!'

'Hi, Becky.'

'How're you doing?'

'Great!'

'Simon, this is Arden; Arden, Simon.'

'Pleased to meet you,' said Simon, but it was clear he only had eyes for Becky, what I could see of them behind his Clark Kent glasses. They twinkled at her above a huge hipster beard and below twitching, bushy eyebrows. 'Would you like another drink?' And Becky and her contender turned to the bar and James returned from the cloakroom and took up his place as Much-Admired Older Man.

'I meant what I said about that lift,' he says to me now, as a girl in an emerald-green dress smiles furtively at him then looks away. I wonder how he can be so *unaware* of it all.

'Thank you,' I reply. 'It's very kind of you. I'll have a think about it.' I wish he hadn't brought it up again. I don't want to think about it at all. I just want to go on the train, get my visit to Marilyn over and done with and come home again. 'Thank you.'

James is on his second beer. He closes his eyes each time he sips from it. I still have the same drink. 'Can I ask you something?' he says.

'Sure.' A woman in a black lace headdress and plum lipstick is taking her place in a dusky corner, behind a microphone. I will welcome a relief to the thudding music which seems to pump right through me.

'Are some of your clothes inspired by characters in movies?'

A slow smile dawns on my face. No one has ever asked

me this before; not even Becky. 'Why would you ask that?' I enquire, all innocent.

'Well, the check coat and beret combo,' says James. 'It's very *Bonnie and Clyde*. Then the shaggy coat the other evening – I could only think of Kate Hudson in *Almost Famous*. And, well, forgive me if I'm wrong, but do I sense a hint of Julia Roberts in *Notting Hill* tonight?'

I laugh. I pat at my hair which is in a plaited chignon thing, the curls restrained – similar to Julia's when she goes to that birthday dinner and causes utter chaos. 'Rumbled,' I say. 'I'm impressed. And quite amazed.'

I've been wearing outfits from the movies for years. When I was with Christian, it was the only thing I had *left* of me. He didn't have a clue. He wasn't a film person and he wasn't that observant anyway, unless it was something he felt was a slight to him, like a look on a face or the wrong kind of smile. I *was* observant. I could name *food* they ate in movies years afterwards. The outfits were even more memorable to me. It was my thing, when all my other things had been taken away by him, and I clung to my secret, as small as it was, as my way of keeping control. When I wore those off-the-shoulder Grace Kelly dresses or those latterly defiant *Annie Hall* waistcoat-and-tie outfits at the appalling date night dinners Christian and I used to have (four courses and a lecture in self-improvement, anyone?), I was still me. When I wore my glam Hepburn wide-legged trousers and white shirt (Katharine) to our weekly finance 'meetings', I was still me. When Julian and I left the house for that fortnight in the women's refuge, and I wore a Hepburn black polo neck and capri pants, with flats (Audrey), I still had a little bit of me left.

James looks awkwardly pleased to have his hunch confirmed. 'I knew it!' he says, like a small boy, and I worry for a minute he is going to make me do a fist bump, but he appears to think better of it.

'You know a lot about films,' I say. He knows *Bonnie and Clyde* and *Notting Hill* and *Almost Famous*, at least. He hasn't seen *The Graduate*. Still, he must be quite a movie-lover. And an oddity, too, to both notice and remember the *clothes*.

'Not really. I've just seen quite a few. I spend a lot of time on my own.'

I thought as much. 'You never said,' I press, 'about being a movie buff, when I told you Mac was a Film Studies lecturer, and when we went to his house and saw all those books.'

'Lots of people watch movies.' He shrugs. 'It's nothing out of the ordinary.' No, I think, but he *is*, isn't he?

'What's your favourite genre?' I ask.

'It's quite specific.'

'Try me.'

'American war films from the seventies and eighties,' he says, '*Apocalypse Now*, *Full Metal Jacket*, *The Deer Hunter* . . .'

'Yes, quite specific,' I acknowledge.

'I know, but I *will* watch anything. I just like films.'

'Well, me too,' I say, 'and as you say, there are loads of us. We're not anything special, are we? Cheers!' I add, unexpectedly, and we clumsily chink glasses and smile at each other and I can feel all those sets of green eyes on me.

The lady at the microphone in the corner of the bar starts singing, some old Ella Fitzgerald song, I believe. Dad used to have a few of her albums and would play them on his old-fashioned seventies record player. They are sad, melancholy songs, often popular at funerals, he always told me. He didn't want one at *his* funeral, though; said he didn't want anyone in the crematorium to feel depressed: when the time came, he wanted to go through the curtains of doom to John Cougar Mellencamp. So he did, exactly two weeks after he died. We saw him off to 'Jack and Diane'. Life goes on, as Mellencamp and many others would say, although sometimes it doesn't feel that way.

'Are you single?' I ask James. It is sheer curiosity, but I immediately feel incredibly stupid. What a thing to ask! I am now definitely one of those hair-tossing, head-flicking girls with the green eyes. 'Oh God,' I hurriedly add, 'I'm not *asking* asking, I'm just curious. You seem to be on your own. No significant other . . . ?' Oh dear, what a stupid phrase and why exactly am *I* using it?

'Yes, I'm single,' says James, tapping the thick base of his beer bottle repeatedly against one palm. 'I have been for a year. I was with a girl for fifteen years, we lived together – I wanted to marry her. She kept saying "I'm not ready, I'm not ready", then she left me and was engaged and married within six months, to a DJ! I mean, fuck off!' he says good-naturedly. 'A bloody DJ?'

The 'fuck off' makes me laugh. 'I'm sorry to hear that,' I say. 'Me too; I mean, I've been single for five years. I didn't have anyone run off with a DJ, though. I was married. Abusive relationship.' I shrug. 'They happen.'

'Sadly they do,' says James. 'Physical . . . ?' he asks hesitantly.

'No. Verbal, emotional, financial. The unholy trinity.'

James nods. 'Are you OK now?'

'Yes. Yes, I think so.' *Am I?* I still don't know. 'And I have my son, of course. He isn't the abuser's' – (the *abuser* . . . I wish it hadn't taken me so long to realize what he was) – 'he's from a previous relationship. I don't have to see my ex-husband again.'

James nods. 'That's good. And Mac? Just an affair or was it love?' Very to the point, I think.

'I loved him once,' I said. 'And he loved me.'

'I thought so,' says James. 'I can feel there was something really special between you. Even if it was just "plastics".'

I laugh, even though his comment doesn't really make sense, then sip the tingling remains of my ice-cold drink. I haven't examined exactly why it is I'm visiting Mac every night. What I feel for him. If it's plain nostalgia or something more; if it's a hankering for a happier, more exciting time because of all I've endured with Christian. Do I still love Mac? I don't think so, though I feel a steady need to be near him. Do I need him to remind me of who I once was and all that I could be? Probably. But I know I'll be visiting him again tomorrow night, and the next.

'Would you like another drink?' James asks.

'Yes, please.'

THEN

Chapter 11: The Graduate

The second autumn term rolled around at last, after an interminable August and September mostly spent hiding in my room at home with rounds of cheese and tomato toasted sandwiches done in the Breville sandwich toaster, a video of *The Breakfast Club* and the listless working through of the reading list for next term.

Mac and I took up where we left off. There was always a worry when I returned after the university holidays, with no contact from him, that things would fizzle out, that I would turn up at his little flat on the first night back, after half a bottle of Lambrusco and a boogie at the Welcome Back disco to be told I was no longer wanted. That it was over. Especially after my last sulky, dramatic exit in the station car park. But when I pitched up in my cut-off jeans, embroidered plimsolls and a new Soup Dragons T-shirt, Mac opened the door to me with a grin, then immediately tried to take off my bra, so all was good.

We resumed normal service: watching movies, sleeping with each other and remaining undetected by anyone, but there was now a slight obstacle to our affair, as second-year students had to live off campus . . . The other reason I was fearful Mac wouldn't take me in on that first night – a waif and stray, an inebriated urchin clutching a plastic pint of cider and black – was I didn't want to return to my new and splendidly hideous student digs.

Becky and I had ballsed things up. There had been an accommodation ballot in the summer term, to allocate housing in the second year, which our names had been in, along with three other girls we wanted to share with. If you did well in the ballot, you got 'top end' of Leamington Spa – nice Georgian houses, central heating, carpets. If you didn't, you got 'bottom end' – dodgy terraces, gas fires you had to throw lit matches at, mouldy carpets. We came out in the top three, or something, in the ballot. We had a Monday-morning appointment to be allocated our beautiful Georgian villa, but got pissed the night before, overslept and didn't turn up for it. We were awarded a terraced house, Bottom End Leamington, which had bed bugs, mattresses with nails in, slug trails and a dangerous 1950s gas oven complete with one of those scary overhead grills that threatened to set your hair on fire every time you cooked bacon. The heating was woefully inadequate: we made do with those vile gas heaters (one in each horrible bedroom) and a three-bar electric fire in the damp living room that we all shifted up the sofa in turn to roast ourselves by.

I vowed to spend as little time in this hellhole as possible and sleep as many nights as I could at Mac's, if he would have me (well, of course he would *have* me . . . I knew this without doubt, after that first night back). It was risky, we knew. I would emerge, bleary-eyed, from his flat several mornings a week, hovering in the doorway until the coast looked fairly clear and then running like the wind to classes. If people saw me they never said anything to anyone. Becky knew, of course; the other three girls thought I had a boyfriend in the third year. On the nights I hoped I would be staying I stuffed a toothbrush and a clean pair of knickers into the pocket of my denim jacket . . . I was never the only person to turn up to laborious Brontë sisters lectures wearing the same clothes as the day before, anyway.

Mac and I watched *The Graduate* one night in late

October, on video, in his bedroom. We wheeled in the telly on the cabinet with castors so we could watch it in bed.

'I love this movie,' I said happily, as he snapped the video out of its box. I was propped up against three white pillows in a nightie with *Little Miss Naughty* on the front and had a packet of Hobnobs at the ready. 'The soundtrack, the actors, the saturation of colour. All that *sunlight*.' I slowly peeled the satisfying strip off the Hobnobs' wrapper.

'The "saturation of colour" . . .' Mac smiled, leaning over to grab his notebook and pen from the bedside table. I was still pleasing him in every way.

'Yeah,' I said. 'The swimming pool, the lilo . . .' I was excited about watching this with Mac. I was smiling as soon as the camera panned back from Ben sitting on the aeroplane and positively buzzing by the time Art Garfunkel started singing about his old friend, darkness, and Ben rode the airport travelator. I didn't even eat a Hobnob until he emerged from the house in the scuba suit.

We sang along to the soundtrack. We laughed at 'Plastics'. When Anne Bancroft rolled her stocking up her leg Mac was inside me.

'Such a good moment,' said Mac.

'This?' I said, giving him a long, lazy wink.

'Well, yes,' he whispered, taking a slow intake of breath.

'What were you like as a graduate?' I asked him later. The film had finished and we were hoovering up slice after slice of paté on toast, with super-thin slices of cucumber on top. Still in bed. I wanted chocolate cake, like John and Yoko, but neither of us would make the effort to go to Sainsbury's. 'Horny?' Mac laughed and popped a slice of cucumber in his mouth. 'What about as an undergraduate? Did you get *under* an older lecturer?'

'No. That's a funny thing to ask!'

'Is it? No Mrs Robinsons?'

'No.'

'I just wondered if that's how you got the idea to do the reverse.'

'Cheeky!' said Mac. 'Though it's flattering to be thought of as the male version of Mrs Robinson, I suppose. The woman is seriously sexy.'

I wanted to ask him why he was having this affair with me, but at the same time I didn't want him to think about it too much, to analyse it the way he did his movies. I'd end up as an intense, fucked-up character with a suspect past or something and he'd be a dark, shady brooder with issues that needed to be triumphantly overturned.

'You could argue Anne Bancroft is the ultimate embarrassing mother,' I said flippantly, 'although of course you haven't met mine. Why are you including *The Graduate* on your course?' I added, pitching toast crumbs off my chest and leaning back against the pillows. 'What does it say about women?' I was feeling too full and languid to work it out myself, however much Mac liked my musings.

Mac put his triangle of toast down on his plate and grabbed an edge of pillowcase to clean his glasses with. 'At the time, this film was so controversial. A woman like Mrs Robinson – a woman in control, a woman who feels nothing but is desperate to feel *something* – was new to audiences. She was an absolute pioneer. And the fact she was an older woman – sexually powerful, still sexual *at all*, to be honest – just blew people's minds.' He put his glasses back on. 'But ultimately, she is punished. She is conniving, manipulative. She loses her husband, her toyboy lover and the love and affection of her daughter. She is made to *pay* for her sexual verve, so you could argue that after all its shock and subversion, *The Graduate* is ultimately conservative.'

I rested my thumb under my chin, wedging it into the concave space there; my forefinger resting against my nose. I hoped I looked cute and contemplative. 'Could you also say that Elaine reaches independence and rebellion, but

those silver marathon blankets; I needed to be as far from this doorway as possible. But the scent of Poison and Embassy Lights was refusing to knock me out. My mother was here. *Here*. This was the worst thing to have ever happened to me.

'What on earth are you doing here, Marilyn?' It wasn't my voice, it was the voice of a hysterical woman trying to remain calm; a far-away voice, squeaky and high.

'I thought I'd come up for the weekend,' she said simply, hauling her vanity case over the threshold and into the hall. 'Pretend I'm a student. One of the *gang*.' And she tittered her horrible laugh and her raspberry-pink talons scraped against the side of the case with a sound that would make a cat wince and I wanted to stab her with something, *Psycho*-style.

She'd never given any indication she might just turn up! She'd been sneery about Warwick – yes, she'd shown off about it to her friends, but towards me there had been nothing but disdain. That I was getting above my station. That I was becoming a *student*, like it was the most bourgeois, embarrassing thing in the world. I felt invaded. Every fibre in my being was screaming against her being in this house. I didn't want her *poison* here, infiltrating my new, escaped life. After all these years, *now* she chose to pay me some attention?

She was in. She shut the front door behind her with a decided bang. She was dressed in skin-tight gingham pedal pushers, a mohair jumper and a tragic sort of cape. Her hair was massive, over-rollered. Her toenails were coral and thick-looking, curled over at the ends.

'It's a dump,' she said, looking round her. 'Absolute hell-hole. Where's your room?'

'Upstairs.'

Up the worn carpet to my bedroom I went, the poison following me. Marilyn looked around at the movie and music posters, cast an ironically judgemental eye on my cluttered desk and my scraps of clothes and single socks littering the floor.

153

'Where am I going to sleep?'

What was she expecting? Twin beds with matching eider-downs, like in all those Doris Day movies?

'I don't know,' I said. I didn't want her to *stay*! I didn't want her here at all! 'One of us could sleep on the floor?' I ventured, every part of me in silent revolt.

'Yes, that's what we'll have to do,' she said and I hated the chumminess of the 'we'. We weren't chums. We weren't going to be roomies, giggling at midnight in the dark. Her in my bed, no doubt, me on the floor. She was a woman I had tried and failed to make love me. 'Now, how early can we get a drink around here? I'm up for a really big night.'

'Well, the union opens at six,' I volunteered angrily. 'We have to hitch in.'

'Hitch-hiking? Well, isn't that just *thrilling*! I'll have to show a bit of leg.'

The thought of Marilyn by the side of the road sticking out her leg like Claudette Colbert in *It Happened One Night* was almost too much to bear. 'Yeah,' I said, more unhappy than I'd ever been. Who *was* this woman? I wanted the woman with the floury apron back, the one who'd given me a cuddle and told me I had beautiful curls and a kind heart. 'Before that, I have a bottle of Lambrusco in the fridge downstairs?' There was only one way to survive this: I had to get absolutely hammered. 'You stay there and I'll go and get it.'

I made Marilyn spaghetti bolognaise on the hob of the terrible oven. She complained it wasn't tasty enough. That the sauce was too runny. I sat in silence, pushing mine round my plate and knocking back glass after glass of Lambrusco until I had to steal Becky's Mateus Rosé from the back of the fridge, while Marilyn judged, judged, judged. I felt sick when I heard the front door open and Zara, one of my housemates, came bustling in with a load of bags.

'This is Marilyn,' I said weakly, 'she's come up for the weekend.'

'Hi!' trilled Marilyn, waving her fork in the air. Zara went to put a Fray Bentos pie in the oven. 'Ooh, she *looks* like a student, doesn't she?' Marilyn remarked. 'A bit hempy.'

There was no point trying to shush her. She was impervious to a kick under the table, too. I just let the wheels come off, and sat drunkenly at the table while she mithered about her meal and slagged my housemates off one by one as they came home.

Last in was Becky; she'd brought Fisher Boy with her.

'This is Doug,' she said.

'This is Marilyn,' I muttered. Marilyn's face was bright red now and she'd just reapplied a matching red lipstick so everything kind of blended in. She was now up at the furnace end of the sofa watching a Jason Donovan video; I was nursing my last glass of Mateus. 'Sorry, I drank your Mateus. I'll replace it tomorrow.'

'That's OK.' Becky looked stupefied. 'And Marilyn is . . . ?'

'My mother,' I said, though it killed me to do so.

'Oh! Well, what a surprise! Actually, you do really look alike.'

This was true and I absolutely hated it. I didn't want Marilyn's mouth, nose or almond-shaped eyes, but I had them. It disgusted me. I willed Becky to take Fisher Boy to her room and she did, and Marilyn and I got ready to go out – me in jeans and a stripy T-shirt, her in a very tight off-the-shoulder black dress and a ridiculous pair of shoes.

'Nobody wears heels in the union,' I said.

'Well, I'll get noticed then.'

She certainly did. She got noticed at the hitching point, where she *did* hitch up her skirt and shove a leg out; she got noticed walking into the union, where she got a wolf-whistle she absorbed like syrup into a sponge pudding. She was *highly* noticeable and completely out of place amongst the jeans and DMs and the Ramones T-shirts. And she made a complete show of herself. She ordered a 'whiskey and American' at the bar – no one knew what that was; it turned out to be whisky and ginger beer. She flirted with random people, including two goths. Danced inappropriately to Salt-N-Pepa's 'Push It'. Went into the porters' lodge at the end of the disco and wrestled the tannoy off porter Paul to announce a party back at 68 Tachbrook Street (why had I ever written home and given them my address. *Why?*), to which a gaggle of pissed and excited students turned up at half one, brandishing cans of Guinness. There she danced on a chair in the kitchen to Sinitta, before making a round of fried egg sandwiches and doling them out to everyone on tea plates. I was drunk as a skunk by then. I slept on my own floor, thoroughly pissed off. Marilyn collapsed into my bed sometime later, a gnarly, clawed foot suspended above me.

The next morning I thought I'd get rid of her early, but she insisted we go back into the union because last night someone she'd been flirting with had told her there was a little place which sold fantastic milkshakes and the best ever American-style pancakes and she didn't want to eat anything else from my kitchen, quite frankly. (*What about the fried egg sandwiches?* I thought. She had no trouble wolfing those down last night.)

I was so hungover I could barely move. I told Marilyn to go on her own but she threatened to make Becky take her so I had to escort her. We had the pancakes and the milkshakes, somehow, without heaving. We walked back to the hitching point. It was sunny and my eyes hurt. We stood there and waited, doing controlled breathing (that may have just been me). I was desperate to be picked up so I could get away from here and send Marilyn off to catch her train. I was also worried some hot young thing she liked the look of would pick us up and I'd find out a week later she was still up here, in Bottom End Leamington with a matching Argos kettle and toaster. And then Mac's car came around the furthest corner. Oh God, I prayed he wasn't going to Leamington, as then he'd be required by student law to pick us up.

I realized how ridiculous we must look. Me in rolled-up jeans, DMs and a huge red lambswool jumper down to my knees; Marilyn in hot-pink capri pants, red slingbacks and a cropped jumper with cherries on it, plus the bouffant electric-white hair and the vanity case. He'd think I was standing here with a souped-up bloody Myra Hindley.

Marilyn had a fag on and was blowing smoke over the heads of the incredulous students in the queue behind us. I tried to step away and pretend I wasn't with her but she grabbed my arm and hung off me, adjusting one of her slingbacks because she was getting a blister. Mac drove past. I could see the eyebrows raise behind the rimless glasses, the half-smile curve of curiosity and amusement. My only salvation was that he was clearly not going to Leamington, so he didn't stop. But he'd seen her. He'd seen Marilyn. We looked so much alike he'd know now who I was and I hated it.

I did not want to be my mother's daughter.

NOW

Chapter 12

It's the morning after the night at Gatsby's and I wake up with a terrible hangover. I'm groggy and my mouth is dry. My nightie has Nutella stains on it. My hair looks like a giant, electrified dandelion clock and reminds me I need to get my roots done. None of it is a good look.

I lurch from my bed and into the bathroom, then back to bed to turn on the radio where Cher, in turn, is turning back time, so I turn it off again. It's not like me to get so drunk, these days, although at least I am free to do so, since Christian. I'm not quite sure what happened. James left as he said it was late and he had an early viewing in the morning – watched by several pairs of disappointed eyes, I noticed – and then Becky handed me another drink and another and then a dance floor formed itself like an amoeba, over by the front window, with a huge triffid plant bearing down on everyone, and we danced until 3 a.m., with Dominic briefly joining us to stomp on crutches to The Pointer Sisters. It was fabulous, actually.

I wonder briefly if James would have danced, had he stayed. Would he have done the imaginary knocks on the door to 'Love Shack' and the doggy paddle-esque *running away* hand gestures to 'Tainted Love'? Would he have whoo-hooed to the Black Eyed Peas? I'm not sure; somehow I don't imagine him to be the dancing kind, though he may have surprised me.

I really enjoyed it. I haven't danced for ages. I have a vague memory of whirling round and round with Becky as disco lights flashed a kaleidoscope of half-moons above our heads and cast dots and dashes on our faces. I felt free and alive and a little like my old self, to be honest. I never expected that to happen. For those few hours it was like Becky and I had gone back in time.

Becky left with her prospect, in the end, and I shared a taxi home with Dominic and the Leg, which by now had its own fan club and about fifty signatures, phone numbers and propositions written on it, mostly in liquid eyeliner. *I did it*. I have been out. I have been out with friends and I survived. I'll give Becky a call from work, later – the first I will have initiated since Christian; it was a shame we didn't get a chance to talk more last night, about the things that really matter, but maybe today we can. I had an illuminating thought in Gatsby's on the dance floor running away to 'Tainted Love' – one I may share with Becky today, if the call goes well – that I had been *targeted* by Christian. Recruited: he'd made a career of it, after all. It's all so obvious now. I was a single mum who had just been left by a cheater; I had an unfeeling, narcissistic mother, a depressed father (did Christian even have some kind of sixth sense that he would leave us in the worst possible way?) . . . no anchor to cling to in life's storms to stop me being stripped away to nothing. I was vulnerable, I was easy prey. He saw me coming.

For now I can email Becky at the Opera House, to say thanks for a great evening. I get out of bed and flop to the sitting room where I open the laptop to send her an email, but as I click on to Outlook, three emails down in my inbox, making my heart stutter, is something from Stewart Whittaker.

Dear Arden,
  Thank you for your email. I'm so sorry to hear Mac is in hospital. I send him my warm regards and wish him

a speedy recovery; if you let me know which hospital I'll make a visit when I get back from New York in a couple of weeks. I'm afraid I don't know his son Lloyd's current whereabouts. As far as I was aware, he was running a bar in London somewhere and I don't know anything beyond that.

There is someone you can try, if you can track her down. A former student of Mac's, Perrie Turque, who I once met at a barbecue at his house. I believe she was Lloyd's girlfriend for a while and as such may know where he is. I'm afraid I don't have any contact details for her but I believe she is a travel writer and has a blog.

Yours,

Stewart Whittaker

PS. You have an unusual name. Did we meet once, many years ago, in Soho?

These Film Studies buggers have bloody good memories, I think, as I bash out a quick reply. Yes, we did meet once, many years ago, and it was outside the Wiltshire Hotel in Soho. I was terribly polite and desperately trying to look as though I wasn't having an affair with Mac; *you* were a big man in a big overcoat, with a curious expression on your face.

It was on one of the best weekends of my life.

I don't write this, of course. I thank Stewart for his information, tell him Mac is in St Katherine's and say I will pass on his best wishes.

I then google Perrie Turque and she pops up straight away. She has a travel blog, an Instagram account, and both Twitter and Facebook pages. I wonder if she met Lloyd in his bar and why she went to a barbecue at Mac's after they were no longer together. I'm not on Twitter or Facebook, but I email her via the blog, with the necessary details, and then collapse back into bed for ten minutes before I have to get up for work.

*

When I get to the hospital that night, straight from work, Mac is not in his bed. A fear grips me like a cold, gnarly hand round my heart, squeezing it too tightly. I look around wildly for Fran, for anyone. Where is she? Where is *he*? I run to the nurses' station and someone I don't recognize is there, nodding an auburn curly head over a computer.

'What's happened to Mac Bartley-Thomas?' I breathlessly ask.

'Oh, sorry, love!' Thank God. It's Fran, emerging from a cupboard set into the wall and wielding a bed pan. 'I was looking out for you but I got distracted by Mr Hussain in bed two. Hey! Mac's fine, he's fine. He had some bleeding overnight, on the brain, and he's just having a little operation to release the pressure.'

'A little operation?' I realize I am gripping the edge of the desk.

'More a procedure. It's pretty standard. Routine. He's going to be fine.' Fran touches my arm, to reassure. Her eyes look kind and unfazed. Unfazed enough that I allow my breathing to relax a little.

'I was so scared when I saw his bed was empty!'

'Oh, I can imagine. More of a worry if there's someone else entirely in it, though, to be honest!'

I laugh but the fear hasn't quite left me. It's a residue surrounding me – a churning fog I can't reach out from. I wish Julian was here. Or Becky. *Becky*. I didn't even call her today, I realize, or email her. Instead, I spent the day musing about Perrie Turque and Mac's son, but now the regret that I didn't contact her pierces through the fog like a lance.

I hear another familiar voice, saying, 'Good evening.' It's James. In another suit, hair combed and careful. I'm in my dog-tooth one, black cashmere jumper. My hair is a bit of a mess as it's wet and windy out.

'Mac's not dead,' I say hurriedly. 'He's just having an operation.'

'Oh?' I realize James has actually had a haircut; everything's even shorter and neater. 'Everything OK?'

'I think so. How long will he be?' I ask Fran.

'Couple more hours, I expect.'

I wonder why no one has called us then I remember we are not family. No one here has our phone numbers; we are not next of kin.

'You look tired,' says James, once Fran has explained everything again to him, patted me on the arm once more and squished off down the ward.

'Do I? Hungover, more like!' I remember how all those young girls had looked at him last night, how his soot-grey eyes had been oblivious to them.

'What time did you stay at that bar till?'

'About three.'

'Oh, a big night.'

'Kind of.'

He hesitates for a moment. Neither of us knows what to do, I think, with Mac not on the ward. We are hovering by the nurses' station like a couple of awkward spare parts. 'Do you want to go to the café? Get something to eat?'

'OK.' I don't want to go home. If I did I would only want to come back again.

We leave the ward and navigate the yellow corridors to the infrequently signposted café. In the last corridor, where a casual piece of green tinsel still clings to the wall, we pass an open door and a sign saying 'Hospital Chapel', and I sneak a look inside.

It looks peach-painted creepy. Apricot-sterile. There's a modern stained-glass window at the front – depicting a seascape, three rows of woolly upholstered chairs and a cross suspended on a pleated sage curtain, on the right. If God is supposed to be in this room I can't see his hand or any other part of him; it looks like it was all done up cheaply at B&Q. Still, people find it comforting, I expect.

A woman comes out in a navy anorak, a tissue balled up in one hand. Poor love, I think, and pray I won't ever have to go in there. Once, at another hospital, after we lost Dad, was enough. 'Sorry,' the woman says, as she brushes past us and I don't know what to say. She doesn't look at all comforted. I'm not religious; I don't come from a religious family. 'A load of old hokum,' Dad always said and Marilyn would add, 'Opium of the people', quoting Marx to try to make herself look clever. She had *a lot* of pretensions, that woman. She still has a Goya painting from her old bedroom in Essex in her room at The Cedars – *The Naked Maja*, the one the real Marilyn had. Actually, the Chapel of Rest reminds me of my mother's room there: all 'comforting' textiles and 'soothing' pastels.

It's busy in the café, there's a lot of steam rising from behind the counter; lots of different accents ordering hot drinks and lots of kinds of people squatting at cluttered tables. The bustling, bright nature of it actually *is* comforting. The walls are not the stale peach of the Chapel of Rest, but a vibrant ochre which bathes the café in a cheery tropical sunset, despite the driving rain outside.

'I always liked the café in *Brief Encounter*,' says James. 'You seen that?'

'Yes,' I say, not surprised *he* has, after what he told me at Gatsby's. 'Carnforth station. I didn't think you'd like that sort of film.'

'I like all kinds of films,' says James.

'I love it,' I say. 'All that black-and-white angst. The repression . . . And no, you don't have anything in your eye.' I laugh, remembering how Celia Johnson and Trevor Howard first meet in that movie. 'What do you fancy?'

I look up from my purse and at him, and the expression on his face – warm, amused, almost tender? – makes me wonder for the merest of split seconds what it would be like if I *did* have grit in my eye and he were to take a look at it for me. Then I order a sticky bun and a cup of weak tea and James asks for a chocolate brownie and a hot chocolate.

'A bit girly?' he suggests, after he has ordered whipped cream to go on the top. 'I'm one of those unsociable weirdos that don't like tea or coffee, and I'm a bit of a chocoholic.'

'No, of course not,' I say. 'Of course it's not girly.' He's different, I think. He's not like everyone else.

'And do you want marshmallows on that, dear?' the elderly lady behind the counter asks. Shrill, old-fashioned, a hefty nose. She looks like she'd fit in quite well at Carnforth.

'Yes, please.'

We go and sit down. There's a free small table by a large radiator.

'It's terrible,' says James.

'What's terrible?' I ask, although I can think of a range of answers, to be honest.

'Mac. The head injury. The operation. Poor bloke.'

'I know.' I sip my scalding tea. 'I hope it goes OK. I'm worried – really worried – that he won't come round, that this is it, that even if he does I won't ever get the chance to speak to him again. I know this is totally self-absorbed but so much is missing for me,' I add. 'There's so much I want to know. It's a big gap, isn't it? Thirty years? Well, twenty-eight, actually, since I last had a conversation with Mac. I don't have a clue what's *in* all those years.'

'How do you mean?'

'Well, I have no idea what Mac did for the last three decades,' I say. 'So many pieces to fill in. There's the London Film School, lecturing at UEA, possibly, but that's about it. What about before that? And what about before *that*?'

'I don't know,' says James. 'I've only lived next door to him for four years, and even if it had been much longer I probably still wouldn't know a lot. I'm sorry.'

'It's OK.' I stir my tea, pick at my sticky bun. 'It's just

weird to have this void; that he can't fill it by simply telling me about it. It makes me feel . . . discombobulated.'

'That's a big word.' James smiles.

'It is, isn't it?' I break off a piece of my bun. 'Did you meet someone called Perrie Turque when you went to Mac's barbecue that time?'

'Perrie Turque? Yes, that was her! Mac's former student. Not you.' He smiles at me, releases a marshmallow from a mound of cream and pops it in his mouth. 'Perrie. Feisty kind of woman. Pushy, I thought. I didn't really speak to her. I was a bit scared of her, to be honest.'

I laugh. 'It does seem to be that sort of name, doesn't it? Perrie Turque? Forceful, slightly sinister. Did she have a severe fringe?'

'Yes, I believe she did. And a very stern cardigan.' James's eyes are lit up, teasing.

I laugh again. 'Did you know she was the ex-girlfriend of Mac's son?'

James looks surprised. 'I didn't know he had a son!'

I nod. 'He does.'

'I'm surprised. He never mentioned anyone, ever. Though Mac and I didn't talk that much, it has to be said. I was only at that barbecue in the first place by default, because I was in my garden pretending I knew what to do with a rose bush and I think he felt sorry for me. I could have been a rose bush for all Perrie Turque cared. I remember she started barking on about her journey from Crystal Palace or something and her voice was too loud so I made my excuses and escaped to the bottom of the garden.' I smile; I can imagine James keeping clear at the bottom of Mac's garden. 'I was spared her life story, which I could imagine would be quite long. Where is his son now?'

'I don't know,' I say.

'Missing?'

'He's not *missing*.' I frown. 'At least I hope not. A missing son would be unbearable, wouldn't it?'

'You have a son,' he acknowledges.

'I do,' I say. 'And I can't think of Mac's son being missing, it's just that he's not able to be *located*, at the moment. Listen, you said you also met a man there from the London Film School. Was he called Stewart Whittaker?' I ask. 'A big guy, with a beard, possibly? Looks a bit like a bear?'

'A bear called Stewart . . .' James smiles as he stirs his hot chocolate. 'Yes, I think that was the chap from the London Film School. Why do you ask? Why all the interest in these attendees at a long-forgotten barbecue?'

'I've been playing amateur detective,' I say. 'I'm trying to *find* Lloyd – Mac's son.'

'Oh, right. I see. Any luck?'

'Not yet.'

'Maybe he doesn't want to be found.' James shrugs.

'How do you mean?'

'Maybe they're estranged.'

'I'll find out,' I say. 'I'll find out what the situation is. If Mac is in hospital his son will want to come to him, I believe.'

'Not if they are estranged.'

'You're not helping!'

'Sorry!'

'They'll just have to become *un*-estranged,' I conclude. I can't imagine being without Julian. I can't imagine him not coming to my bedside if I was in a car accident.

'You sound determined.'

'I *am* determined.' And the fact surprises me. I haven't felt like this in a while, that I have a purpose. I quite like it. Mac wrote so much of my life for me – those intricate, plot-heavy eighteen months of our affair – I realize I want to write a bit of his for *him*, something good, something wonderful. A plot twist (not a denouement, no!), and a plot twist created by me, lifted from the pages of my screenplay. I wonder if it's the memory of the old Arden coming back that's making me do it, too. The scrappy, annoying me. The girl who went after what she wanted, at any cost. I want this for Mac. I really do. I'm going to find Lloyd. 'Can I ask you something else?'

'Sure.'

'Why do you keep coming to visit Mac if you hardly know him?'

James is silent for a moment. He places his hot chocolate on the table and a thick ribbon of cream creeps down the side of the mug. 'Because I know what loneliness feels like. To have no one bothering about you. Wondering how you are. Looking out for you. I know how it feels to be alone.'

'Oh.' I remember the ex-girlfriend and the fucking DJ. James's eyes are grey and steadfast and I avoid staring into them by focusing on tapping my teaspoon on the edge of my saucer. 'I'm sorry.' It troubles me that Mac was lonely and I wonder how it could have happened to such a colossus of a man. I wonder why James is lonely, too. Doesn't he have any friends, nice work colleagues? Where is his family? I know there is the mum down in Kent, but doesn't he have anyone else?

'It's OK,' says James and as I glance up he almost does a little start, recovers himself. His voice lightens and his eyes crinkle into a smile. 'So, have you thought any more about letting me give you a lift to see your mum? You're still going, aren't you?'

'Yes, I'm still going. And she's not my "mum",' I say, trying not to sound indignant but failing. 'Well, she is, but I don't call her that. I call her "my mother", or Marilyn.'

'Oh, I see,' says James, looking at me with curiosity. Those grey eyes flicker. 'Not the greatest relationship, then?'

'No, not the greatest. I don't like my mother,' I add. 'But that's OK. Some people don't.'

'Well, no,' he says. 'That's very true. So, would you like a lift? I wouldn't mind the company, to be honest. Being a lonely old soul and all that shit . . .'

I laugh, but my mind is racing. I like being on the train by myself, gazing out of the window. I don't like being tied to someone else's plans, their times. I like to eat messy junk food on the journey, from a carrier bag. Read a dog-eared book. I'm not sure I can sit in a car with James for two hours and make small talk although, actually, I now wonder if the talk *would* be that small. Now I know him a little better.

'Well, think about it,' he says finally, while my mind continues to race round its own endless track, with no safety car in sight. 'The offer is still there.'

'Thank you,' I say.

James slurps at his chocolate again. He gets a chocolatey moustache, which looks quite cute. I decide not to tell him it's there. Not for a bit.

'How do you know Mac has a son in the first place?' he asks me.

'Google,' I say. I wasn't going to tell him that Mac's son is the reason we couldn't stay together.

The neighbour and I, the ex-lover, wait either side of Mac's bed – somehow we found ourselves back at the ward again, two spare parts – and finally Mac is wheeled into the ward, on a different kind of bed, with high sides, and lifted carefully by two orderlies on to his own.

He doesn't look that good. He is pale; his lips are dry. His eyes are firmly shut. James and I stay with him for an hour; there's an old film on one of the TV channels, *Overboard* with Kurt Russell and Goldie Hawn – one of Dad's favourites, actually – and we gawp at it, periodically, until we start watching it properly. I catch James smiling occasionally. Now and again he breaks into a chuckle. Towards the end, we realize Mac has his eyes open and is watching it too, but he is not smiling. His dry lips are set into a cracked line.

James has to go.

'I'll see you tomorrow, Arden,' he says, 'won't I?'

'Yes, you will,' I say, and I like the thought of arranging to meet him here. I can't imagine visiting Mac without him now. We're like some kind of tragic double act. 'Bye, James.'

He leaves the ward. I watch him holding the door for a family of five who have just been buzzed in, before he leaves. Fran glides over. She is in super-efficient, bustling mode, fussing with the sheets and blankets, patting back hair, gently chiding Mac for his absence.

'Ah, you're back with us, Mac. I'm glad to see it. You *are* naughty, giving us a little scare like that!' Scare? She implied earlier it wasn't a *scare*. She said it was a 'procedure', routine. 'I expect to see you up and about tomorrow and eating all your dinner, Mac, my boy. I'm going to hold you to it.' Oh, she really is giving him a good telling-off. Mac simply stares at her, unblinking. There's no twinkle today; the ghost of his charisma gives no flicker, no hint of its former magnificence.

Once Fran has soft-shoed away, I lean close to him and place my lips a fraction from his ear. I don't know if he can hear me or not, but I know the next movie on The List and I want him to remember it, too. I also want him to know that to me he is not a bad boy but one of the very best. I lean over to whisper in his ear and I say, 'Nobody's perfect.'

THEN

Chapter 13: Some Like It Hot

The worst thing about my mother's hideous visit in the autumn term (well, not the *worst* – that would be her cavorting near the front of the stage to Erasure's 'Respect' while pretending to ride an invisible pony) was that when the Christmas holidays rolled round again – dreaded and inevitable – Marilyn had a new weapon.

Christmas was the same old same old – indifference, disdain, dullness, damage, disillusion, despair and too much Drambuie – except this time Marilyn knew something about me I had fiercely wanted to keep to myself.

Where I lived. What my life was like at Warwick.

I *hated* that. She had infiltrated a part of me I never expected her to even get close to. She had rocked up to my *escape* – my refuge away from her – gleefully planted her flag and casually moon-walked away. Warwick and everything that came with it was supposed to be *mine*, but she had claimed a portion of it for herself, which made me absolutely rage inside. I couldn't bear it that she could envisage me there, in that horrible house, in my horrible bedroom, in the brilliantly horrible bathroom with the one-bar electric heater precariously attached to the ceiling and operated by a single fraying cord. That she'd stayed there, gatecrashed a night out. The fact we had had a shared experience made me shudder, and she could now afflict me with a whole series of 'remember when's:

'Remember when we queued at the bar and that lad said I looked like a movie star?' *He was taking the piss, but yeah.*

'Remember when I drank that pint down in one and then put the empty glass on my head?' *Er, yes, as it was one of the most embarrassing moments of my life!*

'Remember when I fell up those stairs?' *Yes, yes, yes, I do bloody remember! I will never, ever live it down!*

And of course every 'remember when' had her in the spotlight, with me playing a bit part in the shadows, just where she liked me. I was tempted to come up with some of my own: remember when I fell outside the butcher's and hurt my knee and you took me in to ask the man for a plaster? Remember when you used to look really happy when I came out of school, especially that time I had made peppermint creams and saved all the smoothest ones for you? Remember when you loved me?

I knew Marilyn was tempted to send her own round robin, boasting about her 'wonderful' weekend in October with her daughter at university. I could see her thinking about it, as she scowled and read the Bankses' latest offering. She even lifted a biro and reached for an A4 notepad – usually reserved for scribbling incoherent shopping lists. But she laid down the pen after writing 'painkillers' and 'cottage cheese with pineapple in'. She probably couldn't be bothered, when it came to it. Too much effort. But still, it was round robin material, wasn't it? Mother-and-daughter adventures in Academia Land. Ugh. The hideous fake camaraderie of it made me sick to my stomach.

Dad didn't say a lot about her little escapade. He was probably pleased she'd gone away for two days, so he could potter in his shed in peace, drinking his beer and wondering what the hell had happened to the woman he'd married. All he said to me that Christmas was he was glad I was home.

The only very small, microscopic saving grace of it all was that I don't think Marilyn had set eyes on Mac that autumn

171

Sunday, so preoccupied had she been with her blister when he cruised past in his MG, but I also hated that she had kept me from him that weekend. As soon as I'd dumped her and her vanity case at the ticket office of Leamington station, I'd hitched back to campus and run straight to Mac's flat, where of course he wasn't in. Hungover and desperate for him, I'd skulked around and waited for him for over an hour and when he finally turned up, with a Sainsbury's bag and a grin that re-ignited my soul, I'd uttered, 'Thank God,' and had almost wrestled him to the ground with relief.

The first movie on The List we saw in the new spring term – so fresh, so full of possibility, and me so relieved to be far away from home – was *Some Like It Hot*. When Mac showed me the reels, in the screening room, having promised me a black-and-white comedy, I smiled, although it could have been a grimace.

'Not keen?' Mac asked.

'My mother thinks she's Marilyn Monroe,' I said.

'Really?' said Mac, an amused look on his face, his right eyebrow raised into his floppy fringe. 'Well, that *is* interesting. Tell me, your mother wasn't that woman standing at the hitching point with you late last term, was she? You know, the one with the white-hot barnet and the heels?'

'Er . . . no,' I tried to bluff.

'Hmm. She looked a lot like you,' said Mac. 'Similar build, same face . . .'

'All right, all right, that was my mother!' I cried, not liking that I sounded so hysterical. 'She ambushed me for the weekend. It was horrible.'

'I'm sorry,' said Mac. 'I must admit you didn't look pleased to be seen with her. Why does she think she's Marilyn Monroe?'

'She thinks she should be a movie star.' I shrugged. 'She thinks she's someone special.'

'Everyone's someone special,' said Mac, stepping towards me and teasing one of my curls between his thumb and forefinger. 'But not everyone's Marilyn Monroe.'

'She's a fantasist,' I concluded. 'Now are we going to watch the movie or not?'

'A fantasist and someone with *fidelity issues*,' said Mac, infuriating me by still not taking the first reel out of the box. 'Not good for a daughter, I should imagine.'

'No, not brilliant,' I said.

'So coming to Warwick was an escape for you?'

'Well, I *would* quite like to get a degree,' I said, 'they *can* be quite useful in life . . .'

'But you also wanted to escape from home.'

'Yes, *Freud*, I also wanted to escape from home.'

'Am I part of your escape? This affair? Us?'

'Don't try to psychoanalyse me, Mac! I'm not a character in one of your films! Are you trying to say I'm an empty husk of a girl, damaged by her home life and seeking to fill the hole – don't say anything rude! – with an older, wiser mentor figure, as an act both of rebellion and of self-flagellation? If so, what's *your* excuse? Why are you doing this? I just fancied you, that's all. It happens.'

'Whoa,' said Mac. 'It was only a question! And one that's hit a bit of a nerve, I see.' He sat down on one of the bristly sofa-chairs and rubbed a hand across his chin. 'And why am *I* doing this?' he added quietly, staring up into that husk of a soul of mine and filling in every cracked corner of it. 'Because I can't not. Come here.'

And he put his arms out to me and pulled me on to his lap and I was determined not to let his closeness feel restorative, salvationary, everything I needed, but it did. I wondered if he loved me but I still didn't dare ask.

'And now I'll thread up the movie,' he said. 'If you can bear to watch Ms Monroe in action.'

'I can bear it,' I replied.

I loved it, actually; adored it. I'd last watched *Some Like It Hot* when I was about twelve and couldn't even countenance thinking about it since, so Marilyn-y had Marilyn become – in looks if not in sweetness – but I did enjoy it, watching it with Mac. We laughed a lot; I loved Marilyn's character, Sugar, in this movie, how she played up to the camera, how she let it swallow her whole.

'Themes.' I clicked my fingers at Mac, when it had finished. 'Go!'

'Hmm. Let me see.' He pretended to muse, stroking his chin. 'Subversion of expectations of gender identity. The objectification of women. Misogyny. The male gaze . . .'

'Laura Mulvey,' I offered. I had read the book Mac had given me. Cover to cover. I had considered Mac's male gaze towards me, wallowed in it, how he gazed at me, feasted upon me. His gaze was everything. I still couldn't see it as a negative – sorry, Ms Mulvey. Mac's view of me brought me *alive*. And in *Some Like It Hot*, there was no image more male gazeable than Marilyn Monroe waddling up the platform with her cases; even the train is not impervious to her charms as it lets off a shot of steam. Sublime, really. *My* Marilyn would see a moment like that as the pinnacle of her absolute *life*.

'Quite,' agreed Mac. 'You know, the Hays Code did *not* like this movie. It was basically the middle finger to it. Gender bending, sexual innuendo . . . It was banned in Kansas, you know.'

'We're not in Kansas now, Toto,' I trilled. 'I love how Lemmon and Curtis [hark at me, *Lemmon and Curtis* . . . !] discuss how women are treated. What was it they said? Something like all you have to do is put on a frock and men become animals?'

'Pretty much that. Great, isn't it? That script. I'm sorry your mother thinks she's Marilyn Monroe,' he added, looking at me curiously. 'Do you still need her in your life? Could you *actually* escape her?'

'Seems I can't,' I said. 'As she'll just turn up anyway.'

'But you're a grown-up now; you could cut yourself off from her if you wanted.'

'I could,' I said thoughtfully, 'but I keep hoping my real mother will come back.'

'She used to be a good one?'

'Yes, she did. A long time ago.'

'I'm sorry she thinks she's Marilyn Monroe,' repeated Mac.

'Well, nobody's perfect,' I said, with a wink, mimicking the last line of the film and lightening the mood to a shade I was happy with. 'What's next on The List?'

'*The Witches of Eastwick*,' said Mac. He got up and headed for the projection room to retrieve the reels.

'Ooh, I love that,' I said. I'd seen it last year. 'How exciting.'

'But I haven't got the print of it yet. It'll have to be next term.'

Next term, next term . . . I hated the way my life was divided into Term Time and Hell; life interspersed with a slow death. I only existed for the *terms*; all those other weeks were just a waste of time, space to be filled, somehow, before I could live again. Slave to the calendar, with alarming regularity it plotted against me, reducing me to a surly, aggrieved lump just waiting, waiting, waiting. I soaked up every minute of the rest of that spring term, often willing time to pause, just for a second, so I could hold it in my hand and squeeze it so tightly it couldn't escape.

And then the Easter holidays crept up, like one of the slugs on our damp living-room floor in Leamington. I didn't want to go home. I didn't want to crawl back to Dad and Marilyn to have to wait, wait, wait all over again. I begged Mac to meet me in the holidays again, anywhere he liked, but, one afternoon in his flat, he told me he was going on a trip with Helen. A trip! Where? To Paris. Romantic bloody Paris, for three whole weeks. I was incensed, I kicked out, I lashed out, I screamed at him that *we* should be going to Paris, not him and her, that I couldn't live without him in the weeks apart, that I simply couldn't bear it, and he should feel like that too, and why didn't he? Why didn't he? Why was he going on a *trip*?

He tried to joke and say *he* had wanted to go to America, to cowboy country, but he had been overruled by his Francophile wife. This didn't help me. I kicked off again. I said he should say he didn't want to go, lose his passport, invent a conference somewhere or something. I wanted to say I loved him, but I didn't dare. I told him I hated him. And then, when I was contrite, I sat in the corner of his room, near the standard lamp and in a very small, meek voice begged him to forgive me for my outburst and made him promise me we could carry on after the holidays, just as we were. That's all I wanted, just to carry on.

While Mac and Helen were traipsing around iconic Paris landscapes in matching Alain Delon trench coats, I decided to get myself a holiday job, to get me out of the house if nothing else. I got a job in Boots developing photos and I thought as it was a job based on photography, it might be kind of interesting, but it was far from interesting or glamorous. How glamorous is developing photos of screeching babies in paddling pools, dumb families standing in front of castles eating ice creams and a bloke sitting in the front of a dirty lorry doing a thumbs-up? There were no arty black-and-white shots, no art at all – just banal family life and, once, a whole series of pictures of the junctions of the M25, taken from inside a car. The only exciting moment was when a photo emerged of a naked man slapping a woman dressed in a maid's outfit with a swing ball racket, and, as she looked like she wasn't enjoying it, my boss called the police.

The summer term was like a beacon on my horizon. A hot ball of happy fire waiting for me in the distance. Day by day I flew towards it, like Icarus. Summer was my time, anyway. My happy season. I loved the sun on my face, feeling hot; wearing fewer clothes. Last summer had been magical, lying in Mac's bed, the heavily leaved branch languidly swiping against his open window in a soft breeze. And we could meet in the summer holidays again, couldn't we? Surely there would be no *trip* that could take up all those weeks? I had all sorts of plans. The first of which, when we arrived back on 23 April, was persuading Mac to come with me to the lido at Finchworth.

'Really? Do we have to?' he complained.

'Summer' had arrived early; the first Saturday of term was blisteringly hot and students were stripping off down by Tocil Lake and dangling their feet in the water, or strolling round campus in shorts and T-shirts and sandals. I wanted to go to the lido and lie by the pool. Feel the sun on my back. And I wanted Mac there with me.

'You *never* want to leave campus! You're such a stick-in-the-mud.'

'I don't like swimming pools,' said Mac.

'You don't have to go in.'

'I'll get splashed.'

'Now you sound like a baby. We don't have to go near the edge.' I saw Mac give a small shudder. 'You're such a wuss! Come on! Let's go. It's far enough away that no one will see us there and I'll be in a bikini and wearing heart-shaped sunglasses like Lolita.' I was reading it, bored of the books on my course. 'And I'll pack plenty of snacks. *Please!*'

'I don't swim,' Mac said.

'You don't need to,' I'd replied. 'We'll just lie there. It will be . . . sexy.'

I did have a certain image of this encounter in my mind: me looking all cute in my tie-side bikini, Mac rubbing carrot oil into my back, the sun dazzling our eyes and making us both look gorgeous.

'OK,' Mac finally conceded. 'I'll come, but I *will* just lie there.'

We drove there in Mac's red MG, breezing past a busy hitching point with me cowering in the passenger seat, my head low to avoid detection. He fished a tape from his glovebox and put some God-awful music on his tape player. Glen Campbell or some other old fart. Country music; I was not impressed.

'What do you mean this is shit?' Mac laughed. We had the top down and his hair was flip-flapping across his forehead; mine was unrestrainable. '"Rhinestone Cowboy" is one of the best songs ever written.'

'It's shit,' I shouted above the rushing air. 'Can't we have Radio One on?'

'My car, my music,' said Mac, 'and I shall brainwash you. If you hear this stuff enough you'll come to appreciate how genius it is.'

'Doubt it.' I pouted.

I'd brought my stripy towel and Mac had a terrible Arsenal one, which luckily most of his body covered when he lay down. As we walked into the lido, nice and early, he'd eyed the surface of the water suspiciously, so we claimed a spot at the back of the paved area to the right of the pool, where the concrete sloped upwards giving us a nice incline to lie on. It was *hot*. Gorgeous.

We lay there for ages, my canvas bag to one side, a selection of snacks laid out. We'd already had an apple each and some Kia-Ora. It was boiling hot and I could feel my skin burning under its sheen of carrot.

I sat up.

'I'm going for a quick dip. Are you sure I can't tempt you in?'

'I'm sure,' said Mac. He was on his front reading *Film as Film*, a film studies textbook. Typical Mac! Why couldn't he bring a Harold Robbins like everyone else? Actually, I had *Tess of the d'Urbervilles* in the bottom of my bag, the book I was *supposed* to be reading, but I wasn't getting it out.

The water was freezing; 'bracing' was a good word for it. I planned to slither in, all mermaid-like – I could see Mac had one eye on me, from above his book – but it was too cold for such an aesthetically pleasing entry. I decided to toe-it down the steps and then plomp in at the last moment. More Ethel Merman than pretty mermaid.

Five lengths were required just to feel even sub-human again. Mac wasn't looking at me now, but there was someone in the pool I knew. Damn, the boy in the Smiths T-shirt, the philosophy student who'd tried to snog me in the union in the first term of the first year. He was diving for a pair of goggles with some girl. Laughing. Pushing his thick hair back with a wet hand. I hoped he didn't recognize me behind my heart-shaped glasses; he was not someone I saw around all that much. I turned my back on him and swam to the side, determined not to worry about it.

'Hey, water baby?' Mac said as I plonked down next to him. I remembered his words about all the lost water babies and wondered if he realized what he'd said. 'Good?'

'Lovely,' I said.

I lay on my back, enjoying the feeling of the water droplets on my body evaporating in the sun. We had the whole, glorious day here together, in the heat, and it was fabulous not to be hidden away in Mac's room. I really should get him out of his comfort zone more often, I thought. It would probably get chilly about four, but glorious freak days like today – a slice of summer in April – had to be made the most of.

'Ah, heaven,' I exhaled. 'It's so nice here,' and because Mac was still absorbed in his book and I wasn't sure if he'd even hear me or not, I said, 'My mother works in a leisure centre. She screws the lifeguards.'

'Oh?' said Mac, his face looming into view and blocking my sun. I'd got his attention, then. OK, now I would have to talk about her.

'Yeah,' I said, closing my eyes behind my sunglasses. 'A kid nearly drowned a few days before I started in the first year because she was out the back *doing* one of them and he wasn't at his post. I mean, really? Silly cow! Talk about inappropriate! She's one of these women who's just got to have attention the whole time, who just has to be adored. And she takes it way too far, she just can't help herself!'

I opened my eyes. Mac's face wasn't there now. I sat up. He was staring out across the water, rubbing his fingers together. The sun in his face. A passing kid splashed water on to his arm and he didn't move a muscle. He looked anxious, unsettled.

'Are you OK?' I asked. He was bothered, wasn't he, by me talking about an age-inappropriate, cross-rank relationship? He was having an unprecedented attack of conscience about us, here outside of his comfort zone, at the pool. He hated what we were doing, suddenly. But that wasn't *us*! Marilyn shagging a lifeguard was nothing to do with *us*.

'I'd like to go back to campus now,' he said. 'It's not as hot as I thought it would be.' He rubbed at the arm that had been splashed; his wet hairs were standing on end, like trees in a plantation.

'We haven't been here very long,' I said. 'And it's *boiling*!'

'I know, but I'd like to go.' He was looking at a boy, in the water, doing handstands over and over. Behind him was the philosophy student from Warwick, just emerging from another dive. Is that who Mac was really looking at? Had he recognized him, too? Is that why he wanted to go? I caught Smiths Boy's eye – briefly but damningly – and he looked away.

'We haven't even eaten any of my snacks,' I said with a pout, but I too was now feeling a shadow of unease over us.

'We can eat them back in my flat.'

Smiths Boy looked over again, for longer this time. He drew his hand up to his forehead in a visor gesture, to get a better look, maybe. The sun was in his eyes. We needed to get out of here.

'OK,' I said, and I began gathering up our things. The sausage rolls we hadn't yet eaten, the Kettle Chips, the bottle of cloudy lemonade I had laid out so cheerfully. I shoved them all into my stripy canvas bag. The bottle fell open, fizzing everywhere; I mopped at it with my towel, fearing ants. I rolled up my towel and put it under my arm. Mac was already standing there with his when I got to my feet.

'Let's go home and go to bed, Midlands girl,' he said, not looking at the water, and we walked quickly out of there, the splashing and shrieks echoing behind us in the warm April sunshine.

NOW

Chapter 14

I have a surprise tonight. Julian turns up as I am leaving work, the collar turned up on his coat, his shoes brown and shiny and a sheepish grin on his face. He's had a – minor, he puts it – row with Sam and wants to ask if I'll cook him dinner, seeing as he's having the night off. I grin, too, and hug him tight to me, breathing in the charcoal wool of his heavy coat and his end-of-the-day aftershave. I'm really pleased to see him.

'What did you row about?' I ask Julian as I turn up my own collar – my black *Love Story* Ali MacGraw pea coat – James would appreciate it – and we brave the bitter January wind that spitefully slices through us as we walk home. Julian still has a room at my house, in case he ever needs to come back. His Foo Fighters and Kelly Brook posters are still on the walls; his Spurs duvet is still on the bed; there will always be room at the house for Julian.

'Me failing – in one *very* small instance – to pull my weight around the house.' Julian shrugs.

'Ah,' I say. 'What did you *not* do?'

'*Un*load the dishwasher.'

I laugh. 'She's a good girl, that Sam. It's right she brings you up on these things.'

I link my arm through his and am pleased he is old enough to not be fiercely embarrassed by this; I'm also happy to cook something for him, but it means I won't be able to go to the hospital tonight and that makes me a little anxious, especially after Mac's operation. Will he wonder where I am? Will he be disappointed? And how would anyone know?

'How's work going?' I ask Julian. I still worry about my son being in the City environment. I know first-hand those City boys can turn out to be not such great men, but I feel I've done a pretty good job in steering him towards Good Man territory. He is courteous, he aims to be respectful; he has integrity. Julian seems to have broken the template Felix and Christian laid out before him. Despite the occasional dishwasher lapse, he's a really great kid.

'Good. Great, actually. There might be a small promotion on the cards.'

'Wow. That's fantastic, Julian!' I may not understand Futures but I understand promotion, not that it's happened to me for a long time. I've been stuck in my role at work for years now. I have become a plodder, a coaster. I know I should do something about it, but it requires confidence I simply don't have in the tank. 'I'm so pleased for you.'

I withdraw my arm from the crook of his and instead scope it tightly round his back and snuggle him into me. I am desperate to kiss his soft, pale cheek but I know that's probably a step too far. I adore him. He has brought me nothing but joy. He was a dream baby, a heavenly juxtaposition to Felix, who was far from a dream father; a cute toddler – there were no terrible twos to speak of – no flinging himself to the floor of Sainsbury's, nothing like that; he was a cute, sensitive small boy, who always made me laugh with the disarmingly funny things he said. He also survived Christian. Cold, hard Christian who was all over him when we first met, who said he would protect him, do the whole swooping-in hero bit and then was cold, ignored him, saw him as a pest, a pain, an obstacle between us. He made him stand in the corner of the room, his face to the wall, for 'disrespect', for looking at him 'like that' (how else would you look at someone who was telling you over and over how stupid and useless you were?), but it was when that happened one too many times I – finally – became a lioness. Julian was standing in the corner of the kitchen, his face to the wall, when that knife glinted on the table and I thought *I* might kill *Christian*.

'How are *you*, Mum?' Julian asks. He has a concerned look on his lovely face. It's often there when he looks at me, when it should be the other way round.

'I'm good, thank you.'

'Sure?' He asked me this question every morning in the refuge. Was I OK, was I sure? Each day that passed when I said 'Yes' I meant it a tiny bit more and each day that passed when I looked at his lovely face I knew *he* was better, too. We *survived*. Together. I'm just sorry it took so long, and I'm even *more* sorry for letting Christian happen to us in the first place.

'Yes, I'm sure.' I consider telling Julian about Mac but I worry about the light in which the story will paint me, how bad I might look, when my track record with men is already so terrible. Mac is a part of my life Julian knows nothing about.

'Good. So, what shall we have?'

'To eat? Sausages, mash and beans?' I've never been much of a cook. I tried to be, when I was married; my husband and breadwinner (Lord, did he go on about that. There was *never* so much bacon brought home by anyone, *ever*) said it was only fair, after he'd 'worked so hard for us' (my work never counted) that I provide him with a 'decent dinner at the end of the day'. I studied Oliver, Stein, Kerridge, Ramsey and Blanc – all books that arrived on the doorstep via Amazon, ordered by Christian – but something always went wrong, or even if it miraculously didn't,

Christian would find something somewhere to complain about. The satisfying fact I was a terrible cook was another wooden spoon with which to beat me.

'Some things never change, Mum!' says Julian. He'd loved it when I'd reverted to sausage and mash, after Christian had gone. 'How's Becky?'

Julian adores Becky. When he was little she was round our house a lot, and always bringing Julian something. He missed her when I wasn't allowed to see her any more and he is thrilled she's back in my life, not that he's seen her yet. How can he, when I barely have? It's just so difficult. I don't know if I can expect her to get over what happened; I don't know if I can either. When you've chucked a cherished possession down the stairs and it shatters into a million pieces, how can you put it together again?

'She's good, thanks.' Despite our night out – a good start, and our first since bumping into each other again – I don't really know. Not yet. But I hope to. It's up to me now.

'That's good.'

Such a nice, polite boy. He has turned out well, all things considered (and what a lot of things there were to consider, and to consider still. *I'm so sorry, Julian*), and the ferocity of my love for him will never dwindle, whatever bastards come our way. I squeeze Julian again. And wonder again where *Mac*'s son is. I hope I hear from redoubtable, globetrotting Perrie Turque soon, with news.

We have our sausage and mash, the overdone beans that formed a crust round the edge of the microwave dish, the sausages that are on the wrong side of cremated, and then Julian gets a call from Sam which he takes in the other room and there is a lot of chuckling and giggling and he comes back in the kitchen and says they've made up and do I mind if he goes? I am a little disappointed, but pleased for him and say 'no', I don't mind. And I think, *At least I can go and see Mac now*.

I wrestle that kiss on the cheek from Julian, wave him off from the front door and decide to check my emails before I head off to the hospital.

Yes! There's an email from Perrie Turque. Below it is one from Becky and, again guilty I didn't send her one first, I read it quickly.

> Hi Ardie! Was such a cool night on Monday! Felt dreadful yesterday . . . Prospective love interest was a complete loser, though. I didn't even bother asking him in for coffee. Happy you came – we must do it again soon. Becky xx

So uncomplicated, I think, so forgiving. How wonderful she can see past the terrible role I had to play; she certainly does it better than me. I reply, finally feeling I can take a step towards her. I can do this; I can deserve my friend again. I just have to open up. Push past my guilt, which is hurting us both, be more friendly, say 'yes' to more things. We'll get there. We can repair what we had . . .

> Yes, loved it too, sorry about prospective love interest! Yes please, we must do it again! xx

I feel happy as I send it. Hopeful. Then I click, with an excited intake of breath, on to Perrie's email.

> Hi there Arden! (Cool name, by the way!!!)

From the off she's feisty, over the top. I can just see her, typing away under that fringe. I'm surprised she's not writing the whole thing in shouty capitals.

> Yes I went out with Lloyd for a while – a bit of a toyboy for me, ha ha! I met him when he was running a bar in

Thailand – Koh Samui. [Oh, not London then, as Stewart Whittaker had said – so was that before or after?] He was still Bartley-Thomas then. I found out Mac was his dad – I had him at Sheffield Uni. [I hope she *hadn't* . . .] Lloyd said they weren't speaking, and didn't want his dad to know where he was. After Lloyd and I broke up I contacted Mac – I was curious about him, you know – once such a brilliant lecturer, I don't know if you know? [Oh, she thinks I'm a neighbour or something, a concerned friend . . .] I got in touch with him when he was lecturing at UEA [definitely before the London Film School, then] and we've corresponded some since then. He invited me to a barbecue at his house a few years ago. [By letter? Mac never wrote *letters*. I don't like the thought of this Perrie writing to him, going to his barbecue where he was all quiet and not like Mac at all.] So, anyway, no I don't know where the elusive Lloyd currently is but I hear on the travel grapevine he was going to become a scuba dive instructor though I have no idea where – knowing Lloyd it could be any country in the world! Would you like me to dig around for you? I'm happy to. Would be fabulous to finally bring them together if Mac is on his deathbed or whatever.

Perrie xx

On his deathbed or whatever? I decide this Perrie is quite precocious. I'm also jealous she may have had a fling with Mac, after me, at Sheffield – despite the fringe. I have an irrational and probably destructive urge to ask James to let me into Mac's house again so I can hunt around it for her letters. But, still, she has offered to help me, and yes, I would like Perrie to dig around.

I type a sweet reply.

Yes please, if you could, that would be great and very
much appreciated. Do you happen to know why the two
of them weren't speaking?

I am surprised by an email pinging back straight away. I wonder where Perrie is. On a dramatic beach somewhere, her toes
in the surf? Halfway up a palm tree? Typing up copy in an
internet café with free mango *lassis* and an electric fan in the
corner, blowing a local diplomat's papers around?

I'm not overly surprised by her reply.

Mac's affairs.

Mac is brighter this evening. He has that glint in his eye again.
The old Mac sparkle, the sparkle that could make me melt
into a glistening puddle of double cream just by looking at
him. I wonder for the first time if it's *me* that has brought it
back. By being here. By sparking memories of his most golden
days. But perhaps I'm giving myself far too much credit.

I'm relieved to see him looking better, but I can't stop
thinking about what Perrie said. *Affairs* . . . This would
mean plural, more than *me*, definitely – possibly Perrie, possibly dozens of others – enough for Mac's son to not want to
speak to him again. Is she right? I know she is – isn't Perrie
just the sort of woman to be absolutely crystal-clear sure of
herself, like the tropical waters she's currently bathing her
big toe in? Mac has a *glint*. Mac has had affairs with dozens
of women, passing himself lazily between them like a shining baton for God knows how long.

I know she's right. I may once have been arrogant enough to
believe that after the immense, intense, cinematic nature of our
romance Mac would be sated; there would be no one else like
me; he would resume a conventional life of husbandry and
fatherhood with poor Helen, with only his sinful memories to
give him a warm glow on cold winter evenings. But not now.

Things are different now. *Then* the universe revolved around me. I couldn't see beyond my own entity. I was the archetypal legend in my own (cheese salad baguette, with loads of mayonnaise) lunchtime. *Now* the universe does as it pleases and is nothing to do with me. I can believe Mac continued to have affairs.

Mac smiles a slow-formed smile at me as I come and take my seat. It's a different one today and I don't feel quite comfortable on it. This chair is bright orange and the back is too straight; my usual one is brown and it bends with me happily when I lean on it. I look around for *my* chair. I'm sure there's a woman with a large bottom plonked on it on the other side of the ward, where Dominic was, but as she looks quite formidable and is waving a bunch of grapes around like a weapon, I decide it would be churlish of me to go over and ask for it back.

'Hello, Mac,' I say, resisting the urge to add, 'you old bastard'. There is no mention of Helen in Perrie's email. From all the evidence, and the lack of it, I get the feeling she moved out of the picture a long time ago, and who would blame her if she had divorced Mac? If she had left him after one too many betrayals? When exactly did *Lloyd* do the same? I wonder. I may feel remorse now about the affair, about Helen, but it seems Mac has not been afflicted by any such conscience. He carried on and on ... I wonder if Mac played around when Lloyd was a baby, a small child, a teenager ... if he was still enjoying dalliances right up until the car crash. If so, why is he alone? Why am I the only former lover and nostalgic idiot to visit him?

Instead I say, 'It's good to see you back on the ward. I hope you're feeling better.' I look at him and I worry that *our* affair is included in Perrie's curt two-worder – *Mac's affairs* – whether I should cancel finding Lloyd, somehow, if he knows about his father and the girl at Warwick. But it's not about me; it's about Mac. He's the one lying in hospital, without his son, unable to speak. I try and fail to be angry with him. I have been cheated on and shouldered the sear of its pain; I know how that goes. I have committed treachery myself and carried the shadow of it on my back for years. But I realize that if Mac had a thousand affairs, before *or* after me, it wouldn't affect how I feel about him. It can't. I can only see him in isolation. I *do* only remember him in relation to me; that he matters only in the context of that spinning cosmos which bathed me in light for that brief, golden time when I had youth and power and the world at my DMed feet. This man taught me how to love. This man gave me some of the best moments of my *life*. And I'm afraid, for me, it is only *our* moments that matter (sorry, Helen, and I truly *am* sorry). I can't change what happened to us. I can't turn down the brightness of everything we meant to each other. The past is a landscape that cannot be altered, however much we'd like to get our hands on it.

I take off my coat, smooth my cream pin-striped skirt over my knees. Fran soft-shuffles over. She's got a pen behind her ear, like a builder; I'm pretty sure that's breaking some kind of Health and Safety regulation.

'He ate his dinner,' she says cheerfully. 'Fish pie followed by apple crumble.'

Fran is lovely but, like sitting in the wrong chair, I feel uncomfortable with this infantilizing of Mac. I don't care that Mac has finished his apple crumble and I suddenly feel quite angry, for a totally different reason. I just want him *back*. I want him to come back to me – properly – even if it's just for ten minutes. To sit up, smile, wrap his arms around me and talk to me. I want to hear a complete sentence, the raw beauty of that northern accent involved in a proper, rhythmic, tennis-match back-and-forth conversation with my flat, Essex-tinged one. I want him to tell me what he remembers about us. All of it. I'm shamefully going old-school Arden and want to talk about *me*.

Fran walks on. I take Mac's hand. *The Chase* is on, above us; Bradley Walsh laughs at something one of the contestants says until he cries. I don't let go of Mac's hand. We are me and him, just as we once were, no one else allowed in the picture. I wish I had taken a screen shot of that photo of us in his house so I could keep it on my phone and look at it every day.

'Hi, Arden.' It's James. He's in a navy suit, a cornflower-blue polka-dot tie. I wonder what his flash of socks will be today. He looks handsome, unsure of himself. I'm pleased to see him but I realize I still haven't made a decision about the lift up to Walsall on Saturday.

'Hi, James.'

James has brought biscuits and coconut milk, film magazines *Empire* and *Sight & Sound*, and some cherries in a large brown paper bag. He unrolls the top of the bag and shows them to Mac who nods approvingly, but I don't think he'll be able to eat them.

James is kind, I think. Maybe it would be nice to have someone to witter on to, after I've seen my mother, so I can banish her from my brain. Light-hearted conversation with someone who doesn't talk all that much, so I can chitter and chatter on until she is gone. On the train, she always swills around my head for ages, like cold coffee. Perhaps I should take James up on his offer. I never used to be so fearful; Mac and The List are reminding me exactly how fear*less* I used to be. Perhaps the old-school Arden – the best part of her, at least – should make a guest appearance in the present day, a small cameo. I could at least *pretend* I am as unworried as she was, as nonchalant and confident about everything, if only for a little while. It's only a trip in a car, what's the big deal?

Mac has turned a little paler, suddenly. He gives a slow exhalation of breath then closes his eyes. Within seconds his chest is rising and falling and he is fast asleep. I lean across the bed. James is sitting the other side, in his usual position.

'I'd like to take you up on your offer, James,' I say. 'For the lift up to Walsall on Saturday. I can give you petrol money.'

'Great,' says James, looking pleased. 'And, well, we can work something out. Shall I pick you up outside the hospital that morning, say, ten?'

'OK.' Now I've said it, I don't want to do it, but it's too late. I'm committed.

'If you get hungry we can stop somewhere on the way.'

'Sure.' I wasn't planning on food stops. I'm even more sorry I've said 'yes' now – all of a sudden it's turning into a *road trip*. But he's being so kind.

'And bring any CDs you like. Even if it's something dreadful like Adele we can sing along.'

James doesn't strike me as the sing-along type so I'm already amused at the prospect of *that* happening. I remember Glen Campbell in Mac's red MG. How much I hated it, but how if I hear 'Rhinestone Cowboy' now it makes me cry.

'OK,' I say.

James reaches into the bag of cherries and pops one in his mouth. There is nowhere to put the stones, except back in the same paper bag. I decline to take one; I would get into all kinds of mess.

'Go on,' says James, 'have one. I'm sure Fran has a petri dish or something we can put the stones in.'

I take a cherry while James leaps up to bother Fran for a dish, purple socks peeping. I eat round the stone. It is delicious. James returns, laughing, with something and we sit in silence for a few moments, eating more cherries and lobbing the stones into a kidney-shaped dish, as Mac sleeps. A rubber shoe squeaks on the polished floor; Bradley Walsh asks if any of the viewers think they're clever enough to have a go; the tea trolley careers round the corner. A knife or fork clatters to the floor; there is insistent coughing, spreading down one side of the ward like a Mexican wave.

Eventually Mac opens his eyes. I am holding the open

bag of cherries, the dish of stones is on Mac's bedside table; James is childishly dangling a cherry above his mouth, unaware he is being observed. I will Mac to speak. His favourite line from the next movie on The List – *The Witches of Eastwick* – is a little too rude for the sterile confines of the hospital ward but his second favourite is so brilliantly apt at this moment. He must feel it like I do.

I *urge* Mac to say it, by some kind of brain osmosis, mine to his, but, although he is staring at the bag of cherries, he says nothing, so I do it for him. Well, *our* version of the line. I want to try out nonchalant, confident and fearless for size, put them on like my old denim jacket. I want to make Mac laugh – even if that's currently impossible – like he made *me* laugh so many, many times.

'Have another devil's spawn,' I say brightly to a bemused James, holding the bag of cherries out to him, and the corners of Mac's dry lips slowly curl into the hint of a wolfish smile.

THEN

Chapter 15: The Witches of Eastwick

Jack Nicholson in *The Witches of Eastwick* was probably the most brilliant and sexiest thing I had ever seen. I mean, I'd loved him in *The Shining* ('all work and no play makes Jack a dull boy' indeed) and I'd loved him in *One Flew Over the Cuckoo's Nest* (the fishing trip!), but as Daryl Van Horne in *The Witches of Eastwick* he was simply sublime. Mooching around with that devilishly impish grin; seducing Cher and Susan Sarandon and Michelle Pfeiffer, individually, then all at once; stretching and writhing on his bed in a silky dressing gown and a silly little ponytail, purring that he liked something very naughty indeed 'after lunch' ... Outrageous, sexy, cheeky, wicked and arrogant ... Oh, I was Jack's for the duration of that film, every second. And his eyebrows should have got an Oscar, even if he didn't.

Mac and I watched *The Witches of Eastwick* in the screening room one afternoon at the height of summer. We were six weeks into the summer term, with four weeks to go until the end of the second year.

'So, what do you think?' Mac asked as the credits rolled.

'That cherries are definitely the devil's spawn and I'm never eating them again as long as I live.'

Mac laughed. I had tried to hide under his arm during the cherry-vomiting scenes. I *may* have done a bit of screeching.

'Ah, my second favourite line in the film is the one about the cherries,' he said. 'Good old Jack.'

'What's your *favourite* line?' I asked. 'No, you don't need to tell me. It's the one about the pussy, isn't it?'

Mac clutched a hand to his chest. '*Arden!* This from a *lady*! Now, come on, tell me your thoughts on the film.'

'Well . . .' I considered; I was getting really great at this, I thought. 'On the face of it, this is a movie about female empowerment, the triumphant and potent release of their latent sexuality, et cetera, et cetera, et cetera . . .'

'Yes, yes,' said Mac, stroking his chin like a mickey-taking learned professor.

'But . . .' I took a dramatic pause, languidly stretched my tanned, smooth left leg up and over his knee and ran my hand slowly up my calf. I had his full attention.

'But?'

'It takes a man to release it.'

'Oh, interesting.' Mac's hand followed mine up my leg, but overtook it and headed towards my thigh. I was wearing cute denim dungaree shorts, a white Kate Bush T-shirt underneath.

'Yes,' I said, warming to my theme, as Mac's hand warmed my skin, under denim. 'It's under his touch that they're released, isn't it?'

'True,' said Mac. His eyebrow was up, not as high as Jack's, but still pretty impressive; he was looking at me intently. The buckles of my dungarees were almost voluntarily coming undone. 'But *they* conjured him up.'

'Well, yes,' I said. I was finding it hard to focus on my train of thought; Mac's fingers were burrowing under the edge of my knickers; my breathing was becoming heavy. 'But he completely steals the show!' I argued, not without some difficulty. 'It's all about *him*! None of them are a match for Daryl Van *Horny*! And the whole thing is pure male fantasy, isn't it?'

'Or is it a *satire* of it?' asked Mac, keeping his fingers where they were and leaning in to kiss me with those soft lips.

Now he had got me. When he had finished kissing me, which was quite a while later, I gathered my hair back from my face and said, 'It should be very interesting for your students, anyway. Lots for them to get their teeth into.'

'Yes,' said Mac. '"*Female empowerment or women kept in their traditional place?* Discuss." A good essay title, no?'

I laughed, a little weakly. I had my own essay on the New Woman in nineteenth-century literature – due in next Tuesday – burning a hole in my terrible bedroom carpet in Leamington Spa. 'A very entertaining romp of a movie, though,' I said; 'Hollywood at its best.'

'You know I have one student who's a complete chump,' said Mac, standing up and dusting imaginary crumbs off his trousers. 'All he says in seminars, in a long-drawn-out voice is "well, I really *liked* it", although he doesn't really ever say why. Over-earnest, but actually says nothing. There's always one of those. I've got another one who's always late and keeps falling asleep in lectures. He actually *snores*.'

'What would it be like if *I* was on the course?' I asked, leaning back in my seat and giving Mac a fine view of my chest, straining under those buckles. 'Really? If I was in your lectures, or sitting opposite you in one of your seminars?'

'I wouldn't be able to keep my eyes off you,' said Mac, pausing at the steps to the projection booth. 'I'd be showing off, grandstanding. I would make sure you were mesmerized by my every word. I'd be like a panther – a caged one – pacing. It probably wouldn't be good for either of us. I'd have to have you, and often, and it would be as clear as day. I'm not sure the other students would like it and it would be really distracting for all concerned.'

'Probably best I'm not on it, then,' I said, faux-haughty, 'don't want to *distract* anyone.'

'Have another devil's spawn,' Mac laughed, bastardizing his second favourite line, and of *course* I would eat cherries again. He turned to go up the steps then turned back. 'Hey, I've got to go to London in a week's time to do a talk at the British Film Institute. Can you bunk off? Come with me?'

'Oh my God, yes! I'd love to.' I leapt up, excited, like a child. 'A road trip! Will we drive?'

'Yes, we'll drive. I know somewhere cheap to park in Hammersmith, then we'll get the tube into town.'

'Oh yes!' I was so excited. 'So there and back in one day?'

'No, I thought we'd stay the night in a hotel.'

'A hotel! Oh, Mac.' I was aware I sounded unbelievably childish but I couldn't give a monkey's. I was absolutely thrilled.

'You'll come with me, then?'

'Of course I will!' Oh, this was going to be absolutely fantastic. A night away in London, with *Mac*, this was pure *female* wish fulfilment. I felt like all the silk-pyjama-clad *Witches* rolled into one when Jack Nicholson rode into town in a thunderstorm – not everything had to be given a feminist slant and jotted down in a notebook, you know. And I decided to distract Mac there and then by taking him by the hand and leading him into the projection room. We could celebrate our upcoming trip by doing it up against one of the projectors.

Mac waited for me in the car park. The boot of his MG was open, and as I walked towards it I saw his battered brown bowling bag waiting for mine. He looked like Ryan O'Neal in *Love Story*. He was wearing a preppy chambray shirt with a beige jumper over the top and jumbo-cord trousers. It was a bit chilly, despite the season, but I'd gone for a Baby in *Dirty Dancing* look, if you were to say I looked like anyone: rolled-up jeans shorts, a sleeveless little seersucker camisole top and white plimsolls. I was cold but I hoped I looked cute.

It was eight in the morning, before most people were up. I'd been lucky to hitch a lift in with a maths nerd going straight to the library to work on a dissertation; unlucky that he'd spent most of the journey talking about it. The sun was pale in the sky and yet to emit any heat.

'Ready to go?' Mac asked me.

'Ready to go.'

I threw my carpet bag in the boot and we set off. We drove past the hitching point and it was blessedly empty, just a couple of joggers with their backs to us, and Mac pressed the Play button on his cassette player.

'Not this rubbish again!' I scoffed.

'A different kind of rubbish,' he said. 'John Denver. You'll appreciate it when you're older.'

'Ugh, I won't! I can't *stand* country music! It's cheesy and sappy and just *terrible*!'

'Oh, the ignorance of youth.' Mac smiled. 'There's quiet, absolute beauty in this music, especially the stuff from the seventies . . . I'm going to go and just stand on one of those ranches one of these days, my foot up on a fence, looking across cowboy country . . .'

'You keep saying that,' I said, bored. 'Why don't you go and do that with *Helen*?'

Mac indicated and turned left out of the campus. 'She likes Paris.'

I had brought some spicy Nik Naks and some mints, a bottle of water to wash it all down with; I'd eaten everything before we'd left the A46. It was raining now, Mac's wipers were lulling me into a hypnotic trance; John Denver was leaving on a jet plane – I hoped he'd stay wherever he'd buggered off to and never come back. But I was happy – I was with Mac.

After we'd been on the M40 a while, I noticed Mac was a

slightly nervous driver. He left a massive gap between him and the car in front, he checked his mirror constantly; he nervously touched at his neck with his right hand, now and again, like he was feeling for a pulse. I examined him, curious. He was nothing like the humming, tootling-along-happily driver of my dad, or the ball-breaking, shouty driver of Steven from Home who constantly tailgated and swerved across lanes without indicating.

'Are you all right?' I asked Mac.

'Yes, fine.'

I wondered again about him hating being away from campus. Was he driving further and further from his comfort zone? His 'happy place'? 'What's your talk at the BFI about?'

'Japanese cinema and its influence on modern British cinema.' Mac tucked a nervous thumb under the seat belt across his chest, as though making sure it was there.

'Ooh, heavy.'

'No, good fun actually.'

'When did you write that? Your speech?'

'While you were sleeping. Last week sometime, no big deal.' I knew Mac could run up something like that in about five minutes.

'Are you nervous?'

'No!'

He was *now*, though, I think. Driving. I decided to not concentrate on what he was doing, but look out of the window. There was a steep bank to our left, rising upwards, with cows on it. I counted them. It started to rain more heavily. A song came on the stereo. Still John Denver. Something about sunshine, something about him giving someone a day like today, if he could – soppy and sappy as hell, but it was actually quite beautiful, after a while. I gazed at the fields and the cows and realized I was crying, just a little. It must have been all those violins, hamming it up in the background.

After the song finished the rhythmic swish-swish of the wipers sent me to sleep.

When we arrived on the outskirts of London the sun was out and everything looked bright and brilliant. Mac found the little NCP car park he'd mentioned and squeezed the MG into the tiniest, lowest-ceilinged space I'd ever seen; I had to climb over to the driver's side to expel myself, like toothpaste from a tube.

We walked to Hammersmith tube station and got on a packed train to central London. Mac was due at the BFI at half two and I was going to sit in Bar Italia, ten minutes away on Frith Street, and drink fancy coffee and look out for famous people while I waited for him. I begged to be allowed to sit in on his talk but Mac said no, he'd be too sidetracked.

'But it would make you *grandstand*,' I said. 'Be your best you.'

'I need to concentrate,' was all he said.

We changed on to the Central Line and hung off the straps like lemurs. It was hot down there; I liked it. Humid, warm air buffeted in from the next carriage via grimy, lowered ventilation windows. It looked out of control, the next carriage – from across the rocking junction. A hurtling fairground ride unimpressing stony-faced riders; a mirror image of the people in our own carriage – brightly lit, mostly silent, staring ahead. Mac and I, in high contrast, grinned at each other. We were in a happy London bubble, although now and again Mac rubbed his fingers together and looked anxious. I was thrilled, giddy; a little sweaty. I couldn't wait for the afternoon to begin.

We got off at Tottenham Court Road. Mac would go to the BFI in Stephen Street; I would walk to Soho, clutching my brand-new *A to Z*, but first I accompanied Mac to Stephen Street and kissed him outside the Film Institute building, challenging someone to see us. He was uncomfortable and told me to stop it.

'Treat it like campus round here,' he said. 'Anyone coming in might know I'm married.'

I felt surprised. I had mentioned Helen in the car but only as a passing annoyance. She didn't feature in our lives. Apart from the photo in his wallet, which she'd probably tucked there herself – there was no evidence of Helen in Mac's life on campus – so why was he bringing her up here, on a colourful, bustling Soho street, where I had never been so full of life and excitement? And full of *us*. When he is mine and only mine? *Married?* I hated the word. It was everything I despised.

Mac looked around. Behind us, three people trickled into the building. 'You need to go now,' he said and I was indignant and a bit pissed off but off I trotted into the crowds to find Bar Italia and to wait.

Three coffees and two Italian layer cakes later, I was sitting with a curved china cup and an empty plate at a Formica bench, chatting to a girl in her late twenties who said she was trying to make it as an actress. She had just been for a casting; she was beautiful and looked like Patsy Kensit. Behind us, a nonchalant Gaggia coffee machine hissed and steamed; above us an aloof retro ceiling fan whirred.

Mac sauntered in. He was smiling.

'You found it, then,' he said, coming to stand next to me. He had a spot of colour on each cheek.

'Yeah. Did it go well?' I was looking at Mac but Mac was looking at Patsy. She really was very beautiful.

'Very well. I think they liked me.'

'Never mind that, did they like your talk?'

'Yes, I think so.'

'I'm just going,' said the girl. 'Lovely talking to you,' she said to me. She slid from her stool and slipped out of the café, Mac watching her leave.

'Eyes front!' I said, nudging him. 'So, what sort of people were there?'

'All sorts of people. Young, old, in the middle. What have you been doing?'

'Drinking coffee, chatting to actresses. Looking at old boxers.' There was a large photo of Rocky Marciano behind the bar. 'Yeah, I could get used to London life.'

'Shall we go out to dinner tonight?'

'*Out?* I thought just coming down to London *at all* would take it *out* of you!' I cried, but I could see that he was high on his speech, positively buzzing, and I was buzzing too. 'But yes, I would absolutely love to.'

He stepped towards me and weaved his hands under the hem of my cropped top, then slid them round to my back, where he let them overlap; I could feel his fingers lacing together, pulling me in close.

'I'll show you the best night of your life, kid,' he said.

NOW

Chapter 16

On Saturday morning, James is waiting outside the hospital in driving rain, hanging off a black umbrella so massive it could easily shelter a family of five.

'Nice day for it,' he says as I approach. It has rained since Thursday. The last two evenings I've turned up at St Katherine's like a saturated poodle. And there's never a nice day for visiting Marilyn, I think. 'My car's in the car park. I'm living dangerously and didn't get a ticket.'

'You rebel,' I say. I pull my charity-shop Burberry trench coat round me and wish I'd worn something more sensible, with a hood. My own umbrella is not *quite* inside out, but almost, and its spikes have already proven Bond-movie deadly.

'*Breakfast at Tiffany's* or *Kramer vs. Kramer*?' asks James, looking at my raincoat, and I laugh.

'*Breakfast at Tiffany's*, definitely.' I prefer the aesthetics of Holly Golightly to Meryl Streep's tug-of-love divorcee. I aspire to extrovert socialite and can't relate to deserting wife and mother. I'm not sure Audrey Hepburn's trench coat had a little tear at the back, though, mended with iron-on tape.

James's car is dark grey and quite small; I have no idea what make. It's very clean inside; unlike my tip. After my marriage ended I almost revelled in scuzzing up my little Golf again. Eating chocolate bars and dropping the wrappers. Getting it muddy. My mess, my life. I'm not sure I would let someone like James in it, though.

I feel nervous, putting my seat belt on, and wonder again why I'm doing this; I could be on the train by now, with a revolting pack of sandwiches and a fizzy drink, and all that time to myself to avoid thinking about Marilyn.

'OK?' asks James, when we are ready to go. He's got one of those pine tree air fresheners dangling from his rear-view mirror. It rocks back and forth as he reverses out of the parking space.

'Yes, thank you,' I say, though my stomach is in knots. I feel trapped, I want to get out. I'm reminded of all those terrible car journeys when I looked at my husband in profile and thought, *I can't do this*. The only thing to do now is start prattling on about nothing and James gives me the cue.

'Off we go, then,' he says, indicating left. 'Duty visit!' It's never been a duty with Mac, I think. Visiting him. Though often a worry. He's remained pale and sleepy the past two nights; James and I have reluctantly exchanged concerned looks over the bed.

I take my cue. 'My mother's been in this home for four years,' I say. 'It's called The Cedars.' OK, this is interesting, I think. I'm talking about her when I didn't even want to *think* about her. I must be *desperate* to unravel the knots in my gut. All right, I'll go with it. 'I presume that's because it has cedars in the grounds. I don't know. I wouldn't know a cedar if it came up and bit me on the bum.' James laughs. He has a nice profile. It's friendly. 'She's seventy-three. She has kidney problems and rheumatoid arthritis that's always flaring up. Often she has trouble walking so is bedbound a lot of the time. I go to The Cedars as infrequently as I can get away with. I hate going there, in fact. It's a depressing place and she's a depressing mother – I'm afraid I've got nothing good to say about her.' Just a lot of *bad*. I'm sorry. I may as well carry on. 'She was just one of those mothers. Mothers who should never have had kids, who just weren't cut out for it. Sorry, I'm waffling; I don't know where all that came from.' I do know; it came from a desire to distract myself from the fact I'm stuck on a two-and-a-half-hour car journey with an almost complete stranger. And we haven't even got on to the South Circular yet. I'd better shut up or it will *all* come out.

'I'm sorry to hear that,' says James, his eyes on the road. 'Relationships with parents are tough. I had one of those *dads*.'

'What, not cut out for kids?' I ask.

'Yep.' He indicated, tick-tock, tick-tock, to overtake a white van. It's going to take us ages to even get out of London, I think. The traffic is diabolical. I should be letting the train take the strain. I shouldn't be in this car. 'And one of those that beat you up.'

'Oh God, really? I'm so sorry.' James's face hasn't changed; his eyes are still on the road. He still looks *friendly*. I don't know what to say. Violence wasn't an item in the catalogue of my parents' many parenting failures. I got the odd slap on the back of the leg with a giant hair roller, of course; who didn't? I got screeched at plenty of times, often by a half-dressed harridan whose spittle landed on my cheek. And sometimes Dad slurred benign nonsense at me before falling over on the kitchen floor, which wasn't that great. But nobody laid a finger on me. I can't imagine having a dad who *beat you up*.

'Well, yeah, it's OK,' says James. Eyes on the road, face forward. 'I've had a shitload of therapy. My mother did the evening shift in Budgens to pay for the sessions. Moira, that was her name. American. She wore a different-coloured scarf every time and sensible shoes. I talked and talked it all out and still thank my wonderful Mum for the chance to, as it helped me a lot. These days I don't think about it too much; you don't exactly want something like that becoming the thing that defines your whole life, do you?'

'No,' I say. I have experience of this. Trying not to let past experiences define your life. A nightmare parent. How the shape of my mother has threatened to become the shape of me. But I'm not Marilyn. I've spent the best part of my life trying not to be her and I hope I've been pretty successful at it. I'm not a narcissist. I like to think my relationship with Julian is a fantastic one, and far from toxic. We're OK, despite my recurring guilt about his childhood; I'm a good mum, despite once having allowed the horrors of Christian. Patterns don't have to be repeated, I think. You can just use a different fabric. 'So, is that what you do, not think about it too much?'

'He whacked me with the belt of a circular saw.'

'Are you joking?' James still hasn't looked at me. He's mirroring, signalling, manoeuvring like he hasn't just told me his father used to beat him with the belt of a saw.

'Nope, I'm not joking.'

'Bloody hell!'

'Yeah. He didn't like geeks, apparently.' And James actually laughs.

'*Were* you a geek?'

'I've always been a geek,' says James. 'Stamp collector, maths boffin, chemistry-set maestro. My dad even thought the *Guinness Book of Records* was for geeks and to be despised. Now I'm geeky about the energy performance of houses, amongst other things.'

'Oh, mine's *good*,' I interject. 'Great insulation and a solar panel.' I don't need to lighten the mood, though, as James is already light, and talking in breezy tones like this is all just a frothy coffee. 'When my little brother came along my mum couldn't bear it any longer. I was ten. He hadn't been planned, I don't think – the last thing she wanted was another victim. She knew *she* would be beaten, *I* would be beaten and Ollie would probably be beaten too. Another one on the conveyor belt of abuse. Or circular-saw belt, I should say.' He laughs, I don't join in. 'We left in the middle of the night. She was in her dressing gown, we were barefoot and in our pyjamas. All she kept saying after was that she'd left him the best pillow-cases and she wished she hadn't.'

'Where did you go?' I ask.

'Kent,' he says. 'To my Auntie June's. Mum drove Dad's automatic for the very first time all the way from Maccles-field. She tucked her left leg under her right so she wouldn't forget she mustn't use it.'

'Wow,' I say. I think of the women's refuge, the Erin Martin Women in Need, to be specific. Julian and I had a blue room with a single bed, a pull-out metal camp bed and a kettle. We were there for two weeks – just me and him, both each other's world when the rest of it was too fragile and frightening to consider – until the court order came through and we could move back to my house. The refuge wasn't far from home, geographically – not like Macclesfield to Kent – but a million light years away from the prison Christian had made it.

'Yes,' says James. 'We started again, left our old life behind. My brother lives in Florida now, moved there ten years ago. I stayed in Kent until I moved to London in 2001. I've always kept my northern accent, though.' He grins, shyly, and I wonder if he was determined to keep that accent, as one thing from his old life, his boyhood.

This is the most he has ever said to me. The car has become a confession box, as they often do. My own was a great place for some of my most awkward conversations with Julian – frank discussions about some of the more hairy aspects of puberty, the importance of contraception at music festivals, the absence or not of heaven and Father Christmas . . . A person can say what they want without having to look someone in the eye, talk freely against the buffering mobile scenery of traffic and trees; use low-level school-run radio as a shock absorber for revealed secrets and fears.

'I'm very sorry,' I say. 'Is your father still alive?'

'No,' James says. 'In an ironic twist of fate and karma a tree fell on him, during the storm of eighty-seven – remember that one – Michael Fish saying it was a storm in a teacup?'

I do remember it. Marilyn had been furious that a fence had blown down and a pair of her knickers had flown into next door's garden. 'Oh God.'

'A happy day,' says James. '*Oh, happy day!*' he sings, and gives a little smile as he taps two skittering fingers on the steering wheel. It reminds me that my car was also where I told Julian we were finally leaving Christian and his excited 'Really?' both broke my heart and put it back together. Perhaps James will sing along to Adele, after all, I muse, although I've brought Johnny Cash. 'Is *your* dad still alive?' he asks. 'I haven't asked.'

'No,' I say. 'He died several years ago.'

'I'm sorry.'

'It's OK.' It wasn't, though, not at all. Every day I missed Dad or remembered some little thing about him. How he licked along the edge of the crackly thin paper to seal his roll-ups. How he chuckled often, at something he heard on the radio. How he must have felt so utterly, utterly hopeless and beyond miserable, that day, to want to end his own life.

'Did you also have a difficult relationship with him?'

'No. Well, he wasn't perfect – far from it – but I loved my dad.' I had loved him, despite all that he was and all he could never be.

'That's good. It would be awful to have *two* parents you couldn't stand – it would require an awful lot of counselling.' Wry smile. Indicate left. 'I was fourteen when my dad was killed. It meant he could no longer try and come after us. It meant we were free. But sometimes I'm not sure I really am. Free, I mean. Not quite.'

'Why?' I ask. I know *I'm* not free, I'm heading for my ball and chain (or is it apron strings? No, Marilyn wouldn't be seen dead in an apron these days) right now. Counselling has never appealed to me. Why would I want to sit and talk to a stranger about Marilyn for an hour at a time? Or about Christian? And if I had to talk about my dad for that long I would just cry and cry, and I can do that at home.

'Do you want to talk more about your mum?'

'No,' I say. 'I'm good.'

James nods. 'OK. I'll just carry on talking about myself.' He smiles at the corner of his mouth, checks the rear-view mirror. 'Confession time – there's something about being in a car, don't you think? I became an estate agent for a reason,' he says. 'I'm not good in groups, not good in social environments, lots of people, meeting people. I hated that bar the other night.'

'Sorry,' I say. I wonder why he came, and I wonder if it was because of me, then tell myself off for being stupid.

'I know a lot of us can be wankers but I chose that career carefully. It's a job that suits me. I like to be a one-man band. Come and go. In and out. I can't be in a job where I have to be a team leader, go to the pub all the time, attend meetings. I get nervous in social situations.' I understand it now, why, like me, he is happy to sit in the hospital night after night with Mac. There's comfort and safety in the routine of it. 'My little brother is the complete opposite. Funny, eh?'

'He wasn't beaten up,' I offer.

'No,' he adds, and we laugh and I'm not sure why. 'When I was a young kid I was always dragged to this terrible working men's club,' James continues. 'You know the places – cheap beer, awful karaoke nights and enforced discos.' He's talking fast; he's really on a roll. But I let him roll – if it's good for him, I will watch him roll all the way down the hill, wrapped tight around himself, then when he reaches the bottom he can laugh and unfurl and stretch out, maybe. 'My old man was a nightmare – all the time. He'd kick off, make a show of me and Mum. There would always

209

be some sort of scene. We were judged all the time. Stared at. Usually we limped out of there like we'd just been in a shoot-out at the OK Corral.'

'Why didn't they just ban him?' I ask. 'He sounds horrible.' Marilyn was banned once, from the local village hall. She'd got up on stage, drunk, during a quiz night and had tried to pull the compere's trousers down.

'I'm not sure. I think he spent a lot of money in there, or they liked the drama?'

'Who knows?' I say.

'Anyway,' and James turns to look at me at last, just briefly, 'it's one of the reasons I'm socially awkward. And that's pretty much my story. You already know the whole "my girlfriend left me" strand. We're done here, I'd say, unless you want to add anything?'

That sideways smile again. I'm sure he's probably *not* done, but I don't say so. There's always more.

'Will you be OK at the expo?' I ask, thinking about what he's just told me.

'I don't know. I'll have to see when I get there.'

James has told me a lot about his life in a very short space of time, and I do feel pressure to reciprocate. Should I tell him more about Marilyn? The rest of the journey wouldn't be long enough. Or how my dad took his life, one sunny June afternoon, in the shed at the bottom of the garden, taking part of mine with him? I really don't want to start something I can't finish. There's no neat endings to either of these stories; they just go on and on.

'And no,' I say again. 'To adding anything. Thank you.' James glances over at me and I look away. I could always talk about Christian, but I can't bear to. Perhaps, instead, I should start talking about Mac. The search for his son. My silly need to find him so I can generate a moment for Mac, worthy of the movies . . . That's what I'm doing, isn't it? I think, as I stare out of the window at an incongruous Vanmaster caravan shunting past in the dense traffic. I'm trying to engineer a wonderful movie moment for Mac. I will manipulate scenery, flood light on to a dark corner, stage-manage the best of scenes . . . The scene where his long-lost son shows up . . . I peer into a brown-curtained motorhome window, my stories untold. James is now silent. He is a careful driver, courteous. He always indicates before he switches lanes, always checks his mirror. I lean back into my seat. After a while the swish-swish of the wipers, fighting an endless battle against the rain, make it hard to resist closing my eyes.

'Shall we stop?'

'Hmm?' I open my eyes. We're on the motorway and rapidly approaching a large services sign. I must have been asleep for ages. I don't want to stop; it's warm in the car and cold outside. I just want to get there and get home again. 'OK, yes, I don't mind.'

We find a space in a rammed car park. The rain has sulkily decided to become drizzle and a fine spray of it coats me as I squeeze out of the car, trying not to scrape the door against the car next to us.

'It's rammed,' says James, pulling his umbrella from the footwell of the back seat. 'Where is everyone *going*?'

Inside it's worse. Women are snaking in a long, stoically disgruntled queue for the Ladies'; truckers and lone drivers and families queue for Wok U Like and KFC and Burger King and Subway, their damp hair and downcast, grumpy faces above dark, padded coats and grim-grey scarves. This is not the pleasure dome. No male *or* female fantasy here, nobody's fantasy at all. This is hell on earth.

'What's your poison?' James asks. 'Early lunch, brunch, whatever.'

'Oh God, I don't care.' I would rather eat soggy shepherd's pie and questionable jam roly-poly at The Cedars, to be honest, than anything here. 'KFC?'

We eat popcorn chicken and fries. I'm not very hungry.

Perched at a too-high round table with a sticky unwiped surface, I look at James and consider whether he looks a changed man to me, after all he has told me. A beaten boy. An escapee. A survivor. A man sometimes frightened of going out. I can see it all in his eyes if I look hard enough – everything flickering behind the screen of them. At the same time, he looks just the same as he did before.

'How is it?' he asks.

'How's what?' I reply and I look down, feeling caught out at staring at him. Does he regret telling me what he has? It is hard to know.

'Your food.'

'Oh, great thanks. You?'

'Great.'

There is a kerfuffle, a sea change, over by the queue for Burger King. A rustle of excitement, a whoop. Someone is down on one knee in front of a startled-looking girl in a beige faux-fur coat. She looks like a teddy bear. The person on one knee looks like an orange chrysalis folded uncomfortably in half, a flapping corner of his padded jacket sweeping the grubby floor.

'Who on earth would propose in a queue at a service station Burger King?' says James. He looks tickled, quite delighted.

'He's insane!' I say. 'But at least it's something different. And look how *happy* they are!'

I probably looked that happy when Christian proposed. It was a more conventional setting – an Italian restaurant. A ring in a tiramisu. A polite round of applause from fellow diners. *This* crowd is going wild. Orange Chrysalis has scooped up Teddy Bear and is running round the perimeter of the food court with her, to people clapping and cheering. It's probably the happiest moment this place has ever seen. Customers' faces light up over their junk food; they grin at each other as a pair of brown knee-high boots go rushing past them, the toes pointed upwards in ecstasy.

'Good for you, Paula!' a rotund man bursting from a red duffel coat in front of Marks & Spencer drolly calls out. Most of the audience turn and look thoroughly bemused at this misquote, but I smile in recognition, and so does James.

THEN

Chapter 17: An Officer and a Gentleman

Mac and I stopped off at a tiny minimart on Frith Street and picked up the cheapest bottle of wine we could find. We smuggled it into the Wiltshire Hotel, Soho Square, under his coat and into our room on the first floor. We had twin beds – an error – so we pushed them together and I jumped, laughing, on the newly formed double bed, too close to its seam, and they wheeled apart again. As I slipped down the ravine in the middle with my hand waving not drowning in the air I had never felt so happy.

Mac pushed the beds back together. We poured the wine into the smeared water glasses we found upside down on the vanity unit in the bathroom.

'To us,' said Mac.

'To us!'

I pulled back the covers of one of the beds and got in, fully clothed. Mac squeezed in next to me so we were a couple of hot sardines, packed close. We were high on life and each other. We breathed each other in. We drank wine, made love, drank some more wine, made some more love. We were all that existed.

'What time shall we go out?' I asked later, naked and stretched out on the other side of the seam, where the sheets were still smooth and unromped on.

'Ten-ish?' said Mac. 'Everything's open until late.' I felt all decadent. I'd been to London before, of course. I'd been dragged to see *Starlight Express* with Marilyn (although she missed most of the second half because she was chatting up a Rob Lowe lookalike in the bar); I'd been up on the train to go shopping in Topshop at Oxford Circus – there was a photo at home somewhere of me wearing round turquoise plastic earrings and standing outside the shop with a random group of girls; I'd been to the Tower of London when I was ten, followed by Madame Tussauds, where I was frightened to death by Christie and Crippen. But this was real London – this was night-life, hot-in-the-city London.

Mac switched on the telly.

'Oh look,' he said, '*An Officer and a Gentleman*. It's not next on my list but it is *on* my list. You seen it?'

'No,' I said, 'well, bits of it.' Someone had put it on at someone's house one drunken night, after getting back from an Essex house party. My memory of it was sketchy. Becky had told me it was one of her all-time favourites – she said Richard Gere was hot in it and she totally had a thing for men in white uniform.

'Do you want to watch it? It's only just started.'

'All right. Have you brought your notepad?'

'Of course,' said Mac, leaning over to the side of the bed and pulling it from his leather bag, along with his trusted Parker pen.

'Always prepared,' I laughed.

'*Always* prepared.'

We pulled off the sheets and rearranged them so it was like we were in a proper double bed and we propped ourselves up against as many pillows as we could find – some stashed high in the wardrobe, hoping not to be used – and watched the film. I'd always had mixed feelings about Richard Gere. I'd seen him in *American Gigolo* and *Yanks*, and I'd thought he was just OK, although obviously very

215

good-looking, but all that changed now: I *loved* him as Mayo in *An Officer and a Gentleman.* All that DOR business, the shouting, the drills, the crying as he did press-ups; and my, Debra Winger was so sexy. I was crying a bit at the end. I couldn't help it.

'Well *done*, Paula,' Mac said, as the credits rolled.

I sniffed away my tears with a bit of toilet roll and said, 'Right, Mac, down to business. Portrayal of women in the movie . . . What do you have in your notes?'

Mac turned to lie on his front and read from his pad. 'Men and women both flawed, can behave better. Two gits, one male, one female. Two nice people – one male, one female. Working-class women as the enemy.'

I climbed on to Mac's back, like a porpoise. I lay flat and still and rested my chin on his right shoulder blade. 'The character of Seeger,' I said. 'A female character wanting to be a man and accepted as one at the end.'

'Entrapment via pregnancy,' read Mac. 'Economically motivated. Paula is saved by Mayo without having to do any of that; she gets economic elevation just for being nice.'

'Seems all very straightforward,' I say. 'And lots of good discussion points here, Mac.'

'Yep. It's a goody. What do you think, about Paula's rescue by Mayo at the end?'

'It's a great movie moment.' I sighed, tickling Mac's upper arm with the tip of my index finger. 'It makes me a little angry, though. That she needs a man to save her, and all that, but at the same time I was suckered right in.'

'Is it a fantasy of *yours*, to be rescued?' He turned his head to the side and grinned at me.

'I already have been,' I said. 'But not by you.' I poked him, in the armpit.

'Ouch!'

'I rescued *myself* when I got into university. You were the cherry on the cake.'

'I thought cherries were the devil's spawn.'

'Ha. I'm back on them. I like cherries.'

'And I like being *your* cherry.'

'Good. And I like your *choices*,' I said. 'Of movies. Well, so far. You've got a bit of everything.'

'Thank you, student.'

'How many more do we have?'

'Oh, you're bored!'

'I'm not! I don't want them to come to an end, if anything.'

'Two more,' said Mac.

'And then what?'

'What do you mean?'

'*Then what?*' I flattened myself to him, flanked my arms down his sides. 'What happens after we've seen them all?'

'I start the course, in October. We carry on. I don't know, Ardie. There are *always* more movies to watch.' He shifted his arm free of me and checked the time. 'Come on, let's go out. Soho awaits, my darling.'

I'd packed a dress for the evening, a red dress with a halter neck and a full skirt: fifties style. I'd never worn it and God knows why I'd brought it up to Warwick in the first place – I could hardly rock up in it to the Cholo Bar on a Wednesday night, and it was even a bit too flash for the occasional student balls that were held at nearby Chesford Grange.

Mac gave a wolf whistle when I emerged from the bathroom in it.

'Wow,' he said and I lit up like a Regent Street Christmas tree. I had never felt so attractive, so desired. I was a Hollywood starlet standing on a grand staircase ready for my close-up; I was the glamorous star of my own show. I was *Paula*, and I wanted this feeling to last for ever.

We went for dinner in a tiny Lebanese restaurant. There were only about six tables; the whole place was the size of

217

our bathroom at the Wiltshire. We had meze and wine and goat curry and baklava and it was amazing. Our waiter was hilariously gossipy and over-attentive; at one point he sat down at the table with us and started telling us about the time Al Pacino came into the restaurant. At least, he thought it was him – somebody else thought it was Bobby Ball. Mac laughed his head off. He loosened up, unbuttoned his shirt. I could tell he was having a really good time. We were the last to leave but Mac still wasn't done with the night.

'Come on! Let's go dancing!' he said and he took me by the hand and pulled me through the streets of Soho where we dodged slow-moving sports cars with dazzling head-lights, and people crowding the pavements and spilling out on to the streets holding pint glasses. There were clouds of cigarette smoke, jostling, shouting, people calling to each other. A girl, swivelling on her heel and tumbling into the street, caught by a couple of men in dungarees and Caterpillar boots. I got whistled at and I loved it. I felt like Rita Hayworth.

'Where are we going?' I shouted.

'You'll see!'

Mac dragged me, laughing, into a small dark doorway, music throbbing beyond it. The black door, featuring a painted-on spider's web and a skew-whiff brass number '6', opened to expel both a girl in a black tutu and white T-shirt and a muffled bass-y beat that was in danger of causing a seismic tremor beneath my sandalled feet.

'What is this place?' I asked. There was no sign about the door.

'The Electrifonic,' Mac said. 'Early eighties electronic music. It's pretty cool.'

'Far from the cowboy plains of Glen Campbell,' I teased, amused. 'I wouldn't have thought this was your bag.'

'Lots of things are my bag,' said Mac. 'I'm a man of eternal surprises.'

He yanked open the door and we stepped into a black womb of an entrance, three steps to a further matt-black door, the throbbing base straining behind it. To our right a girl in a booth – blonde quiff, red lipstick, look of utter disdain – took our money.

'Friendly,' I remarked, as we walked from her, and Mac laughed. 'How do you even know about this place?'

'I read about it in the *NME*,' Mac said, pushing open the matt-black door.

I was whacked in the face by a rush of heat and a pulsing beat that went straight through my body: *boom boom boom*. The place was heaving, compressed; an organic mass, shifting and swaying. Made-up boys and girls out-pouted one another in brief kaleidoscopic sweeps of disco lights; sprayed-on silver jeans rubbed against chain mail and competed with New Romantic ruffles and snappy suits with skinny leather ties; post-punk hair topped curious, glittery-hard stares.

Mac was smiling, laughing, already moving his hips. He looked incongruous in here . . . preppy, American almost, in his chinos and unfashionable white shirt. But he was so uncool he *was* cool and being ridiculously, stupidly handsome helped, of course. He was getting glances from both men and women – eyebrows raised, the curl of new smiles – and I fitted in pretty well in my fifties dress and my wild hair because, it seemed, anything went in that place.

We weaved to the bar, queued for Alabama Slammers – Southern Comfort, sloe gin, Amaretto and orange juice. We grinned at each other, drank in each other with our eyes. I reached behind Mac and slid my hand into his back pocket; he pulled me into him and kissed me on the nose while a man dressed as a pirate dandy winked at us both over a pina colada.

Holding our huge drinks, we squeezed our way to the dance floor and joined the throng. It was only the second time I'd ever danced with Mac; tonight it was making me laugh.

'What?'

'Nothing!'

'What're you laughing at?' I adored the flat vowels of Mac's northern 'laffing' – I adored Mac; at this moment, I knew I would never love anyone as much again.

'You're cute when you dance.'

'Is that a good thing?'

'Yes!'

The music changed to Tubeway Army's 'Are "Friends" Electric', and whether he was responding to me laughing at his cute dancing or just because he wanted to, Mac wrapped his arms round me and we slow-danced, in a slow-turning circle, like we were at a wedding. I was in temporary, disco light-flecked heaven – Mac's floppy fringe already damp and lilting against my humid curls; me pressed close to his shirt, his warmth, his heat. The music was deafening, thudding, enveloping us and holding us in its sweaty, electric palm as colourful strangers pulsed and grazed around us.

'I love you,' said Mac.

'What?' I shouted above the music, although I had heard each of those three words and the combination of them was unexpected, delicious, mind-blowing and everything I had ever wanted. 'I can't hear you!' I was grinning from ear to ecstatic ear as I shouted that.

'I said I love you. I love you! I love you.' Mac pulled me to him, breathless. 'I've never felt this way about anyone. Ever. I *love* you.'

I laid my cheek on his. I breathed him in.

'I love you too,' I said. And I knew that whatever happened, and whatever might come to rip us apart, Mac and I were *supposed* to be in love. It was written . . . somewhere. It was recorded. It felt right and it *was* right, for this moment and always.

NOW

Chapter 18

The Cedars looks as depressing as I remember it, except last time I came it had been August so the trees at least had leaves on them and the lawn at the front was a chirpy bright green. Now, the trees are bare and scary-looking and the lawn is brown and churned up in parts as though a massive mole has burrowed through it. They are building something to the right of the squat beige new build – an additional wing or something – there is scaffolding and orange tape and piles of dusty, rust-coloured bricks. It's ugly. A little girl clinging on to a father stares at the scaffolding as she walks past. A tiny lady on a walking frame, accompanied by a huge carer, comes out of the front doors of The Cedars bundled up in a coat too heavy for her.

I don't want to go in. James has parked the car over on the far side of the car park, under the willow tree – my back is to the front of The Cedars but I am eyeing it suspiciously in the little square mirror on the inside of the sun visor.

'So, we're here,' he says.

'Yes.'

'We've been here about five minutes.'

'I know.'

'Are you going to go in?'

'I don't know.' I flick down the sun visor and turn to face him. 'I suppose I have to.'

I feel unreasonably annoyed with him, despite the soul-baring confession of the journey, the funny anecdote-providing trip to the services. If I'd come by myself I'd have a choice whether to go in or not. I could just walk away if I wanted to. Of course, I'd still get the phone calls, the wheedling letters, but I'd have a choice. I've done it before – walked away. I'd stood outside the lobby, looking in and then had turned and walked back to the train station. But as James has kindly brought me here – all this way – I know I have to go through with it.

I stay in my seat.

'So, I've got that expo . . . *fairly* soon,' says James, after a few seconds.

'Yes, yeah, OK, I'm going,' I say. 'Thank you so much for the lift.' I put my hand on the door handle, ready to open the door.

'Pick you up at five?'

'Yes, thank you.' Gosh, that's an awfully long time, I think. I wonder how long I can feasibly sit on that bench over there, waiting for him. It's one o'clock and there's no way I'm spending four hours with my mother.

I open the door and get out. The air is cold, after the cocoon of James's warm car, unpleasant. I walk to the entrance, with a heavy heart and the dragging feet of a moody teenager. I can hear James's car nosing out of the car park.

As soon as I am inside The Cedars the smell hits me: peach air freshener layered over burnt egg. Tea bags. Bleach. There's a mug of tea on the reception desk, half drunk, as I sign in, no receptionist to be seen. I buzz myself through, pressing the sticky buzzer under the desk and then quickly availing myself of the watermelon-fragranced antibacterial handwash in the grubby wall-mounted dispenser, before I push open the door.

The corridor down to Marilyn's room has been painted a hopeful but rotting pale apricot and dotted with funereal nosegays of artificial flowers shoved into vases in waist-height alcoves. The whole place is shrouded and dipped in stinky, sticky artificial peach; the upholstery a universal dirty cappuccino.

Marilyn's room, by contrast, is pink; a sickly blancmange. She's lying in the middle of it in a pink bed and wearing a primrose nightdress, done up to the neck. Her hair is frizzy – a Marilyn-Monroe-gone-wild halo; red lipstick dries and bleeds into the lines around her mouth. Her face is white. Now I know *What Ever Happened to Baby Jane*. I always feel like I've stepped on to the set of that movie when I come here. There's a woman in the room next door now who actually looks a bit like Joan Crawford . . . she has a brown wig like a motorcycle helmet and an imperious smile – it's terrible but I enjoy imagining her and Marilyn threatening to push each other down the three steps to the depressing little café here, when no one is looking.

As I step towards the bed and the suspiciously stained 'easy' chair beside it (nothing 'easy' about this place) I want to turn and run.

'Arden.' The voice is tremulous, husky and put on.

'Hello, Marilyn.'

'Please sit down.'

I'm already sitting. I don't want to touch the armrests of the chair. I don't want to take off my coat, which is now definitely more *Kramer vs. Kramer* (Mother vs. Daughter?) than *Breakfast at Tiffany's*. 'How have you been?' I ask. I'm looking around me so I don't have to look at her. There are photos on the Queen Anne dressing table. None of me or Dad; they are all of Marilyn in her heyday. Marilyn on a donkey at Southend-on-Sea, in a gingham shirt tied at the waist; Marilyn raising a glass of something to a lip-glossed mouth on holiday at an outside restaurant table on the Costa del Sol; Marilyn reclining on the sofa with a book, legs entwined like snakes, and I know she straight-copied this pose from

223

the real Marilyn – I've seen the original. I'm reminded of Rose, the old lady in *Titanic*, and all the photos in her bedroom at the end of the movie. But Rose's life was fulfilled, crammed with love and adventure; Marilyn's has just been fluff and treachery.

'I've not been so good,' says Marilyn. 'It's really terrible in here now. It smells. And some of the other residents are just witches. That one next door, well, you've never heard anything like it. She just moans, moans, moans, all day long. To be frank with you . . .' Marilyn struggles to sit up, trying to lean forward. A spindly arm startles me by cantilevering out, clutching on to mine. I have no choice but to steady it – its skin feels like a dry doily from a vintage tea tray – and Marilyn's breath is hot and sweet, like gone-off cloves. 'I think she's trying to kill me.'

I can't help but laugh, into the cloves. I imagine Joan in the bed next door, in a cloud of polyester and lavender talcum powder, having exactly the same conversation about Marilyn.

'I doubt it, Marilyn. And how exactly would she do that?' Pillow over the head? A trip-up with an errant walking stick?

'She's trying to poison me. She's got some from somewhere – her son's a chemist, you know – and she's slipping it in my tea and sprinkling it on to my biscuits of an afternoon, when they're still on that trolley, outside. She's always got that evil look on her face, nasty old cow. Well, I've got the measure of her. I refuse to drink the tea and I throw the bloody biscuits on the floor!'

'You're imagining it, Marilyn.' I *really* want to leave.

'I'm telling you, *poison*. On my *biscuits*!'

I extract Marilyn's hand from my arm, put it down on the bed. 'For God's sake,' I say, 'this is not *Murder on the Orient Express*! It's a care home in the west Midlands. I'll talk to one of the carers about it,' I add, but I won't. The whole notion is quite ludicrous.

'*Thank you.*'

Marilyn leans back with a *plompf* on her pillow, satisfied. Reaches for a cough drop from a little tin on the tiny bedside table. She struggles to open it with long, burgundy talons but I don't help her. When one is finally free – a shiny prune – she pops it in her gaping mouth.

'How's *Christian*?' she asks.

'Well, I don't know, Marilyn. I'm not married to him any more.'

'Such a nice man.' She flicks the sweet from one side of her mouth to the other, with a clacking tongue.

'He really isn't.'

'He looked after you.' She revolts me by spitting the cough drop into a tissue she's unearthed from under the bed covers. She drops the tissue parcel, a tongued-edge of sweet poking through, on her bedside table.

I almost splutter, outraged. 'No, he didn't! He did the opposite of looking after me. How can you say that?' Of course, she says the same thing to me every time I visit but this is the first time I have retaliated beyond smiling tightly and changing the subject.

'I think you were stupid to throw it all away. You had a good life with that man.' She is actually tutting.

I save my breath. It is no use trying to explain to the woman, even though I now seem to have the strength to do so. She won't listen to how it was. The abuse. The control. The reduction of me, over those long years, until there was only a shell left. She is deaf to it all.

'Oh, for God's sake!' is all I bother saying. I am considering the pillow myself, to be honest, though it's me who feels suffocated. I want to go. I'm going to go. I'm going to say the words any second.

'It's lunchtime in a minute,' says Marilyn. 'It's shepherd's pie.'

'That's nice.'

'Will you stay for some?'

'I don't think so.'

'Did you come on the train?'

'No. I got a lift.'

'Who with?' I should have just said 'yes'.

'A friend.'

'Christian didn't bring you up, then?'

'No! Why would he? We're *divorced*. I've got a restraining order against him!'

'You always were a melodramatic child.'

I snort, so preposterous are these words, so ironic. Then I stand up. 'I think I'm going to go, Marilyn.'

'What do you mean? You've only just got here! I was going to ask you to look at my feet. *They* say there's nothing wrong with them, but I think I've got a touch of athlete's foot, round my big toes. You could pop out and get me some cream . . . rub it in for me.'

'I don't want to look at your feet, Marilyn,' I say. 'I don't want to *rub cream* on your feet. I'm going.' I check the back of my coat for stains.

'You never stay long.'

'No, well. *I don't want to.*'

Her face falls but I can't find it in me to feel guilty for being so horrible. I'm not going to kiss her on the cheek, like I usually make myself do. Her cheek is always rough, like the sugar paper at school, and her skin slightly sour. I'm already at the open door.

She squints at me until no part of her irises are visible. 'Why won't you stay a bit longer?'

'I can't, I'm sorry.' I pause. My hand is on the germ-ridden handle of the door and I don't even know why I'm touching it. 'Did you ever actually like me?' I ask.

'What?'

'Did you ever actually like me? Did you enjoy spending time with me, ever?'

Marilyn purses her dry red lips and seems to consider my question for a moment. She tips her head to one side like a semi-reflective Jack Russell.

'I *loved* you,' she says tersely, 'in my own way.'

This is astonishing, coming from her – the mere mention of the 'L' word (her 'L' words were more customarily 'lazy', 'licentious' and 'liar'). It simply wasn't in the vocabulary of our lives, growing up. Oh, she had loved me *once* – she of the apron and the cuddles – then, nothing. No more. I felt love from Dad but he would have been far too embarrassed to say it; Marilyn flounced around in contempt of the very notion for years and *years*. It's quite a shock to hear the word 'love' from my mother, even if it nestles sourly amongst the other tart words of this dismissively strangled sentence, and the accompanying look of acid distaste on her face under-lines how much its utterance pains her.

What she's said – however lacking, embittered and the most backward of terribly backward compliments – must have shocked her too as she goes into a temporary coughing fit; dry, hacking. I don't even wait for her to compose herself before I say, 'Your *way* was never good enough, I'm afraid, Marilyn,' and I'm absolutely horrified to feel tears bothering my eyes. I'm about to *cry*? Why? I despise her. It's far too late for any kind of volte-face on her part, however badly exe-cuted. She never loved me in any kind of way that I needed.

I grip the grimy door handle. I look at her, swatting at her mouth with a tissue. It kills me, but I know why I'm in dan-ger of crying. Because there was a long, long time when I desperately *wanted* her to love me, when her love was all I craved, because I *remembered it*. I remembered her love before it turned as sour as the lemons she looks like she's sucking now. But she could never do it. She simply didn't have it in her.

While I'm still here – I feel stuck to the spot, actually; maybe it's the sticky carpet – I say, 'Also . . .' I take a deep

227

breath. 'I'll never forgive you for what you put Dad through. I just want to say that to you. Now.'

I watch her face for a reaction but, as usual, she disappoints. There's a 'So what?' shrug from bony shoulders. A closed face. My questions about Dad won't be answered. Questions like, was it one affair too many? As he neared old age did Dad look back over his life and calculate how much of it he had wasted on my mother? From the look of her, Marilyn doesn't have the answer to why Dad committed suicide, nor does she much care. It was me who found him, that afternoon, when the buzzing of sun-scorched bees competed with the indifferent splutter of next door's lawnmower and a distant ice-cream van tinkling 'Greensleeves', on a loop. She was in the house, where it was cool, having a G&T. She screamed blue murder for two hours when I told her, but three weeks later she was moving to Walsall with a man – her last man – she'd met at the post office. Following me to the Midlands again, although I was no longer there.

I sigh. Her silence and her shrug are my cue to depart.

'I'm going now.'

'Goodbye then, *Arden*.' Incomprehensibly, she is angry now and almost spits at me. She is claiming my name, reminding me she chose it and every word she spits is a tiny, poisoned arrow intended to puncture my heart, but I don't want the arrows to find me. They can fall to the sticky carpet, along with Joan's cyanide biscuits.

'Goodbye, Marilyn.'

Like we always have, we sound like we are in some terrible, tragic play. I leave the set. I close the door behind me and walk down the cloying peach corridor. With each step, I breathe away my threatening tears and will my identity to come back to me. My own life, apart from hers. I need to step into lightness again otherwise she will weigh me down, this woman I am attached to by invisible, viscous cords. I want to play loud music, watch a film I love. Dance like everyone's watching. I will not be dragged down by her. I will not slip all the way back in time to when she was my mother.

It's still cold outside. I sit on the bench. I watch a robin, his bright red flashing at me amongst all this grey and dull muddy green like a tease. He is more cheerful than me; he has far more purpose. I see a tall woman in a fur hat take an elderly gentleman out to a car. He is shouting about someone called Tina; the woman bundles him in the car. That man once had a whole life, I think; a whole life that was fun and vital and rich and full. Or maybe he didn't. Maybe it was a sad life, like my dad's. I'm still haunted by the image of him, on the dusty floor of the shed where lost nails and blades of grass congregated in webby corners, the bodybuilder's resistance band that broke his neck still attached to the splintered beam that fell with him. I'm *always* haunted by it.

James's car pulls into the car park. He's an hour early, thank God. I haven't been sitting on this bench the whole time. I wandered up the road to nurse three cups of weak tea and a deflated piece of lemon meringue pie in a dingy café. Perused a mobile library. Stared at some graffiti. I get into the car; it's warm and the radio is on.

'You weren't keen on sticking to the full four hours, then,' he says. 'How was it?'

'Awful. I didn't manage long. I've been wandering around.'

'Is she well?'

'Unfortunately, yes. How come you're early? How was the expo?'

'Not too bad,' he says. I'm pleased to see him, I think. His friendly handsome face is a nice one to see after Marilyn's bile-wizened one. 'A lot of people but nothing breathing into a paper bag couldn't help me deal with.'

'Oh God, really?'

'No,' says James. 'Not this time. I'm joking. It was OK. I was free to mooch around at my leisure, really. I left early because it was a bit boring.' He reverses out of the same space we were in earlier. The pine tree air freshener rocks and a branch of the willow tree droopingly trails along the bonnet of the car, then flops free.

I look at him. 'Can we go somewhere nice on the way back?' I ask. 'Somewhere cheery. My treat.'

'Of course.'

James comes off the motorway after only three junctions. We cruise down an endless slip road, circuit about six mini roundabouts and soon we are on a country road, which ends at a low, one-storey building with a pitched roof and picnic tables out the front.

'Where are we?'

'It's a butterfly farm and café,' says James. 'It's called "Happy Hills". Cheery enough?'

'Oh, absolutely!' I say, and I actually clap my hands together. 'What could be more cheery than butterflies?'

We get out of the car and go in. To get to the café you have to walk through the winding atrium of a butterfly farm; it has a gabled glass roof with netted canopies, bridges, brooks, clusters of tropical ferns and wooden walkways – I used to go somewhere similar with Julian when he was a child. Butterflies flick and flutter around us, and land prettily on laddered leaves to preen and be marvelled over.

'There are fifty-nine species of butterfly in the UK, over twenty thousand in the world,' offers James.

'Thank you, geek boy,' I say as a red admiral alights coquettishly on the back of my hand. It's about the only one I would recognize. There's tinny music in the background, unrelated to butterflies. Depeche Mode, currently. British electronic music from Basildon's finest. I am reminded of that club I went to with Mac in Soho, all the colours and the lights there. It's as hot in here, to be honest. It's baking. I slip off my coat and put it over my arm.

'Too warm for you?' asks James.

'No, I like it.'

The café is as bright and cheery as it could be. Huge overlapping fabric butterflies in sapphire, ruby and topaz create a mural on three walls. The fourth wall is painted a rich emerald green — sponge effect, like something from a nineties makeover show. The strong jewel colours are far removed from the sickly pastels of The Cedars and I breathe a massive sigh of relief that comes out much louder than I intend.

'I feel . . . rescued,' I say, with a big smile, and I think of Paula being carried out of that factory by Richard Gere and laugh because I must be easily pleased — a slice of carrot cake and some butterflies and apparently I've been rescued! 'I'm just so pleased to be away from The Cedars.'

'You look it,' he says. 'You look like a burden has been lifted from your shoulders.'

'It has,' I reply. 'The burden of another hideous duty visit.'

James's face is thoughtful. 'If it's that bad maybe you don't have to go again,' he says.

'Of course I do!' I say. 'Let's change the subject. Do you think Mac's going to die?'

James laughs. 'Well, that's a nice subject change!' he says. 'From the *hideous* to the downright depressing . . .'

'I want to know what you think,' I continue. 'I've been thinking about it a lot.'

'I don't know,' says James, stirring the thick cream on the top of his hot chocolate. 'What have they said to you?'

'Not a lot. That it's fifty-fifty; that they don't really know.'

'Fran said the same to me.'

'I'm not sure I can bear it, if something bad happens,' I say. I'm not sure why I've shifted the conversation down this road. I have the horrible feeling again that I might start crying, and I really don't want to do this in the Happy Hills café.

'He's really special to you, isn't he?' says James, not realizing he has a Charlie Chaplin moustache of cream above his top lip. 'Not just then, but now.'

'Yes,' I say. 'Seeing him again is reminding me exactly how much. And he's still special to me now *because* of how I felt about him then. *Thirty years* . . . God, I'm old! The whole thing is wrapped up in rose-tinted nostalgia, and because he can't talk to me, I can't tell the *then* and the *now* apart. Like if he was to actually speak to me today some kind of spell would be broken. Oh, I don't know what I'm saying, really.'

'I think *I* do,' says James, wiping his mouth. 'Seeing him has transported you back into the past and because he's not able to talk to you in the present you're kind of stuck there, feeling what you felt back then.'

'Absolutely! That's exactly it, James! There's also the fact he saw something in me nobody else could see. Oh, that reminds me of a line from a movie!' I say. It could be from anything, but I think it's from a movie on The List . . . 'I can't remember which one – that's going to bug me.'

'Can't help you on that one,' says James. 'My encyclopaedic memory only goes so far . . . *Scarface*?'

I laugh, shaking my head. I know he is joking. 'No, not *Scarface*.'

'Do you think you'd start something up again if he gets better? Get back together?'

That's a very direct question, but James, I've noticed, is a very direct character. His eyes question mine, unblinking. 'After all these years? No, I can't see it,' I say, 'but sometimes I think about it.'

We finish our drinks and our cake and walk out of the café. There's a small aviary outside the rear entrance – it's noisy with cheeping and chirping and claws scratching as birds alight on the tiny wire squares of the cage. Parakeets and canaries ribbon from top to bottom and blue budgies pivot like circus performers from swinging bamboo perches.

'Oh, lovebirds!' I cry. 'My favourites!' There's a pair at the back, yellow and orange chests puffed out, wedged together on top of a square wooden bird box.

'Everybody loves a lovebird,' says James. 'Did you know they not only mate for life but can live up to twenty-five years?'

'Really? No, I didn't know that.'

James places his little fingers in one of the small wire squares and coos to the lovebirds. They refuse to come over and say 'hi'. 'Ever seen the Hitchcock movie *The Birds*?'

I smile. An outfit of mine James didn't pick up on was the green sleeveless Tippi-Hedren-in-*The-Birds* dress I wore to the hospital the first night I met him. It would have astonished me if he had, to be honest – that one was pretty obscure, although hopefully Mac noticed. 'Yes, I have.'

'You know Hitchcock's use of the lovebirds, then. My favourite is how they lean into the turns together in Tippi Hedren's convertible as she drives to Bodega Bay. It's very sweet and funny, considering the carnage that's to come.'

'Yes, I remember that,' I say. I don't think I've ever discussed the movie with anyone but Mac. I peek and coo at the lovebirds, on their perch at the back of the aviary. 'They're so cute,' I say. 'I love how Melanie brings them to Mitch's door in that film. First to his house in the city, but he's not there, then to his place by the lake. You're right, the film is almost a romantic comedy at the beginning, before the claws come out . . . and I remember how the lovebirds stay calm throughout, when all the other birds are kicking off!' I remember a lot about that film, I think, and most of it is tied up with Mac.

'Has anyone ever brought lovebirds to your door?' asks James. I realize he's standing quite close to me now and as I look up at him I can see darting flecks in his grey eyes, picked out by the watery winter sun.

'Yes,' I reply, 'they've brought them and then, like the movie, everything has gone horribly wrong!'

James laughs, then gives a little frown and looks thoughtful. 'Shall we go?' he says, stepping back. 'We should hit the road.'

We walk to the car. 'There's always something to see in everyone,' says James, almost to himself, as we put our seat belts on, 'even people that think there's nothing.' And I suddenly remember where that line is from – prompted by the memory of Mac seeing something in me – and I'm cleverer than I thought, or perhaps my subconscious is just working on overdrive, because it's something Judy Garland says about James Mason in the next film on The List.

THEN

Chapter 19: A Star Is Born

The morning after the Lebanese restaurant and the tiny electronica club, Mac ordered room service. We had croissants and jams and toast and cold meats and I sat cross-legged on our pushed-together double bed in my Madonna *True Blue* T-shirt and simply thought, over and over again: *He loves me, he loves me, he loves me.*

Mac kept asking me, 'What do you keep smiling at?' in dour, delicious northern tones; I kept saying, 'Nothing', and hugged my delight to me like an enormous soft toy. I was giddy. I kept breaking into spontaneous, idiotic grins. If I was by myself I would have jumped up and down on that bed, screeching, and probably fallen straight down the middle again.

Check out was at twelve, which seemed far too draconian. We hadn't woken up until half ten – student hours, natch – and until breakfast had lain in the fluffy white cloud of a bed playing with each other and dozing. At ten to twelve we jumped in the shower and threw our stuff into our bags. We laughed and kissed as we came down in the lift, watched by a po-faced middle-aged couple who looked like they hadn't done either for years. We held hands and crossed the street, our bags bumping against our legs. I was giggling; Mac was smiling at me. I was as happy as I had ever been.

'Mac!'

There was a huge man standing in front of us, in the middle of the road. He had a massive beard, astonishingly bushy eyebrows and was wearing a voluminous brown overcoat. He was tall; my head only came up to his lapels. In short, he looked like a big brown bear.

'What are you doing here?'

Mac dropped my hand, like it was a cold stone.

'Stewart,' he said, shaking the bear's paw. 'Good to see you, I came down to do a talk at the BFI yesterday – Japanese cinema.' He was effusive, pleased to have been apprehended; there was no suggestion in his voice he had been caught out in any way. Meanwhile, my heart was in my mouth, being chewed over.

'Oh excellent, excellent. Let's get out of the road, shall we?'

A black cab was impatient behind Stewart, beeping its horn.

Mac didn't steer me to the side of the road. He walked over with Stewart and I had to trail behind. The three of us teetered at the edge of the busy pavement, me with one foot in the gutter.

'How are you enjoying your retirement?' Mac asked Stewart.

'Oh, I decided not to call it a day, in the end,' said the man, giving me a curious glance. He only looked about fifty. 'You know how it is. It's like a drug, film.' He laughed a mighty laugh, clapped a grinning Mac on the back; I ventured a hesitant, joining-in giggle. 'I'm lecturing at the London Film School now. How are things at Warwick?'

'Oh, rolling on; you know how it goes,' said Mac, all jolly and brimming with bonhomie. 'This is Arden,' he added reluctantly. 'Arden Hall. A research student. I met her to talk her through a few notes.' I cringed really badly, we'd just come skipping out of a hotel, for God's sake! We had been holding *hands*. And what he said didn't even make any kind of sense. 'This is Stewart Whittaker,' he said to me.

'Nice to meet you, Arden,' said Stewart Whittaker. He

knew exactly what we had been doing, I thought. He could see it in my face. The flush at my neck. The shine in my eyes. He knew we were in love and we shouldn't have been. 'How's Helen?' he asked and he raised his eyebrows slightly at Mac, at the same time shaking my hand with a padded palm. I could feel the hairs on the back of his fingers as mine went loosely round them.

'Oh, you know,' said Mac, 'brilliant as ever. Going great guns at Sheffield.'

'Great, great, good to hear it. Yes. Well, good luck to you both,' Stewart said and he meant Mac and I, not Mac and Helen, the way he was looking at me and he *definitely* knew what we were doing. 'Great to see you, Mac. Nice to meet you, Arden.'

'Likewise,' I replied. Wasn't that the sort of thing grown-ups were supposed to say? And Stewart lumbered back over the road, dodging cars and bicycles, and disappeared into the Soho crowd.

'Oh dear,' said Mac. He stood there, on the pavement, his arms at his sides, his leather bag dangling from one defeated hand. He looked agitated. Twitchy. He lifted his free hand and ran it through his fringe until it flopped back in his eyes. He blew his fringe skywards, his mouth a worried 'O'. He glanced across the street as though more Stewarts might be coming. I realized he actually looked *frightened*.

'You're terrified of us being found out, aren't you?' I couldn't help it, I was mocking, scathing. Last night he'd told me he loved me. This morning I wanted to tell the world Mac and I were together – not only shout it from the rooftops but string a banner between the earth and the sun, announcing it to the universe. Why didn't *he*? What did it matter that some crusty old fart had seen us together? What *would* it matter if the Dean found out, or *Helen*, or the other students? I didn't bloody well care. Let them all know! Let them all know; then Mac and I could be together for ever.

'If we were found out, we would have to end it,' said Mac. 'It's as simple as that.'

'But it's not against the rules,' I protested. 'Frowned upon, you said.'

'If we were found out we would have to end it,' Mac repeated, and he said it so quietly I became scared too. He meant it, didn't he? He loved me but he wouldn't risk everything for me, after all. Helen, his reputation . . .

I pulled myself together. This had been a short false alarm; nothing had changed. 'Well, we *weren't* found out,' I said with forced jollity. 'We got away with it, didn't we?'

'Yes,' replied Mac. 'Seeing Stewart did take me by surprise, though. He's always been up north in some bloody garret, writing theses!' He frowned, looked disconsolate, frowned again, but then slapped on a smile and said, in sunny tones, 'Oh well, never mind, worse things happen at sea. Let's go and get on the tube!'

I could tell he was trying to be jolly but wasn't feeling it. That was fine, I thought, I could feel it for both of us and I decided everything was going to be OK. I knew we had to be careful, but this accidental near-discovery shouldn't derail us. The Dean hadn't seen us that time, no one else but Becky knew about us and I knew she wouldn't tell anyone as I said I'd give her a Chinese burn and eat all her Frosties if she did.

On the Central Line, Mac was distracted. His hand went from the handrail to the overhead strap to the handrail behind him. His other hand was at his face, rubbing at his nose, his chin, his eyelids under his glasses. I couldn't talk to him; I tried to say something bubbly about the heat, something flirty about having to take all my clothes off, but he just made a kind of grunting 'huh' sound, and kept staring at nothing.

At Marble Arch, a boy of about seven or eight got on the tube. He surged in amongst a small sea of people but they all trickled away from him, to stand or to sit, and then he seemed to be on his own. Mac and I were at the end of a carriage, by the interconnecting door. The boy was to our left. There was a five-pound note half sticking out of the side pocket of his jeans, looking like it was about to fall. He had a little rucksack on his back. He was grinning to himself and tapping his feet on the floor, left right, left right. I kept looking at him, trying to see who he was with. So did Mac, but nobody else on the carriage bothered him with a glance. There was a woman, to our right, perched on a half-seat. She had orange Sony Walkman headphones on and was staring straight ahead. Was she with him? I kept looking at her, looking at the boy, wondering. Mac was doing the same. But he was sweating, really sweating. Rubbing the fingers of his right hand together like he was making pastry.

'Who's that boy with?' he asked me.

'I don't know.'

'Should we say something?' Mac wiped his brow; he looked unnerved.

'What would we say?'

'Well, ask him who's he with?'

'He *must* be with someone,' I said. I looked around. I really didn't know who. 'He's probably with that woman there.' We both looked at the young woman with the head-phones. She still stared straight ahead. The boy was smiling, tapping; he'd noticed the falling fiver now and had stuffed it back inside his pocket. 'Anyway, we're getting off now.'

'I think we should say something to someone.'

'Who?'

The tube rattled into White City where we had to change; the brick walls, the advertising posters, the waiting people. The door swept open. 'Mind the gap between the platform and the train,' a voice said.

Mac hesitated, looked distressed.

'Come on then!' I took his hand and pulled him off the train.

239

As the door shut behind us, Mac said, 'We should have asked him. We should have asked that boy who he was with. We should have asked that woman.' He was running his fingers through his floppy hair, his eyes wild; he was frightening me.

'Don't worry about it!' I cried. 'There are probably loads of streetwise kids running around London, hopping on and off the tubes. Who cares?'

'Maybe we should tell a guard?' There was one behind us talking to an elderly lady; she was saying something in a plummy voice about the Palace Theatre.

'And say what? Come on, Mac. You're being silly.'

'Yes, yes, you're probably right,' said Mac, but he looked anguished all the way to Hammersmith and I got cross with him, because he was ruining the last hours of our special trip that Stewart Whittaker had already put a dent in and it was all rather ridiculous.

'Stop it now,' I said, quite sternly. 'Please.' He dropped the anguished look, and by the time we walked to the NCP car park he was trying and failing to be charismatic and good-humoured again – but he didn't fool me.

The drive back to Warwick was pretty awful: the traffic horrendous, Mac's mood indefinable. Yes, he spoke, he laughed, he sang along to the songs on Radio 1 (which I put on), but I could tell his mind was elsewhere. He drew a barely disguised sigh of relief when we turned into campus and *I* could barely disguise my annoyance.

'So, I'm going to go home.' I shrugged, standing behind his car and hefting my carpet bag on to my shoulder under dappled sunlight. 'Back to the slug-infested hovel.'

'OK,' said Mac. He was looking around him. What was wrong with him? Was he worried the Dean was going to jump out at us from a bush and snare us in a net? 'I've got some work to catch up on anyway, so . . .'

'Thank you for a lovely time,' I said tersely, giving my best pout.

'Thank *you*,' said Mac. He was glancing over to his building, ready to scurry inside. He'd said he loved me yesterday, I thought, as I walked away. *Last night*. How could things have gone so ever so slightly wrong since then? Because of a man on the street and a boy on the tube? I felt there had been an unravelling in London, like when a spool of film runs out from one of those clunking grey projectors – whipping to its end with an unsettling clatter. We were reduced, somehow. We were not quite what we had been.

Mac was weird for a few days after that. When I was next at his flat I noticed a copy of the *Evening Standard* on his little side table next to the sofa, and he casually told me he'd placed a subscription for it, from London.

'Why?' I asked.

'Keep me abreast of London news,' he said, but I didn't believe him. I suspected he was scouring that paper daily for news of that boy. Some tragic accident, a murder? God knows what Mac was looking for but it became a temporary kind of obsession for him.

'You watch too many movies, Mac!' I said, after I had seen the paper on his side table for the third time. He was on the sofa taking notes on Jimmy Cagney in *The Public Enemy*, while I lounged next to him with a cup of tea and attempted to read *Middlemarch*. Mac didn't laugh. He popped his glasses on the top of his head and looked at me with clear, cool eyes.

'No. But I have encountered real life,' he said.

'I know you're looking for news of that boy. It's ridiculous!'

'Is it? Bad things happen to people all the time, Arden,' he said, rubbing at his eyes. 'To children. We should have said something. We could have done something.'

'We didn't need to do anything!' I protested. 'That boy was fine. He *is* fine!'

'I lost my brother, when I was a kid.' Mac put his glasses back on and stared at Cagney shoving a grapefruit into his girlfriend's face at breakfast.

'Lost? What do you mean? Lost in a supermarket or something?'

'Not lost, *lost*. Died. Drowned.'

My heart contracted for a millisecond. I put my book on my lap. I remembered Mac's distaste for the lido, his nervy unease, his declaration he wouldn't be getting in the water. 'How awful. What happened?'

Mac looked away. He fiddled with the corner of his shirt, rubbing at it between index finger and thumb. Then he looked back at me and started talking.

'There was a group of us, when we were kids, my little brother and me and a load of other kids from school. We used to go to this pond not far from us, in the middle of some woods. Swim in it, particularly on hot summer days. It was always in the shade, it was always lovely and cool. We went there in the summer holidays one time when I was about fifteen. We were all larking around, as boys do. Diving to the bottom for a big stone we'd found, over and over again. There were too many of us. Too many boys.' He paused. 'Reggie didn't come up, but we didn't realize for ages that he hadn't. He'd got tangled in the weeds. He was lying on the bottom of the pond. I guess no one noticed.' He laughed bitterly. 'It took all of us to pull him out and get him to the surface, but by then, of course, it was too late. He was only seven.'

'Oh God, Mac,' I said. 'That's so terrible.'

'Yeah. It was bloody awful. I don't think I'll ever get over it. That I didn't notice. How could I have not *noticed* that my brother didn't come up again?' Mac looked wretched, broken. I had never seen that look on his face before.

'Because you were a boy,' I said softly, surprised at how caring I sounded. 'Because you were playing with loads of your mates and you just didn't notice.'

He'd noticed that boy on the tube, though, hadn't he? He'd *noticed* and hadn't done anything. I got it now. The panic on his face, the agitation, the *Evening Standard*. I felt sick; this was an awful story. Poor Mac.

'We never went back to that pond again,' he said. 'I think of it sometimes. Still there in the shade. It'll probably be there for ever.'

My heart contracted again. I recalled with horror my flippant anecdote about my mother and the boy who'd nearly drowned at the leisure centre. *That* was why Mac had wanted to flee the lido: my story, delivered against the splashy scenery of pool shouts, merry screams, tomfoolery and laughter. A story where I'd got the focus all wrong – it should have been on the poor boy who had nearly died, or at least his worried family, not my own acid indignation towards my mother. I also remembered *The Water Babies* and *all* the lost children Mac had been unable to rescue, and my heart ached for him.

'I'm so sorry, Mac,' I said, and I really meant it.

'It's just one of those things,' he said. 'Just one of those terrible, terrible things.' And he got up and left the sofa to walk to the kitchen, where I heard him flick the kettle on.

A few days later, it was over. I didn't see another copy of the *Evening Standard* and Mac didn't mention that boy on the tube or poor Reggie again. Still, I felt like something had shifted. We had gone into a patch of shade which hovered over us, biding its time. A little colour had drained from our affair, like from a seventies caravan curtain left flapping in a sunny plastic window too long. I was even scared I had fallen out of love with him, just a little, so when Mac mentioned the next movie on The List – *A Star Is Born* – I jumped at the chance of watching it with him so we could get ourselves back on track.

Mac and I saw the Judy Garland and James Mason version of *A Star Is Born* – the Technicolor one, from 1954, where Judy dances for James in tights and a button-down shirt and announces herself in a moment of high drama at the end of the movie as *Mrs Norman Maine*. We watched it in the hot screening room, two weeks after Soho, with a large bag of M&M's and noisy cans of Dr Pepper, but despite our attempt at all-American movie-going high spirits, there was a swirl of unacknowledged disquiet and unease around us.

The film is super-charged with high-colour vibrancy and big-band numbers, but I found it sad and quite depressing. When Judy Garland sings her torch song, 'The Man That Got Away', I wondered how soon Mac might become mine. When Judy as Esther Blodgett goes to the studio lot in Hollywood, after James Mason – who sees something in her no one else can – sends her, and the backstage elements of artifice are revealed: lighting, gaudy make-up, wigs and being given an arbitrary, more glamorous new name, I felt deflated. The drinking, the despair, the hollowness of surface-sparkly Hollywood left me feeling strangely bereft and the melancholy of Judy's voice went right through me, haunted me. I cried at the end as yes, it was a very sad ending, but also because of my own fear and sadness, which I'd nursed since London, that Mac and I were reaching the end of something.

We didn't even discuss the movie afterwards, as we warily walked back to Westwood under intermittent street lights. I couldn't be bothered to give Mac my brilliant thoughts on the movie's portrayal of women – how it was pre-feminist, with its self-denial and its keeper-of-the-flame Mrs Norman Maine business. I didn't mention how I had never seen a movie more about the trials, the drive and terror of failure of one woman. How the sheer *power* of Esther Blodgett becoming Vicki Lester frightened me. Mac was walking in front of me, two paces, as though making sure he could easily extend them to five, or six, if someone came the other way.

Everything felt vulnerable, fragile, impermanent and a little fake. With both his revelation about his brother and his fear of the discovery of our affair revealed to me, Mac was now fallible and not the giant I had imagined him to be. When your rescuer needs rescuing himself, the fairy tale gets shattered . . . *I* was supposed to be the brittle damaged one who needed stuff seeing in me. I couldn't be any kind of salve to Mac. I just didn't have it in me.

'Would you say *A Star Is Born* is melodrama?' Mac asked me, hands in pockets.

'I'm not sure.' I thought it was but I wasn't in the mood to talk.

'A melodrama should bring out heightened emotions,' he said, as we walked. 'There's another film I was debating having on The List, *Imitation of Life*. Do you know it?'

'Nope,' I said, wishing I did, to impress and get some of *us* back. I wanted *all* of us back – the laughter, the carefree joy, but I was worried the fun and fearlessness of Mac and I had disappeared.

'It's a Douglas Sirk movie,' says Mac. 'His last, and what a way to go out! Lana Turner's in it. She has a black maid whose daughter passes herself off as white. It's highly emotional, a real weepie – you'll weep buckets, I guarantee it. There's a funeral scene that is just "wow". We should watch it sometime.'

'OK,' I said. The end of term was fast approaching. I wondered exactly how much time we had left together, if we would last another year, and whether the best of us had already passed. God, I hated myself like this – morose, flattened. I decided there was another way to get back on track. As soon as we got through the door of his flat I took my top off and led Mac into his bedroom, where I seduced him as the languid branch at his window tap-tapped a lazy finger down the pane in the mid-summer dusk.

NOW

Chapter 20

James and I are on the home stretch. There is about a mile of the journey left. We are stop-start at traffic lights, we are wedged between hissing and belching buses, we are assaulted by fumes and skimmed by weekend Boris bikes flashing by in the dark – but I lace my fingers and stretch my arms lazily out in front of me as I am quite content. I am cheered by carrot cake and the butterflies. I am far from Marilyn again.

'Why *do* you keep going?'

'Sorry?'

James is fiddling with the radio, we've got bored of pop and inane, breathy DJ-chat; we've been thoroughly geeked out by a presentation on Radio 4 about quantum physics and the application of amplitudes, or something. I quite enjoyed that, actually – at least, I'd loved how consumed James was by it, how concentrated. He was nodding at things I didn't even understand and it made me smile. James finally settles on something classical, a piece I know but cannot name.

'Going to see your mother?' he says. 'You say you don't like her. You looked miserable before you went in, even more miserable when you came out. You needed the help of the butterflies to get over it.'

'True,' I say, with a laugh. A bus draws up alongside us,

about an inch from the car. Inside, so brightly lit I feel like a voyeur, passengers are sullen under headphones or chatting to each other, laughing. I see a girl pull something from a Topshop bag and show it to her friend.

'I broached it in the café and I'll broach it again now. You don't have to go again, you know. Why do you?'

'The honest answer is I don't know,' I say, as the bus pulls away with a wheeze. 'Duty. That someone will tell me off if I don't.'

'Who's going to tell you off?' James brakes suddenly, for a wobbling pizza delivery bike. 'All right, mate, take it easy, there you go . . . You're not a child, Arden.'

'I know. And I don't know.' My jolly mood has collapsed; I don't want to talk about her any more today. I have moved on. I have had carrot cake and butterflies.

There's a kid and a dog in the back seat of the black cab in front of us. Both are waving at us – well, there's a paw and a hand at the back window, anyway. Perhaps they're playing rock, paper, scissors.

'You feel a duty between daughter and mother,' continues James. 'But there doesn't need to be one. You could simply cut and run.'

'*Cut and run?*' Cut the choking apron strings and run for my life? I think. Where would I go, to escape her? She's always back there, to be drawn to, like a flame to a dull, brown moth, which is what I am. Or at least what I was until Mac came back into my life. I'd like to think at least one of my wings is tipped with a little colour now.

'Yeah. You don't have to see her any more if you don't want to.' The traffic is moving so slowly James is literally holding the steering wheel with one thumb.

'Don't I?'

The kid waggles a lolly at us; the dog, a tongue.

'Do you owe her anything?'

'She's all alone.'

247

'I suspect that's her choice. Or rather, the consequence of all her choices. Whatever they are.' He beeps and gestures good-naturedly at a professional cyclist weaving too close to the car on a spindly road bike. '*You* now have a choice. Mac is lonely – you want to sit with him. You feel something for him. You have a history you feel fondness towards. It warms your heart.'

'Yes.'

'Your mother is also lonely, I'm guessing. But you have an awful history with her, don't you? Well, you haven't told me much about it – almost nothing – but she's been cold to you, and you now feel cold towards her. That's evident. If you don't want to see her any more then choose not to.'

'Wow,' I say. The more I'm with him the more he surprises me. He is so very black and white – none of this analysing things for a hundred years like I do. 'You make it sound so simple.'

'It *is* simple, Arden.' And I like the way my name sounds in his accent. He overtakes a white van. 'Am I right or am I right?'

'*Groundhog Day.*' I smile.

'I *am* right,' he says, and he is smiling. 'Don't continue to be a supporting artist to all her drama. Sorry, I'm guessing that too. That there's drama.'

'There's always drama,' I agree.

'She made a mistake. Being a bad mother to you. Don't make a bigger mistake by letting yourself suffer for it for the rest of your life.'

'Colossal,' I mutter, looking out of the window as I remember the last film on Mac's list. A car streaks past us in the other direction, windows down despite the dark and cold, Drake or some other rapper Julian is into blaring. 'Do you really think I can never see her again? That I can get away with it?' It would be like a crime, I think. Like *Bonnie and Clyde* in their getaway car, on a killing spree.

'Your choice,' he says, 'but it's within your own power to make it. Do what's right for you. My mother did. She did the right thing for us and for her. You can do the right thing.'

I think of Vicki Lester, all the strong women in the movies. I wonder how *I* would have been discussed in a 'Portrayal of Women' seminar, if I was in the movie of my own life. At one time strong, unapologetic and fearless, if rather cold and more than a little sinful. Now? *Pathetic?*

'Do you need her in your life? That's what you need to ask yourself.'

I heard the same question, many moons ago, from Mac, not long after Marilyn's terrible gatecrashing visit to Warwick. The answer had clearly been an echoing 'yes' as I have kept her in it for a long, long time – if only in the shadows, like a dark spectre. A bird, waiting high on a telephone wire, to come and rip at my hair. A woman with a knife, glinting in sunlight. Someone with more power than me because I had let her have it.

Nobody has ever said to me before that I can just *not* see her again. It seems so simple. Is it something I've been waiting for permission for? I don't *want* her to wield any power over me. Not any more. My real mother is never coming back.

'Do you ever wonder what happens after the end of the movie?' I say. 'After all the decisions have been made, all the kissing has been done, the baddies have been banged up, the goodies have found the treasure? Do you wonder what comes next?'

'Yeah, all the time,' says James, and I smile to myself – so different to Mac, who saw everything as self-contained and every film as its own entity. 'That's a funny question, though. I thought we were talking about your mother.'

'I still am,' I say. 'It's kind of like the story of me and her finished years ago, with my dad dying, her moving away then going into that home, but I've hung around to see if anything else is going to happen, if she's going to change . . . Of course, she hasn't – the movie's just gone on and on and on – no editing, no closing scenes, endless rushes of just *the same* – and I've realized nothing else *does* happen. That was it.'

'So why hang around any more?'

Yes, why am I still hanging around? Taking the abuse from her? Haven't I taken enough? I can stop the movie right here, right now, and move on with my life, free of her. I would like to give a different answer to the question.

'No,' I say.

'No?'

'No, I don't need her in my life.' And, as we pull up at another red light, I do what I should have done a long, long time ago. I decide to cut her from my life – for me, for Dad and every sad, terrible moment she gave him – and it's already done before I've even properly thought it. There is no process, no soul-searching, no long-drawn-out debating with myself. I decide – right here and right now – and Marilyn is gone, severed from me, like snapping a carrot in half, the rotten end falling and gone. As base and as un-Hollywood and as simple as that. 'OK,' I say breezily, glancing my hands off each other like I am dusting off flour, 'I've done it. She's gone.'

'Just like that?' He smiles.

'Just like that,' I say. I know I'm probably being far too flippant. Is it really done? Am I really free of her *just like that*? I stare out of the window as the lights turn orange and another black cab nudges its way forward to our left. Yes, it can be that simple. It *could* be. If I want to be free of her, then I am. The decision is under my own control. I am free. I haven't been free for a long, long time.

'I've done it,' I say. *I've done it, Dad. I've done it for me and I've done it for you. Now we are* both *free.* 'Thank you, James.'

'I haven't done that much,' he says.

'You have,' I say. 'You've taken me up there today and more importantly, you've brought me back.' Despite my flippancy, my free, lightened spirit, I suddenly feel I could cry. That something feral and primeval and totally, bloody embarrassing could burst out of me in this car and take me over. That I could lay my head against the glass of the window next to me and let everything out in giant, heaving sobs of regret and misery and relief. For a few seconds I am on the brink of it, but then the feeling just stops.

'Are you OK?' asks James.

'Yes,' I say, and I take a deep breath. 'Yes. I'm OK.'

My phone chimes in my bag, with the signal that I've got an email. I suspect it's The Cedars detailing a list of complaints about my visit my mother 'forgot' to mention while I was there. I usually get one. Last time I visited there were ten bullet points, ranging from I moved the pot plant on the windowsill, to she didn't like my perfume and it had given her a sinus reaction. The emails were always signed 'Iris'; I suspected Iris had far too much time on her hands, or Marilyn had been bribing her. If it *is* from The Cedars it's nothing to do with me now. I won't reply to it. I will delete it. I can delete any others that come. I can stop answering the phone from them, too, at work. I won't be stepping foot in The Cedars again and the shiny bright new knowledge of this makes me want to leap from the car and out into the traffic, to dance in the dark drizzle light of foot and free of heart, like an outdoor Riverdancer.

'Do you need to check your phone?' asks James.

'No.' In fact, I decide, ignoring my bag as it squats in the footwell, I'm not even going to look at the email; that's how much I have moved on. It can sit benign in my inbox, as I am totally indifferent to it, and I will delete it later.

I'm surprised James wants to go and visit Mac after such a long drive, but he says we should pop in, if just for a little while.

'To see the old boy,' he says. 'He might miss us otherwise.'

'Well, I'd like to,' I say. 'If you're sure you want to.'

'Of course.'

James stretches his legs in the hospital car park, literally. He touches his toes and does some gym-like limb flexing. A passing elderly couple nudge each other and stare. While I watch and wait, thinking again what a strange one he is, the email notification on my phone chimes again. I'll check it, I think. If it's from The Cedars I'll not only delete it but also strike their address from my contacts.

The top email is from Dorothy Perkins. They have a sale on: 25 per cent off all shoes. The one below it is from Perrie Turque and it is short and very sweet.

I've found him, it says.

THEN

Chapter 21: Pretty Woman

The last film on Mac's list was a biggie. A popular favourite. A colossal hit. I had already seen it when Mac and I settled down to watch it in the screening room; I think half the world had, since its release a few weeks before. Most of them had bought the soundtrack, too. Lots of luckless lovers had left the twelve-inch of 'The King of Wishful Thinking' outside their intended's front door. Well, Becky had. Hers was Dhruv Henderson, a history student in Top End Leamington she'd sat next to on the coach back from a trip to the Birmingham Hippodrome. 'Wishful Thinking' hadn't worked; she'd discovered the slightly soggy record still there when skulking past his house two days later. Maybe he wasn't a Go West fan, I had suggested, giving her a consolatory hug when she arrived back at the Slug House, the offending article back in her bag, and we commiserated with Asti Spumante and breaded chicken, as we often did.

'Richard Gere again?' I remarked to Mac, stretching my legs over his in the screening room, one hot afternoon. I was in short shorts and a cropped white T-shirt; I was tanned from topless sunbathing in the tiny back yard of the Slug House, on a beach towel. There was only a week until the end of term and I was soaking up *everything*, while I could.

'Richard Gere again,' he replied.

'The eternal rescuer of impoverished women . . .' I mused, heeling off my plimsolls with the opposite foot and letting them drop to the thin carpet.

Mac laughed. I was really interested in hearing his take on *Pretty Woman*. Would he see it as damning of feminism or all for it? Vivian as a passive rescuee saved only by a man's wealth, or an independent, feisty heroine who knows exactly what she wants?

I hadn't made my mind up, myself, although I'd already seen *Pretty Woman* three times at the cinema with Becky. We loved it. We constantly quoted from and exaggerated the script. Julia Roberts' scathing 'huge!' to the Rodeo Drive shop assistants became 'colossal!' in our re-enactments in the clothes shops of Coventry; her proposition to rescue Richard Gere 'right back' pompously became 'the reciprocation of liberation' in our hammy spoofs. We sometimes, for a laugh, even pretended to students who didn't know us that Becky's name was Kit and my name was Vivian. The first time we watched it, I'd been semi-outraged at the ending and had scoffed at it as a Cinderella-load of hokum. The second time I thought Julia Roberts had kicked arse; she had said how she wanted her fairy-tale ending to be and that's what she'd got. The third time I'd just enjoyed it.

Mac placed a warm hand on my left thigh and the credits rolled. I decided I could watch the opening of this movie every year for the rest of my life and still be excited by it. I wondered if it would still be a favourite in twenty or thirty years' time. I was also apprehensive that our analytical discussion on this movie would be our last. As film number ten on The List, and, as things currently stood in our relationship, it could be the last film we *ever* saw together.

We were acting as though everything was the same – larking around, having sex, sprawling on Mac's bed, eating grapes and cheese and biscuits – but things hadn't been right since the BFI trip. I was struggling with trying to adjust to my new version of Mac – a romantic hero tarnished, to me, around the edges. Charismatic, fabulous, sexy as hell, yes, but also a man with anxieties: twitchy when not in his safe kingdom of campus; haunted by a dead brother he did not save; afraid of discovery; fallible. He was not the undented knight in shining armour I had imagined him to be and I didn't know if I could adjust to the new image in my viewfinder. I kept wanting to wipe the lens with a soft cloth, to clear all the fog that had clouded it, or to give it a shake, like a snow globe, and restore him.

I looked at him, and I shunted up the sofa of two chairs pushed together and flanked the side of my body to his. I wedged my chin in the soft cotton where his armpit met his chest and stretched my arm across him. I realized, as Richard Gere pulled up to the kerb in Stuckey's sports car, I was gripping Mac's biceps on the other side.

I ungripped my hand and sat up. I really needed to *loosen* up, I thought, so I giggled at all the funny bits, shouted, 'Yes!' at Julia's rebuff to the snooty shop assistants, sang along badly to 'It Must Have Been Love' (trying to ignore the bit about it being 'over now', in the context of Mac and me) and shed a secret tear at that disgustingly satisfying fairy-tale ending, which I disguised by rubbing at my face and pretending I had an itch.

'What do you think?' Mac asked me, at the end. He hadn't been fooled by the itch; he had just pulled me in closer to him, until the beating of his heart was louder than my own silly romantic notions and the feeling he wasn't quite the man I thought he was.

I think we're on shaky ground, is what I wanted to answer. *I think we're in trouble.* But what I said, into his chest, was, 'Well, there are two sides to it.' My voice was all muffled so I shifted upright again. 'On the one hand, it's a conventional Hollywood story of a *tart with a heart* rescued by a rich man. On the other, Vivian completely calls the shots. She's feisty, she's independent, she dictates the conditions of her rescue and it has to be on her terms. And the whole "she says which men and how much she charges" business. All that.'

'Yes, I agree,' said Mac. His legs were still stretched out in front of him, in chinos. 'There are totally two sides to it. So, do you think Richard Gere was a worthy partner for her? Did he deserve the spirited and beautiful Vivian?' He looked at me. 'It got to you, didn't it? The fairy-tale ending? It gets to *me*.'

'Yes,' I said. 'Bloody Richard Gere, again! What a sucker I am! Ugh! I kind of hate myself for it!'

'That's Hollywood for you!' laughed Mac and, despite myself, I realized how much I still wanted that laugh in my life. How much I still wanted Mac.

'Well, I *do* hate myself.' But I couldn't help it, could I? Not now I had watched this movie with Mac. 'And in answer to your question, yes, he does deserve her and I think it's because he's flawed . . . *The flawed hero. Discuss . . .*' Now I understood. I paused for an instant, thought about it. 'His insecurities, the whole father thing . . . Isn't everyone flawed?' I asked, looking carefully at those pale eyes with the pistachio flecks, under rimless glasses. Of *course* we were. Mac was flawed and I was too. I was selfish, a brat, unapologetic, unfeeling, expecting everything to be picture-perfect when there was no way it could be . . . Nobody was perfect, least of all me, but Mac *loved* me. What was the difficulty in loving him back if he was a dented knight, a tarnished hero? As Vivian – and Becky and I – said, he could rescue me and I could *reciprocate*.

'*You're* not,' he said, 'you're just perfect.'

He was wrong, but that he believed so was good enough. I didn't need to shake the snow globe or wipe the lens to get a better picture. Weren't the flawed heroes always the best?

'What's so funny?' asked Mac softly. I realized I had a huge grin on my face, that I was giggling a little to myself.

256

'Nothing,' I said. 'Richard Gere, that's all.'

We could do this. We had the dreadful summer holidays to get through, then I would be back in halls on campus for the third year and everything would be OK. We wouldn't go to London; I wouldn't make him take me to restaurants or to that stupid pool. We could stay in our bubble on campus for another whole year, and after that, who knew? But I knew for certain my future would have Mac in it. I simply couldn't visualize it without him.

'I wonder what happened afterwards,' I said, happily stroking Mac's knee through his creased chinos. 'After Edward rescued Vivian and *she* rescued *him*. Did they live happily ever after or did her past come back and haunt her? I wonder what Vivian's life was like after the film ended.'

'*Not again*.' Mac smiled. 'You always want to know what happens after the happy ever after!'

I did, and I had more people on my list to wonder about now: Mayo and Paula, Ilsa and Laszlo, Ben and Elaine, Vicki Lester . . . Jack Lemmon and his beau at the end of *Some Like It Hot* . . . 'And I think Vivian's life turned out to be just brilliant,' said Mac. 'As will yours. You're going to have the best life.' He pulled me back down to his chest; stroked the curls at the back of my hair as I buried my face in the cotton of his shirt. 'The best and most brilliant life. Make sure you do, Ardie. Make sure you go out there and have the best time, the best career, the best of everything. Be the best friend. The best lover. The best mother. The best of everything.' *Go out there? Make sure you do, Ardie?* He didn't see himself in that life, then? I'd be on my own? 'I don't believe in a whole lot in this world, but I believe in you. Life can be harsh. It doesn't always have a happy ending, but go out and be *brilliant*.'

I thought Mac believed in the magic of the movies, the finite Hollywood ending. But I also knew what he was saying was true – there were some things that weren't magical, or

257

turned out the way you wanted. Sometimes a pond in the milky light of the moon was just a pond, and a deadly one, too, in the shade of a summer's day. Sometimes a cherry was just a cherry. And sometimes the hero does not swoop into the factory at the end and carry you away to a better life. Sometimes he's not even quite the hero you want him to be . . .

'Do you really believe in me?' I asked, raising my head a little. 'Do you really believe I'm going to have the best life?'

'Yes I do, I really believe that. You've got it all, Ardie. You've got everything you'll ever need.'

'You sound like you won't *be* there. In this best life. Please don't tell me I'll have a bigger love than you, again.'

'You will.'

And he said it so gently I was filled with sorrow. I lay in his arms, my head on his shoulder, and curled my legs up on to his lap like a child.

The next morning I crept out of Mac's flat early. After the screening we'd had a restorative night, fuelled by my own purpose, that was, to restore our relationship to what it had been: lots of wine, lots of sex, lots of laughing until our faces ached, some chocolate cake, and at one point, naked, me putting on Mac's cowboy boots, just because it was funny. At 5 a.m. we'd lain in bed entwined like tree roots, listening to the birds chirping outside Mac's window as they alighted on the branch, tapped giddily on the glass then skittered off again.

I'd decided with relief to simply love Mac again in the here and now, to not worry about my future as *he* clearly wasn't; to put aside fears of what would happen to *us* after our shifting, gossamer-thin but sheeny bubble of a happy-ever-after. I was happy just to love him again, be in his company, learn from him and embrace all that he was. Everything felt wonderful.

Mac said he'd be busy for the rest of the day: he had back-to-back seminars, an appraisal with the faculty head and tonight he had to mark a million essays on Avant Garde Cinema. He was dusting his living room as I left; I laughed at him being all domesticated, said it made him look sexy and I would love to see him doing it naked, under a frilly apron. I almost didn't leave, but Mac shooed me away, laughing, with his duster.

I would spend the rest of my day productively, too. Go back to the Slug House, wash my sheets at the local launderette, tidy my hideously messy room, finish my George Eliot essay, make a start on the better, more shiny person Mac said I was going to turn out to be. Although I was already pretty perfect, as he had said that too.

First I had to walk to the centre of campus to get some money out and I was actually whistling – something by Kylie Minogue – as I headed to the courtyard with the little cluster of banks and cash machines, the campus launderette I had used in the first year and the tiny supermarket visited for exam-writing munchies and extortionate back-up supplies when a trek to Sainsbury's was too much for hungover bones. I got out ten pounds from the NatWest cashpoint and decided to nip into the supermarket for a packet of chocolate digestives. I held open the door for the person coming out. She took her time coming through, encumbered as she was by a straining carrier bag dangling from each hand, a bunch of flowers shoved under one arm and a very noticeable pregnancy.

I stopped. I stared. A pregnant woman was a rarity on campus; this was my first ever sighting of one. The woman had long straight blonde hair in an Alice band. She was wearing a pale denim shirt dress, loose over her bump, and under it her legs were pale and laced up to the calves with Roman-style sandals. She had a tight smile, wide-set blue or possibly green eyes, and an aquiline nose with the shadow of a line across it, like Adam Ant's make-up or the marking of a tiger.

It was Helen.

NOW

Chapter 22

It's really hot on the ward this evening; someone must have turned up the radiators. I immediately shrug off my charity-shop Burberry, flop it over my arm and push up the sleeves of my cream Diane-Keaton-in-*Something's-Gotta-Give* roll neck. A man at the nurses' station standing in front of James and me drags his long black puffa coat further round him as he loiters at the visitors' book. He rakes a finger through shaggy, curly hair, then tugs on the front of it as though trying to straighten it out.

We're waiting to use the anti-bac, but the man is in the way. I want to wash my hands of the long, cathartic journey and go in and sit down on my chair so I can take a breath, get my head round Perrie's email. Where is Lloyd? How did she find him? Has she actually told him his father is in hospital? I'm a little annoyed, but not surprised by her propensity for the enigmatically dramatic. She has become quite a character, in my mind. With that fringe and that cardigan. I had said as much to James as we were buzzed in.

'She's a drama llama,' I'd said. 'Fancy just sending *that*! *I've found him*. Didn't she have time to write anything else?' I'd rolled my eyes, but at the same time I was excited. *She'd found him*. She'd found Lloyd!

'Our Perrie is very mysterious indeed,' James had replied, like an elderly scholar.

'Cryptic!' I'd qualified, but I couldn't wait to hear more. I'd bashed an email back to Perrie on the way into the hospital – *Where is he?* – and I keep checking my phone to see if there's a response.

The man in front of us is now doing his hands carefully and way, *way* too slowly at the wall-mounted dispenser. His coat is almost down to his ankles but his ankles are bare and tanned; one them has a multicoloured tweedy band wound round it. He's wearing very white, new-looking trainers. His thick head of blonde hair is wavy and sun-streaked and when he turns his head slightly to one side I see that he is bearded – a young Father Christmas.

'Oh, hi, you two!' It's Fran, bustling up to the desk. Her hair is in a little blonde-tipped topknot today so she resembles Pebbles from *The Flintstones*. 'You've arrived together, tonight!'

'We've been to the Midlands,' I say.

'Oh, right. Anything nice?' She looks excited.

'Work,' I say, smiling at James.

The man finally finishes doing his hands. He shoves them in his pockets and looks around him as though he is lost.

'Can I help you?' Fran asks him, as I turn to use the dispenser. 'Who are you visiting?'

'Mac Bartley-Thomas,' says the man, from behind me. 'I'm his son.'

My heart takes a sideways lurch, like a kettlebell in one of those God-awful classes I used to take when Christian accused me of getting fat. I turn around. 'You're Lloyd?' I ask. I horrify myself by clutching at his arm with a still sticky hand and he looks rightly horrified, too.

'Yes, I'm Lloyd,' he says, now adding puzzlement and who-the-hell-are-*you* to his glare. He takes his hands from both pockets but makes no move to shake either mine or James's, who is standing like a sentry and staring at us both.

'I'm a friend of Mac's,' I say. 'I've been visiting him almost every day. Did Perrie contact you?'

'Perrie Turque.' He nods and I notice he has a slight Australian accent. 'Turque' goes up at the end. 'That woman's quite the detective.' Actually, that was me, at least initially, I want to say, though I know I won't get credit for this historic reunion, with the forthright Ms Turque in the picture. How come she's only just emailed me when he is already here?

'Where's Dad?' Lloyd's eyes are scanning the beds in the ward one by one, left to right.

'Over there,' I say, 'in the middle.' Lloyd's eyes travel along the beds and he starts when they alight on Mac. I try to see Mac in him. Lloyd would be late twenties, wouldn't he? Is that right? Whatever, he looks older. Weathered. Has he just flown in from *Australia*? If so, Perrie must have found him at least twenty-four hours ago.

'Have you flown in from Australia?' I ask.

'Yeah, the Whitsundays.' Again his voice rises at the end but his words mean nothing to me. 'They're *islands*? I run a scuba diving *school*?'

'I know,' I say. 'Perrie said.' Lloyd is looking at me oddly; it's making me feel really uneasy. 'This is James.'

'And what's your name?' The sentry is ignored. No handshake is offered. Lloyd's eyes, periwinkle blue like Mac's, are lasers on me above his bleached beard and his freckled nose.

'I'm Arden.'

Lloyd's blue eyes with their fan of crinkly ripples at the corners widen. It's hard to tell how he is feeling. He looks vindicated, somehow, indignant, slightly *repulsed*. Does he know about me? Does he know who I am? I feel all panicky, a bit faint. His eyes are asking so many questions I can't process them all. Oh God, I think he *knows*.

He starts walking towards Mac's bed. James and I fall into step with him.

'It's fantastic, really fantastic. I didn't know *what* would happen. We've just travelled back from the Midlands. I'm so glad you've come.' I am talking utter nonsense, a defence of mine that has never achieved very much. At the same time I'm frantically wondering if Perrie mentioned my name to Lloyd, but why his look of revulsion? He can't know, can he?

He just walks, his expression in profile stern yet unfathomable. We are at the bed now. Mac is fast asleep, his hair flopped above a pale face and parted lips. Lloyd goes and sits down by his side, on my brown chair. James and I stay back. We don't need to gatecrash the moment when Mac opens his eyes and sees his son. I feel we shouldn't be witnessing it at all. But we can't exactly turn and leave so we hang back awkwardly – shuffling supporting cast in a silent movie, widening our eyes and rolling our lips in at each other.

Lloyd places his hand on Mac's, which is palm down on the bed, fingers splayed.

'Dad?'

Nothing happens. Mac is dreaming, I think. There's a rapid flickering under his eyelids. He's dreaming of the movies, not knowing a cinematic moment of his own is about to take place, if he would just open his eyes.

'Dad?'

The flickering stops. Very slowly, and like his body is fighting against it happening, Mac opens his eyes. Lloyd is smiling uncertainly at him and Mac's eyes are widening and his mouth forms the shape of a smile, in return, and he is crying silent tears which course down his face. Lloyd leans down towards his father. His enormous coat is restrictive and it creaks as he bends forward to place his hands on Mac's upper arms; he is shiny creaking polyester to Mac's laundered cotton. Lloyd moves his hands to Mac's shoulders; he rests them there as he looks into Mac's face. Mac is just smiling, smiling; his arms still down by his sides and his fingers flickering, like they are skating across piano keys.

Several seconds pass – fleeting, endless – and Mac's tears continue to run their silent river down colourless cheeks.

Lloyd's face is all red when he straightens up, squeaking in that coat like an unoiled door. He gets a tissue from the box on the side of the bed and dabs it under Mac's eyes. It has been a moment, one of those rare ones in life that really, really matter. I want to cry for the second time today – for Mac, for me and for *my* dad, again – but resist; I can't go there and I can't over-egg someone else's pudding. Nobody wants my saccharine tears over someone else's drama. It's not like *Imitation of Life*, that weepie film Mac had talked about all those years ago, a melodrama for others to weep over; this is Mac's life. Love is pinned and hangs on moments like this.

We pause, held in an awkward tableau. Lloyd and Mac now just staring at each other; James and I are standing back like a couple of incidental pawns in a nothing-to-do-with-us chess game.

Lloyd beckons us over to them with his index finger. It has a gold signet ring on it.

'Dad and I haven't seen each other for a very long time,' he says, as we arrive at Mac's bed.

Mac – looking utterly exhausted by it all – is tearing up again, his blue eyes flecked pink where there once was pistachio. This time I pull a tissue from the box and he blinks as I gently blot his eyes with it. I wonder exactly how many years it has been, father and son?

Lloyd pulls two chairs over from the next bed, one in each hand, scraping them noisily along the floor. He gestures for James and me to sit down so we do, although I feel we should really go. I only sit for a few seconds.

'I'll go to the coffee machine,' I say, hoiking my bag on to my shoulder. 'I might go to the café as well, get some cake. Do you want to come, James?'

'No, I'm OK here,' James says. He has his legs stretched

out in front of him, probably resting after the long drive. I can see why he's reluctant to get up, but surely he must want to leave Mac and Lloyd to it?

'Really?'

'OK, I'll come.'

We wander to the café along the yellow corridors.

'Quite something,' he says. 'A father-and-son reunion.' I wonder how James feels about it, considering his own history – that he never saw his father again after he and his brother left with their mum in the middle of the night. I still can't think about *mine* – too difficult, today – but I realize, with a jolt, that I'll never see my *mother* again, after the decision I made in James's car. I consider this brand-new fact, hold it up to the light in my mind. It looks pretty good, actually. I don't think it will ever make me cry.

'It was lovely,' I agree. Mac has no idea I was responsible, but I have given him his movie moment, from my metaphorical director's chair, and I'm *proud* of myself – another brand-new fact, or at least one I haven't seen around for a while.

We buy cake, a hot chocolate, a tea. Something for Lloyd (I'm still worrying about his indignant eyes), in a paper bag – the default combo of a sticky bun and a milky coffee in a lidded Styrofoam cup.

'Oh heck, I forgot to turn off my phone; someone's calling me,' says James, as we trail away from the counter with our stash. We deposit everything hurriedly on a table and he pulls his phone from his jacket pocket. 'Hello?

'Urgent estate agent wankery,' he says, with a handsome grimace, after the call has ended, a deal which might fall through unless he legs it to a house half an hour away and placates a high-maintenance woman who carries a tweed-wearing dachshund puppy in her handbag – and he dashes from the café saying he hopes to see me tomorrow, at visiting, and thanks me for my company today.

'You're welcome,' I call after him. *And thank you*, I add silently to myself.

I sit at the table; I eat half of my cake and drink my tea. Lloyd walks in, glancing around him. He's still got his coat on.

'Oh,' I say, looking up. 'I was going to bring you a coffee.'

'It's all right. Dad's really sleepy, after all the excitement. I thought I'd come and find you.' He sits down in James's vacated chair. 'I won't beat about the *bush*?' he says, fixing those blue eyes on me. His beard is ridiculous, I think. It's not even hipster but full-on Grizzly Adams. 'I know who you are.'

'Oh?' I say. I open the paper bag and put the milky coffee and the sticky bun on the table.

'I know Dad had an affair with you, at Warwick, when Mum was pregnant with me, and before.'

'Oh.' I'm shaking a little, suddenly. All my historic guilt about Mac and Helen and Helen's pregnancy floods back to me and threatens to knock me off my chair.

'It is you, isn't it? You used to be that girl.'

I don't like his crinkly eyes and his silly beard. I don't like the way he is looking at me, like I'm responsible for all the ills in this world. 'Yes, I did,' I say. Well, I can hardly deny it. Why else would I be visiting Mac if I wasn't *that girl*? 'Sorry.' My 'sorry' is as weak as my tea, and I realize I sound a bit surly. Something about this man is making me layer defiance on top of guilt, and I wonder just how badly Lloyd needed to come and have his say that he left the bedside of his just-rediscovered father, sleepy or not.

'You were the first but you weren't the last,' he says. I know this, of course: Mac had told me he hadn't had an affair before me; Perrie had told me he'd had loads after. If Lloyd is trying to shock me with this revelation he can shock elsewhere. I'm still shaking, though; this is pretty awful, being confronted by your former lover's son, after nearly thirty years. The son of the woman that lover betrayed. The innocent victim of your crime. It might be something dramas are made of, but it's *not* a particularly great movie moment for me, and the remorse bubbles up again. 'Dad had affairs up until I was seventeen. I don't know why, to tell the truth. He and Mum seemed fairly happy on the surface. As people can be.' He sips at his coffee, through one of those annoying little holes in the lid. 'I found out about *you* just after he and Mum got divorced.' *Divorced* . . . I thought so. That had to be the only outcome for Mac and Helen, didn't it? I feel pleased Helen got the chance to make a new life for herself, after me, and after all Mac's affairs. I imagine her living happily alone in a garret somewhere, an elegant long grey plait over one shoulder, frowning over a complicated thesis. The tiger woman.

'I'm sorry,' I say again, with a bit more feeling. I *want* a happy ending for Helen; she deserves one. Lloyd ignores me.

'I was helping Dad sort out the attic and amongst his Warwick photos I found one of you and him, in his bed, inside a copy of that book he wrote, *The Language of Celluloid*. I asked him who you were and when it was, and he told me about you . . . He was caught out at first, uneasy, but then he sounded proud about it – all misty-eyed and nostalgic – and I hated him for being like that. "*Arden* . . ." he kept saying, like he couldn't help himself . . . I asked him why he had ended it with you and he told me it was because of me. Because I was coming. I don't know if that's the truth.'

Well, the truth is it was because I *found out* about you, I think. But his father is already not coming across very well – nor me, obviously – so I leave it there.

'I guess he thought I could handle it because I was seventeen but the truth is I couldn't. He made it sound as though I was the saviour of the marriage, but I knew that wasn't right because I knew about all the other affairs, after you. He thought he'd covered them up for all of those years but I knew, and so did Mum. All that stuff about them drifting apart, divorcing "amicably" was nonsense. He'd been playing around for years, starting with you.'

'Starting with me,' I repeat. I feel sick. 'Did Helen . . . did your mum know about me?'

'No, and I didn't tell her. Why make things worse?'

'No,' I reply, at a loss at what else to say. Helen knew about all the other affairs but she never knew about me. She was saved the worst of the pain.

Lloyd sighs, almost a huff. 'Look, my mum's a fantastic woman. She's a fantastic *mother*, kind, clever . . . I don't know what he was doing with you, or anyone else . . .' Well, I'm not going to spell it out for him . . . 'All wrapped up in ego, probably, knowing Dad.' Yes, I could believe that. Mac liked to be adored, that was pretty much gospel. But he *had* adored me; that was history. 'I hated my dad for what he'd done. I couldn't see him after that, after finding out about you. The fact he was with someone when Mum was actually *pregnant* with me was just too much, after everything else I knew. I was pretty angry. After seeing that photo of you and Dad I went travelling and never came back. Well, I came back for a while, ran a bar in London, but I never told him – though I think he found out, after I'd moved on. I just kept moving on. Not talking to Dad just became a part of being away, my new life. He just didn't feature and that was OK by me. It was so easy not to think about him. To just let the time drip on and on without making contact.'

How awful for Mac, I think, whatever he'd done, to have his boy gradually slip further and further away from him. I wonder if it was from this moment – the moment Lloyd left him – that Mac's light began to dim; that he started to slowly fade, to lose his charisma, his 'Macness' . . .

'I'm sorry,' I say – again – aware I'm beginning to sound

how I was with Christian. Always apologizing. I'm desperate to change the subject but the subject is too big. Mac was sleeping with someone else when his wife was pregnant. It's pretty huge; I felt it when I *discovered* it, twenty-eight years ago. I have no mitigating circumstances, not for the son of my lover, except that Mac and I loved each other and it was everything to us. Was it an ego thing? Did that play a part for *both* of us, at the start? I was in need of validation, to have my presence in the world acknowledged and revered in a way my parents never could. In Mac's case, was there simply too *much* of him to confine to one person, too much Macness to be admired and adored for only one relationship to satisfy? Was kind, confident Helen – his intellectual equal, his opposite bookend on the academia bookshelf – up on her own pedestal, out there somewhere, and Mac needed someone in his thrall? Possibly. I was definitely that *someone*. Did we need each other in a way we couldn't even articulate?

'Have you been in touch with him all along?'

'No,' I say. 'It was completely accidental, me finding him here.'

'How come?'

'Well,' I say, 'I was visiting someone else and Mac was here.'

'A happy coincidence,' says Lloyd sarcastically.

'Something like that.' I really want to go back to the ward now.

'How did Perrie find *you*?' I ask him. There, a subject change . . .

'Ah,' he says, with a smile that looks a little like Mac's. Good, he's happy to change the subject, but I worry he will return to it. That he isn't done. 'Her network of spies. She's always had them. The backpacking, jet-setting community. She put out her long feelers, I guess, and she somehow found me, in my tiny dive school, on the north shore of a tiny island in the Whitsundays.' He sounds so proud. He flashes me a bigger

269

smile and I think, Oh God, there's Mac, and I wonder if Perrie's feelers had ever tried to find Lloyd before, for Mac – his literal water baby. 'She called me and told me about Dad, about the accident. It was the day before yesterday, I think, my time frame is screwed.'

Perrie's obviously was too. Or she just forgot to tell me. 'And you dropped everything and came back?'

'Yes, pretty much, despite the fact I was in the middle of running a course. I got on a plane as soon as I could, after a lot of rearranging and logistics. Shall we go back to the ward?' he says, standing up and abandoning his half-finished coffee and untouched bun. 'I just wanted to tell you I know who you are. Put you in the picture, as they say. There's no point in me pretending.'

'No,' I say – I would add, *I appreciate it*, but I don't. We walk back to the ward without speaking. As we sit down on two chairs at the same side of Mac's bed, where he lies awake and unblinking, Lloyd pulls an envelope from his coat pocket.

'Dad, look, here are your grandchildren.' I'm glad he is focusing on the future now, not the past. Showing his dad his legacy. There are four grandchildren, from what I can make out from the photos, all with unusual names – Lloyd doesn't let me see. Mac's face lights up as he sees their faces, as much as it can, and I smile as I am so, so happy for him, but – despite me trying to hang on to it – my heart can't help but break at the thought that *my* father's face will never light up again at the sight of Julian, his only grandson. I let tears fill my eyes and I'm reminded of my first night on Ward 10, when I witnessed the patients with their children, and their grandchildren – families whole and not ripped apart. Oh dear, I think, shaking my head to banish my tears; this is turning out to be quite the emotional rollercoaster of a day for me, one I had no idea of when I strapped myself into James's car this morning. I'm glad he's not here to see me making an exhibition of myself.

Lloyd goes through the photographs twice; at the end he flicks the stack of them like it's a flicker book from the pre-dawn days of cinema, those ones with the stick people. Mac will appreciate that, I think, although he looks tired. Then Lloyd puts the photos back in his wallet and Mac immediately closes his eyes. My tears now gone, I am just wondering why Lloyd has come back, considering everything, considering how far he was from his father, considering he had decided to never talk to him again, when Lloyd leans towards me and says, in an almost inaudible whisper, 'I've spent a long time trying to distance myself from him. Moving to Australia was about as far away as I could get. Yet here I am. The pull of family; it always brings you back eventually. It's really quite annoying, actually, but there you go.'

He shrugs those shiny black padded shoulders and gives me another smile and he looks just like Mac again. They both ripped their family apart – Mac and Lloyd – I hope their reunion now is not too late to heal something for each of them. Funny, I think, how the day they reunited is the day my mother and I severed for good, but Lloyd is *not* quite right – the pull of family doesn't always bring you back; sometimes, it releases you, like a smooth pebble from a catapult.

'Is there a chance he'll get out of this?' Lloyd asks.

He makes it sound like a funk, like something self-inflicted almost. Or a tunnel Mac simply has to walk through to reach the other side.

'I don't know. You'll have to ask the nurses.'

'And the not-being-able-to-speak thing?'

'No one seems to know, I'm afraid. How long are you back for?'

'A week or so. I'm staying with a mate. On their sofa. No biggie.'

He looks older, but he is young for his age, I decide. A kind

271

of eternal teenager. I bet he still rides a skateboard and surfs as well as scuba dives. 'OK, and then you'll just go back?'

The whispering is becoming almost comedic now. 'I live in Oz, my wife and kids are there. I have to go back.' I wonder how long Mac will be in hospital. It's been over three weeks now – how many more, or will it be months? Will they move him somewhere else? Will it be close by so I can still visit? Will he get better and walk out of here before that happens?

Lloyd stands up. 'I'm going to go now,' he says, in a normal voice. 'I'll be back tomorrow. Bye, Dad,' he shouts, spoiling it.

Mac's eyes slowly open and Lloyd leaves the ward, a rustling caterpillar in that bloody coat.

I sit back down on my chair.

'Good, eh?' I smile, taking Mac's hand and giving it a gentle squeeze.

A single tear slips out of the corner of his eye and travels down the side of his face to a slightly stubbly jaw. I hope the nurses will give him a shave again tomorrow. I grab a tissue and catch the tear.

'He says he'll come back tomorrow. There's a few of us now, eh? We'll have to queue up. You still want me to come?' I am doubtful, suddenly. Does Mac want me coming to see him every day? Does he care if I am here or not? Has he just been happy to see a friendly face, *any* friendly face? Has he just been mentioning the movies because he *could*, because it is the most economical way to communicate with me, in a fit of convenient nostalgia? The girl he once loved. *Once.* Perhaps that's all it is; I have been proved unlovable time and time again by Christian, after all. Mac's simply in *Remembrance of Things Past* mode, like Proust and the bloody madeleines, that's all. My self-doubt attacks me with beady claws, ripping at any feeling I have a right to be here. How easy it is to slip back.

'Do you still want me to come?' I ask him again.

Mac looks at me and his dry lips part into a smile. It takes a long time for him to get his words out but when he does they mean everything.

'Depends on the pie.'

THEN

Chapter 23: The Way We Were

It was my favourite moment in *The Way We Were*, the moment Katie (Barbra Streisand) gets an unexpected call from the delicious Hubbell (Robert Redford), at work – after not hearing from him for ages – asking her if he can stay on her couch for the night. Having told Hubbell to let himself in, she frantically shops for dinner and wine and flowers and treats for an evening in together – because she is utterly in love with him – but as she approaches her apartment he is walking down the road away from it, his hands in his pockets. She calls him, dashes across the street; protests, gabbling, her words tumbling over one another – that he absolutely *can't* go as she has bought all this stuff: the steaks, the baked potatoes, the salad, the pie . . . There is a wonderful pause and Hubbell's eyes flick from left to right and he looks down at the bags and back up to Katie and he asks her what kind of pie it is.

I loved that scene. I loved the movie. Mac said he'd seen *The Way We Were* a million times – it was not on The List; he wasn't planning to teach it on his course – but *I* said he'd never seen it with *me*. I put it on my *own* list. As we watched it, on video in Mac's bedroom, me with my legs across his and he with his glasses on, annoyingly marking some essays while looking up for all the good bits, I pondered if the movies Mac and I watched made our affair seem more romantic. If I was living through them, seeing myself in them, taking the lead role in our own love story, was that making things more intense? Or was it our *affair* that made the movies we saw together more meaningful; infusing them with reflected passion and the feeling they had been created just for us? It was hard to tell.

The Way We Were was just heaven. As we watched, I was pretty much open-mouthed, throughout, at Robert Redford's beauty. I mean, Mac was beautiful, in his own way, but then there's *subliminal*. In his white uniform, drunk and asleep at the end of that bar, Hubbell was just irresistible; you couldn't take your eyes off him – anyone watching felt the same as Katie, surely? I'd seen this film with my mother who had declared it a crock of shit. She was jealous because she'd never experienced anything like it – not in her marriage or any of her affairs. That real kind of love, that beauty, that truth. All her encounters were grubby and fleeting, or disappointing to her, in the case of my dad. They were her searching for an illusion. Searching for a self that didn't exist.

Hubbell could never disappoint anyone, that's the *point* of him. To me, anyway. When Hubbell asks her about the pie, I loved how Katie is not afraid to show her desperation, how happy she is he'll stay and have dinner with her, signalled by a cheeky, almost childish, smile and a kind of ecstatic bob, in the street – her arms full of flowers and grocery bags. Mac looked up for that bit and we both smiled. After the movie finished I asked him if he was going to stop marking essays now and could we go out somewhere, maybe, and he looked at me lazily and said, 'Depends on the pie.'

Was it sometime before London, sometime after the trip to the pool, when Mac and I saw *The Way We Were*? It was definitely when things were as romantic between us as they were between Katie and Hubbell, at least at the beginning of the movie. I didn't like the last scene – I didn't like that she couldn't have Hubbell, in the end. That they weren't right, that their relationship was doomed from the start. I wanted a happy ending, but sometimes people don't get one.

Mac and I didn't. After I saw Helen coming out of the supermarket I went in and, on devastated automatic pilot, where I kept dropping my purse and almost knocked over a half-hearted pyramid display of kidney beans, bought chocolate digestives, a large pack of salt and vinegar crisps and a giant, much-needed bottle of hock. I walked like a zombie to the hitching point, my head down, praying I wouldn't see anyone I knew. Someone I knew picked me up in a green car. I actually laughed at some of their jokes; I pretended to enjoy their prog rock mix tape. I made it home to the Slug House. Becky wasn't there, but the other girls were in the fire-hazard kitchen, burning meatballs in a wok. I went straight to my room and sat with the door closed all day, until the hock was gone. I alternated between swigging straight from the bottle and lying on my bed staring at the ceiling.

At 7 p.m. I put on some bright red lipstick and my jeans shorts, hitched back to campus and headed to the students' union where I downed three snakebites and black and flailed around on the dance floor to the Communards. 'Don't Leave Me This Way', Jimmy Somerville sang, he couldn't survive otherwise, you know, and I realized I couldn't either, but this was the way I was being left by Mac. Because of a pregnant Helen with a tight smile and Roman sandals.

Emotions got the better of me. I made it to the ladies' loos and sobbed wretchedly in a cubicle with trails of loo roll criss-crossing the floor. I couldn't compete with this; Helen being pregnant was insurmountable. She had Mac's child growing inside her; *my* insides had been viciously ripped from me and thrown to the ground. I was empty, I was desolate; I was abandoned. I had lost him. I had lost Mac.

I sobbed and remembered another line I had adored from

The Way We Were. It was an entreaty, from Barbra Streisand to Robert Redford, something like Hubbell never finding anyone as good as Katie, who would believe in him and love him as much as she did. It had been true for me and Mac. I had never believed in someone so much or loved someone so much, and he felt the same way about me. He'd told me so, hadn't he? He'd told me only *last night* he believed in me; in that London club he'd told me he loved me and he'd never felt this way about anyone before. So why, *why* did Helen, pregnant fucking *Helen*, have to come along and spoil everything?

I didn't care that one of the white tissue trails was gleefully clinging to the back of my plimsoll as I staggered out, tears still wet on my cheeks, pain pulsating through my body. When someone laughingly pointed out my trailing glory to me – a blurry looming balloon with crescent-thin eyebrows and brown lip liner – I nearly punched them in the face. What did it matter? What did anything matter? It was over. It was all over. No more storms in a white bed, dodging cracker crumbs and listening to the branch at the window – *tap tap tap* – no more screening room and black-and-white movies and stars long dead. No more cowboy music and delicious Mac–Arden banter that made my heart soar like a bird. I didn't want a Bigger Love, to go on 'out there' to live my brilliant, fabulous future. Like Mac, I wanted to be institutionalized, in the four walls of his room and preferably for ever. I didn't *want* a future if he wasn't in it. I didn't want anything except him and going back to the way we were.

I lurched outside into the sticky air and headed, like a homing pigeon, to Mac's room. I knew *she* might be there but I didn't care. She should not have come here! To our place! But as I swayed round the last corner to Mac's building, he was coming down the little path from it. Sauntering almost. Looking so amazingly calm and unbothered by this seismic shift in *everything*, I could have screamed. I could have rushed up to him pulling out my hair and thrashing around and wailing. Instead, I shouted, 'Mac!' and he started and saw me and I marched up to him.

'She's pregnant.'

'Who's pregnant?' Mac took me by the wrist, to steady me, I suppose, but I took it as an infliction, an intent to burn, and shook off his hand.

'Oh, come on! Your *wife*.' I was aware I was spitting my words. I was aware I was drunk and deranged, but I didn't care.

'Oh.' Mac never just said 'oh'. He always said important things, things of weight, funny things. Why the fuck was he saying 'oh'?

'Yes, *oh*. I've seen her. I've seen her and she's pregnant.' I was slurring so badly it was terrible but not as terrible as I felt. I had never felt so bad.

'I'm sorry.' Mac rubbed at his face and looked behind him as though she might suddenly appear. With her tiger stripe and her baby belly. I hated her.

'Don't worry. I'm not going to do anything!' I said. I was not sure what I meant. What *could* I have done? Stormed into his little flat? Surprised her over cheese and biscuits and a glass of weak orange squash? Told her who I was? And then what? She was his wife and she was pregnant; I was just some student Mac was having sex with. 'Will you leave her for me?' I asked, knowing he wouldn't. He was being supplied with his water baby. He was having all those lost children replaced. And he had known about this pregnancy for months but he had never told me.

Mac looked at me, his eyes saying everything and nothing.

'I won't leave her,' said Mac. 'I can't. We've wanted it for so long.'

The 'we' sliced into me like a big, steel, glittering knife. 'Big of you,' I slurred.

'It's a boy,' said Mac, as if that would make a difference to

278

me. What would *I* care? 'We went for a private scan. We've been having lots of scans, actually. The baby is a boy.'

'Wonderful,' I said. 'Congratulations.' He was having his lost boy come back to him at last, his little brother, almost. Joy, finally. 'Were you *ever* going to leave her for me?'

'You never asked me to.' He grooved a finger at his forehead, through his fringe. Why was he being so pathetic? So un-Mac? Where was my brilliant, charismatic man? My firebrand?

'Of course I didn't!' I cried. 'I didn't care about *her*! She was no threat to me!' I was the vampy bit on the side, I thought, the one with all the power – full to the brim with it; she barely crossed my mind. That's why he liked me, because while I was demanding everything of him I asked for nothing. 'Were you going to tell me? About the baby?'

'I was stalling.' He attempted a grin. He looked sheepish, like a little boy. It was a look of his I'd loved so often. Now it made me want to knock him clean to the floor, like I was one of his fucking cowboy heroes in a fucking saloon bar – doors swinging, chairs flying, pistols smoking. 'I didn't want to; I didn't want us to end.'

'You said you loved me.' I hated him. Now I knew he was slipping away I loved him more than ever.

'Oh God, Arden, I do love you. I love you, Arden.' He tried to take both my hands; I slapped his away with force, hoping it stung like hell. 'I'm sorry she's here, I'm sorry you've seen her.'

'Because otherwise you would have got away with it?' He was a moron. He was a fucking joke. He was a liar and an utter, utter coward.

'No, I'm just sorry. It's been killing me, all this lying. How I've betrayed Helen, how I've loved you so much but couldn't tell you. How I've had to keep everything going.'

'*Keep everything going?* What, like spinning plates? I'm not a *plate*, Mac!'

'Could you please keep your voice down?'

'Why? Because *she* might hear?' I raise it even louder. 'I could just go into your flat and tell her, you know. There's nothing stopping me.'

'Don't do that,' said Mac calmly. 'And you're not a plate.' He smiled slowly at me, like he always did when I made a brilliant joke or said something clever, and that smile broke me into a million pieces. 'You're not a plate.'

'Brilliant,' I muttered. 'So what am I, then?'

'I love you,' said Mac, as though that explained everything in the universe and beyond.

'Love is not enough,' I said. I thought it had been but it wasn't.

'I'm sorry, Arden. You'll never know how sorry I am. I wanted everything. I needed you. I . . .' He paused. 'Look, there's something else you should know.'

'Something else? What could be more *something* than this?' I was finding it difficult to stand. I wanted to lean on something, lie down. If that staple of the drunken student, the shopping trolley, had been to hand I would have jumped in it and curled up like a baby. No, not a baby. Not a fucking baby.

'The Dean knows about us.' Mac had stepped forward and was holding me now and I was letting him or I would have fallen over, but I hated the feel of his hands on my waist. If I could have done, I would have kicked him off, like a donkey, but I couldn't. I didn't feel well.

'What?' I was finding it hard to focus. Mac's beautiful, treacherous face was swimming before my sickly, devastated eyes.

'The Dean has found out.'

'What? How?'

'He heard.' In my drunken brain I imagined the Dean's shuffling figure, walking sideways and listening at doorways until the swell of whispers was a squall loud enough for him to hear. His beetle belly swelling with indignation.

His forefinger going to the bridge of his nose to hitch his glasses up in an 'I knew it!' manner. Then him marching to his office, wherever the hell that was, and standing angrily at the window like a detective in a film noir, shadows from blinds casting lines across his face. *Mise en scène.* It was everything.

'You mean someone told him?'

'Yes.'

'Who?'

'A student. Jonathan Flemmings.'

'Who the hell's that?'

'Philosophy student. Third year. That's all I know.'

It dawns on me like a forbidding early dusk. The boy in the Smiths T-shirt. I bet it was that weasel. He'd seen us, hadn't he, at the pool? Fuck. How empty would his sad, student life have to be to tell someone about us?

'Well, the Dean can't *do* anything. It's not against the law! It's not even against university rules!' I cried, but I was already anticipating a sea of faces, lining up against the sides of the Arts Centre, or somewhere equally exposing – the local press having been alerted – to stare at me, heads shaking in slow, repulsed motion . . . I was furious some little rat had snitched on us. This, and the pregnant *Helen* had conspired to doom Mac and me – I knew the two truths combined were enough to bring us down and destroy everything.

'I'm staying with Helen,' said Mac, still holding me at the waist. 'I need you to understand that. She's pregnant and I have to stay with her.' The word 'pregnant' was so soul-rippingly gutting it made me attempt a short derisive laugh, but I thought I might be sick. 'I'm so sorry, Arden, but I'm afraid this brings things to a natural end for us.'

A natural end? There was nothing natural about us ending. It was highly unnatural. Jarring, man-made; like a jagged snag of metal scraping against glass. Mac and I weren't something to just peter out, like the end of a frayed piece of string, or a scene in a movie fading to black . . . We were strong, we were everything, there could be no *end*.

'We can't end,' I said, and I knew I sounded absolutely pitiful, but I didn't care. I was full of pity, for myself and for us. This was it – this was the greatest love I would ever know and he didn't want it any more. 'I love you.'

'And I love you. But it has to, Ardie. We have to finish this now.'

I was being locked out. Ejected. Exiled. I had become Alex Forrest in *Fatal Attraction*, the movie that had started all this. My calls would be unanswered, my pleading ignored; I would be forced to metaphorically wait in office receptions – for ever – in a long leather coat.

Like Alex, I erupted. 'This is not a "this"! This is *us*! I hate you for doing this! You were supposed to want me over everything, but you're as boring as everyone else. You're choosing *conformity*. I never thought you would do that! The safe option, respectability . . . *family*. Ugh!' Family sickened me. It always had. I was different, or I was supposed to have been. I didn't want to tie Mac down, have his babies. I just wanted to *be* with him. If there was a wall near enough I would have punched it. I was so frustrated, my blood was boiling like sticky hot tar, about to spill over and make a hot mess everywhere. I knew Mac was willing me to keep my voice down again.

'I have to,' was all he said. That was all he'd got. So much for my charismatic hero. When push came to shove he would give up love for life.

'You're doing a *Casablanca*!' I cried quietly. 'You're giving me up for the greater good.' And I laughed, then, a little hysterically, because it just sounded so ridiculous. 'And how can we stop the feelings we have? We can't just *stop*.'

Mac sighed and ran his fingers through his hair.

'Do you think no one else has felt what we're feeling right now, that no one else has had to put an end to a love affair?

Thousands, millions of people have, and we have to, too. Ardie . . . I—'

'Leave me *alone*!' I wrenched myself free of his consoling grip and lurched away.

'I'm sorry,' he said, one final, bloody time.

'Good*bye*, Mac!'

I was dramatic, I was pathetic; I was a performer playing a part, but I knew I would never know this again. This love. I ran back to the hitching point as I had run home to White-fields so many nights in the first year, but this time I was sobbing my heart out and my legs were not those of a giddy lover, tumbling home after hours of passion and illicit excite-ment, but those of a wretch who had come undone. I slumped in the back of some unknown girl's 2CV and was transported back to Leamington. I staggered in and ignored the line-up of people on the sofa, now eating limp fried egg sandwiches – one of whom was Becky, who asked me what on earth the matter was. She followed me upstairs but I simply told her it was over, it was over, and I shut my door and got into my bed and pulled the duvet high up over my head.

NOW

Chapter 24

We don't exactly have to queue up, but there's quite a merry band of us round Mac's bed tonight – the atmosphere is almost festive, despite the fact it's a rainy Sunday in mid-January and people are not feeling festive at all but cold, miserable, fat and totally fed up at all that winter still to be trudged through.

There's me, of course – where else would I be? James, for once not in suit and tie but a pair of dark blue jeans and a teal lambswool jumper – he does smart casual pretty well. He brings *me* a gift tonight – a packet of Polos and a *Bella* magazine – which finds me surprised and quite touched. Lloyd, on his second visit, seems to have been to the shops and bought more clothes: he is wearing a brand-new bright red sweatshirt and a pair of cargo trousers with a thousand pockets on them. He still hasn't managed socks. Fran is sitting with us, too; she's come in for the last ten minutes of her break and is showing everyone a complicated card trick that looks unlikely to succeed. Hooting with laughter and slapping her own thigh, she has already dropped three cards on the floor.

Mac is sitting up, bolstered on pillows. The doctors have reported that the opposing, positive fifty per cent is taking charge today and he's having what is known in medical terms as a 'very good day'. He is smiling; his left hand managed to form itself into a surprising, half thumbs-up when I came into the ward, and his eyes are bright. 'His lordship's behaving himself,' says Fran, and his bloods are equally well behaved this evening, apparently; I imagine them giving each other a thumbs-up, too. The ward feels . . . happy. It's like it's New Year's Eve again; I feel everyone should have party hats on. The nurses are upbeat; the tea trolley rattles gleefully like it's on a victory tour; cheeks are pink and eyes bright; even the coughs sound pretty merry tonight. Ward 10 is bright and light, free of gloom and foreboding, sickness and dread. With almost Dickensian cheer, there is a roar of laughter from somewhere behind us; next someone will be bringing out a giant roasted goose on a silver platter . . . This is how I'm choosing to see it, anyway; if I want to shine a bright convivial light on Ward 10 then I will.

Julian is also here. My boy. He turned up at home about five o'clock – Sam's on a girls' cinema night out – and I know he was on a Sunday roast dinner-beg but I told him I was coming to St Katherine's and he said he'd come with me, if there was a café. Food overrides everything for him, even the universal dislike of hospitals. He asked who 'this Mac' was, as we walked; I gave him a sunny-as-I-could potted history of the story of Mac and me, aware of a bad light painting us black, up to me yelling drunkenly at Mac outside his flat, that summer's evening, a pregnant *Helen* inside. I tried to give it a comic spin, that final scene, for Julian's benefit, said I had screeched like a banshee, almost had a bucket of water chucked on me from an upstairs window and had fallen head first into a flower bed. Inside, I was dying all over again.

'Wow,' Julian said. 'So he lied to you, carried on seeing you even though his wife was pregnant . . . must be some bloke! I'm *definitely* coming to the hospital, out of curiosity! Why on earth are you visiting him?'

I laughed and then frowned. It's a question I have asked myself many times since my first visit. Why come and visit a man who once betrayed me?

'I admit Mac doesn't come across particularly well in this story,' I said.

'Er, *understatement*!'

I laughed again, although I felt a little sick as I added, 'Nor me.'

'*You* weren't married! Why are you visiting him?' he asked again.

'I'm visiting him because I remember what came before the end of our affair,' I said, 'or I *choose* to. How good it was, the year and a half I was with him, how enveloped it all is in memories of my youth, in the magic of movies, in the promise of myself. You don't have to play the film until the final scene, if you don't want to.' Yes, that's it, I think – stop the movie while things are still amazing. 'He gave me so much – believed in me – so I don't like to think about the end, but what came before. I try to do the same with Grandad.' This is true – I've always tried to imagine my dad pottering in the shed at the bottom of the garden, arranging his ice-cream tubs of nuts and bolts, smoking his roll-up cigarettes, using his set of hand weights to do his biceps curls with; not what he did there at the end. I've failed at this; I have remained haunted. But now Marilyn is gone from my life I will try harder to remember my father as he was and keep him in my memory in relation to *me* and not to her. He deserves it.

His name was William Richard Hall and he was my dad.

'I know you do,' said Julian, sadness glazing his eyes. He was ten years old and bewildered when Dad died, but we got through it. The shock, the emptiness, the swiping away of everything we held certain about life and ourselves – which Christian had already carved a deep and dangerous gorge into. Julian and I can get through anything. I hope he can understand about Mac.

'Mac loved me. And, oh God, you're probably going to be embarrassed by this – sorry! – but I'd forgotten how that feels and what it means. It's been so lovely to be reminded.'

'That *is* cringe,' said Julian with a wide smile, slipping his arm through mine. 'How embarrassing.' He winked at me and then nodded. 'But I understand. I was there, Mum,' he said, looking at me with serious eyes. 'I was there all those years with Christian.'

'I know you were. It's something I think about every single day. What he put you through. What *I* put you through. I'm sorry.' I have said 'sorry' to my boy for Christian so many times.

'It wasn't your fault,' he said, and it is not the first time he's said it, my forgiving, wonderful, generous boy. 'With that kind of man you don't realize they're that kind of man until it's too late. That's sort of the point.'

'I'm still sorry,' I said. I'll *always* be sorry.

'I know.'

'Are you OK now, Julian?' I asked, searching his face for an answer. 'Are you really OK?' It's one thing to survive, I think, another not to be *haunted*.

'Yes, I'm fine, Mum. I really am fine.'

'Sure?'

'*Sure*. I bumped into him, you know, Christian. The other day. In a pub in the City. Lunchtime.'

I froze. This has been a recurring nightmare of mine: Julian running into Christian. Felix, he wouldn't recognize, hopefully. 'What? Oh God. What happened?'

'Nothing happened. I saw him. I'm sure he didn't know who I was. I looked at him, looked away and that was that.'

'Were you OK?' I was shaking, a little. 'God, Julian, how did you feel?'

'I felt nothing, absolutely nothing. The man means absolutely nothing to me. Don't look so worried. I'm telling you to prove a point. You don't have to worry about me, Mum. I

287

really *am* fine.' He smiled at me. 'We're natural born survivors, Mum. You and me against the world, right?'

'Right.' I smiled uncertainly back at him, my heart flooding with love and that measure of regret that will always be there, whatever points are proved and however many times I'm told not to worry. 'You and me against the world.'

'Anyway, look, *be* reminded,' he said, 'with this Mac person. Be more than reminded, if it makes you feel wonderful. Perhaps you'll feel so wonderful one day you'll go out there and look for love again.'

I laughed, disbelieving. I also have an image of Christian in a City pub I need to shake from my mind. 'Oh, I don't know about that.'

'No, I know you don't,' Julian said, 'but you can think about it.'

'Hmm,' I replied. My son saw Christian in a pub and he is unscathed. I can't think about much else.

'Hmm,' Julian echoed, gently mocking me. 'Well, *I* love you, anyway, Mum, which is possibly even *more* cringe.' Yes, he does. His love has been a constant, through everything. It has been my oxygen. I'd like to think my love has been enough to sustain *him*, to arm him for those nightmare moments in life, in the City and elsewhere, but maybe he has armed him*self*, all on his own.

'There's no need to *creep*,' I replied, mocking him back. I shook the image of Christian. Lightened up. 'I promise I'll be buying you dinner anyway. But, thank you,' I said, squeezing his arm. 'About Mac.' *He understands*, I thought. He may understand everything. 'Thank you, Julian.'

The tea trolley rattles past the end of Mac's bed. Julian looks at the plate of digestive biscuits longingly as they sail by. When he came in Julian nodded at Mac as I stood by and proudly announced him as my son. Mac smiled at Julian and smiled at me. He understands, too, I hope. Julian has been staring at him curiously ever since, though it might just be

288

hunger and boredom. We'll go to the café once we've finished our visit; not for a while yet.

We all laugh at the bodged flourished finale of Fran's card trick and she felts back to the nurses' station in soft shoes, then Lloyd shows Mac more photos of his grandchildren, on his phone. This is a good, good day. Everyone is basking in Mac's light. Even though he is silent and has no words with which to embroider them, his magnetism and presence are here; he's just making people feel good, somehow, like he used to. Perhaps that's another reason I have kept on coming.

'Mac looks happy,' James remarks to me. Due to there being so many of us, his chair is quite close to mine; our legs are almost touching. I have red woolly tights on, a tartan skirt – yes, Ali MacGraw again. James's legs are crossed at the ankle, his socks yellow with ladybirds on.

'He does, doesn't he?' I reply, smiling at the ladybirds. 'What a difference a Lloyd makes, eh? How did you get on with Dachshund Woman?'

'Offer made and accepted,' he says. 'With the aid of some puppy chocolate drops I picked up from a corner shop en route.'

'Bribe the dog, always works.'

He grins a boyish grin and I grin back. I catch Julian throwing me a curious glance as a result and I pretend I haven't seen it. 'Have you relented?' James asks.

'Relented?'

'Your mother?'

We are talking quietly – I don't think anyone can hear us – but I sneak another look at Julian, on the other side of the bed. He hasn't seen Marilyn for years; after Christian I didn't want him damaged any more so I stopped taking him to The Cedars, where she still sung that man's praises and tutted over the fact we'd left him. I don't want Julian to hear me talking about her now. I don't want him tainted by her, although

289

having seen how strong he is today, maybe her name would just bounce off him like a penny from armour plate.

'No, I haven't relented.' It's a fait accompli as far as I am concerned. Job done, no going back. I've felt so free since I made my decision, like Marilyn was hanging off me, her scrawny arms grasping round my neck, and now I have prised them off and stepped away into the light and fresh air. She is not my problem now. She is being looked after, but not by me. I have also let go of the notion she might ever love me. It's about time.

'Good,' says James and I detect a slight wink, just a small one, then reckon I have imagined it.

We sit, we chat, we laugh – all Mac's visitors. After a while, Lloyd announces he's going to the coffee machine and asks if I'll give him a hand. I say, 'Yes,' but he marches off ahead of me, leaving me to trail behind like *I'm* a puppy hoping for chocolate drops.

'You're still here, then, after I told you about all Dad's affairs. I thought it might put you off coming,' he says, irritated, pressing at random buttons until his cup drops down and waits for hot liquid to cascade into it. I stand next to him, feeling like a told-off child, suddenly, in my tartan skirt and red tights. 'I'm impressed by your loyalty.'

'Don't be,' I reply. 'I've got nothing better to do.' He doesn't laugh or smile. His 'you're still here, then?' isn't very nice and the 'I'm impressed by your loyalty' makes him sound like a not-very-good Bond villain.

'You obviously felt a great deal for him.'

'Yes, I did.'

'I suppose that never goes away.'

'No, not really.' I watch as black liquid whooshes into the cup, which is vibrating a little. Lloyd is staring at me. I want to look away but instead I stare back at him, until it eventually becomes a challenge: one of those childhood stare-outs where you mustn't blink.

'There's something else,' he says. His coffee is waiting for him but he is not reaching for it.

'Something else?' That's exactly what Mac once said. About the beetle-ish Dean and his discovery of us.

'I have a theory, on seeing that photo – you know: the two of you in bed . . .'

'Yes . . . ?' OK, does he *have* to keep bringing that up?

'And how Dad's face lit up when he was looking at you, talking about you.' He pauses, pulls quickly at his Father Christmas beard, his coffee still sitting waiting. 'I think he was continually searching for another *you*.'

'Oh,' I say. What else *can* I say? I wish I was wearing something other than my cutesy Ali MacGraw get-up, like an eighties power suit with shoulder pads, from *Working Girl*, or something. I feel I need to be *stronger* for this.

'I saw one of his women once,' he continues, watching milk tumble into his cup. 'Blonde curly hair, petite, getting into his car outside the library – he didn't know I was there, of course – and when I saw your photo I thought, Ah yes, that library woman looked just like this girl. I think he was looking for you in every one of his affairs.'

'But you don't know what any of the *others* looked like, do you?'

He shrugs. 'It's just a theory.'

'I don't know what to say.' I really *don't* know what to say. So, I was not only the cause of one affair, but the catalyst for dozens of others? That's a very big burden for someone to carry. It's hard to get my head around, but I'm not saying 'sorry' again; I can't. And if Mac was searching for another me, why didn't he just come looking for *me*? I know the answer to this question. Mac had chosen Helen over me; he'd let me go to have a 'bigger love', and the 'best life'. He wouldn't have felt he had the right to play a part in that. Not after everything.

'*I'd* say you were the love of his life.'

291

'What? Is that what you think?'

'That's what he *told* me, in the attic. I was too mad to say anything about it to you yesterday, but now I think you might be all right, really, so I'm putting it out there.' He flashes me another Mac smile, which I fear may disarm me just as I'm thinking how rude he is. Perhaps the way he expresses himself is just Aussie-style bluntness. Perhaps I am simply shocked. I was the love of Mac's *life*? Well, I have always suspected he was mine, particularly as I can't see anyone *else* showing up to supersede him, not now . . . There are no Bigger Loves, before or after.

'That's what he told you?'

'Yes.'

This is *huge*, I think, if it's true. Colossal. I will Lloyd to fetch his damn coffee but he just stands looking at me. I was the love of Mac's life and he was mine. It *should* make me feel great, considering all I said to Julian, about stopping the movie before the end, not playing things out to the final scene, remembering things in a nostalgic vacuum, but I realize that sometimes you can't deny how things turned out, how things went on to be. And how much hurt surrounds something that had once felt so wonderful.

Our affair came at a price. Mac was a charismatic adulterer; I was a spoilt brat who casually betrayed another woman. He went on to repeat offend, over and over again – because of me – and because of *him*, I went in search of men opposite to Mac and found, first, ineffectual Felix and then horrible, horrible Christian who nearly destroyed my life. Discovering you are the love of someone's life doesn't quite bring the thrill it should when it's shaded by betrayal and selfishness and consequences. You can't always focus on the 'before' when the 'after' is smacking you in the face with a sledgehammer.

'Cheer up,' says Lloyd, but it's too late. I feel sadness creep into my heart on soft slippers and take up residence, a crouching shrouded figure. 'What does it all matter, anyway? We've all moved on.' *Well,* you *didn't,* I think. *You moved away; as far as you could get. And you've hardly kept quiet about my involvement in your father's life since your return.*

Lloyd finally takes his coffee and sniffs at the plastic cup. He ordered coffee; surely it will smell like coffee? 'I reckon I can have a relationship with the old fella again. Seeing him like this, in hospital, has made me realize Dad should still have a place in my life. I wouldn't actually want to lose him.'

'No, of course not,' I say, but I have a sudden and very naughty urge to tell him to 'piss off', as the old Arden would have. Or she would have given him a look of utter disdain and then flounced off. I wish she was here – the *best*, most triumphant part of her, of course; the selfish and callous Arden can stay there, in the past – but I sense she might be lurking somewhere, just out of reach. She's certainly the closest she's been for a very long time.

We leave Mac at eight, now actually *doing* that queuing up to shake his hand or kiss his cheek. Well, it's only me that does that. I do it to annoy Lloyd.

'I'll see you tomorrow, Dad,' says Lloyd.

'See you, mate,' says James. 'I'll pop in and pick up your post when I get home.'

'Bye, Mac,' says Julian. I'm going to take him to the café now, for his dinner.

Mac nods and half-smiles. He looks tired after all the excitement. As I reach him in the queue, I notice a stray eyelash on his cheek and wipe it away with my thumb. Then I smooth back his hair from his face. As I kiss him, I want to say the line of a movie, but I don't know which one. I can't think of anything perfect enough, the perfect line to say now in case I forget to say it later, but I can feel his love, from the past, and I can see the ghost of it, in the present. It surrounds me like a velvet cloak. It helps me to remember.

How can I possibly sum up how I feel? So I simply look at him and we hold each other's gaze for a few seconds and I say, 'See you tomorrow, Mac.'

Then, on impulse I kiss him again.

'See you tomorrow,' says Fran chirpily as we walk out of the door. I look back and there he is, for better or worse – the love of my life.

THEN

Chapter 25

My third year at Warwick was pretty wild. If Mac wanted me to have the best time I decided I would *have* the best time. I drank from both barrels, burned all the ends of all the candles I could lay my greedy, drunken hands on. I embraced student friendship, finally. I extended my circle of trust from just Becky to the other three girls I had lived with for the last year. We were all together again, for the third year, in halls across the road from main campus. I bothered to get to know them, enjoyed wild nights out with them. I even went on holiday with one of the girls, Ruth, in the Easter holidays, Interrailing across France and Germany. I became what I considered to be a *proper* student, not one whose main module was shagging a lecturer and turning up for a few seminars on the side. It was a convincingly good pretence.

I also went for fun, uncomplicated boys, mainly for drunken snogs and some light playing around. There was a succession of boys, banned from having actual intercourse with me, in my bed, and bicycles parked outside my halls; once, a motorbike, after I met a biker accountant in a pub in Coventry. I got through it, that year. The year without Mac. And I left Warwick University with a 2:2, which I thought was pretty good going, considering.

The moment I found out he had gone was pretty awful. I hadn't spoken to Mac since the night the affair ended, but

I thought about him every day and I missed him every minute of the eternally long and miserable summer holidays. The first night back on campus, I broke off from a giggling gang walking back from the Westwood Bop – including a very pissed Becky, and a newly made friend, Dominic the Roadie – to give crouching attention to a fake undone DM lace and, making sure the gang had disappeared round a corner, skittered up Mac's stairs to peer into what had been his window. He had gone. The blinds had been replaced by thick curtains. His door had a silly mat saying 'Welcome' in bristles outside it. When I caught up with the giggling gang, I wondered aloud, with a weak attempt at a tragic chuckle layered under my sing-song voice, if the legendary Mac Bartley-Thomas would be holding any of his legendary parties this term, already knowing the answer.

'Oh, he's left,' said some bastard. 'Gone to Sheffield to lecture there, apparently. Media Studies. His wife's having a baby.'

I smiled above a severed and bleeding heart, uttered some kind of squeaky exclamation usually reserved for dyspeptic Labradors, and snarled inside at the thought of Mac treating his lucky, lucky students at Sheffield to The List – *our* list – which at least diverted me from black, black thoughts about Helen and the baby and the three of them together in a cosy house in Sheffield, and the knowledge I had lost Mac for ever.

'Lucky them,' I said, in an attempt to be something other than devastated, and I ignored Becky's drunken look of concern but instead nicked a bottle of beer from Dominic's jacket pocket and started necking it down like I was having the best night of my life.

Another awful moment was when I bumped into the Dean, sometime in the spring term. It was the first time I'd ever come face to face with him and it was on the little set of stairs that led to the Cholo Bar. He looked at me and

I could see his eyebrows rise ever so slightly behind his glasses. He gave me a polite, acknowledging nod, which I was perplexed and mortified by. What did *that* mean? I scuttled away from him, red-cheeked and desperate for a cider and black.

The only time I overindulged in thoughts of Mac was when I sat in my room and watched the video of *Imitation of Life* I'd pretend-casually picked up from a local charity shop. The other girls were out, at Super Bowl night or something. I locked my door, opened a packet of M&M's and prepared to weep buckets, as Mac said I would. But nothing happened. Yes, it was a sweeping lachrymose melodrama but, as I'd decided high emotion was not for me – not any more – I remained unmoved. When Sarah Jane rejects her mother I just stared blankly at the screen; when she runs up to the coffin at Annie's funeral, distraught and sobbing, I rolled a melting M&M around my mouth with my tongue. Without Mac to watch with, to love with, I was left cold.

I somehow made it to the end of the year, although it was a stagger rather than a glide. On the very last morning all my possessions were in boxes at the side of my stripped bed and Dad came to pick me up at ten o'clock sharp. I didn't want to go home; I wanted to stay here for ever. Do it all again, especially my affair with Mac – God, I missed him! Sometimes it was almost unbearable. When I thought of him in Sheffield with Helen and the baby I almost had to stuff my own fist into my mouth to stop myself screaming – but Dad knocked on the door and I had to go home.

I saw Mac, just once more, and it was when I was in London with Felix sometime in the mid-nineties. I'd been dating him for a while and he was taking me to some flash lunch at some flash restaurant off Cavendish Square – showing off; that was his thing. We were holding hands, crossing the street, and I saw Mac and that man again, Stewart

Whittaker, coming out of a hotel. Stewart was chatting to the red-coated doorman; Mac was carrying that same brown battered bag and looking up the street. My heart gave a massive, high-voltage jolt when I saw his face and almost immediately Mac saw me too. He attempted a half smile; I gave a half wave I didn't want Felix to clock.

'Who's that?' he demanded. I thrust my hand back in my coat pocket.

'Nobody. Just an old lecturer from university.'

'Ugh. Academia.' Felix shuddered. He was a City boy; he dealt with money and commodities, stocks and shares. He wouldn't know a Cukor or a Minnelli if they came up and slapped him in the face. 'Why's he smiling at you like that?'

Mac wasn't smiling at me now. Stewart, who I was sure hadn't seen me, had turned to him and they were both laughing about something with the doorman. A black cab pulled up and they clambered in, but Mac went to the near-side window and just for a brief second he looked at me as the cab pulled away.

'Tossers,' muttered Felix. 'I prefer the University of Life. I've got a degree in *that*. Not you, of course,' he said, squeezing my hand. '*You're* all right.'

We went for lunch but I didn't eat all that much. I drank too much white wine and had to be put into my own black cab, at three o'clock. I remember how I leant my face against the cool glass of the window, how I stared at every single person I saw on the pavement, all the way home, in case one of them was Mac. That day was the last time I saw his face. I missed it. I missed all of him. He was now just a face in a distant crowd, a man I had once loved.

NOW

Chapter 26

Monday turns up mild again – another lucky dip in the typical yoyo-ing English weather. The pavements are slick and unimpressed, the drizzle half-hearted; it's an uninspiring something-and-nothing day, just like the day I first saw Mac again, at St Katherine's. There is still a long, long way to go until spring.

When I get to work Charlie is at my desk. He's twanging at a paperclip, hopping from one big shiny black foot to another. He's clearly up to something, as he often is.

'Nice outfit,' he says.

'Thanks. I'm channelling Hedy Lamarr today – off-duty look, of course.'

'I have no idea what you just said.' Charlie twangs the paperclip again. 'Hey, there's a job going in the script department, a script reader, with a chance to progress to script editor,' he says. 'Didn't you do something English-related at uni, back in the days of the dinosaurs?' He raises his arms at the side, like he is attempting an impression of a pterodactyl. He is closer to resembling a zombie in the *Thriller* video.

'Oi, cheeky!' I tap him lightly on the leg with a handy ruler. 'But, yes, I did English Lit.'

'Yeah, I thought so. You should apply. You must be bored of phoning up grumpy old gits about their lock-ups.'

I tuck my bag under my chair and make a well in the

middle of a pile of papers on my desk I might be able to work from. 'Well, of course I am. But I wouldn't get it.'

'Why not?' He flicks the paperclip and it flies through the air and on to the carpet. He bends to pick it up.

'I don't know.'

'You don't know until you *try*,' he says. 'It's on the intranet whatsit. You should take a look. Promise me you will, Hall?'

'OK, I'll take a look.' Maybe I will. Maybe it's time to fulfil some of those promises Mac made for me. Stop being scared; try something new. If he's come back into my life perhaps there's a reason for it, perhaps I'm supposed to *do* something, as a result. Why else has he made me remember? Why else has he come back to me? 'I'll take a look,' I repeat, to no one in particular, because Charlie has already gone.

I get to the hospital at half seven, via the Stop 'n' Shop where I've picked up a tube of sour cream and onion Pringles as James has mentioned he likes them, and a bottle of Lucozade as a joke present for Mac. As I walk to the main entrance, I spot Fran lolling against the wall outside it, wearing a red padded jacket over her uniform and drawing on an alarmingly long, virgin-fresh cigarette, under artificial light. I've never seen her out of the ward before; she looks different out of context, and it makes me smile. If you have to be in hospital you should have a nurse like Fran.

As I get nearer, I see she looks preoccupied, unaware of the bustle of people going in and out around her, like she has the cares of the world on her shoulders, which she actually does, to be fair. All those people; all those lives. When she spots me amongst a slow-moving trail of people heading into the hospital – coats and scarves, bags and boots – her face suddenly looks really odd. She gives me a weird turned-down smile, with her lips closed, and immediately drops her barely dragged-on cigarette, driving it into the ground with a soft white heel. Then she steps slowly towards me. Why is she doing this? Why is she doing this unnatural, slow-motion walk? She looks weird.

'What's up?' I say, walking towards her. But even as I am asking the question I think I know the answer. Tears spring to her eyes, making them red. The down-turned smile stretches down to her chin. She shakes her head and I begin to shake mine back at her, a mirror image. Faster. But not as fast as my heart, which is lurching from side to side like a lettuce in a spinner.

Oh God. No, no, no. 'Please don't say the words, don't say those words to me,' I beg her. I can feel my legs going. I'm not sure I can reach her . . .

'Oh love, love, no, no, it's not that,' breathes Fran. She has clutched me in a padded embrace. I have my face in her neck and she smells of cigarettes and cough sweets. Eventually she takes me by the shoulders and lifts me away from her. 'But Mac's in theatre again. I'm so sorry. He's had a haemorrhage – right hemisphere. Caused by a sudden brain abscess, the consultant said. It's not looking too great, lovely, but they're doing the best they can for him. I promise you they are.'

I am relieved – so relieved – Mac is not dead when I was so, so convinced of it, but I am utterly terrified he is in theatre, fighting for his life. I semi-collapse on to Fran's neck again, the zip of her padded jacket a train track in my cheek.

'How long has he been in theatre?' I whisper, my voice a terrified croak.

'A couple of hours, and it could be a couple more. I'm not really sure, my love.' Fran pats my shoulder, like she is burping a baby. 'His son's here, somewhere. We called him in the night.' They don't have my number, I think. Only family.

'What should I do?' I ask her. I don't know what to do now. Do I go in? Do I just go home? I can't just turn around and walk back home, can I? How can I do that?

'All you can do now is wait,' says Fran. 'Do you knit?'

Random, and the second person to ask me this. Do I *look* like a knitter? 'Er . . . no.'

'Shame, it's a great soul-soother. Why don't you come in, go to the hospital chapel?'

'That awful place?' She is stroking my arm under the wing of my wool wrap.

'It's not so bad. It's a quiet place, a place where you can think. It might help . . . maybe.'

'OK.' I nod. I'll go where anyone tells me at this point. At least I can go inside, where it's warm and it's light. Closer to him. I have become institutionalized, too. My social life – give or take a night in an awkward bar and a bizarre road trip – is St Katherine's. My life is Mac at the moment. I don't want to return to my soaps and my shortbread – to the cold grey life I have made for myself since I kicked Christian out of it. I feel panicked, flighty, my heart is racing – perhaps the hospital chapel *is* a good idea. Perhaps internally tutting at the plastic décor of the Chapel of Rest will calm me down.

Fran is studying me closely, with a nurse's concern. I probably look unhinged.

'Will you come and find me if there's any news?' I ask.

'Of course I will. And give me your mobile number, too. I'll call you if you've already left.'

'I won't leave.'

'Well, if you do. It could be a long time, Arden.'

Fran pulls her phone from her coat pocket – it has a blinged-up cover, pink sequins –and hands it to me with Contacts open so I can key in my number. As she stuffs it back in her pocket she looks at me intently.

'Are you really just a former student of his?' she asks.

'No,' I say, and tears leap to my eyes. 'I was much, much more than that. I loved him and he loved me. It was a long, long time ago but it was a massive, massive love affair, me and Mac.'

'I knew it.' She smiles.

'You could see it in my eyes?'

'No,' she says. 'I could see it in his.'

I head through the catacombs of the hospital and into the chapel. The seascape is still looming; the sage curtain looks like it has something awful hiding behind it. Lloyd is in there, sitting on one of the woolly chairs. He has his back to me and his head in his hands.

'Hi,' I say.

'Oh, hi,' he says, turning round. He's in long shorts and a T-shirt and those same trainers, which are not quite so white today. His puffa jacket is squatting on the back of the chair next to him.

'Do you think he'll be OK?'

'I don't know.'

I sit down on the coatless chair the other side of him and sigh. 'I don't know what to do or say,' I venture. 'Last night was almost like a party and now . . .'

'I know.'

'He'll be OK,' I say. 'He *has* to be.'

'Let's hope so.' Lloyd looks at his watch as though he has a flight to catch. Perhaps he has. Perhaps he's desperate to get back to the other side of the world. To sunshine and his kids and wife and away from the dad he doesn't like too much. Away from all this hurt and drama.

'What date are you supposed to be going back to Australia?'

'I haven't booked a return flight yet. I was going to see how things go.'

'I see.'

'I can't stay too long, though, you know.' He takes his head from his hands and looks at me. His eyes are all red; his face looks like a crumpled cushion. 'I have a course starting next Wednesday. Six people. Extensive dive course with a three-night trip to the Reef at the end of it.'

303

'Sounds great,' I mutter. 'Hopefully there'll be good news and you'll be back way before then.'

'Yes.'

'Thank you for visiting him,' says Lloyd, looking at me. 'All those nights. You didn't have to.' He makes it sound like it's final, like there will be no more visiting. Like it's over. *It's not over!* I want to scream. *He's going to be OK!*

'I wanted to. I've liked sitting on my chair in the ward and being with Mac,' I say. I realize there's a single tear hesitating in the corner of my left eye. I sniff it away and attempt a smile. 'And like Mayo in *An Officer and a Gentleman* I had nowhere else to go.'

'What?'

'Oh nothing. Film stuff,' I say. I have clearly lost my mind.

'I've seen that movie, too, you know,' he says. 'One of Dad's favourites, right?'

I nod pitifully. I feel I'm being told off for my feeble, incriminating attempt at a private joke and quite right, too. Despite Lloyd saying he liked me a little – though that could be a lie – anything that reminds him of my affair with his father must sting. 'He'll be OK,' I repeat numbly.

'Yeah.'

It's weird how Lloyd and I are two strangers worrying over the fate of a life we have known two separate halves of. Me: the young Mac, the maverick King of Campus; Lloyd: a dad, a whole different kind of man altogether. We cannot relate to each other's experiences and the gulf between us is massive. Yet, here we are, side by side on woolly chairs in a plastic chapel.

I realize I don't feel good. I wish I *did* knit, so I can distract my hands, which are shaking slightly and rubbing at my sides like wobbly hams.

'Yes. Well, I'm going to go out for a bit,' says Lloyd, standing up. 'Walk around London, see a few sights. I can't handle it in here any longer.' He looks around him. The cross on the curtain. The laminated psalms, stuck on the wall with Sellotape. 'I don't like hospitals.'

'Well, no . . .' I say. I'm not sure how he can go wandering round London staring up at buildings and ooh-ing and aah-ing when he doesn't know if his father will live or die, but he will be called, won't he, and he'll come back, unless he gets *really* spooked and by the time Fran calls him he's on a plane eating nut-free snacks and settling down to the latest blockbuster . . .

We swiftly shake hands like we are at the close of a business meeting flogging paper supplies or something and he is gone and I am grateful, for Mac's sake, that his lost boy came back. Mac saw his son, he saw his grandchildren. There had been a bedside moment to treasure and replay and if Mac can't then I will replay it, in my mind, for him.

Oh God, am I thinking he won't make it? I slump further down in my chair, at a loss to know what to do with myself. I clearly can't be trusted with my own thoughts. There's a noise behind me, someone else coming in. I get up; let a real person use this room properly, I think. I'm an imposter; I'm just a woman potentially grieving for a man she had an affair with thirty years ago. I don't know what I'm doing.

'Arden.'

It's James. 'They told you?'

'Yes. I came here early today, just been showing a house. An old wreck, I'm not sure anyone will want it.' He comes and stands next to me, his brow furrowed. 'Will Mac be OK?'

'They don't know.'

He nods. 'Shall we go to the café?'

'Yes, please,' I say with relief.

I toy with sponge and consider cream cheese frosting, but my slice of carrot cake goes largely untouched. I sip at my tea but it brings me no comfort. I just want Mac to be all right. I don't want this to be the end; I want to know what happens next and I'm willing it not to be something bad. James and I don't say a lot; it's just nice to be together. And the sounds of the café are a buzzing, cheerful backdrop to our uncertainty and worry. Not cancelling them out, obviously, but providing a happier slice of life: warmth, chatter, the hiss and steam of the coffee machine; bickering women behind the counter shouting to each other about the whereabouts of the 'sliced white'. Life is going on regardless, always just going on.

'How long shall we sit here?' asks James eventually. 'We've already been here an hour and a half. They'll have to kick us out at some point.'

I smile and lay down my fidgety spoon. 'Yes, they might. I suppose we ought to go fairly soon.'

'Do you want me to walk you home?'

I'm about to say 'no, thank you' but I change my mind.

'Yes, please. Just ten more minutes, though? Just in case we hear?'

'OK.'

We step outside the hospital. The night is coal black, the drizzle unremitting. The same as any other unremarkable British winter night, really, but the world looks slightly different when you fear someone you have loved may not be in it for much longer.

James walks me home. I wave goodbye to him from the front door as he walks up the street and I wonder, should Mac not make it, if I would still see him. Probably not, is the answer, but I don't want to think about that, or indeed about Mac not making it. I've got a headache. I close the door and go to the kitchen where I take four halves of chalky paracetamol, as they have broken and splintered in their blister pack at the bottom of my bag, and go to bed.

NOW

Chapter 27

It isn't the best timing, I think, as I try to drink my tea the next morning. I have a thing today. A leave-the-office thing — a rare treat, usually. I have to travel to Richmond and check out a three-storey family mansion we may do a week's shoot at, for a *Coppers* episode which will feature domestic violence. I have to be cheery all day. Make notes. Check power points and access. Drink lots of hot drinks made for me by a woman in a jolly print Boden skirt with a matching scarf. I don't know how I'm going to get through it. I've packed tissues and mascara and the darkest sunglasses I own, not that I'll wear them as it's another dull, charcoal-grey day. I wish I could stay in the office and spend the day hiding behind my PC and all my junk.

Mac survived the operation — just — but is in a coma; I called the hospital first thing and some faceless person, with not the greatest bedside or consoling manner in the world, gave me the news while the voice of another person shrieked 'How long will you be, Sheila?' in the background.

I walk to the tube. The word 'coma', when the horrible staff member said it to me, like she was simply declaring Mac had gone off on a walking holiday in the Lake District or something, chilled me to the bone, not that I'm an expert on them. All I know of comas is the movie *Coma*, which was terrifying, and that some people are in comas for years and years and then wake up, twenty years later, and everyone around them has got old and they don't know what's going on any more and they have to learn all about the new technology and stuff. Or, they don't wake up.

I'm utterly petrified. I have on my swishing skirt, my black gloves and my black New Look coat (the style from the forties and launched by Dior – full skirts and cinched-in waists – not the high street shop) and try to style out my fear and my worry. Sometimes Mac used to say to me, 'What would Katharine Hepburn do?' She was his favourite of all the feisty, plucky Hollywood heroines and occasionally this was his mantra. I'll give it a go today. I'll try to emulate Ms Hepburn's no-nonsense, keep-going, independent spirit but it will take everything I've got.

I laugh at the twitterings of three-storey Boden woman, accept and drink endless cups of tea, measure up door-frames and count electric sockets. Tears are behind my eyes the whole day but I ignore them. I return to the office to hand in my notes to Nigel, like homework. He's on the phone and does that condescending nodding thing, holding his arm out for the file, too important to say 'thanks'. At five o'clock, when I come out into the tiny car park, James is waiting for me.

'Hello?' I say. I'm pleased to see his face but really surprised. 'How do you know where I work?'

'*Coppers*, you said, and I was in the area so I thought I'd meet you. I hope I haven't stepped into some kind of stalker territory?' He looks worried.

'No, no, not at all,' I say. 'How did you know what time I'd come out, though?'

He shrugs. 'I didn't. I just thought I'd wait around. I'm hungry,' he says. 'Shall we go and get something?'

'OK,' I say, 'let's try that new burger bar on Colman Street.' Typical man, I think. Everything revolving around their stomach. I've barely eaten all day and am not sure I could manage even a couple of chips, let alone a burger, but I could do with the company.

'I phoned the hospital and Fran told me about the coma,' James says, as we walk.

'What did she say his chances were?' I ask. 'The woman I talked to didn't seem to know.'

'Fair to not great,' says James. 'Fran didn't seem to know either. Are you OK?'

'Not really,' I say.

'Me neither,' says James. 'I like the old boy. I don't want him to die.'

'Don't even say the words, James.'

'Sorry.'

We keep walking. We're in the park now. It's cold. My work bag is bashing against my leg. The same spot each time: upper right thigh. I will have an almighty bruise there tomorrow but I don't care. I relish the comforting, rhythmic *thwack thwack thwack* of the pain. It keeps my mind off everything.

'How's your job?' asks James, an attempt at deflection, I know. 'You said there aren't many thrills. You don't enjoy it?'

'Not really,' I say.

'Why not?'

'I'm bored, I guess. Unchallenged. A colleague has told me about a position that's come up in the script department. I'm thinking of applying but I'm not sure if there's any point.'

'Why not?' he asks. James the Direct again. 'Would you *like* to work in the script department?'

'Well, yes, I would. The position's for a reader. I think I'd enjoy it.' My voice is flat, I feel cold and sick inside. Mac is in a *coma*.

'Then why not apply?'

'I'm scared they'll say no.'

'Yes, they might, but they might also say yes. What have you got to lose?'

My safety, my boring monotony that I have been wrapping round me like a blanket, I think. For God's sake! I know James is trying to take my mind off it, but Mac is in a *coma*!

We walk past The Parade. The kebab shop is surprisingly busy for this time of day and there's a scrum of schoolchildren outside Tesco; skirts rolled up, socks rolled down, scuffing shoes, the odd swear word. One of the girls drops a packet of sweets; I pick it up and hand it to her. 'Thanks,' she mutters.

'You're welcome.'

A telly in the hi-fi shop window is playing an old movie. It's one of those massive ones with the whole HD thing going on; you can see every pore on Robert Redford's face. He's drunk at the end of the bar. He's asleep and looking absolutely beautiful. I stop to look at him, my bag thwacking to a stop against my leg. This would be a good time to cry, but I'm not going to.

'You might need to prepare yourself,' says James, and he doesn't say anything more but I know exactly what he means.

'I don't want to be prepared,' I say. 'Look, can we swerve the burger bar, go to the hospital instead?' I ask him. 'I just need to be there. The café does toasted sandwiches?'

'Oh, I love a toasted sandwich,' says James. 'Let's do it.'

I have cheese and tomato and James has ham and cheese and I have a tea and he has a hot chocolate. The ladies behind the counter now call me 'ducky' and James 'pet'. We have virtually moved in, after all. After we've eaten, I check my mobile phone but there's nothing from Fran. After we've finished our drinks, James gets a call on his.

'Oh God, Arden,' he says, slipping the phone back into his jacket pocket, 'I'm so sorry to do this to you again, but I've got an emergency second viewing and I really have to go. Will you be all right? What will you do, stay here?'

'I'll stay for a bit,' I say, 'nothing much to go home for. Television, bed. Nothing.'

He stands up, pushes back his chair. 'Sorry,' he says again, then he hesitates. He looks at me, his gaze steady. 'What did Mac think you'd do with your life?' he asks.

This is a bit random. 'What do you mean?'

'When you were with him, all those years ago, that photo . . . When you were young. Did he see this as your life, going to work, coming home again? Doing nothing? Did *you*?'

'He thought I'd have a brilliant life,' I say, *and a Bigger Love*, I think. 'But things happen. Like my ex-husband. Like normality.' Like real life that sometimes has no brilliance or sheen, it's just life . . .

'There's still time,' James says.

'Is there? Time for what?'

'To do exciting things, new things, fall in love . . .'

'Yeah, right,' I say, remembering Julian said something equally ridiculous about going out looking for love, 'like *that's* going to happen!'

I look at James and pull a face. He pulls a silly one back at me, then smiles. We look at each other for a while, and then I look away and he leaves the café, waving cheerily to the ladies. I push what's left of my sandwich around my plate, like it's a packed bus in slow-moving traffic.

When I emerge from the double doors of St Katherine's entrance, I am surprised to spy Dominic hobbling in through them, on crutches.

'Dominic!' I am pleased to see an open and friendly face untouched by life's misery.

'Hey, Arden! What are you doing here? I've been a bad boy – I got the cast wet, messing about with a girl and a bottle of champagne, you know how it is. I'm coming in to get it changed before the clinic closes.'

'I'm visiting someone,' I say, my heart breaking. And, as I'd quite like to be swallowed back into the warmth and buttery light of the hospital, I add, 'Do you want me to come in with you or anything?'

He checks his watch. 'Nah, you're all right. I've got a girl – a different one – meeting me in there. I met her at the last fracture clinic.'

'You old rogue,' I say, mimicking a Dominic-esque cheeriness I'm not feeling.

'Yeah.' He shrugs. 'I probably *am* too old for all this nonsense, but there we go. How's Becky? You spoken to her today?'

'Today? No, but she's fine, I guess,' I say.

'I hope so. She's all right, then?' I notice he looks quite earnest, for Dominic.

'Well, yes, as far as I know. I haven't seen her since that night at the bar.' Dominic has an even odder look on his face. Concerned; a very rare look for him. 'Why, *shouldn't* she be?'

'You do know about her relapse?'

'*Relapse?* What on earth are you talking about?' My heart starts to race.

'She's had a bit of another breakdown. Because of the attack.' Dominic must know from my face that he's completely lost me now. His turns pale. 'Shit, you don't *know*, do you?'

'No,' I say, shaking my head. *Attack?*

'Christ, Ardie. Just over a year ago Becky got mugged on the way home from work. She got jumped from behind and wrestled to the ground, by two men, all for her mobile phone.'

'Oh God.'

'She broke a rib. Was severely traumatized for ages. I think it's PTSD, myself. Surely she must have told you?'

'No, she didn't.' *Mugged, a broken rib, severely traumatized . . . ? No, she didn't tell me*, and as I am processing this news I fold up inside because I know why. Of course I do. Because since I bumped into her that day in M&S eighteen months ago I have not only kept her at arm's length but actively

312

pushed her away. Why on earth *would* she tell me? 'I need to call her, I need to go to her,' I say. I am agitated, totally bewildered. She told me a lie about her mobile phone rather than share this with me. All this has happened and I didn't even deserve to know. I am still the same selfish, terrible Arden.

'You can't,' says Dominic. 'Not unless you get on a plane to Tenerife. She's gone to her cousin's apartment for a few days. That place helped her when it happened. She went there for three weeks. You really don't know any of this?'

'No.' I am more ashamed than I have ever been. 'I'll call her,' I say. I am already striding away from him, if you can call it that – in truth my legs can barely hold me up. 'I'll call her.'

I remember Becky drinking more than usual at Gatsby's, her jumping out of her skin when that Simon came up behind her and put his hand on her shoulder . . . I thought *I* was the one who had suffered, who had been through the mill, who needed care and kid gloves and could be arrogant and unfeeling enough to push people away. But all the time it was her, and *she* hadn't been arrogant or unfeeling at all, just reluctant to tell her worst experience to someone who wasn't a real friend any more.

I hurry home. I have the number for that apartment in Tenerife because years ago Becky and I both went there, for a riotous girls' holiday – just before I met Felix. The number's in my ancient black leather Filofax. It rings and rings and I don't blame it for its Spanish cold shoulder; it probably knows Becky only wants her real friends around her.

After texting Dominic, asking him to let me know when Becky's coming back, I'm at a loss. I don't want to watch the soaps tonight. I flick through my DVD collection and, with a grim smile, decide to torture myself with *Imitation of Life*. I'd replaced my video of it with the DVD years ago, when I'd had an Amazon voucher. Christian had scoffed at it, on the shelf, next to his *Die Hard*s and his *Pulp Fiction*.

This time – the fickle nonchalance of my youth departed, and my current sadnesses bearing down on me like a thick fog – I am overcome. The story of the two mothers and daughters and the tragedy of Sarah Jane denying Annie and then weeping at her funeral swamps me and I sob into the silky back of a linen cushion. Funny how you view things differently, depending where you are in your life. I had been proud of seeing nothing in this film the first time around – now it claws at me on so many raw and painful levels.

I cry for the person I used to be and who I am now, and I don't know which of the two is better, and which is worse. I cry for Becky and how I have let her down. I cry for the mother I should have had – sweet, kind, remotely interested – and at the injury of being lumbered with the one I actually got. I cry for all the ways in which I have imitated life and not done it justice.

And the *funeral scene* . . . As Mac once said, 'wow'. It kills me. Totally wipes me out. All I can think is that I do not want to be at Mac's funeral. I don't want to see the practised grim faces of the undertakers, glum and solemn but secretly looking forward to lunch at the chippy. I don't want to see the dreadful curtains, oscillating – ever so slightly, just there at the bottom – as they close, like they did on the day of my father's. I don't want to say goodbye to Mac, not yet.

I cry for him and I think I'll never stop. James is right, I need to be prepared, let a little practice-run grief seep out, so I am used to the taste of it, but I hope I'm overdoing it.

There is *hope*, isn't there? Hope that Mac will come round and everything will be OK. As I dry my last tears on a long piece of toilet roll from the downstairs loo, I cling to this hope like a barnacle to a shipwreck. I turn off the telly and reel my way up to bed, done in, telling myself he *must* pull through, or why has he come back to me at all?

I awake at half seven to my mobile ringing. My heart jolts in its cage, thrashes about, and I know, from the way the phone is ringing, from the early hour, it won't be still again for a while.

'Hello?' I croak, terrified.

'Hi, lovely.' It's Fran and her voice sounds weird, like she is a million miles away, across continents. 'I'm so sorry to have to tell you this, but I'm afraid Mac has died.'

NOW

Chapter 28

I fly to the hospital in an old pair of jogging bottoms, grubby trainers and a Spencer Tracy T-shirt, an over-sized, slightly stained duster coat only just staying on my shoulders. I run through the early-morning streets like a ghoul. It's raining; my curls are soaked to my head. I try to distract myself with thoughts I must look like a blonde Andie MacDowell at the end of *Four Weddings and a Funeral*, despite all the horrible irony that entails.

There's the usual hubbub around the hospital entrance. Faces both relieved and worried coming out; faces both hopeful and worried going in. A man on crutches, laughing with a mate. Not Dominic – he's probably straddled between a chesterfield sofa and a footstool somewhere having his plaster of Paris stroked. I scuttle through the catacombs, my coat wrapped round me like a superhero's cape, but it is too late for all that. The only hero was Mac and he is gone.

I buzz at Ward 10, over and over again, until Fran – looking weary but as though she's made an attempt to disguise the fact with a chalky coral lipstick I'm sure is against the rules – appears in the frame of the door's window and it swings open.

'Arden.'

'Please don't tell me to go to the chapel again, Fran,' I rush, 'I can't bear that place.'

'No, I won't. Go home now, pet. Go home and grieve for him.' She places a hand on my arm; I don't want it there.

'I don't want to go home!' I peer behind her, into Ward 10, as though Mac is there and all I have to do is take my seat.

'You have to, my love. You have to go home.'

Home is where I wanted to escape from, for the second time in my life. I liked coming to St Katherine's; it gave me a reason and a purpose. I felt needed and comfortable. Home to me is a cold, grey place where all roads lead even if I don't want them to. I wonder if I can call Julian, if he can come over, but I know he'll be on his way to work and who wants their mother calling them and begging them to come home because some old bloke she knew a million years ago has died?

'I don't know what to do,' I say. I should be going to work today myself, but I know I won't be able to. 'Where to go . . .' I know I'm not making much sense. I need to call Nigel, call in sick for the day, the week, the life . . . 'Will I see you again?' I ask Fran. It won't just be Mac who has gone from me, but Fran and James, the people I've been with every day. I won't see them again. I'll be back alone in my dark, sad world, which I didn't even realize *was* quite so dark and grey until Mac blasted in to illuminate it.

'I don't know.' Fran shrugs in a kind-nurse way, so I take that as a 'no'. She meets hundreds of people like Mac, hundreds of people like me; she is not my *friend*. I've made damn sure I don't have any of those, haven't I?

I don't look back as I walk away, back through the corridors, out through the *swish* of the double doors into the cold and the morning. I hesitate there, at the front of the hospital. I pull my phone from my coat pocket and text Nigel quickly, saying I won't be in today. Then I just stand there, completely paralysed.

There has been no Hollywood ending, not for Mac. There's no point pondering on what happens next, once the

317

story is over, because the story *is* over and *nothing* comes next. I wrap my coat around me but still I don't move. I have seen my whole life through the prism of the movies, I realize – as a lonely young girl yearning for escape, especially; as an up-for-excitement and self-centred young woman, definitely. Christian put a long stop to that prism – delighting in showing me reality could be very harsh indeed – but encountering Mac again I began to see life in terms of movie moments once more: the framed serendipity of finding him in Ward 10; the thrill of a whispered, nostalgia-evoking line; the wondrous, slow-motion reunion of Mac and Lloyd, father and son . . . I had even imagined the ready-for-your-close-up miracle of Mac waking from the coma and reaching for me. But movie moments fade to black and wither to nothing – seeing Mac in the hospital was just coincidence; a line from a movie is just a line from a movie; Lloyd is a rather lacklustre prodigal son . . . and Mac has died.

I walk home and I let the tears fall, unchecked. He has gone; he has gone, just when he had come back to me. There had been so much to say and be said, so much to remember, and now there is nothing.

My phone buzzes in my pocket and I ignore it. It buzzes again and I reach to look at it. There's a text from Dominic, and I run like a ghoul for the second time that morning.

The airport dash. It happens a lot in movies. It usually involves the hero or heroine – sometimes in a wedding dress – hurtling through departure lounges and jumping over barriers and pushing past airline staff to reach The One That's Getting Away so they can declare their love and stop them getting on the plane. It doesn't usually involve a bewildered attempt by a deranged and bereaved middle-aged woman in a Spencer Tracy T-shirt to meet her best friend on a flight from Tenerife, without even knowing what she will say to her when she does.

318

Becky will be on Flight FR3516 from Tenerife South. After I run back home, arriving dishevelled and quite sweaty, I realize I actually have quite a lot of time, so it's not really a dash in the end – more an unwieldy schlep. The first part of my quest is a drive to Stansted in my knackered old Golf littered with old Costa coffee cups. I can't cope with the radio, like James and I had, and my Tom Petty CD doesn't seem appropriate for how I am feeling – dazed, sad, determined – so I drive in anxious silence, my eyes literally on the road ahead; three feet in front of the bonnet, to be precise. I drive slowly, through arduous London traffic, and, then, the motorway, fearful of crashing.

Parking is a nightmare. I pay £3.50 to dump my heap in the drop-off area. You're only supposed to be there for ten minutes and I'll probably get a massive fine but I don't care . . . Of course, I'm running slightly late now and I can't be faffing about in some Jenga multi-storey and miss Becky. Nor do I want to wait outside for her to come out. I want to be in Arrivals. I want to see Becky coming through the doors and round the corner, with all the backpackers and the red-eyed businessmen. And then I will decide what on earth I'm going to do to make it up to her.

I head along the concourse, doing a stupid half-run and aiming for the far right end, which has the big yellow sign above it proclaiming 'Arrivals'. I am aware I am dressed extremely badly. Baby Boom Brexiteers wheeling cases and wearing sombreros in the January chill may think I am a wayward immigrant making for some unseen border. Instead, I walk-run past the window of 'Arrivals'; there's a Starbucks, the huge lozenge desk of a taxi office . . . And then I see her – she's leaning against the window in a pink coat, her back to the glass, rummaging in her massive bag for something; knowing Becky, a tissue, an Extra Strong Mint or her tin of Vaseline. Her suede coat suckers from the window; she is moving away, not in the direction of the exit but the other way, WHSmith? I can't risk her mooching off for a coffee, a cake, a browse for a magazine, where I can't find her . . . so I bang on the window, startling a couple of pecking seagulls bickering over the egg mayonnaise part of a Meal Deal on the ground outside and I yell her name.

'Becky! Becky!'

She pauses, but only to tuck a remnant of tissue into the corner of her bag and zip it up before continuing. I rap again, harder, and shout, 'Becky!' She turns and sees me and I try to sum up everything I am feeling in my facial expression – contrition, shame, love and the asking for forgiveness I don't even know how to formulate – but it all just comes out as a huge, heartbroken grin and she looks surprised, but she smiles too – although it is an uncertain one, not fully executed – and I see her hurrying towards the exit, to the right, and I'm running to it, too, and I'm in and I am flinging myself at her and launching myself into her neck.

'Becky,' is all I can manage to utter at this point, into what looks like a fluffy purple snood.

'It's all right, it's all right,' she is saying, and I am close to it but I don't want to cry – not yet – and she is trying to pull her head free from mine, which is clamped somewhere in her furry collarbone and she says, 'Let's get a coffee.' So we lurch, our arms round each other like in a three-legged race – although it is lopsided and we probably wouldn't win, as I am leaning heavily on her and staggering a little – into Starbucks.

'I didn't know, I didn't know,' I say, and she makes me give a choked, laughing, truncated sob at the counter by telling the friendly server asking us our names – so they can be scribbled on our drinks – that her name is Kit, and I say my name is Vivian. That kills me as I don't deserve to be, and the thought reaches me that *no one* will be rescuing me, not now. We decide to sit down at a just-wiped small, round table. 'Dominic told me. I'm so sorry about what happened to you.' The words

320

gush out of me, shame speeding their passage. She nods, settling her coffee named Kit and her muffin down on the table; placing a stack of napkins near my unaccompanied Vivian tea (I can't eat). 'And I don't blame you for not telling me.' Yet, even now, as I look at her face – Becky's face, that I know so well, shadowed currently with anguish and apprehension – I am selfish. As I am talking to my friend my brain is screaming, *Mac is dead, Mac is dead, Mac is dead*, but I *can't* think about him, not now. 'Are you OK? How are you feeling?'

'Yes, I'm OK,' Becky says. 'I just had a bit of a wobble. Although I must admit it was quite a big one. Dramatic.' She attempts a light-hearted grimace, but she is not light-hearted; my friend had a dramatic wobble over something catastrophic and I wasn't there. I didn't even know. 'A bit of winter sun and some sangria has done me the world of good, though,' she says, running the base of her thumb down the outside of her cup. 'I can go on now.'

(Like Mac said *I* must, I think. I'm thinking about him, I'm sorry. How can I go on, now, when he is not here? How can I even do *this*, right now, with Becky?)

'I don't blame you for not telling me,' I repeat. I am selfish and I am a terrible person. Despite how terrible I've been, Becky has tried to be there for me and I have utterly refused to return the favour. 'I've been a useless friend. I've pushed you away.' I swallow down the tears that are near again. I want to tell her about Mac but I am equally desperate not to make any of this moment about *me*. I need Becky back in my life; I need her more than ever. And if she still needs me – and God, I hope she does – I want to show up for her. I hope showing up for her today will be enough.

'I tried,' says Becky. 'With you. I really have tried. But it was exhausting. Every time I reached out, there was just nothing. Nothing at all.' She sighs, and the look on her face breaks my heart. 'I just couldn't tell you about the attack because . . .'

'. . . we weren't close enough,' I say. My tea is untouched; I flick at the cupboard cuff of my cup. 'You didn't feel you could confide in me.'

'Well, no, I couldn't.' Her face, again, has a look on it I never want to see again. 'I'm sorry, Arden.'

'For God's sake, don't be sorry! I *deserve* it!'

'The only people I told were my family and Dominic, as he was around at the time.'

'And he's been around for you since. I've been neither.'

She nods sadly. 'You never wanted to meet up, get together. It was like pulling teeth, Ardie! I couldn't tell you. You've been . . .' I look down, ashamed, and wait for her to continue. 'You've been bloody awful, Arden!' There. She is angry with me and I'm glad. I *have* been bloody awful. But I love her even more for her anger because I know that however bloody awful I've been and how weary and exasperated she's been for trying with me, she *has* kept trying. 'Even you coming to Gatsby's with me, a miracle in itself, us dancing, like old times, it just wasn't the same. I tried to make it feel like it was, but it wasn't. You've been lost from me. I just couldn't tell you.'

Showing up is not enough, I think. So much more is required. I want and need to apologize, to start over, to build a bridge I'm not sure I have the tools for. I simply don't know where or how to start. 'I realize now why you were different that night,' I say. I was a blind idiot; I was blind to everything. How she acted, how she drank . . . I was blind to her because I wouldn't let myself see her.

'Yes, I'm different,' says Becky. 'I jump at my own shadow, I drink too much, I'm frightened, Ardie. I'm frightened it will happen to me again.'

She is confiding in me and my heart takes a small leap. 'It won't, Becky; it won't happen again.'

'That's what Dom says, but it *might*!' She looks a little wild, frantic almost. I have never seen my calm, funny, beautiful Becky like this. I wish I had known.

'If it does, we'll be here to look after you. *I'll* be here to look after you. I feel *sick* that I wasn't. That I wasn't there for you.'

'I know Christian made you do everything,' she says quietly. 'When you were married to him. Blanking me, hiding from me in your kitchen. Yes, I saw you,' she says with a sad grin. 'Sending me that message telling me you never wanted to see me again.' A very sad grin. 'I know that wasn't you, Ardie.'

'No,' I say, feeling wretched. I take a sip of my tea and welcome its scalding sting. The message she's referring to fills me with a recurrent horror; the message Christian made me write as he sat behind me, a smiling assassin eating a strawberry Cornetto and tapping his right, bare foot in the air, on a crossed knee. The message he even – shamefully, oh so shamefully – made me believe I *meant*, as he had chip, chipped away at me until there was nothing left to do except exactly as he told me. But the real horror is how I have behaved since that moment. Since I've been free of him. I have been behaving terribly all on my own. 'But it *has* been me since, hasn't it?' I say. 'Hiding from you. Rejecting you . . .'

I remember that day, some three years after my marriage ended, when I bumped into Becky in M&S. How, shocked by seeing her, I had garbled out a quick apology to her about what happened with my marriage, and with Christian. It had been pathetic, inadequate, embarrassing; surface shallow, a reflecting puddle not a deep, searched pond. I couldn't bear to go into the pain of specifics. I was too ashamed to explain myself to her properly. And because I had not said a proper 'sorry', that shame festered and grew, until it became the disease that separates us now. It has been a grey, cold and uninspiring life since Christian. Devoid of drama, yes, but also devoid of *anything*. Until Mac showed up. He made me feel again, gave me back some colour and some light. Can I *feel* my way back to being a good friend to Becky? Not just show up for her but *be* there, in every sense of the word? For Mac (oh, Mac, Mac) I decide to try.

'I'm so sorry,' I say. 'I'm so sorry for everything that happened and I'm so sorry that I've been too ashamed *since* to let you in. I've been an utter idiot. You came back to me, you offered me your friendship again, but I couldn't cope with it, after what I'd done. The shame . . . it just possessed me. I couldn't see beyond it. I couldn't *be* beyond it. I just don't know what to say, really, except I'm so very, very sorry and I hope you can forgive me.'

I wait, searching her face for a response. I can be a proper person again now, can't I, because of Mac? For Mac. *Through* Mac. I can be a friend, a confidante, someone to believe in. I hope Becky can see it; I hope she can believe in me again.

'Becky?'

I am terrified, I am waiting.

'You've been an absolute nightmare, but, yes, I can forgive you,' she says, finally, my lovely Becky, and she smiles at me; a smile I just want to swim in. 'I don't want to be angry any more. I want us to get back to how we were. To be honest, I've just bloody well *missed* you.'

'Oh God, me too — so much — and we can!' I urge. 'We really can.' Relief fills me like welcome air into a deflated balloon. 'I've been so stupid. So incredibly stupid.' The relief is making me gabble. 'I'm even more stupid for not letting you back into my life than I was for marrying *Christian*!'

'Oh, I hardly think *that's* true,' says Becky and she is still smiling but her eyes are glinting now in a very 'Becky' way, so I know she is joking. 'Look, Christian was a con man of the worst kind, a manipulator and an abuser. He targeted you and he made your life a misery, but it was you who took charge and made him leave. You're stronger than you think, Ardie.'

'I'm not strong at all,' I say and I know I am on the verge of collapse if I think about Mac and the fact he has died. I

324

still can't think about it; I don't have room in my brain – the crash that is coming will have to wait. Wait until I get home, like Fran said.

'You have to forgive yourself for getting into that relationship,' Becky says, munching now on her chocolate muffin – is she relieved too? Crumbs litter the table like confetti. 'You survived it but now you have to let go of the guilt. All of it. None of this was your fault, you know. It's not your *fault*.'

I smile. I am Matt Damon in *Good Will Hunting*. And Becky is wise, lovely Robin Williams.

'What happened to you is not *your* fault either,' I say.

'Oh God,' she groans, slapping herself on the forehead, 'we're *victims*.'

And because the way she says it is really funny and so, so Becky, I laugh, and then to my horror my face sort of collapses and I realize that crash cannot be put off – it is here, it is now – and before I can think anything else at all, I say, 'Mac has died,' and Becky says, 'Oh, Arden, I'm so, so sorry,' and I have an urge to do a kind of flop across the table, laying my arms in parentheses round the empty cups and the muffin crumbs, and sob and sob and sob, but I don't as I know that as I have lost one person from my life – and it is a great, great loss – I have regained another, and she is alive and she is here in front of me, in a pink coat and a purple snood, so I haul my face up into a smile and lean across the table to let her hug me, and I hug her back like I never want to let her go.

NOW

Chapter 29

What would I have said to Mac, had he regained consciousness, got better, recovered his speech? What would he have said to me? Would he have said, 'Come in!' as I knocked on the door of his new private room at St Katherine's and found him sitting up in bed, his head all wrapped in bandages like Jack and his vinegar and brown paper, after he fell down that hill, his eyes underscored by two heavy black shadows, but twinkling at me nonetheless.

Would he say, 'Hello, Arden,' croaky but clear. 'I guess I've come back.'

Would I reply, 'I look a mess!' with a little, nervous laugh, and would he say he hardly looks picture perfect, that he feels as rough as a dog, 'a medical term'? Would I give him water and would he say, 'Why don't you sit down, Ardie?' making me feel weird as it's the first time he's said my name in almost thirty years. Would we try to make small talk, although we never did it, as everything we said to each other was big, and had a purpose – to shock or seduce, impress or amaze? Everything had to *mean* something.

'Thanks for coming to see me, Arden, I really appreciate it,' he would say, with tears in his eyes, and I wouldn't know if he meant *now* or *then*, all those evenings I had sat by his bed in Ward 10, on my chair. 'Thanks for finding me.'

'I wasn't *looking* for you,' I would teasingly reply – the old

Arden, 'I wasn't *ever* looking for you,' which we'd both know was a lie, as wasn't he once *exactly* what I was looking for? And I would smile and he would smile and then he would look sad, suddenly, and I would ask 'Why?' and he would shake his head and say he would be in a wheelchair now as he had lost the use of his legs, as a result of the coma, the haemorrhage – that he would be Lieutenant Dan in *Forrest Gump*, Luke Martin in *Coming Home*, Ron Kovic in *Born on the Fourth of July*.

'Are you just going to name every character in a wheelchair in every bloody movie since the beginning of time?' I would enquire. Then I would suggest he would make a better Daryl Van Horne, if only we could get him the dressing gown, and that he watches too many movies.

He'd chuckle – a throaty one – and say I must go on with my life without him, that he wouldn't want to be a burden, a Norman Maine to my Vicki Lester, and the old Arden would say, 'Bit presumptuous, really, Mac. Who says that I *want* you?' And I would not be sure if I did or not, as he was still a hero, but he was a flawed one, and I didn't know. But he would laugh because he had loved the old Arden, and I had loved the old Mac.

He would say sorry for betraying me, all those years ago. That he was young, morally reprehensible and full of ego. I would say I was a selfish, infuriating, annoying brat, that nobody was perfect. But also that I *wasn't* like that now, I hoped, as I had experienced so much since him – that those experiences had made me dull and colourless and empty, uninspired, but he had fired me back up with the memory of us, brought colour into my life and made me want to live – *properly* – again; to fulfil all those promises he had for me. And I would be tempted to get in that bed with him, my flawed hero, and stow my chin in his armpit, although really I knew we would have a bitter-sweet parting, but remain close friends until the end of our lives . . .

None of that script would be followed.

He isn't here.

He didn't make it.

He is gone.

It's an unexpected morning, the morning of Mac's memorial service. It's the first morning it has snowed for a long, long time, certainly the first time this winter. When I pull back the curtains I am so surprised to see that glaring, blinding whiteness everywhere, as snow hasn't been forecast. There's a flat royal icing loaf of about three inches squatting on my car, scattered arrows of bird prints across my tiny front garden and the trees spaced along the road have white piping on their branches and half of their trunks coated in white shadow.

As I stand at the window, I remember a day Mac and I had when he'd watched all afternoon at his flat for snow, like a child, and when it finally came, at midnight, alighting softly on that winter-spindly branch at his bedroom window, he dressed me up in his coat and took me outside on to the patch of grass behind his building at Westwood and made me stand there as he flapped himself into a snow angel. I had laughed – a bit – but mostly I had scowled and been a miserable so-and-so because I hated the cold. And he had hugged me, back in his flat, and made me a hot-water bottle that had a fluffy mock-cowhide cover before wrapping me up so tight in so many of his prairie blankets I had formed a startled tepee, with a tiny head sticking out of the top.

'Are you OK? Shall I make us a cup of tea?'

I smile at my best friend Becky and close my bedroom curtain again, trying not to feel desperately sad that Mac and I can't remember that day together, or any of the days and the nights we spent, in love and lust. That I will never speak to Mac again.

'Yes, please.'

Becky stayed here last night. She said she wants to support me as much as she can today and I thank her with all my heart and continually try to swallow down the thought that threatens to derail me, that I wasn't there to support *her* when she needed me, but I will now, every single day.

'A cup of tea sounds amazing,' I add. Becky is in fleecy pyjamas with a polar bear on the front and looks like she did in the mornings at Warwick – hair sticking up, blinking and slightly dazed, like a newly hatched chick.

There will be no more secrets between us – she will get sick of me telling her absolutely everything in my life; and I hope she can tell me everything in hers, like we once did. She knows for a week after Mac died I walked to the hospital every night but didn't go in, that I loitered, outside the automatic doors, watching people get swallowed up into the warmth and light within and wishing I could follow them to Ward 10, to sit with Mac. She knows how on a few occasions I walked further still and stood outside Mac's house, staring up at the windows he wouldn't look out of any more, imagining him pottering round the house and garden, loping through the rooms practising his lectures out loud, employing all those emphatic hand and arm gestures he used to make; wondering if he ever slid our photo from between the pages of his book and stared at it, remembering . . . She knows how after a few moments I turned and went home again. 'And I'll do us a bacon sandwich.'

We didn't go to the short service at the crematorium as it was family members only – Lloyd, basically, and two nieces of Helen's I knew nothing about, who live in Ireland and were apparently combining the funeral with a trip to see Michael Bublé at the O2, and I was relieved not to go as I couldn't bear the whole shuntingly, sub-gothic curtain thing – but Lloyd and James and I met up in Costa a few days later to discuss the details of Mac's memorial service.

I was surprised and gladdened that Lloyd asked me to contribute – the former harlot, the wanton affair-igniter – but maybe he has forgiven me, or maybe he likes me enough to bear to have me involved. At least he's still in the country. And it was good to see James, although at that stage, nothing really felt good. Apparently he called round to see me when I was at the airport with Becky, and he turned up at my house the evening after that, but I had been crying and I looked awful, so I didn't open the door. Hiding again; it seems I will never learn. But what would have been the point, really? In seeing him? Yes, we have shared a couple of semi-confessions and he helped me see how simple it could be to free myself from my mother, but we are not *friends*. We have never even exchanged mobile phone numbers. We're just two people who met through wildly disparate connections to a man in a hospital bed. And without Mac, what reason would we have to stay in touch? When I met James at Costa, when we sat with Lloyd and talked through plans and logistics, I knew that today, at the memorial service, will be the last time I see him.

Becky and I have our tea and our bacon sandwiches, shower and get dressed in warm hats and coats and walk to Larkspur Hill. As we step in the snow-grooves already made by others, I wonder how I would feel if I had read somewhere Mac had died, having not seen him for so many years; would I feel the same choking grief I feel now, having seen him every day for three weeks? I know the answer is 'no'. I would have been shocked to read it, and tearful, probably, and I would have spent a few days feeling sad and looking back and feeling sentimental, but I have had such an intense few weeks remembering *everything*, with Mac's prompting: The List, the laughter, the love – all so immediate and so real – that now he is gone I feel utterly bereft. Yet, I am glad we had these days. And I'm glad he prompted me to bathe in the golden nostalgic glow of our affair. To long, once more, for how he made me feel.

The movie references he spoke to me – *our* movie references – will have to be his last will and testament. His will that I remember him, his testament that what we had together is something worth remembering.

We are the first here and it is bitterly cold. There is no sun and the sky is low and dove grey. There is a slanting soft blizzard of snow; if you stare at the swirling snowflakes too long – like dust from a projector in a dark screening room – you start to feel you might lose your balance and fall into a parallel, wreathing universe. Varying icing-sugar flakes make a soft landing on Becky's black coat and fade one by one to a wet nothing.

I'm not wearing a black coat, but a camel-coloured wool one, self-tied at the waist, over a black polo-neck sweater dress. Plus brown seventies boots; I've got to be practical, in all this snow. I know Mac will appreciate it, as I say goodbye to him. That I am here to figuratively smooth the hair from his face and hold him tight for the very last time.

'*The Way We Were*?' says James, and I am surprised at how pleased I am to see him, as he walks up to me, his shoes making long commas in the snow. It's been two weeks or so since I have. Last time, in the coffee shop, I couldn't even really focus on him; today he is bundled up in a long grey wool coat, leather gloves and an unflattering deerstalker hat with a furry lining, which really makes me smile.

'Bloody hell, you're good,' I say, as Mac once did to me.

'Seen it fifty times,' he says. 'The perfect Saturday-afternoon movie. You look great, actually.'

'Is that appropriate?' I tease. 'Compliments at a memorial service?' I'm really quite amazed he got the reference, actually, but I know, as I've pinned my curls up at the back, that I've also given myself a blonde version of Katie's shorty curly hairstyle. Still, he's *good* and his compliment makes me feel . . . well, I don't know.

James shrugs and smiles. A snowflake lands on his chin

331

and he laughs and flicks at it with one of his leathery fingers. His eyes look really intense, I think, in the almost fairy-tale, blizzardy gloom. Almost petrol blue. It's like they have been lit from behind. 'How are you doing?' he asks and I realize I've missed him. I like his earnest easy-going nature and his little quirks. I like his face. I hope, suddenly – and it's a strange little hope that sparks within me like a pilot light – this is not the last time I see him.

'I'm OK. You?'

'I'm OK. It's so quiet, next door. I mean, it was while he was in hospital, but now I know he's not coming back . . .'

'I went there,' I say. 'To Mac's house. I stood outside like a bloody idiot. More than once, actually.'

'You should have knocked,' said James, 'come in for a cup of tea.'

'You don't drink tea.'

'I keep it in for guests.'

I smile; I enjoy the light dancing in his grey eyes, but they are also making me feel strangely shy. 'Oh, you were probably out, doing the estate agency thing. And I wouldn't have wanted to disturb you.' The truth was, when I'd stood outside, my eyes had been red raw and my emotions all over the place; I hadn't dared knock.

'You wouldn't have disturbed me.' He looks at me, holds his gaze. I need to look away.

'Hello, Arden.' It's Lloyd. He's finally got socks on and is bundled up in a massive black overcoat and a brown beanie hat. There are two women standing with him, twenty-somethings. 'This is Kelly and Scarlett,' he says. They must be Mac's nieces, I think, still in London somehow, the Bublé fans who went to the service at the crematorium. I wonder how the concert went and scour their faces for resemblances to their aunt. Lloyd told me that Helen sent flowers to that service, from her home in Paris; that she didn't want to attend then or today as she wasn't sure what she could 'contribute'. I'd smiled and thought, *Sounds like Helen*. I wish her well – *so* well – but I'm relieved she's not here. There are only so many emotions a person can feel in one day.

'Nice to meet you,' Kelly and Scarlett – in unison – say politely. They are wearing a lot of make-up.

'I'll just go and set up,' says Lloyd. He has a large carrier bag dangling from one gloved hand. In the other he holds a folded-up stripy camping chair. He wanders off with his kit and the nieces stand staring at James, despite his ridiculous hat.

'Fran's here,' says James.

I turn around and she is in front of me, looking smart in a grey wool coat and a red scarf, her hair tucked under a matching woolly hat with a big faux-fur bobble on it. I'm surprised to see her as I didn't think she'd make it.

'Fran! Thanks so much for coming!'

'I swapped shifts,' she says. 'I really wanted to come.' She squeezes my arm. 'He was quite a guy. I'll miss him.'

Julian, who has brought Sam – all wide-eyed and excited, but trying to hide it, as a blissfully unaffected onlooker on such an occasion might – walks up the hill. I smile as I look down at them, a snow-globed London behind them. There is certainly something epic about being up here, I think. Cinematic. I can see why Mac loved the view from here.

I'm beginning to not be able to feel my toes in my boots. Becky is hopping from side to side slightly, to keep warm. And the snow continues to come down, soft and unrelenting.

'All right?' I ask her.

'Cold,' she says with a smile, and she takes my hand. She has woolly gloves on, I have leather; I give her hand a squeeze.

A burly man, elderly, and like a bear in a huge black overcoat and a fedora, approaches and shakes my hand. 'Stewart Whittaker,' he says, his voice more gruff and tremulous than I recall it. 'Thank you for letting me know about today. I'm glad you found Lloyd.' There are two middle-aged women with him, in hats and scarves – I wonder if one of them is the woman who answered my phone call at the London Film School – and a couple of young men around Julian's age, who may be current students.

'With your help,' I say to Stewart. 'Thanks so much.' I've emailed him twice, since he wrote from New York: firstly to tell him Mac had died and about Lloyd; secondly to invite him here today. In neither was I brave enough to answer his question about whether he'd met me before, but I get the feeling he knows exactly who I am, and does it really matter now? He's not looking at me in a judgemental way, certainly. He looks kind and he is smiling, snowflakes alighting on his big bushy beard.

We take our places in a small circle – me, James, Fran, Becky, Kelly and Scarlett (who are still trying not to stare at James), Stewart and the women and the two young men. The wooden bench Mac sat on forms the final plane of our semicircle, which I thought was a nice touch when James suggested it; we might get one of those plaques made, later on. Lloyd is opposite us and is unrolling a white screen upwards from a metal stand which he has planted into the ground. He pulls a cube-shaped mobile projector from his carrier bag, unwraps it from what look like two navy jumpers and places it, facing the screen, on the camping chair.

'Are we expecting anyone else?' asks Becky, to my right.

'I don't think so,' I say.

'Who are that lot, then?'

At the bottom of Larkspur Hill, seven or eight people, broad brush-stroked by dark daubs of coats, hats and scarves, arrange themselves in a silent cluster. There's some quick handshaking, some light hugs, then the small army begins to move up the hill towards us. At their head is a diminutive figure, with dark hair and a long straight fringe, who strides with long, booted steps and purpose.

James, to my left, glances at me. 'Is that a severe fringe I see before me?' he queries.

'Looks like it,' I say, incredulous.

As they get nearer, I notice most of the dark, blizzard-muffled flock seem to be clutching the same rectangular-shaped item in their hands. The small marching figure at their head carries one too. Fringe and flock reach us. The small figure – gimlet eyes, fitted double-breasted military coat – thrusts out an ungloved hand to me.

'I'm Perrie Turque,' she says crisply, 'and these are some of Mac's old Film students, from the glory days. I tracked them down via Facebook.'

The flock – fifty-somethings down to early forties, perhaps; there are touches of grey and eyes crinkled by time – nod at me and smile. 'Hello, Perrie,' I reply, shaking her hand. 'I'm Arden.'

'Thought you might be. I looked up your photo on LinkedIn.' Of course she did. A lacy trim of snow edges the bottom of Perrie's formidable fringe. She swipes at it with an index finger and it disperses into the air. I let her know Mac had died and when the memorial was, but I never heard anything back from her . . . enigmatic and infuriating woman . . . yet here she is.

'Hello,' trills one of Perrie's tribe, a slight woman with lank grey-blonde hair overlaid with a doily of snow. I look at the hardback book she's holding in her hand, the red cover polka-dotted with melted snowflakes; it's the book Mac wrote – *The Language of Celluloid*. All the other ex-students are holding the same, some hardback, some paperback, snow-flakes glancing off them or disintegrating on its navy spine.

'How amazing!' says Lloyd, coming over to shake hands with them all. 'Absolutely great. And you all have Dad's book! That's so cool! *Perrie*,' says Lloyd, surprised, when he gets to her.

'Lloyd.' Perrie nods curtly. 'Nice to see you.'

Lloyd blushes and beats a rather blustery retreat. I venture a smile at Perrie and she smiles back, brisk but not unfriendly.

'Thank you for coming,' I say to her, when the flock has dispersed a little, and I realize I have so much to thank her for. 'I didn't even know you were in the country.'

'I flew back for this,' she says, 'Belize. I'm off to New Zealand tomorrow. Mac was a fantastic lecturer and should never be forgotten,' she adds, not a trace of emotion in her clipped voice.

'He won't be,' I say, refusing to choke up – not yet. 'Not ever.'

Perrie and her small band of Glory Days students are directed to elongate the semicircle and Lloyd crouches at the side of the striped camping chair and starts the projector. White light tunnels through the whirling snow and lands as a square on the screen; there's a flickering silence, then one of those spluttering ticking countdown begins, just like on the old movies – eight, seven, six, five . . . Lloyd adjusts the focus. The screen remains pure white and the soundtrack starts and, oh God, it's 'Everybody's Talkin', from *Midnight Cowboy*.

I'm a mess before an image even comes on the screen and when it does, it's Mac's cowboy boots. A photo of them, taken on Mac's kitchen table. There's a small ripple of laughter from the semicircle, whipped by the wind, but from me, immediately, tears, which turn to unchecked sobs when the image cuts to a photo of Mac looking typically Mac, older than I remember him, but younger than he was in these last weeks – maybe early fifties? He's looking pretty *Midnight Cowboy* himself; he's leaning on a fence, in jeans and a white shirt, one foot up on the second rail, and looking into the middle distance like a matinee idol in a movie still, as long thin clouds scud above his head and tail off into a far-off dusty tan horizon. Is he on a *ranch*? Did Mac achieve his dream and make it out to the prairies after all?

The thought makes me cry even harder. I try to keep the tears in but it's impossible. He got there; he got to the prairies. I'm so happy for Mac, that he made it, but God I miss him. I miss the time I spent with him and all the years I didn't.

I'm probably making an utter, jibbering fool of myself so I daren't look at anybody else. Nilsson is already singing about going where the sun keeps shining and now on the screen is Mac, as a child in bib and braces, on what could be the steps of a nursery; then, in a sepia school uniform, perched on a high stool with a birthday cake and candles in front of him; as a teenager, bell-bottomed trousers and a lairy shirt – quite the dedicated follower of fashion; then – twenty-something? Beard, top off, sitting in the front seat of a car that may be a Ford Capri. I smile through the tears that simply won't stop.

'Wow.' I glance to my left; Scarlett and Kelly are looking at each other, their mouths open and tears in their eyes, too, clearly marvelling at just how handsome Mac was. It's an amazing photo – the sun is in Mac's eyes and he is grinning like life was just rolling out in front of him like a country road, which of course it was. Now he's with Lloyd as a baby, leaning over the side of a paddling pool in a suburban back garden and handing his son a plastic watering can. Helen is half in the photo, in a black swimsuit; Mac is in shorts and a Spencer Tracy T-shirt. Now Mac stands towering next to Lloyd, who's puffing out his chest in a Boy Scout's uniform and long socks. Now Mac and Helen have their arms round each other on a sofa and Lloyd – a teenager – has his head sticking in from the side of the photo, laughing.

I see Mac through a veil of smattering, sliding snowflakes which soften him and give him that ethereal quality he will always have for me now. My Mac, the Mac who belonged to others. The final picture, as Nilsson warbles to a close, is Mac looking about eight or nine, grinning with a wide-eyed baby on his lap, who is happily chewing his own fist. *Reggie*. Oh God, Reggie. My heart is officially broken. Sadness envelops me like the whirling snow. I simply don't have enough tissues in my bag for the tears I need to cry.

The image fades and John Denver's 'Sunshine on my Shoulders' starts with its gentle, lilting twang of guitar chords and I have to stop myself from gasping through my never-ending tears as here is Mac as I remember him, in his early thirties at Warwick University. He's on the steps outside the Arts Centre, he's in chinos and desert boots and a pink shirt and his tweedy blazer and my heart gives a great lurch and I smile, as that's him, that's my Mac – there he is. Mac in a seminar room, on one of those low, woolly chairs, in mid discussion with a handful of enthralled students, his arm raised in animation, a photo I'd seen in his room. A photo I'd loved. Mac giving a speech at the BFI – was it the one I went to London with him for? No, wrong clothes, and he has an amusing hint of a goatee. It's after me, I think; *it's after me*. Mac below a big sign for the UEA; Mac, laughing his head off, with his arm round Stewart Whittaker, and standing in the doorway of the London Film School. That one makes me smile through my tears. He still had it; he still had flashes of light in these later years when life may have faded for him. Oh God, and when the song gets to the part about giving you a day just like today, I am in silent floods, holding poor Becky's hand so, so tight. Mac gave me so many wonderful days. He wished so very much for me. The man who made me who I am, who brought back some of the girl I used to be. My flawed hero, my memory creator and memory jogger; the man whose life was carried as a trophy before him by others; the man who carried a piece of my heart, always. I loved him, I loved him.

For the last minute of the song we stay on a photo of Mac

sitting on the steps outside his flat at Warwick. I've never seen this photo before. He's squinting into winter sun. One arm floats on a knee, his other, bent, offers him a hand to rest his chin on. He looks happy. Amused. Content. He was everything to me and I'm so thankful he came back to me, however briefly. To remind me of us.

We remain with him on the steps until the final few bars of the song fade away, and I can't bear it. I don't want him to go. I don't want him to go. The picture slowly, awfully fades to black, in one of those circles that decrease to nothing, and the circle of us quietly applaud for a very long time as we stand there in front of a white screen in the swirling snow and the bitter, beautiful cold and remember him.

As we make our way silently back down the hill, a troop of dark-coated soldiers, heads bent, I see Lloyd take his phone from his pocket and he must hate us because he hits us with one more song to break our hearts and the rousing strings of the opening bars of 'Rhinestone Cowboy' echo softly through the snow.

'Oh no!' I say to Becky and I'm crying all over again and letting the tears run down my face, mingling with downy flakes of cold, as we make fresh footsteps in the snow – Becky and I, James, Lloyd, Fran, Stewart Whittaker and friends, Julian and Sam, Helen's nieces and Perrie Turque and her merry band, still clutching their books. As Glen sings about being where lights are shining on him, I feel a hand take mine, but it's not Becky, as she's the wrong side; it's James, and I look up at him, surprised, and he smiles gently at me and we walk down the hill to 'Rhinestone Cowboy', glove in glove.

The place where we have come to celebrate Mac's life is called The Ellipsis and, beautifully apt, it's a tiny, converted art deco cinema, three streets from Mac's house; a snug building with beautiful ceilings and a lobby with an original carpet patterned with overlapping fans like pistachio-green halos. The downstairs restaurant is in what must have been the stalls and it is plush and walled in panels of red and gold, with a polished wood floor and white-tableclothed round tables radiating from the arched stage, but we walk through it – where elegant people in luxury knitwear are having coffee and brunch – to a bronze staircase which leads up to the old circle and the Hollywood glamour of the Crescent Bar. Here, the curved back wall is draped with red velvet curtains and bordered with padded raspberry leather banquettes, either side of a shiny, lit-up bar; dimmed, golden chandeliers preside above our heads; and at the front of this fan-shaped space, where once cinema-goers gazed from the front-row in the circle at the silver screen, are gilt railings, like those on an ocean liner, to keep us from falling on the glamorous people in their rosy nest below. Up here, we are to have cocktails and canapés and an attempt at fun, as Mac would have wanted.

We cluster at the bright bar, ordering drinks. Becky has gone back downstairs to the loo, Fran with her. Julian and Sam stare at the contents of his wallet, then realize it's a free bar. Perrie is gripping Stewart's arm and talking intently at him, her students mingling with his colleagues and the two young men.

There's a strange air of gaiety and relief amongst our small crowd, as waitresses glide round with tiny trays of smoked salmon and cucumber canapés, coats are heaved off and thrown on to banquettes and snowy hats are shaken and stowed under high stools at tall round tables. It's warm and it's cocoon-like, under the muted gleam of the chandeliers: the saddest part of the day is done; now is the time to tell stories, to laugh and to joke, to bring back the good times and to remember the beginning, the middle but not the end. The air is definitely charged with something, I feel, as I shrug off my own coat and toss free my hair into its longer curls. Hope and possibility, I

340

decide, as that sounds good to me, and I wonder if life *can* be good once more, for me.

James silently held my hand all the way down the hill and along the street into The Ellipsis, only letting it go as we crossed the art deco threshold and stepped on to that fanned lobby carpet. He's at the bar now, with a barmaid smiling at him, and I want him to take his gloves off, now mine are, and come and hold my hand properly, an unexpected want which terrifies me. I like him, I think, I really like him, but I need to hold his hand again to make sure this terrifying truth is real. That how I felt when he held it was not at all how I felt when Becky did. That he is not just a friend, but has suddenly become something more.

My timing is terrible.

Lloyd appears in front of me. He has a giant pina colada in each hand and passes me one.

'Thank you,' I say, wondering how lethal it is, but then deciding I might need lethal, at this juncture. 'Great venue,' I add. 'It's lovely here.' Lloyd nods. 'You're quite the movie maker, you know, Lloyd. Your tributes were really lovely.'

'I'm not bad,' he admits. His beard is smaller today – has he had it trimmed for the occasion? 'I messed around with that sort of thing as a kid. Then I stopped doing it because I didn't want to be anything like my old man. Oh, sorry,' he says quickly, 'I'm not having a dig, I promise. At you or Dad. You made him happy, for a while.' He looks at me and smiles sadly, before taking a sip of his cocktail.

I'm amazed. 'Thank you, Lloyd,' I say. 'Your dad once made *me* really happy. It wasn't just an affair, you know. I really loved him.' I am about to add that I believe Mac to be the love of my life, too, but I remember what Mac said to me about a Bigger Love to come, so I shut up. I can hear his Northern voice in my ear – *You've got it all, Ardie. You've got everything you'll ever need.* Can I honour him, finally? Can I do

341

something with all those things I've got and be happy again? Is the love of my life *yet to come*? I sip from my drink, eyes lowered and scout the bar for James but I can't see him now.

I am probably a ridiculous idiot.

'I can tell,' says Lloyd. *What, that I'm a ridiculous idiot?* 'That you loved Dad. You wept buckets earlier.'

Mac's phrase. 'Yes, sorry – I was never going to keep it together today.'

Lloyd nods slowly. Then he pats my arm, gives me a winky smile and walks off. I watch him go. Mac's son.

Fran and Becky come back from the loo.

'What are you drinking?' Becky asks.

'A pina colada.'

'Oh, I might get one of those. Do you fancy one, Fran?'

'Why not?'

Their coats are over their arms and I can see they've both touched up their make-up. Becky must have lent Fran her lipstick as they're both sporting a dramatic plum. It suits Fran. I smile at another instant friendship formed in a ladies' loo, but the way Becky is smiling at me – so kind and so concerned – makes my heart swell as I know that hers and mine is for a lifetime.

'Will you be OK if we go to the bar?' asks Becky. 'We'll be as quick as we can.'

'Yes, I'll be OK. Shove your coats under one of those banquette thingies.'

They bustle off and Julian spots me, from across the room. I give him a wave and sip my drink. He gestures that he'll be over in a minute.

'Hello,' says James.

I turn and he is there. He still has his coat on, undone over his black suit and tie, but that terrible hat has gone, as have his gloves. I wish his eyes weren't so grey and the memory of his hand in mine so fresh. He looks absolutely lovely, although part of his hair is sticking up, at the front,

342

and I have to resist the urge to take my hand and smooth it down.

'Hello.' I sound high-pitched, mildly hysterical. I need to act normal. I'm at a function following a bloody memorial service, for God's sake. Mac's memorial service. A few moments ago I was crying my eyes out over him.

'It all went really well,' he says.

'Yes, it did.'

'And a good turnout.'

'Yes.'

'I liked the music.'

'Mac's favourites,' I say. 'You could probably tell. The combination of soundtrack and image totally killed me.'

'Well, yes.' James smiles. 'You got through a lot of tissues.'

Thanks for holding my hand, I want to say, but of course I don't. And then I wonder if he needed a hand-hold too, on the way to this social function, where we would be in a crowd of people and far from his comfort zone. 'Are you OK?' I ask him. 'Here, at this do? Will you be all right?'

'I think so,' he replies with a smile. '*You're* here, aren't you?' And before I can think what to say to this, he looks around him and says, 'I think we picked the right venue. It's very Film Studies. Did you apply for that job, by the way? Script reader?'

'Actually, I did. Thank you for your encouragement.'

'Oh, no problem. Well done. I hope you get it.'

'Thank you.'

I feel a little bashful. I'm still trying to process what he said: *You're here*. As for the job, I might get it, I might not. But I'm glad I've applied. I have the feeling, for the first time in a long time, that I've got nothing to lose. It's a reckless feeling, but exciting. I remember it well.

We look at each other for a few seconds. James has a beer in his hand, hardly touched. I sip at the pina colada, relishing its coldness and its high alcoholic content. Out of nowhere I wonder what it would be like if I told James everything about myself; everything good and everything bad. The story of Marilyn and Dad and Christian and Felix and Julian, and how it was with Mac and me. The *whole* story, no omissions: who I am, really, everything I was before, and who I would like to be. I suddenly feel like I want to.

'Can I ask you something?' James says. *He* suddenly looks nervous. 'Sorry, I'm shit at this.'

Shit at what? I think. Why does he look nervous? 'Yes, you can ask me something.'

'Is it OK to give someone a present on the day of someone's memorial service?'

'A *present*?'

'Yes.'

'Who do you want to give a present to?'

'To *you*. I can give it to you another day, if you'd like. It's just that I saw something this morning and I bought it. Maybe I shouldn't have done.'

I'm so curious. Why has James bought me a present? 'If you've brought it, you'd better give it to me,' I say. 'And I'm sure it's *fine* to give someone a present on the day of a memorial. Who would care, really? I certainly don't – I've been crying my eyes out for almost an hour so anything that can cheer me up will be very welcome, quite honestly.'

'That's what I hoped.' James reaches into the pocket of his coat and pulls out a square of folded gauzy fabric that has vibrant splashes of colour across it – red, orange, yellow and green. 'I've been thinking about the lovebirds,' he says.

'Mum! Are you OK? You cried so *much*!' It's Julian, appearing in front of me, Sam standing next to him, all perfume and pretty eyes. Their coats are off; I'm pleased to see Julian has got a black tie on with his grey suit. He's made the effort, for me.

'Oh, I'm fine,' I say, always prone to be buoyed at the sight of my wonderful boy. 'I was really sad but I'm all right now, I promise.' I sound brave, I realize; I *need* to be brave. Julian followed by Sam leans in to give me a hug. James steps back a little, still holding the square of material. *Sorry*, I mouth at him.

'You've got a drink?' asks Julian.

I waggle my pina colada at him. 'Yes, I've got a drink.'

Julian looks from me to James and back again. 'OK, well, we're just going to get another one. Sam says the margaritas are amazing.' Sam grins at me; I grin at her in return.

They walk away, Julian looking so happy as he smiles at something Sam says and puts his arm round her – my loving, strong boy – and I realize that I need to be strong, too. Stronger than I've ever been, if I'm ever to release my guilt about Julian and his childhood. I can't let it envelop me any more. I can't let it haunt me for ever. Becky is right: I need to try to let it *all* go.

'Arden.' Stewart Whittaker is to my right, holding out a paw for me to shake. 'I'm afraid I've got to leave. Dry, dusty lecturing thing to do, you know how it is.'

'I'm sure you're never dry *or* dusty,' I say, shaking that big warm paw, and I think of the photo of him and Mac outside the London Film School, laughing their heads off. Such a fantastic photograph.

'That's very kind,' says Stewart, in his wavering, rumbling voice. 'And thank you for today. It was an excellent send-off for Mac.'

'Thank you for coming,' I reply, feeling tears spring to my eyes again. In the periphery I see James turn to talk to Fran who has appeared holding an enormous red cocktail with half a pineapple sticking out of the top of it. Stewart looks like he's about to go and then he adds, 'I remember you, you know, from Soho, a long time ago. Do you remember the day we met?'

'Yes, I do,' I say. I feel a blush creep on to both of my cheeks.

'I'd just like to say that I think Mac looked happy with you.'

'Thank you,' I say, surprised. 'I was a very different person back then.' But I was capable of making someone happy, I think. That really counts for something.

'We all were,' says Stewart, 'but in some respects we're all exactly the same. Goodbye, Arden.'

'Goodbye, Stewart.'

Fran is laughing at something James just said. The square he showed me is in his hand, down by his side. She moves away to talk to one of Mac's old students and James turns back to me.

Looking at me with grey, steady eyes and without saying a word, he brings up the square of fabric and shakes it out in front of him like a magician and it's a large fluttering square of almost opaque cream, flocked with pairs of plump and happy red-and-yellow-and-orange-breasted lovebirds, with wings of brilliant green, and dancing between the lovebirds are lilac butterflies, their wings flecked with silver thread.

'Remember *The Birds*? Melanie and Mitch?' I stare at him. I look at the scarf and then back to his earnest face and those soot-grey eyes. 'This morning, on the way here, I passed a little shop called The Emporium, and there was this scarf in the window. I think it would look really nice with your Ali MacGraw *Love Story* pea coat, and the red tights.' I smile; he noticed. 'The butterflies are an extra touch,' he adds.

The scarf is beautiful. The lovebirds are so wrapped up in the gossamer thread of mine and Mac's story. Yes, I remember *The Birds*. Yes, of course I remember Melanie and Mitch. I start to cry again, just a little.

'Don't cry,' he says gently. He takes the scarf and wraps it softly round my neck, gently freeing my escaped curls from it. 'It suits you,' he says. 'You always want to be the girl in the movies, but you don't need to be,' he says. 'You don't need to imitate anyone. You don't need to hide away. You've got a star that shines all on its own.'

346

I don't know what to say. James takes one of my hands and, palm to palm, I feel an electric shock of something delicious and scary travel up my arm and round my body. Does *he* feel it? Does he feel it here in this room with the chatter and laughter of sad but hopeful people around us? People who will go on?

'I've been thinking about leaving lovebirds outside your door,' James says steadily, his hand in mine. 'I've been thinking about it for a while.'

My heart starts to flutter like one of the butterflies on my scarf. My mind races. 'Have you?' Hitchcock didn't do *anything* unless it was laden with meaning . . . What does *this* mean? Is James saying what I think he's saying . . . ?

'Yes. You said you've been brought lovebirds before, but it has all gone horribly wrong. That what started as love ended in nightmare. It doesn't have to. Sometimes things *can* stay full of possibility. Sometimes love ends in *love*, all the way to the final scene and beyond.'

My heart is pounding under the drape of my new scarf. Wrapped in the flashes of these bright colours, I don't speak.

'I want to bring lovebirds to your door, Ardie. Will you accept them?'

I still don't say anything. I just look at James and think that one day really soon, if I dare to, I might love him.

'Oh, fucking hell, Arden,' he says, 'I just really like you! You make me laugh, you make me feel happy, you make me feel that I'm OK, as a person, when others around me don't. I feel like you're good for me, I *know* you are. Will you please go out with me, on a date?'

'A date?' I'm smiling now. He likes me. I make him feel happy. I make him laugh. He's leaving *lovebirds* outside my door! My insides start doing a number from *A Chorus Line*. Somewhere, Judy Garland is singing something upbeat and chirpy. And I dare to start living again – properly.

'Yes, a date. Dinner, the movies . . .'

He winks at me and I beam. The scarf is cool as I stroke it with my hand, a soft cotton under my fingertips. 'I accept your lovebirds,' I say. 'The real thing would have been slightly better,' I add cheekily, 'but you probably didn't pass a pet shop this morning and they *probably* wouldn't have fitted in your pocket.' James laughs. 'I accept your lovebirds and I accept your offer. I'd love to go on a date.'

'You would? So that's a yes?'

'Yes, that's a yes.'

'Well, thank fuck for that!' James sighs a huge sigh and then envelops me in a huge, huge hug. He is warm and smells of lemon and cinnamon. I don't want to let him go but, eventually, I do, and I laugh and pull the scarf tighter around me, embracing its softness. I love my gift and I wonder, suddenly, as James smiles at me, if he is a gift to me, from Mac. Mac has reminded me that I can love and that I can do so with passion and without apology. The old Arden, the 'handful' certainly did – rightly or wrongly, didn't she throw everything into it? Has Mac now brought James to me, so I get to fulfil his promise of having a Bigger Love? Or would that be downright crazy and I have *definitely* watched far too many movies?

'OK,' says James, putting both hands in his coat pockets, 'now I need to go and talk to somebody else otherwise I'm going to blush and grin right in your face for the next hour and that wouldn't be cool.'

'No, it wouldn't be,' I say. 'Go ahead.' And I am blushing and grinning on this day that started with such sadness and is now so full of hope. I decide to nurture that hope, let it grow. All I have experienced has made me who I am, and all I am yet to experience I will greet with open arms. I won't imitate life any more or be content to have it dull and unlit – I will leap into colour and light. I will step away from past hurt and let remorse and regret leave me. I will embrace the hope of love and the promise of everything.

'All right?' says Becky, coming up beside me with her cocktail. 'Bloody hell, I've just been chatting to Perrie. Boy, that woman can talk. It was like being bulldozed by an army tank with a heavy fringe.'

'She's quite a character,' I agree. 'She's flying to New Zealand tomorrow.'

'They can *have* her. She can stand in the middle of a field of sheep and talk at *them*.'

'Ha. She probably would, as well.'

'It's been so sad but somehow good today,' says Becky. 'Perfect, in fact.'

'I think so, too.' I nod. It *has* been perfect. 'What do you think Mac would have made of it, the circle of us at the top of the hill, the movies his son made of his life?'

'I don't know – I'm not the girl who loved him. What do *you* think?'

'He would have absolutely loved it,' I say. 'He would have appreciated it as a real *moment*. All that snow and grey skies – it was so cinematic. I don't think even *he* could have planned it better.'

'Will you be OK, do you think?' Becky is looking at me, over the top of her straw, her eyes full of love and concern.

'Yes, I'll be OK. I have *you*, don't I? How about you?'

'Oh God, yes, I'll be OK. *I have you, don't I?*' She laughs and puts her arm round me. 'Single gals together, all that jazz.'

'Actually, about that . . .' I venture, snaking my arm round her, too. 'James and I are going on a date.'

She shrugs, after pretending to look comically disappointed. 'We don't *both* have to be single,' she laughs. 'And you know my hero is *always* just around the next corner . . . Sod it if he is or isn't, to be honest. But, really, that's great, Ardie. You'd be good together, I reckon, what I've seen of him.'

'I really like him,' I say. 'And I make him *laugh*, apparently.'

'Perfect, then,' says Becky. 'You've found your Richard Gere. *Pretty Woman* or *An Officer and a Gentleman*?'

'Oh, definitely *Pretty Woman*,' I say, 'but if he tries any of that rescuing nonsense I'm just going to have to reciprocate.' I can rescue, too, I think. I can love and be loved. I am a grown-up, a survivor and the lead role in my own narrative.

I can do anything.

Becky laughs. 'Good plan. Excellent. Just think, you'd never have met him if it hadn't been for Mac.'

'I know.' *James is a gift from Mac. Discuss*, I think. Yet, even if this wonderful gift doesn't become the story I'd like it to, if it's just me, after all, I know I'll be OK.

'He won't be forgotten,' says Becky, putting her arm round my back. 'Mac Bartley-Thomas. He's one of those people who never will be.'

'No, he won't,' I say, and I let myself choke up and welcome the tears that flood back to my eyes. I want to feel everything for Mac, for ever. For all that he was and all that he gave to me. 'You're absolutely right.'

And as Lloyd stands on a chair to chink on a glass with a knife and make a speech to the perfect little audience here in this sparkling velveted bar, where silver screen memories are forever held, I'm already raising mine to Mac and thanking him.

I am finally about to find out what happens after the movie ends.

Acknowledgements

Thank you to my brilliant editor Francesca Best. I'm so grateful for your support, kindness and spot-on editorial advice.

To my amazing agent Diana Beaumont. 'My agent' is a phrase I never thought would happen to me and to have such an incredible one surely justifies me saying it about a million times a day (at least in my own head).

To my wonderful writing friend and day-to-day cheerleader, Mary Torjussen – I couldn't do any of this without you.

And, as always, to Matthew.

Read on for the first chapter of
Fiona Collins' new book . . .

Chapter One

Summer 2018

'Did you see it?'

A woman in the recognizable navy and red polyester uniform of a London Transport employee is staring at me. She is so close to my face I can see myself reflected in her milk bottle glasses. I look confused and slightly hostile; she looks concerned and overly earnest. Isn't everyone? I think, as I press my over-heated body against warm pale green tiles, away from her searching eyes. Isn't everyone so bloody earnest all the time, these days? It's like an epidemic. Everyone's concerned or outraged or offended; or sincere or impassioned or making sure every single thing they do is 'from the heart'. Everyone's making memories, feeling blessed, taking photos of themselves while looking out over a glassy lake, then captioning it with some terrible quote. Living their best lives . . .

I'm leaning against the tiled wall inside Warren Street underground station. A busker is in full flow at the bottom of the escalator to my right, strumming on a guitar and murdering 'Streets of London', that terrible song my sister Angela used to love and I can't stand – I mean, as *if* someone's troubles could be erased by traipsing the capital's streets, hand in hand with some earnest do-gooder, gawping at the homeless. He's really going for it; people are chucking coins into his guitar case, despite the slaughter – perhaps they're hoping if they give him enough, he'll call it quits, pack up his guitar and go. If Dad still noticed music (unlikely) and was here with me (even less likely), he'd have his fingers in his ears.

'Have you just come from platform one, northbound?' asks the earnest London Transport worker with the milk bottle glasses. 'Are you OK? Do you need to sit down?'

It's really hot. We're five weeks into an unprecedented, God-knows-how-long London heatwave. I came over a little peculiar further down the tunnel and am catching my breath before I tackle the escalator and the crowds again, but I don't think I need to sit down. I'm not *that* old, am I? Does she think I'm about to keel over?

I look at her and she looks at me. My face, in her glasses, looks red and shiny. My birthmark, under its thick layer of foundation, is a bumpy and sweaty moon landing.

'No, thank you,' I say.

I've been to the dentist. Only an unavoidable appointment gets me out of the flat these days. Sometimes, it's taking Dad two doors down to the doctors on Adelaide Road for one of his eye check-ups when they nod at him and say, 'Yes, Mr Alberta, you're still blind', and we go home again. Sometimes it's for me – smear test, eye test (just to make sure *I'm* not going blind too – joke!) – just general things, to keep me tip top. I'm Dad's only carer. Well, I'm not really a *carer* at all; I'm more of a silent companion – but I don't want to go under. Sometimes I go and see someone to ask if new technologies mean my birthmark can be lasered off me, at last, but the answer is always 'no'. Not in my case. After they've told me 'Sorry, you're staying ugly for ever', sometimes I pop into the dress agency next door to the clinic, to flick through and sometimes buy other people's beautiful cast-offs, but I never wear them.

I don't like my dentist. When he stuck that needle in my gum to numb me for my filling, he tutted at me for wriggling in the chair and I had an overwhelming urge to bite his thumb. Before that, I'd attempted to make small talk with him, but he wasn't interested. Gruff bastard. As he did the filling, I lay back in the Smurf-coloured dentist chair and concentrated on a row of thank you cards on the windowsill and the fly flitting lazily between them. The dental nurse sipped from a mug saying 'Get ready for a great smile' and leant forward to make one of the cards into a ramp for a crossing plump ladybird, then plopped her unceremoniously out of the open window. After my own escape, I walked to the tube with my lips like sausages, extended three feet from my face. The tube was stifling and I successfully avoided the eye of every single person wedged like sweating anchovies – brackish and intermittently hairy – in the carriage. An old lady dropped a book on my toe and I managed to give it back to her without glancing at her face, so she didn't have to glance at mine. Perhaps for the best, I decided, considering the book was *Fifty Shades Freed*.

When I got off at Warren Street to change for the Northern Line, there was a fleet of us, hot and sticky, trudging up the platform like the walking wounded.

'What on earth's going on?'

'Bloody hell!'

'It's too *hot* for this!'

There was a problem. Platform One, northbound to Edgware, was inaccessible. I found myself in a wedged funnel of people all wanting to turn left on to the platform but not being able to budge. We were not happy. We swore a bit under our breath; we scratched at the back of our necks; we sighed theatrically and competitively. As we desperately tried not to touch each other's body parts, we were distracted by a bright red balloon with 'Happy 30th' printed on it, its string tied into a small bow at the end, which bounced and bobbed above our heads. I decided it belonged to some pretty young thing; that right after someone told her *just* how pretty she was, she giggled and lost her grip of it before hurrying off to an early rush hour drink in some swanky bar, to be admired and fussed over.

'Sorry.' A man jostled against me. His hand accidentally landed on my right shoulder, just above my breast. 'Me too,' I wanted to say, as a joke, but I could see he was terrified, and that joke has already been played on me too many times. (*Yeah, Me Too . . .*) Instead I said, 'It's OK' and he smiled sheepishly at me and moved away through the stiffened crowd. He didn't get very far. The balloon bobbed and mocked overhead.

It was *my* birthday last week. My forty-eighth, one toe in the grave . . . It was a small affair, just a few close friends, some finger sandwiches and a three-tiered hand-piped chocolate cake sliced to much delight, as Stevie Wonder sang 'Happy Birthday' to me from a pub's stereo . . . No, not really, it was just Dad and I, eating some shop-bought Battenberg in front of *Countdown*, although I'd splashed out on a bottle of Shloer. We know how to live it up, Dad and I. They could probably hear the whooping all the way down at Dingwalls.

I decided to head the other way, for the exit. I'd walk to Euston and pick up the Northern Line there. I walked quickly; I was starting to feel a bit claustrophobic. Sweat was beginning to drip off me; I knew my mask was melting and I would be exposed. I also wanted to get home for *A Place in the Sun*. People were queuing to get on the escalator. The busker at the bottom was earnestly singing 'Streets of London', his fretting at the guitar vibrating through the heavy air. There *was* no air. My lips still felt weird. I stopped and leant against a tiled wall. Tried to take a deep breath of airless atmosphere. Then *she* approached.

'People react in different ways, you know?' she says, staring into my face. She sounds Welsh. 'It's hard to predict, you know?' No, I don't know, as I have no idea what she's talking about. Her glasses have a smear on one of the lenses; I want to take the hem of my over-sized T-shirt and wipe it clean. 'Here, take this. Call the number on the back if you want to speak to someone.'

She hands me a card and I take it. LTR Counselling Service, it says. It's yellow and red, with a London number underneath.

'You get two, sometimes three free sessions. I think it could really help you, if you, you know, needed help. Someone to talk to.'

'Thanks.' I only take the card as it would be rude not to, and quicker to take it and get on my way. She's clearly got me confused with somebody else. Or else she's a bit nuts and needs some help herself. Why would I need a counsellor? *Therapy?* It all comes under the same umbrella, doesn't it? Do-gooders, therapy, earnest inspiration . . . all those stupid quotes. In my eyes, life is not a destination *or* a journey. Things don't happen for a reason, they just happen. Everyone is *not* beautiful, in their own way. And I don't like lemons and I don't want to make lemonade.

I head for the escalator. The busker smiles at me as I walk past so I give him one of my special glares. I don't find the *world* that inspirational, I'm afraid. I won't dance like nobody's watching. I won't live, laugh, love, in that or any other order. In fact, you know people have those giant letters in their houses spelling 'Live, laugh, love'? I've just put a display on the windowsill that says, 'Live, laugh, bollocks'. I know any day soon Dad will suss it when he's dusting, but until then . . .

A disembodied voice comes over the tannoy – crackly and empathetic as a disembodied London Transport voice can be – apologizing for the closure of Platform One, and the suspension of the Northern Line '. . . due to a person on the tracks.'

Ah, I get it. The woman. The card. Was that what I was supposed to have seen? A jumper? A suicide blonde or brunette? A depressed chap, determined to end it at the end of a busy and pointless day and inconvenience the journey home of several thousand northbound commuters? That's sad. I put the card in my canvas shopper (oh, I know, high fashion) and stand still on the right-hand lane of the escalator as it slowly carries me to the London above.